PENGUIN BOOKS

WRITERS OF THE PURPLE SAGE

Russell Martin lives in the canyon and mesa country of southwestern Colorado. A fourth-generation Coloradan, he is a former Thomas Watson Foundation Fellow and the author of *Cowboy: The Enduring Myth of the Wild West* (1983), an examination of the cowboy's rôle in American culture. His articles and essays have appeared in *The New York Times Magazine*, *Rocky Mountain Magazine*, *Country Journal*, and many other publications.

Marc Barasch is the former editor of *Denver Magazine* and the author of five nonfiction books, most recently *The Little Black Book of Atomic War* (1983) and *Breaking 100: Americans Who Have Lived Over a Century* (1983). After attending Yale, he moved to Colorado, where he spent twelve years working as a journalist, a chef, a musician, and a college administrator, with occasional stints in L.A. to produce television shows. He is currently the editor of *New Age Journal* and lives in Boston, Massachusetts.

WRITERS

of the

PURPLE

SAGE

An Anthology of
Recent Western Writing

Edited and with an Introduction by
RUSSELL MARTIN
MARC BARASCH

Penguin Books

PENGUIN BOOKS
Published by the Penguin Group
Viking Penguin Inc., 40 West 23rd Street, New York, New York 10010, U.S.A.
Penguin Books Ltd, 27 Wrights Lane, London W8 5TZ, England
Penguin Books Australia Ltd, Ringwood, Victoria, Australia
Penguin Books Canada Ltd, 2801 John Street,
Markham, Ontario, Canada L3R 1B4
Penguin Books (N.Z.) Ltd, 182–190 Wairau Road,
Auckland 10, New Zealand

Penguin Books Ltd, Registered Offices:
Harmondsworth, Middlesex, England

First published in the United States of America
in simultaneous hardcover and paperback editions by
Viking Penguin Inc. 1984
Published simultaneously in Canada

3 5 7 9 10 8 6 4

LIBRARY OF CONGRESS CATALOGING IN PUBLICATION DATA
Main entry under title:
Writers of the purple sage.
1. American literature—West (U.S.) 2. American literature—20th century.
3. West (U.S.)—Literary collections. 4. Western stories. I. Martin, Russell.
II. Barasch, Marc.
PS561.W74 1984b   813'.54'080978   84-11081
ISBN 0 14 00.7370 1

Printed in the United States of America by
R. R. Donnelley & Sons Company, Harrisonburg, Virginia
Set in Linotron Goudy Old Style

Pages 339–40 constitute an extension of this copyright page.

SILVER STAR

This is the final resting place of engines,
farm equipment and that rare, never more
than occasional man. Population:
17. Altitude: unknown. For no
good reason you can guess, the woman
in the local store is kind. Old steam trains
have been rusting here so long, you feel
the urge to oil them, to lay new track, to start
the west again. The Jefferson
drifts by in no great hurry on its way
to wed the Madison, to be a tributary
of the ultimately dirty brown Missouri.
This town supports your need to run alone.

What if you'd lived here young, gone full of fear
to that stark brick school, the cruel teacher
supported by your guardian? Think well
of the day you ran away to Whitehall.
Think evil of the cop who found you starving
and returned you, siren open, to the house
you cannot find today. You question
everyone you see. The answer comes back wrong.
There was no house. They never heard your name.

When you leave here, leave in a flashy car
and wave goodbye. You are a stranger
every day. Let the engines and the farm
equipment die, and know that rivers
end and never end, lose and never lose
their famous names. What if your first girl
ended certain she was animal, barking
at the aides and licking floors? You know
you have no answers. The empty school
burns red in heavy snow.

—Richard Hugo

CONTENTS

INTRODUCTION

These subtle stories of the here and now are recent products of the sage-strewn American West; lucid, carefully crafted tales about how contemporary lives are led in this remote region have only lately begun to be written. The writers whose work is sampled in the following pages are the first wave of novelists and essayists in the mountain West solely to concern themselves with the parochial present day, the first to sustain interest in the complex and commonplace events of a region caught in a moment of sudden and suspicious change. But the West that belongs to history and to folklore, the mythical West of action and bold excitement, has been the enduring subject of our national storytelling since this high and haughty region was first explored and its settlement begun.

A hundred years have passed since Buffalo Bill Cody told his first fantastic stories about the frontier. In stage melodramas, Wild West pageants, and dozens of dime novels, the long-haired showman succeeded in capturing the imagination of the American public with depictions of a strange, primeval place where bravery and rough living were the rule, and where lives were lived out on the keen edge of adventure. A rich century of Western storytelling has followed Cody's success. More than a hundred touring Wild West shows that imitated Cody's original had been formed by the turn of the century. A whole stable of writers who worked for New York publisher Erastus Beadle produced thousands of short pulp novels about the daring exploits of the "border men," badmen, cavalry soldiers, and cowboys who inhabited the wild wastelands that rolled west from the fertile plains. Philadelphia lawyer Owen Wister published *The Virginian* in 1902, the first full-length, "serious" cowboy saga, a phenomenally popular book that firmly established gore and gunplay as vital elements of the Western myth. Wister was followed by an Ohio dentist named Zane Grey, whose scores of horse operas were read around the world, and by other novelists such as Max Brand, Ernest Haycox, and Clarence E. Mulford, whose formulaic Westerns emphasized hard-riding excitement. "Action, action, action is the thing," said Brand. "So long as you keep your hero jumping through fiery hoops on every page you're all right. . . . There has to be a woman, but not much of a one. A good horse is much more important."

The Western story was a natural one for the fledgling film industry to tell as well. Galloping horses, blazing gun battles, and the awesome sweep of a far horizon could be vividly depicted onscreen, and the early directors and actors such as William S. Hart helped turn the stoic and stalwart Western leading man into a symbol of American manhood. Celluloid stars Buck Jones, Tom Mix, Gary Cooper, and John Wayne followed Hart and further embellished the burgeoning myths about the hard-bitten and courageous people who inhabited the land that lay way out West. By the time Western moviemaking went into a sharp decline in the 1970s, Hollywood had produced more than two thousand Western feature films, virtually all of them set in a make-believe frontier world.

In the tumultuous decades since Cody first tried to turn the raw material of the American West into what he called "public amusement," the West had become far more a terrain of the imagination than of rock and sand and alkaline soil. The West was, to most minds, simply the mythic locale of the nation's enduring morality plays—ritualistic struggles between the wild and the tame, the individual and the society, the forces of evil and the dutiful defenders of justice. By the second half of the twentieth century, not many people outside the region seriously thought that the West could spawn any literary or artistic endeavors other than those head-'em-off-at-the-pass novels, or movies in which the proud and pillaged homesteaders sought revenge against the savages, or the sentimental music of singing cowboys.

Yet those who actually lived in the sagebrush heartland confronted a latter-day reality that was drastically different from the colorful cowboy myths. It was true that the land seemed to dominate every concern and that isolation could carve lives that were as lean and straight as whittled sticks. But more often than not, adventure was displaced by sober and mundane survival. There were kids as well as horses to shoe, car payments to make, and tenuous truces to be struck between wives and husbands. For the Westerners themselves, the folkloric and formulaic West was nothing more than a wistful set of stories; the mythic West was just an ideal to be dreamed about and to be emulated at weekend rodeos and in booze-bred confrontations in dank and depressing barrooms.

In the imaginations of the Western-born writers at work in the postwar 1940s and 1950s, the pervasive frontier myths hung like a late spring storm over the scrublands, limiting vision and obscuring opportunities to give literary shape to contemporary lives and surroundings. In the midst of Hollywood's horse-opera heyday, writers such as Wallace Stegner, Walter Van Tilburg Clark, Bernard DeVoto, A. B. Guthrie, Jr., Dorothy M. Johnson, Paul Horgan, and Frank Waters had to confront the myths head on, to retell the Western stories in antimythological terms, to by God set the record straight. In books like Stegner's *The Big Rock Candy Mountain* (1943), Clark's *The Ox-Bow Incident* (1940), and Guthrie's *The Way West* (1949), the region's first group of literary novelists went about the business of re-creating a historical West that was a palpable, believable place, a world in which the pioneer inhabitants were complex and compelling individuals whose lives belied the tired stereotypes. But instead of writing about the changing worlds they personally knew, the novelists wrote about the dusk-lit worlds of the Westerners who lived before them. It was as if the contemporary region couldn't be addressed until the historical West had been *correctly* divined and defined in fiction.

In an essay, Stegner himself once complained about Western fiction writers' "disinclination, perhaps an emotional inability to write about the contemporary." And he lamented the fact that "nobody has quite made a Western Yoknapatawpha County, or discovered a historical continuity comparable to that which Faulkner traced from the Chickasaw to the Snopes. Maybe it isn't possible, but I wish someone would try."

No Western writer has as yet taken up Stegner's challenge, in large part because historical continuity in the West is scarce. The region has always been occupied by migrants and immigrants, people for whom the personal distance between *now* and *then* is often indecipherable. Except for the region's native inhabitants (and many Indians have also lost contact with a vibrant sense of the history of their cultures), Westerners nowadays live in a brash and often chaotic present that has little to do with the past that was limned by the mythic stories.

Beginning in the late 1960s, writers in the interior West— natives and immigrants, Anglos, Indians, and Hispanics—began to abandon the stories that unfolded in earlier eras and to pay artistic attention to the lives and land they saw around them. They remained as captivated by the landscape's bold beauty and nagging mystery as writers in the West have always been— neither Western novelists nor their characters have ever escaped the strange tyranny of distance or the quiet crush of isolation. But the new Western writing also began to be shaped by the region's modern mix of gaudy pretensions, glib, get-rich aspirations, and the somber struggles of many rural wage earners to find some psychic safety—to locate a sane and secure place amid the whirl of change.

It wasn't merely coincidental that the work of contemporary Western writers began to assume new power and importance at precisely the time that the West itself began to come awkwardly of age, finding itself the subject of national attention. Energy companies were barreling into vacant terrain to get at the enormous resources that lay beneath the land, continuing the West's frontier legacy of boom and bust. Immigrants from depressed industrial states went west in station wagons instead of wagon trains, searching for jobs, heading in the same hopeful direction that beckoned to the pioneers. Western towns and cities began to ache and swell with booming populations; the ubiquitous oil derricks leaned hard on the last of the ranches. Today that process continues: Cattle go to market and cattlemen go to trailer parks and retirement condominiums; the open spaces close up, and the mythic West very nearly withers away.

Poignant and important fiction—writing that is filled with vitality and heart—is well nurtured by this brand of societal tension and uncertainty. The gothic literature of the American South, shaped by an often grotesque obsession with the Southern plantation legacy, emerged at the same time that region began to examine its history of shame and to begin tentatively to join the mainstream American culture. The region that straddles the Rocky Mountains is now undergoing a similar cathartic process, recognizing that it has always been an exploited and ill-defined backwater, often oddly reveling in that fact, but nonetheless anxious to assert its importance to the rest of the nation, to claim that the lives of its people matter. The new Western writers are chronicling this uneasy shift, the sometimes melancholy slide of one epoch into another, the emergence of the West as a region that extends beyond its myths.

The interior, intermountain West comprises eight Rocky Mountain and Great Basin states—Idaho, Montana, Wyoming, Nevada, Utah, Colorado, Arizona, and New Mexico. That definition, like virtually all geopolitical boundaries in the West, is an arbitrary one. But it is a functional one when it comes to linking the writers scattered across this stark region, which makes up one third of the total land area of the contiguous

United States. And it helps to delineate as well the distinction between the new Western writing and the substantially different literatures of the West Coast and Texas.

The contemporary literature of California (and, to lesser degrees, Oregon and Washington) has an urban and suburban focus. Its characters are immigrant seekers of material ease and spiritual enlightenment who inhabit a milieu of shopping malls and singles' clubs, pristine resorts, and palm-lined avenues filled with the frenetic rush of traffic.

In contrast, the writers of the interior West represented in this collection probe, almost exclusively, the rural outback of their region. Although adolescent cities such as Denver, Phoenix, Albuquerque, and Salt Lake City are the places where the majority of people live in the interior West, and although trendy, urbane resorts like Aspen, Sun Valley, and Jackson Hole grab a large share of the rest of the nation's attention to the region, it is the frowzy small towns and the open, abandoned country that capture these writers' imaginations. But their characters are not all unschooled and toothless hayseeds; few of them are, in fact. They are people of wide-ranging means and aims and backgrounds who were born into the strange caress of the country, or who came to it in middle age seeking a rough-hewn refuge from the rest of the troubled world.

If there is an overriding distinction between the characters created by West Coast writers such as Alice Adams, Herbert Gold, James Houston, and many others, and those created by contemporary writers in the interior West, it is this: In modern California and coastal fiction, people still seek the riches and bliss that were the early promise of the Golden State; utopias still seem palpable enough to struggle for. In the sagebrush heartland, on the other hand, the perfect life is an impossibility, and the best places to be are simply those that register some sort of reassurance—places that are safe homes and harbors from the drab disillusionment that surrounds them.

Texas writers are excluded from this collection because Texas, for all its internal diversity, and for all that it stubbornly shares of the West's enduring cowboy culture, is a region unto itself. Texas belongs not to the South or the West, but only to its own terrain, to the rolling land bounded by the Red River and the Rio Grande. Contemporary Texas writers—John Graves, William Humphrey, Larry McMurtry, and the late playwright Preston Jones, among others—have had to grapple against the confining lariat of the cowboy myth just as other Western writers have; the issues of the settlement and subsequent exploitation of the land and the sudden loss of regional innocence have been examined at length by writers in both regions. But the themes of urbanization, the sometimes stifling web of family, and the Texas-sized effects of newfound wealth are more important and persistent in the work of the Lone Star writers. Texas is now the third most populous state in the nation, and its literature reflects that giddy gallop toward the metropolis; its writers envision a measured mix of positive and negative effects in the transition—unlike the writers in the interior West, who, for the most part, perceive only destruction and depression arriving on the heels of change.

The novelists, short story writers, and essayists whose work is sampled in the following pages belong only loosely to a kind of sagebrush school of American literature. They are a group of men and women whose lives and literary concerns are diverse and often divergent. They are scattered from Kalispell, Montana, to Tucson, Arizona; stationed in lonesome logging towns and in resorts for the nouveau riche; living on ranches and haggard homesteads, near hinterland universities, and beside a few quiet and compelling trout streams. Few, if any, describe themselves as "Western" writers—too much of the myth survives to make that an appropriate appellation—and they certainly don't hang out together in brassy saloons, drinking whiskey out of bottles and pronouncing regional literary truths. In fact, except for a circle of writers who live in or near Missoula, Montana—most of whom have ties to the University of Montana's writing program—there really isn't an identifiable Western literary scene; there is certainly no café society of writers and artists, save those cliques in the resort towns, where the scene is everything and little of the weary work of writing is ever accomplished. Like most of the characters they write about, the writers included here seek a measure of solitude among the open spaces, and each sees a region whose shape and style is defined by his or her particular perspective.

It is surely indicative of the changing demographics of the interior West that only nine of the nineteen writers presented in this anthology were born in the region, and it is interesting that the body of work of those nine stands in distinct stylistic and thematic contrast to the work of the immigrant writers. Perhaps it is because the native writers have known no other regions intimately and completely that they treat the Western land with such quiet reverence—that their characters' relations to the land sometimes become oddly sacramental. Or perhaps it is the fact that the West remains largely unpopulated, too empty to be able to sustain a real society, that it demands its native writers substitute the strong presence of landscape for the complexities of culture.

But whether the Western land is as mighty as it is made out to be, or whether its hugeness makes it an ultimately inescapable literary element, its native writers carve stories, novels, memoirs, and essays directly out of the lodgepole pines and rocky arroyos, always meticulously anchoring their tales to terrain, defining their characters, in part, by describing the land that surrounds them.

Each of the native writers seems intent on creating a simple, lyric, and elegiac prose, a self-conscious writing that is meant to be *heard* while it tells its story. It is no coincidence that the three Indian novelists whose work is included here—Pulitzer Prize–winner N. Scott Momaday, Leslie Marmon Silko, and James Welch—are also successful poets. The three belong to indigenous cultures that continue to revere words—their mysteries, their sonorous strengths. Each is steeped in a tradition that believes in the importance of telling stories and in passing them on, one that asserts that stories form a kind of mystical rope that binds past with present.

The work of native writers Ivan Doig, Norman Maclean, Rudolfo Anaya, Alan Prendergast, and William Kittredge shares the Indian writers' attention to the elegiac quality of language. And in much the same way that the Indian novelists and poets attempt to settle the question of cultural history and to weigh its value, the Anglo and Hispanic natives often address the quiet and intricate issues of familial history and relationships. They work to define their characters in the context of kin, to assert in an unabashedly old-fashioned way that the family is an inescapable force.

Throughout the native writers' work there is a kind of persistent yet unromantic optimism, a notion, indirectly expressed by characters or authorial voices, that amid the chaos of change and conflict there is something important to be gained by somehow sitting out the storms huddled together. There are no Pollyannas among the native writers, and many of them are troubled by the fledgling shape the new Western age is taking, but they nonetheless hold on to a kind of unspoken, parochial hope that is grounded in the strength of individual lives.

The work of the majority of the region's immigrant writers—people who have come to the West because it seemed to be a good place to settle, drawn here by its wacky incongruities, its intriguing mix of land and peoples and epochs—is less hopeful than the stories and novels of the natives. There are exceptions, of course—writers like Gretel Ehrlich, David Long, and David Quammen have much in common stylistically and thematically with the native writers—but the immigrant writers tend to supplant optimism with nagging doubt, and attention to familial relationships is often abandoned in favor of a focus on the struggles of displaced individuals.

Immigrant writers like Edward Abbey, John Nichols, Rick DeMarinis, Richard Ford, Elizabeth Tallent, Robert Mayer, and Thomas McGuane don't seem to possess the same need to paint the shape and texture of the country as do the native writers.

The immigrants care about the landscape, to be sure, but within the context of their fiction the land is much more often simply a setting than a pervasive character in itself. And the immigrant writers seem far more willing than the natives to expose the region's wounds and open sores: its failed promises, its legacy of destroying the best parts of its terrain and cultures, its tendency to turn the ideal of individualism into the mean reality of loneliness.

Employing little of the lyricism that is an elemental aspect of native writing, the language of the immigrant writers is often acerbic, satiric, facetious. It is passionately angry in a few instances, and can be refreshingly comic and quirky as well. The immigrant Western writers demonstrate a wider variety of form and literary intent than do the natives—introducing in the process attitudes and perceptions that the West itself has yet to spawn. What all the immigrants do have in common is a commitment to the West as a literary terrain. Their work reflects an interest in the place not just as a picturesque refuge or suitably scenic backdrop, but as a region of lives made compelling by the remote places in which they are lived, of scattered stories anxious to be told.

In gathering the pieces for this collection no attempt has been made to achieve a particular thematic unity or to define a specific Western point of view. These stories have no single ethical intent, nor do they collectively describe the prototypical Western person—happily, no such critter exists. Included among them are a tale about a Laguna woman who considers whether she is, in fact, the elusive Yellow Woman who figures prominently in her people's mythology. One is a story about a Montana logging-trucker who seeks revenge against a grizzly bear that killed a girl he didn't know; another is the story of an ex-convict and his girlfriend, an inspector for plague in prairie dogs, who together devise a scheme to beat the odds at a Santa Fe racetrack; another, an essay about a real-life outlaw who killed two game wardens in the winter of 1981 because they got in the way of his own warped version of the Western myth. One more is a son's recollection of the relationship between a sheep-ranching father and an insular stepmother, two good people caught in a strange and grueling combat.

Five of the selections are nonfiction. Of these, two are personal memoirs; the other three are eloquent pieces about particular Western places and their particular people. Several of the contributors are nationally known, their work renowned; others of equal talent remain almost anonymous, even within the West. We have chosen each story, novel excerpt, or nonfiction piece because we believe that it is representative of that writer's best work, and because it examines people and predicaments indigenous to the West. Personal preferences have, of course, played a significant role in the selection process.

Taken as a whole, these nineteen selections reflect the fact that Western literature currently finds itself in a period of enormous vitality. Undaunted by the pundits' pronouncements that nobody reads any more and their distance from the center of publishing on the East Coast, these writers are carving an important new niche in American literature. Their work resonates with bedrock attention to the specific details of setting and characterization; it is an empathetic literature that views its subject matter as the poignant and ordinary events of human lives.

In the final analysis, the literature of this region is not at all a "regional literature"—that pejorative term meaning provincial, hidebound, untranscendent. The new Western writing is anchored in a place that is still somewhat exotic, one that remains as strange in some ways as the country that Buffalo Bill encountered, one that harbors a few odd enterprises and more than a few particular prejudices. But its literary concerns—the questions of living and dying, the relationships among families and friends, between people and the places in which they find themselves—are as universal as literature itself. Ultimately, what the rural West offers its writers is a rough, still-forming region whose inhabitants' lives are malleable enough to be carved into invigorating and intriguing shapes. What these writers of the purple sage offer us all are vital stories well worth the telling, stories that rise up out of the coarse Western ground into the warm and clear air of compassion.

R.M.
Dolores, Colorado

WRITERS OF THE
PURPLE SAGE

N. SCOTT MOMADAY

INTRODUCTION TO

THE WAY TO RAINY MOUNTAIN

A single knoll rises out of the plain in Oklahoma, north and west of the Wichita Range. For my people, the Kiowas, it is an old landmark, and they gave it the name Rainy Mountain. The hardest weather in the world is there. Winter brings blizzards, hot tornadic winds arise in the spring, and in summer the prairie is an anvil's edge. The grass turns brittle and brown, and it cracks beneath your feet. There are green belts along the rivers and creeks, linear groves of hickory and pecan, willow and witch hazel. At a distance in July or August the steaming foliage seems almost to writhe in fire. Great green and yellow grasshoppers are everywhere in the tall grass, popping up like corn to sting the flesh, and tortoises crawl about on the red earth, going nowhere in the plenty of time. Loneliness is an aspect of the land. All things in the plain are isolate; there is no confusion of objects in the eye, but *one* hill or *one* tree or *one* man. To look upon that landscape in the early morning, with the sun at your back, is to lose the sense of proportion. Your imagination comes to life, and this, you think, is where Creation was begun.

I returned to Rainy Mountain in July. My grandmother had died in the spring, and I wanted to be at her grave. She had lived to be very old and at last infirm. Her only living daughter was with her when she died, and I was told that in death her face was that of a child.

I like to think of her as a child. When she was born, the Kiowas were living that last great moment of their history. For more than a hundred years they had controlled the open range

1

from the Smoky Hill River to the Red, from the headwaters of the Canadian to the fork of the Arkansas and Cimarron. In alliance with the Comanches, they had ruled the whole of the southern Plains. War was their sacred business, and they were among the finest horsemen the world has ever known. But warfare for the Kiowas was preeminently a matter of disposition rather than of survival, and they never understood the grim, unrelenting advance of the U.S. Cavalry. When at last, divided and ill-provisioned, they were driven onto the Staked Plains in the cold rains of autumn, they fell into panic. In Palo Duro Canyon they abandoned their crucial stores to pillage and had nothing then but their lives. In order to save themselves, they surrendered to the soldiers at Fort Sill and were imprisoned in the old stone corral that now stands as a military museum. My grandmother was spared the humiliation of those high gray walls by eight or ten years, but she must have known from birth the affliction of defeat, the dark brooding of old warriors.

Her name was Aho, and she belonged to the last culture to evolve in North America. Her forebears came down from the high country in western Montana nearly three centuries ago. They were a mountain people, a mysterious tribe of hunters whose language has never been positively classified in any major group. In the late seventeenth century they began a long migration to the south and east. It was a journey toward the dawn, and it led to a golden age. Along the way the Kiowas were befriended by the Crows, who gave them the culture and religion of the Plains. They acquired horses, and their ancient nomadic spirit was suddenly free of the ground. They acquired Tai-me, the sacred Sun Dance doll, from that moment the object and symbol of their worship, and so shared in the divinity of the sun. Not least, they acquired the sense of destiny, therefore courage and pride. When they entered upon the southern Plains they had been transformed. No longer were they slaves to the simple necessity of survival; they were a lordly and dangerous society of fighters and thieves, hunters and priests of the sun. According to their origin myth, they entered the world through a hollow log. From one point of view, their migration was the fruit of an old prophecy, for indeed they emerged from a sunless world.

Although my grandmother lived out her long life in the shadow of Rainy Mountain, the immense landscape of the continental interior lay like memory in her blood. She could tell of the Crows, whom she had never seen, and of the Black Hills, where she had never been. I wanted to see in reality what she had seen more perfectly in the mind's eye, and travelled fifteen hundred miles to begin my pilgrimage.

Yellowstone, it seemed to me, was the top of the world, a region of deep lakes and dark timber, canyons and waterfalls, But, beautiful as it is, one might have the sense of confinement there. The skyline in all directions is close at hand, the high wall of the woods and deep cleavages of shade. There is a perfect freedom in the mountains, but it belongs to the eagle and the elk, the badger and the bear. The Kiowas reckoned their stature by the distance they could see, and they were bent and blind in the wilderness.

Descending eastward, the highland meadows are a stairway to the plain. In July the inland slope of the Rockies is luxuriant with flax and buckwheat, stonecrop and larkspur. The earth unfolds and the limit of the land recedes. Clusters of trees, and animals grazing far in the distance, cause the vision to reach away and wonder to build upon the mind. The sun follows a longer course in the day, and the sky is immense beyond all comparison. The great billowing clouds that sail upon it are shadows that move upon the grain like water, dividing light. Farther down, in the land of the Crows and Blackfeet, the plain is yellow. Sweet clover takes hold of the hills and bends upon itself to cover and seal the soil. There the Kiowas paused on their way; they had come to the place where they must change their lives. The sun is at home on the plains. Precisely there does it have the certain character of a god. When the Kiowas came to the land of the Crows, they could see the dark lees of the hills at dawn across the Bighorn River, the profusion of light on the grain shelves, the oldest deity ranging after the solstices. Not yet would they veer southward to the caldron of the land that lay below; they must wean their blood from the northern winter and hold the mountains a while longer in their view. They bore Tai-me in procession to the east.

A dark mist lay over the Black Hills, and the land was like iron. At the top of a ridge I caught sight of Devil's Tower upthrust against the gray sky as if in the birth of time the core of the earth had broken through its crust and the motion of the world was begun. There are things in nature that engender an awful quiet in the heart of man; Devil's Tower is one of them. Two centuries ago, because they could not do otherwise, the Kiowas made a legend at the base of the rock. My grandmother said:

Eight children were there at play, seven sisters and their brother. Suddenly the boy was struck dumb; he trembled and began to run upon his hands and feet. His fingers became claws, and his body was covered with fur. Directly there was a bear where the boy had been. The sisters were terrified; they ran, and the bear after them. They came to the stump of a great tree, and the tree spoke to them. It bade them climb upon it, and as they did so it began to rise into the air. The bear came to kill them, but they were just beyond its reach. It reared against the tree and scored the bark all around with its claws. The seven sisters were borne into the sky, and they became the stars of the Big Dipper.

From that moment, and so long as the legend lives, the Kiowas have kinsmen in the night sky. Whatever they were in the mountains, they could be no more. However tenuous their well-being, however much they had suffered and would suffer again, they had found a way out of the wilderness.

My grandmother had a reverence for the sun, a holy regard that now is all but gone out of mankind. There was a wariness in her, and an ancient awe. She was a Christian in her later years, but she had come a long way about, and she never forgot her birthright. As a child she had been to the Sun Dances; she

had taken part in those annual rites, and by them she had learned
the restoration of her people in the presence of Tai-me. She
was about seven when the last Kiowa Sun Dance was held in
1887 on the Washita River above Rainy Mountain Creek. The
buffalo were gone. In order to consummate the ancient sacri-
fice—to impale the head of a buffalo bull upon the medicine
tree—a delegation of old men journeyed into Texas, there to
beg and barter for an animal from the Goodnight herd. She was
ten when the Kiowas came together for the last time as a living
Sun Dance culture. They could find no buffalo; they had to
hang an old hide from the sacred tree. Before the dance could
begin, a company of soldiers rode out from Fort Sill under orders
to disperse the tribe. Forbidden without cause the essential act
of their faith, having seen the wild herds slaughtered and left
to rot upon the ground, the Kiowas backed away forever from
the medicine tree. That was July 20, 1890, at the great bend
of the Washita. My grandmother was there. Without bitterness,
and for as long as she lived, she bore a vision of deicide.

Now that I can have her only in memory, I see my grandmother in the several postures that were peculiar to her: standing at the wood stove on a winter morning and turning meat
in a great iron skillet; sitting at the south window, bent above
her beadwork, and afterwards, when her vision failed, looking
down for a long time into the fold of her hands; going out upon
a cane, very slowly as she did when the weight of age came
upon her; praying. I remember her most often at prayer. She
made long, rambling prayers out of suffering and hope, having
seen many things. I was never sure that I had the right to hear,
so exclusive were they of all mere custom and company. The
last time I saw her she prayed standing by the side of her bed
at night, naked to the waist, the light of a kerosene lamp moving
upon her dark skin. Her long, black hair, always drawn and
braided in the day, lay upon her shoulders and against her
breasts like a shawl. I do not speak Kiowa, and I never understood her prayers, but there was something inherently sad in

the sound, some merest hesitation upon the syllables of sorrow. She began in a high and descending pitch, exhausting her breath to silence; then again and again—and always the same intensity of effort, of something that is, and is not, like urgency in the human voice. Transported so in the dancing light among the shadows of her room, she seemed beyond the reach of time. But that was illusion; I think I knew then that I should not see her again.

Houses are like sentinels in the plain, old keepers of the weather watch. There, in a very little while, wood takes on the appearance of great age. All colors wear soon away in the wind and rain, and then the wood is burned gray and the grain appears and the nails turn red with rust. The windowpanes are black and opaque; you imagine there is nothing within, and indeed there are many ghosts, bones given up to the land. They stand here and there against the sky, and you approach them for a longer time than you expect. They belong in the distance; it is their domain.

Once there was a lot of sound in my grandmother's house, a lot of coming and going, feasting and talk. The summers there were full of excitement and reunion. The Kiowas are a summer people; they abide the cold and keep to themselves, but when the season turns and the land becomes warm and vital they cannot hold still; an old love of going returns upon them. The aged visitors who came to my grandmother's house when I was a child were made of lean and leather, and they bore themselves upright. They wore great black hats and bright ample shirts that shook in the wind. They rubbed fat upon their hair and wound their braids with strips of colored cloth. Some of them painted their faces and carried the scars of old and cherished enmities. They were an old council of warlords, come to remind and be reminded of who they were. Their wives and daughters served them well. The women might indulge themselves; gossip was at once the mark and compensation of their servitude. They made loud and elaborate talk among themselves, full of jest and gesture, fright and false alarm. They went abroad in fringed and flowered shawls, bright beadwork and German silver. They were at home in the kitchen, and they prepared meals that were banquets.

There were frequent prayer meetings, and great nocturnal feasts. When I was a child I played with my cousins outside, where the lamplight fell upon the ground and the singing of the old people rose up around us and carried away into the darkness. There were a lot of good things to eat, a lot of laughter and surprise. And afterwards, when the quiet returned, I lay down with my grandmother and could hear the frogs away by the river and feel the motion of the air.

Now there is a funeral silence in the rooms, the endless wake of some final word. The walls have closed in upon my grandmother's house. When I returned to it in mourning, I saw for the first time in my life how small it was. It was late at night, and there was a white moon, nearly full. I sat for a long time on the stone steps by the kitchen door. From there I could see out across the land; I could see the long row of trees by the creek, the low light upon the rolling plains, and the stars of the Big Dipper. Once I looked at the moon and caught sight of a strange thing. A cricket had perched upon the handrail, only a few inches away from me. My line of vision was such that the creature filled the moon like a fossil. It had gone there, I thought, to live and die, for there, of all places, was its small definition made whole and eternal. A warm wind rose up and purled like the longing within me.

The next morning I awoke at dawn and went out on the dirt road to Rainy Mountain. It was already hot, and the grasshoppers began to fill the air. Still, it was early in the morning, and the birds sang out of the shadows. The long yellow grass on the mountain shone in the bright light, and a scissortail hied above the land. There, where it ought to be, at the end of a long and legendary way, was my grandmother's grave. Here and there on the dark stones were ancestral names. Looking back once, I saw the mountain and came away.

LESLIE MARMON SILKO
YELLOW WOMAN

My thigh clung to his with dampness, and I watched the sun rising up through the tamaracks and willows. The small brown water birds came to the river and hopped across the mud, leaving brown scratches in the alkali-white crust. They bathed in the river silently. I could hear the water, almost at our feet where the narrow fast channel bubbled and washed green ragged moss and fern leaves. I looked at him beside me, rolled in the red blanket on the white river sand. I cleaned the sand out of the cracks between my toes, squinting because the sun was above the willow trees. I looked at him for the last time, sleeping on the white river sand.

I felt hungry and followed the river south the way we had come the afternoon before, following our footprints that were already blurred by lizard tracks and bug trails. The horses were still lying down, and the black one whinnied when he saw me but he did not get up—maybe it was because the corral was made out of thick cedar branches and the horses had not yet felt the sun like I had. I tried to look beyond the pale red mesas to the pueblo. I knew it was there, even if I could not see it, on the sandrock hill above the river, the same river that moved past me now and had reflected the moon last night.

The horse felt warm underneath me. He shook his head and pawed the sand. The bay whinnied and leaned against the gate trying to follow, and I remembered him asleep in the red blanket beside the river. I slid off the horse and tied him close to the

8

other horse, I walked north with the river again, and the white sand broke loose in footprints over footprints.

"Wake up."

He moved in the blanket and turned his face to me with his eyes still closed. I knelt down to touch him.

"I'm leaving."

He smiled now, eyes still closed. "You are coming with me, remember?" He sat up now with his bare dark chest and belly in the sun.

"Where?"

"To my place."

"And will I come back?"

He pulled his pants on. I walked away from him, feeling him behind me and smelling the willows.

"Yellow Woman," he said.

I turned to face him. "Who are you?" I asked.

He laughed and knelt on the low, sandy bank, washing his face in the river. "Last night you guessed my name, and you knew why I had come."

I stared past him at the shallow moving water and tried to remember the night, but I could only see the moon in the water and remember his warmth around me.

"But I only said that you were him and that I was Yellow Woman—I'm not really her—I have my own name and I come from the pueblo on the other side of the mesa. Your name is Silva and you are a stranger I met by the river yesterday afternoon."

He laughed softly. "What happened yesterday has nothing to do with what you will do today, Yellow Woman."

"I know—that's what I'm saying—the old stories about the ka'tsina spirit and Yellow Woman can't mean us."

My old grandpa liked to tell those stories best. There is one about Badger and Coyote who went hunting and were gone all day, and when the sun was going down they found a house. There was a girl living there alone, and she had light hair and

eyes and she told them that they could sleep with her. Coyote
wanted to be with her all night so he sent Badger into a prairie-
dog hole, telling him he thought he saw something in it. As
soon as Badger crawled in, Coyote blocked up the entrance with
rocks and hurried back to Yellow Woman.

"Come here," he said gently.

He touched my neck and I moved close to him to feel his
breathing and to hear his heart. I was wondering if Yellow
Woman had known who she was—if she knew that she would
become part of the stories. Maybe she'd had another name that
her husband and relatives called her so that only the ka'tsina
from the north and the storytellers would know her as Yellow
Woman. But I didn't go on; I felt him all around me, pushing
me down into the white river sand.

Yellow Woman went away with the spirit from the north and
lived with him and his relatives. She was gone for a long time,
but then one day she came back and she brought twin boys.

"Do you know the story?"

"What story?" He smiled and pulled me close to him as he
said this. I was afraid lying there on the red blanket. All I could
know was the way he felt, warm, damp, his body beside me.
This is the way it happens in the stories, I was thinking, with
no thought beyond the moment she meets the ka'tsina spirit
and they go.

"I don't have to go. What they tell in stories was real only
then, back in time immemorial, like they say."

He stood up and pointed at my clothes tangled in the blanket.
"Let's go," he said.

I walked beside him, breathing hard because he walked fast,
his hand around my wrist. I had stopped trying to pull away
from him, because his hand felt cool and the sun was high,
drying the river bed into alkali. I will see someone, eventually
I will see someone, and then I will be certain that he is only a
man—some man from nearby—and I will be sure that I am not
Yellow Woman. Because she is from out of time past and I live

now and I've been to school and there are highways and pickup trucks that Yellow Woman never saw.

It was an easy ride north on horseback. I watched the change from the cottonwood trees along the river to the junipers that brushed past us in the foothills, and finally there were only piñons, and when I looked up at the rim of the mountain plateau I could see pine trees growing on the edge. Once I stopped to look down, but the pale sandstone had disappeared and the river was gone and the dark lava hills were all around. He touched my hand, not speaking, but always singing softly a mountain song and looking into my eyes.

I felt hungry and wondered what they were doing at home now—my mother, my grandmother, my husband, and the baby. Cooking breakfast, saying, "Where did she go?—maybe kidnapped." And Al going to the tribal police with the details: "She went walking along the river."

The house was made with black lava rock and red mud. It was high above the spreading miles of arroyos and long mesas. I smelled a mountain smell of pitch and buck brush. I stood there beside the black horse, looking down on the small, dim country we had passed, and I shivered.

"Yellow Woman, come inside where it's warm."

He lit a fire in the stove. It was an old stove with a round belly and an enamel coffeepot on top. There was only the stove, some faded Navajo blankets, and a bedroll and cardboard box. The floor was made of smooth adobe plaster, and there was one small window facing east. He pointed at the box.

"There's some potatoes and the frying pan." He sat on the floor with his arms around his knees pulling them close to his chest and he watched me fry the potatoes. I didn't mind him watching me because he was always watching me—he had been watching me since I came upon him sitting on the river bank trimming leaves from a willow twig with his knife. We ate from the pan and he wiped the grease from his fingers on his Levi's.

"Have you brought women here before?" He smiled and kept chewing, so I said, "Do you always use the same tricks?"

"What tricks?" He looked at me like he didn't understand.

"The story about being a ka'tsina from the mountains. The story about Yellow Woman."

Silva was silent; his face was calm.

"I don't believe it. Those stories couldn't happen now," I said.

He shook his head and said softly, "But someday they will talk about us, and they will say, 'Those two lived long ago when things like that happened.' "

He stood up and went out. I ate the rest of the potatoes and thought about things—about the noise the stove was making and the sound of the mountain wind outside. I remembered yesterday and the day before, and then I went outside.

I walked past the corral to the edge where the narrow trail cut through the black rim rock. I was standing in the sky with nothing around me but the wind that came down from the blue mountain peak behind me. I could see faint mountain images in the distance miles across the vast spread of mesas and valleys and plains. I wondered who was over there to feel the mountain wind on those sheer blue edges—who walks on the pine needles in those blue mountains.

"Can you see the pueblo?" Silva was standing behind me.

I shook my head. "We're too far away."

"From here I can see the world." He stepped out on the edge. "The Navajo reservation begins over there." He pointed to the east. "The Pueblo boundaries are over here." He looked below us to the south, where the narrow trail seemed to come from. "The Texans have their ranches over there, starting with that valley, the Concho Valley. The Mexicans run some cattle over there too."

"Do you ever work for them?"

"I steal from them," Silva answered. The sun was dropping behind us and the shadows were filling the land below. I turned away from the edge that dropped forever into the valleys below.

"I'm cold," I said, "I'm going inside." I started wondering about this man who could speak the Pueblo language so well but who lived on a mountain and rustled cattle. I decided that this man Silva must be Navajo, because Pueblo men didn't do things like that.

"You must be a Navajo."

Silva shook his head gently. "Little Yellow Woman," he said, "you never give up, do you? I have told you who I am. The Navajo people know me, too." He knelt down and unrolled the bedroll and spread the extra blankets out on a piece of canvas. The sun was down, and the only light in the house came from outside—the dim orange light from sundown.

I stood there and waited for him to crawl under the blankets.

"What are you waiting for?" he said, and I lay down beside him. He undressed me slowly like the night before beside the river—kissing my face gently and running his hands up and down my belly and legs. He took off my pants and then he laughed.

"Why are you laughing?"

"You are breathing so hard."

I pulled away from him and turned my back to him.

He pulled me around and pinned me down with his arms and chest. "You don't understand, do you, little Yellow Woman? You will do what I want."

And again he was all around me with his skin slippery against mine, and I was afraid because I understood that his strength could hurt me. I lay underneath him and I knew that he could destroy me. But later, while he slept beside me, I touched his face and I had a feeling—the kind of feeling for him that overcame me that morning along the river. I kissed him on the forehead and he reached out for me.

When I woke up in the morning he was gone. It gave me a strange feeling because for a long time I sat there on the blankets and looked around the little house for some object of his—some proof that he had been there or maybe that he was coming back. Only the blankets and the cardboard box remained. The

.30-30 that had been leaning in the corner was gone, and so was the knife that I had used the night before. He was gone, and I had my chance to go now. But first I had to eat, because I knew it would be a long walk home.

I found some dried apricots in the cardboard box, and I sat down on a rock at the edge of the plateau rim. There was no wind and the sun warmed me. I was surrounded by silence. I drowsed with apricots in my mouth, and I didn't believe that there were highways or railroads or cattle to steal.

When I woke up, I stared down at my feet in the black mountain dirt. Little black ants were swarming over the pine needles around my foot. They must have smelled the apricots. I thought about my family far below me. They would be wondering about me, because this had never happened to me before. The tribal police would file a report. But if old Grandpa weren't dead he would tell them what happened—he would laugh and say, "Stolen by a ka'tsina, a mountain spirit. She'll come home—they usually do." There are enough of them to handle things. My mother and grandmother will raise the baby like they raised me. Al will find someone else, and they will go on like before, except that there will be a story about the day I disappeared while I was walking along the river. Silva had come for me; he said he had. I did not decide to go. I just went. Moonflowers blossom in the sand hills before dawn, just as I followed him. That's what I was thinking as I wandered along the trail through the pine trees.

It was noon when I got back. When I saw the stone house I remembered that I had meant to go home. But that didn't seem important any more, maybe because there were little blue flowers growing in the meadow behind the stone house and the gray squirrels were playing in the pines next to the house. The horses were standing in the corral, and there was a beef carcass hanging on the shady side of a big pine in front of the house. Flies buzzed around the clotted blood that hung from the carcass. Silva was washing his hands in a bucket full of water. He must have heard me coming because he spoke to me without turning to face me.

"I've been waiting for you."

"I went walking in the big pine trees."

I looked into the bucket full of bloody water with brown-and-white animal hairs floating in it. Silva stood there letting his hand drip, examining me intently.

"Are you coming with me?"

"Where?" I asked him.

"To sell the meat in Marquez."

"If you're sure it's O.K."

"I wouldn't ask you if it wasn't," he answered.

He sloshed the water around in the bucket before he dumped it out and set the bucket upside down near the door. I followed him to the corral and watched him saddle the horses. Even beside the horses he looked tall, and I asked him again if he wasn't Navajo. He didn't say anything; he just shook his head and kept cinching up the saddle.

"But Navajos are tall."

"Get on the horse," he said, "and let's go."

The last thing he did before we started down the steep trail was to grab the .30-30 from the corner. He slid the rifle into the scabbard that hung from his saddle.

"Do they ever try to catch you?" I asked.

"They don't know who I am."

"Then why did you bring the rifle?"

"Because we are going to Marquez where the Mexicans live."

The trail leveled out on a narrow ridge that was steep on both sides like an animal spine. On one side I could see where the trail went around the rocky gray hills and disappeared into the southeast where the pale sandrock mesas stood in the distance near my home. On the other side was a trail that went west, and as I looked far into the distance I thought I saw the little town. But Silva said no, that I was looking in the wrong place, that I just thought I saw houses. After that I quit looking off into the distance; it was hot and the wildflowers were closing up their deep-yellow petals. Only the waxy cactus flowers bloomed in the bright sun, and I saw every color that a cactus blossom can be; the white ones and the red ones were still buds, but the purple and the yellow were blossoms, open full and the most beautiful of all.

Silva saw him before I did. The white man was riding a big gray horse, coming up the trail towards us. He was traveling fast and the gray horse's feet sent rocks rolling off the trail into the dry tumbleweeds. Silva motioned for me to stop and we watched the white man. He didn't see us right away, but finally his horse whinnied at our horses and he stopped. He looked at us briefly before he lapped the gray horse across the three hundred yards that separated us. He stopped his horse in front of Silva, and his young fat face was shadowed by the brim of his hat. He didn't look mad, but his small, pale eyes moved from the blood-soaked gunny sacks hanging from my saddle to Silva's face and then back to my face.

"Where did you get the fresh meat?" the white man asked.

"I've been hunting," Silva said, and when he shifted his weight in the saddle the leather creaked.

"The hell you have, Indian. You've been rustling cattle. We've been looking for the thief for a long time."

The rancher was fat, and sweat began to soak through his white cowboy shirt and the wet cloth stuck to the thick rolls of belly fat. He almost seemed to be panting from the exertion of talking, and he smelled rancid, maybe because Silva scared him.

Silva turned to me and smiled. "Go back up the mountain, Yellow Woman."

The white man got angry when he heard Silva speak in a language he couldn't understand. "Don't try anything, Indian. Just keep riding to Marquez. We'll call the state police from there."

The rancher must have been unarmed because he was very frightened and if he had a gun he would have pulled it out then. I turned my horse around and the rancher yelled, "Stop!" I looked at Silva for an instant and there was something ancient and dark—something I could feel in my stomach—in his eyes, and when I glanced at his hand I saw his finger on the trigger of the .30-30 that was still in the saddle scabbard. I slapped my horse across the flank and the sacks of raw meat swung against my knees as the horse leaped up the trail. It was hard to keep my balance, and once I thought I felt the saddle slipping backward; it was because of this that I could not look back.

I didn't stop until I reached the ridge where the trail forked. The horse was breathing deep gasps and there was a dark film of sweat on its neck. I looked down in the direction I had come from, but I couldn't see the place. I waited. The wind came up and pushed warm air past me. I looked up at the sky, pale blue and full of thin clouds and fading vapor trails left by jets.

I think four shots were fired—I remember hearing four hollow explosions that reminded me of deer hunting. There could have been more shots after that, but I couldn't have heard them because my horse was running again and the loose rocks were making too much noise as they scattered around his feet.

Horses have a hard time running downhill, but I went that way instead of uphill to the mountain because I thought it was safer. I felt better with the horse running southeast past the round gray hills that were covered with cedar trees and black lava rock. When I got to the plain in the distance I could see the dark green patches of tamaracks that grew along the river; and beyond the river I could see the beginning of the pale sandrock mesas. I stopped the horse and looked back to see if anyone was coming; then I got off the horse and turned the horse around, wondering if it would go back to its corral under the pines on the mountain. It looked back at me for a moment and then plucked a mouthful of green tumbleweeds before it trotted back up the trail with its ears pointed forward, carrying

its head daintily to one side to avoid stepping on the dragging
reins. When the horse disappeared over the last hill, the gunny
sacks full of meat were still swinging and bouncing.

I walked toward the river on a wood-hauler's road that I knew
would eventually lead to the paved road. I was thinking about
waiting beside the road for someone to drive by, but by the time
I got to the pavement I had decided it wasn't very far to walk
if I followed the river back the way Silva and I had come.
    The river water tasted good, and I sat in the shade under a
cluster of silvery willows. I thought about Silva, and I felt sad
at leaving him; still, there was something strange about him,
and I tried to figure it out all the way back home.
    I came back to the place on the river bank where he had been
sitting the first time I saw him. The green willow leaves that
he had trimmed from the branch were still lying there, wilted
in the sand. I saw the leaves and I wanted to go back to him—
to kiss him and to touch him—but the mountains were too far
away now. And I told myself, because I believe it, he will come
back sometime and be waiting again by the river.

I followed the path up from the river into the village. The sun
was getting low, and I could smell supper cooking when I got
to the screen door of my house. I could hear their voices inside—
my mother was telling my grandmother how to fix the Jell-O
and my husband, Al, was playing with the baby. I decided to
tell them that some Navajo had kidnaped me, but I was sorry
that old Grandpa wasn't alive to hear my story because it was
the Yellow Woman stories he liked to tell best.

IVAN DOIG

FLIP

FROM *THIS HOUSE OF SKY*

Let me call her Ruth here.

She came to the ranch on one of the first pale chilly days of an autumn, hired to cook for us for a few months, and stayed on in our lives for almost three years. Her time with us is a strange season all mist and dusk and half-seen silhouettes, half-heard cries. There is nothing else like it in the sortings of my memory. Nor is there anything now to be learned about why it happened to be her who became my father's second wife and my second mother, for no trace of Ruth—reminiscence, written line, photograph, keepsake—has survived. It is as if my father tried to scour every sign of her from our lives.

But not even scouring can get at the deepest crevices of memory, and in them I glimpse Ruth again. I see best the eyes, large and softly brown with what seemed to be some hurt beginning to happen behind them—the deep trapped look of a doe the instant before she breaks for cover. The face was too oval, plain as a small white platter, but those madonna eyes graced it. Dark-haired—I think brunette. Slim but full breasted. And taller than my mother had been, nearly as tall as Dad. A voice with the grip of experience in it, and a knowing laugh twice as old as herself.

Not quite entirely pretty then, this taut, guarded Ruth, but close enough to earn second looks. And the mystery in her could not be missed, the feeling that being around her somehow was like watching the roulette wheel in the Maverick make its slow, fanlike ambush on chance.

19

Even how Ruth came to be there, straight in our path after
Dad turned our lives toward the valley, seems to have no logic
to it. Never before or since did I see anyone quite like her on
a ranch. Ranch cooks generally were stout spinsters or leathery
widows, worn dour and curt by a life which gave them only the
chore of putting meals on the table for a dozen hungry men
three times a day. So alike were cooks usually that the hired
men seldom bothered to learn their names, simply called each
one *Missus*.

But Ruth didn't fit Missus, she was Ruth to everybody.
Those eyes were the kind which caught your glance on the
streets of Great Falls or Helena, where young women went to
escape to a store job and the start toward marriage and a life
they hoped would be bigger than the hometown had offered—
city eyes, restless eyes. Yet here Ruth was in the valley, passing
the syrup pitcher along the cookhouse table, and for all anyone
could tell, she seemed ready to stay until she came upon whatever she was looking for.

Her first reach had been badly out of aim—a marriage, quickly
broken, to a young soldier. *He was home on a furlough one time,*
a voice from his family tells it, *and met her and married her in
such short time; really they weren't even acquainted.* Dad must have
known about that jagged, too-quick marriage; the valley kept
no such secrets. But living womanless had left us wide open for
Ruth. To me, an eight-year-old, she was someone who might
provide some mothering again. Not *much* mothering, because
she kept a tight, careful mood, like a cat ghosting through new
tall grass. But the purr of a clever voice, fresh cookies and fruit
added to my lunchbox, even a rare open grin from her when I
found an excuse to loiter in the kitchen—all were pettings I
hadn't had. And for Dad, Ruth must have come as a sudden
chance to block the past, a woman to put between him and the
death on the summer mountain.

It happened faster than any of us could follow. This man who
had spent six careful years courting my mother now abruptly
married his young ranch cook.

Ruth, Dad. They were a pairing only the loins could have tugged together, and as with many decisions taken between the thighs, all too soon there were bitterest afterthoughts.

I remember that the drumfire of regret and retaliation began to echo between them before we moved from the ranch in early 1948, only months after the wedding. The ranch itself had plenty of ways to nick away at everyone's nerves. Any sprinkle of rain or snow puttied its mile of road into a slick gumbo, the pickup wallowing and whipping as Dad cussed his way back and forth. Yet the place also was too dry for good hay or grain, and too scabbed with rock up on the slopes where the cattle and sheep had to graze. Dad had begun to call it *this-goddamn-rockpile*, the surest sign that he was talking himself into dropping the lease. For her part, Ruth likely was ready to leave after the first night of howling coyotes, or of a cougar edging out of the Castles to scream down a gulch. Working as a cook on the big ranches out in the open expanse of the valley was one thing, but slogging away here under the tumbled foothills was entirely another. Ruth's mouth could fire words those soft eyes seemed to know nothing about, and the ranch primed her often. I can hear her across the years:

Charlie, I don't have to stay here, I didn't marry this hellforsaken ranch . . . I got other places I can go, don't you doubt it . . . Lots of places, Charlie.

And Dad, the jut notching out his jaw as it always did when he came ready for argument: *Damn it, woman, d'ye think we can walk away from a herd of cattle and a band of sheep? We got to stay until we get the livestock disposed of. You knew what you were getting into . . .* And always at the last, as he would hurl from the house out to another of the ranch's endless chores: *Will-ye-forget-it? Just-forget-it?*

But nothing was forgotten, by either of them. Instead, they stored matters up against one another. *The time that you . . . I told you then . . .* There came to be a full litany of combat, and either one would refer as far back as could be remembered.

If they had fought steadily the marriage might have snapped

apart before long and neither would have been severely hurt.
But they bickered in quick seasons. Weeks, maybe a month,
might pass in calm. Saturday nights, we went to dances in the
little town of Ringling. Dad and Ruth whirled there by the
hour. Often my Uncle Angus called the square dances, and I
would watch Dad in a circle of flying dancers while a burring
voice so close to his cried: *Swing your opposite across the hall, now
swing your corners, now your partners, and promenade all!* Sometime
after midnight, I would stretch on a bench along the dancehall
wall with a coat over me and go to sleep. I would wake up
leaning against Ruth's shoulder as the pickup growled down the
low hill to the ranch buildings. The murmurs I heard then
between Dad and Ruth would go on for a day or two. But
eventually, a blast of argument, then no talking, sulking. Sometimes Ruth would leave for a day or two. Sometimes Dad *told*
her to leave, and she wouldn't. At last, one or the other would
make a truce—never by apology, just some softened oblique
sentence which meant that the argument could be dropped now.
Until Ruth felt restless again; until Dad's unease twisted in
him once more.

I watched this slow bleed of a marriage, not yet old enough
to be afraid of exactly what might happen but with the feeling
creeping in me that the arguments in our house meant more
than I could see. Joking with me as she sometimes did, Ruth
would grin and her face come down close to mine: *If your hair
gets any redder, you're gonna set the town on fire, you know that?*
Dad talked in his usual soft burr when I rode in the pickup
with him: *Son, let's go fix that fence where Rankin's cows got in.
There's not enough grass on this place for our own without that
honyocker's cows in here, too. Hold on, I'm gonna give her snoose
to get up this sidehill*—But when they were together, I so often
heard a hard edge in what they said to each other, a careful
evenness as they talked over plans to leave the ranch as soon
as they could.

For what was happening, I can grasp now, was the misjudg-
ment greater by far than their decision to be married: their

mutual refusal to call it off. Each had a fear blockading that logical retreat. Dad would not admit his mistake because he wanted not to look a fool to the valley. On that he was entirely wrong; the only mystification anyone seemed to have was why he kept on with a hopeless mismatch. *I couldn't see that, going on with that marriage, with that little child you in the midst of it,* a woman of the valley once cried to me. *Ruth thought everything should come in a cloud for her. But she had hate in her, she was full of hatefulness . . . What was Charlie thinking of to let that go on?* For her part, Ruth would not face up to another split, would not let another broken marriage point to her as an impossible wife. Since neither could see how to call a halt to the mismarriage, it somehow was going to have to halt itself. But before it did, the pair of them would make two mighty exertions to stay together.

Perhaps because this arrival of Ruth in our lives is a riffle of time which everyone around me later tried to put from mind, memory hovers stubbornly here. Memory, or the curious nature, perhaps, that keeps asking exactly what the commotion was about. For on the edge of this fray between Dad and Ruth I begin to see myself, and here at the age of eight and nine and ten I was curiosity itself. If I inscribe myself freehand, as Dad did with the unfading stories he told me of his own young years, the words might be these: *I was a boy I would scarcely know on the street today. Chunky, red-haired, freckled—the plump face straight off a jar of strawberry jam. Always wearing a small cowboy hat, because I seared in the sun. Under that hat, and inside a name like no one else's. Ivan: EYE-vun, amid the Frankie-Ronny-Bobby-Jimmy-Larry-Howie trill of my schoolmates. Dad was amazed with himself when he at last discovered that he had spliced Russian onto the Scottish family name; he and my mother simply had known someone named Ivan and liked the sudden soft curl of the word—and besides wanted to show up Dad's least favorite brother, who had recently daubed 'Junior' onto a son.*

The name, together with the hair and freckles, gave me attention I wasn't always sure I wanted. At Dad's side in the saloons I sometimes

met men who would look down at me and sing out: 'Now the heroes
were plenty and well known to fame/Who fought in the ranks of the
Czar/But the bravest of all was a man by the name/Of Ivan . . .
Skavinsky . . . Skavar!' I consoled myself that it was better than being
dubbed Red or Pinky, which I also heard sometimes in the saloons.
And once in a great while, in his thoughtful mood as if remembering
a matter far away, Dad would call me 'Skavinsky.' It made a special
moment, and I prized it that way.

People who remember me at this age say I was something of a small
sentinel: 'You always were such a little sobersides.' 'You was always
so damned bashful it was hard to get a word out of you.' All right,
but how jolly was I supposed to be, with a mother dead and the next
one in a sniping match with my father? I believe that much of what
was taken to be my soberness was simply a feeling of being on guard,
of carefully watching life flame around me. Of trying not to be surprised
at whatever else might happen.

I can tell you a time, as my father storied so many of his into me:
Dad and Ruth and I are walking toward the movie house, on some
night of truce in the family. We are at the end of the block from the
building when I notice Kirkwood coming down the street. Kirkwood
is a school classmate, but a forehead taller than I am, and with that
head round as a cannonball and atop square shoulders you could lay
bricks on. Kirkwood can never be counted on to behave the same from
one minute to the next, and now he bears down on us, yelps 'Hullo,
Ivy!' and takes a swipe at my hat.

The worst prospect I can think of is coming true: the great given
rule of boyhood is not to make you look silly in front of your grownups,
and Kirkwood is toe-dancing all over it. Now he has put on a hyena
grin and falls in step with me. He glances toward Dad and Ruth, then
skips at me and knocks the hat from my head.

'Kirkwood-I'll-murder-you!' I rasp as lethally as I can and clap the
hat down over my ears. It sends his delirium up another notch, and
he skips in for another whack at the hat. Dad and Ruth no longer can
pretend not to notice and begin to glance back at the sniggering and
muttering behind them.

Kirkwood giggles; this time when I hear him scuffling close, I swing

*around with my right arm stiff in what I now understand was a right
jab. Kirkwood runs his round jaw into it and bounces flat onto the
sidewalk. He wobbles up, looks at me dazedly, then trots off in a
steady howl. I hustle toward the movie house where Dad and Ruth
are waiting and watching. Both are grinning as if they have mouths
full of marshmallows.*

*But I was less sure of my feelings. It was as if I had been through
a dream that I knew was going to happen. Not in every detail—who
could foresee even Kirkwood gone that batty?—but in its conclusion:
that from the instant Kirkwood rambled into sight, he was aimed onto
my fist. It somehow seemed to me there ought to be an apprehension
about such certainty, some questioning of why it had to be inexorably
so. But it was a questioning I could not handle, and what I felt most
was the curious intensity of having seen it all unfold, myself somehow
amid the scene as it swept past me. Somehow a pair of me, the one
doing and the one seeing it done.*

*It was exactly that twinned mix—apprehension and interestedness—
that I felt all during Ruth's startling time in our lives.*

Now the awaited move, when we at last would put the ranch
and its zone of combat behind us. Put them behind us, in fact,
in a way as wondrous to me as it was unexpected, for Dad and
Ruth faced toward White Sulphur Springs and undertook the
last livelihood anyone could have predicted of either of them:
they went into the cafe business.

The Grill, across the street from the Stockman, had come up
for rent. It was the third and smallest eating place in a town
which had not quite enough trade for two. There was the barest
smidgin of reason to think of Ruth coping with such an enterprise; with her years of cooking for crews, she at least could
handle a kitchen. But for Dad, the notion had all the logic of
a bosun's mate stumping ashore to open up a candy shop. Yet
somehow Dad and Ruth, this pair who had never been around
a town business of any sort and who already were finding out
that they flinted sparks off each other all too easily—somehow
they talked one another into trying to run the Grill together,
and somehow they turned out to have a knack for it.

The knack, of course, was nine-tenths hard work. *Those two took on that place like a house afire.* But when Dad sorted through his savvy, there was use there, too. From all the ranches behind him, he knew enough about purchasing provisions, and better yet, he knew the valley and its people. He put up new hours for the Grill. It would stay open until after the last saloon had closed.

There at the last of the night and the first hours of morning, the Grill found its customers: truckers on their runs through the pitchy dark, ranchers heading home from late business in Helena or Great Falls, some of the Rainbow crowd trying to sober up on black coffee and T-bone. Steaks and hashbrowns covered Ruth's stove, and Dad dealt platters of food until his arms ached. Saturday nights I was allowed to stay up as late as I wanted—on Dad's principle of fathering, that I might as well have a look at life sooner than later—and I looked forward to the pace of that last night of the week like a long, long parade coming past.

Just at dusk, ranch hands would begin to troop in for supper, minutes-old haircuts shining between their shirt collars and hat brims, because *Well, I gotta go in and get my ears lowered* was the standard excuse to come to town for a night of carousing. As the dark eased down and the war-whoops from the crowds in the Maverick and the Grand Central came oftener, the cafe would begin to receive the staggerers who had decided to forget the haircut after all and get right on with the drinking. They were a pie crowd, usually jabbing blearily at the fluffiest and most meringue-heaped possibilities in the countertop case. Sometime in mid-evening, Lloyd Robinson would arrive, suspiciously fingering down a coin for a cup of coffee and demanding to know if my freckles weren't from a cow's tail having swiped across me. Soon after him, as if the town's two prime bellies couldn't be long apart, it would be Nellie crashing in, chortling with delight and spinning a joke off the first item he spotted: *That jam jar, now—did you hear about the Swede at the breakfast table?* '*Yiminey,*' *he says,* '*I yoost learn to call it yam and now they tell me it's yelly.*'

Then if there was a dance in the hall behind the Rainbow, the night would crest with two tides of customers: one which filled the cafe as soon as the dance ended, and a second made up of those who had gone off to drink some more until the first wave cleared out. And at last, sometime after two in the morning, would come the phone call from Pete McCabe thirty yards across at the Stockman: *Save us three, Charlie.* Dad would put aside a trio of T-bone steaks, and before long, Pete and his night's pair of bar help would be straddling in to the counter and trading the night's news with Dad. A few hours before Sunday dawn, the Grill would close and we would step out the door into the emptied town.

A quieter flow of eaters presented themselves too, I was to notice—the town's oldtimers, the pensioners, the sheepherders and cowpokes hanging on from yesteryear. As I have told, the Stockman, where Pete McCabe was known to be the kind of a fellow who would set up a drink even when the pension check hadn't yet come to pay for it, drew most of these oldtimers, sometime in the night, sometime through the week. Now, over across the street, Dad was good for an emergency meal as well. How many times I heard one or another of them, joking so as not to seem begging, ask Dad for a meal on *account*—on account, that was, of being broke. Weeks and months and even years afterward, one or another of them might stop him on the street and say, *Charlie, here's that Grill money I've been owing you.*

Ruth, I think, never objected to those meals Dad would jot on the tab. They might fight over a spilled holder of toothpicks, but not that long apologetic rank of "accountants." Out on the valley ranches, she had seen in the crews clopping to her supper table the men who were growing too old for the work they had done all their lives, and soon too old for anything but those lame rounds of the saloons along Main Street.

Age was making that same wintry push on the one person

Ruth seemed steadily to hold affection for, too. She had been
raised by her grandmother—her family so poor and at war with
itself it had shunted her off there—and regularly she went across
the Big Belts to the next valley to see the old woman. Several
times, on an afternoon off from the cafe, she took me on those
visits.

Creased and heavy, stiff in the knees and going blind, the
grandmother was the most ancient woman I had ever seen, and
her house the shadowiest and most silent. The grandmother
spent her days entirely in the dim kitchen, finding her way by
habit through a thickening haze of cataract webs. When we
stepped in past the black kitchen stove and the drab cabinets
lining the walls, the grandmother would peer toward us and
then begin to talk in a resigned murmur, eyes and legs giving
way above and below a body not yet quite willing to die, and
Ruth, listening, would be a different person, softer, younger,
seeming to feel the grandmother's aches as her own.

But whatever Ruth took from those visits seemed to stop at
our own doorsill. Time and again, she and Dad faced off, and
then they would go full of silence for a day or more. Or worse,
one would be silent and the other would claw on and on.

If nothing else set them at each other, there always was the
argument about our small herd of cattle, which Dad had kept
after all when we left the ranch and which he was pasturing
now in the foothills of the Big Belts. He drove out each morning
to pitch hay to the cattle, then came back to work in the cafe
from mid-afternoon until closing. On weekends, I went with
him to the cattle, and only then would hear out of him the few
tiny snatches of music he knew, his absentminded sign of contentment. A forkful of alfalfa to the cows, then *But the squaws
ALONG the YuKON* . . . *are-good-enough-for-me;* a tuneless
minute of whistling and looking out across the valley to the
pinnacles of the Castles, then *When it's SPRINGtime in the
ROCKies* . . .

Whether or not Ruth knew he was out there singing and
whistling amid the cows, she did suspect that Dad had not given

up intentions of ranching. Dad suspected, just as rightly, that
neither of them could keep up the day-and-night pace of the
cafe work for long, and that our income soon was going to have
to come from livestock again. . . .

And always, always, the two voices which went at each other
just above my head. *Ruth, where the hell you been? If you think
you can just walk off and leave me with the cafe that way, you got
another think coming . . . Mister, I didn't marry you to spend all my
time in any damn cafe. Where I go is my business . . .* The look in
my direction, then: *Better leave us alone, Ivan.* . . . But the voices
would go on, through the walls, until one more silence set in
between my father and my second mother.

The silences stretched tauter until a day sometime in the
autumn of 1948, when the Grill and our town life came to an
end. Dad and Ruth could agree on one thing: the tremendous
hours of cafe work were grinding them down. They gave up the
lease, and now bought a thousand head of sheep and arranged
to winter them at a ranch on Battle Creek in the Sixteen country, not far from the Basin where Dad had grown up.

There seemed to be no middle ground in the marriage. Not
having managed to make it work while under the stare of the
entire town, now the two of them decided to try a winter truce
out in what was the emptiest corner of the county, just as it
had been when Peter and Annie Doig came there to homestead
a half-century before and as it is whenever I return now to
drive its narrow red-shale road. Gulch-and-sage land, spare,
silent. Out there in the rimming hills beyond the valley, twenty-
five miles from town, Dad and Ruth would have time alone to
see whether their marriage ought to last. *Could* last.

And I began what would be a theme of my life, staying in
town in the living arrangement we called *boarding out.* It meant
that someone or other, friend or relative or simply whoever
looked reliable, would be paid by Dad to provide me room-and-
board during the weekdays of school. It reminds me now of a
long visit, the in-between feeling of having the freedom to wan-

der in and out but never quite garnering any space of your own.
But I had some knack then for living at the edges of other
people's existences, and in this first span of boarding out—
with friends of Ruth, the Jordan family—I found a household
which teemed in its comings-and-goings almost as the cafe had.

Indeed, *We call it the short-order house around here,* Helen Jordan
said as deer season opened and a surge of her out-of-town relatives, armed like a guerrilla platoon, swept through. Ralph
Jordan himself came and went at uneven hours of the day and
night, black with coal dust and so weary he could hardly talk:
he was fireman on the belching old locomotive called Sagebrush
Annie which snailed down the branch-line from White Sulphur
to the main railroad at Ringling. Ralph with a shovelful of coal
perpetually in hand, Helen forever up to her wrists in bread
dough or dishwater—the Jordans were an instructive couple
about the labor that life could demand.

And under their busy roof, I was living for the first time
with other children, their two sons and a daughter. The older
boy, Curtis, thin and giggly, was my age, and we slept in the
same bed and snickered in the dark at each other's jokes. Boarding out at the Jordans went smoothly enough, then, except at
the end of each week when Dad was to arrive and take me to
the Battle Creek ranch with him. Friday night after Friday night,
he did not arrive.

Whatever Dad or Ruth or I had expected of this testing
winter, the unlooked-for happened: the worst weather of thirty
years blasted into the Sixteen country, and Dad and Ruth found
themselves in contest not so much with each other now, but
with the screaming white wilderness outside.

As bad winters are apt to do, this one of 1948–49 whipped
in early and hard. Snow fell, drifted, crusted into gray crystal
windrows, then fell and drifted and crusted gray again. Dad and
his hired man pushed the sheep in from the pastures to a big
shed at the ranch buildings. Nothing could root grass out of
that solid snow. The county road began to block for weeks at

a time. Winter was sealing the Sixteen country into long frozen months of aloneness, and I was cordoned from the life of Dad and Ruth there.

At last, on the sixth Friday night, long after I had given up hope again, Dad appeared. Even then he couldn't take me to the ranch with him; he had spent ten hours fighting his way through the snow, and there was the risk that the countryside would close off entirely again before he could bring me back to town Sunday night. *Tell ye what we'll do, Skavinsky. Talk to that teacher of yours and see if you can work ahead in your schoolwork. If she'll let you, I'll come in somehow next Friday and you can come spend a couple of weeks out at the ranch.*

All week, whenever the recess bell rang I stayed at my desk and flipped ahead in one text or another, piling up lesson sheets to hand to the bemused teacher. Before school was out on Friday, Dad came to the door of the classroom for me, cocking his grin about clacking in with snowy overshoes and a girth of sheepskin coat.

The highway down the valley was bare, a black dike above the snow, as he drove the pickup to the turnoff toward Battle Creek. Then the white drifts stretched in front of us like a wide storm-frothed lake whose waves had suddenly stopped motion to hang in billows and peaks where the wind had lashed them against the sky.

The very tops of fenceposts, old gray cedar heads with rounded snow caps, showed where the road was buried. Between the post tops, a set of ruts had been rammed and hacked by Dad and the few other ranchers who lived in the Sixteen country.

Dad drove into the sea of snow with big turns of the steering wheel, keeping the front wheels grooved in the ruts while the rear end of the pickup jittered back and forth spinning snow out behind us. Sometimes the pickup growled to a halt. We would climb out and shovel away heavy chunks like pieces of an igloo. Then Dad would back the pickup a few feet for a running start and bash into the ruts again. Once we went over a snowdrift on twin rows of planks another of the ranchers had laid for support, a bridge in midsea. Once we drove entirely over the top of a drift without planks at all.

Where the road led up to the low ridge near the old Jap Stewart ranch, we angled between cliffs of snow higher than the pickup. Near Battle Creek, with our headlights fingering past the dark into the white blankness, Dad swerved off the road entirely and sent the pickup butting through the smaller drifts in a hayfield. It had started to snow heavily, the wind out of the Basin snaking the flurries down to sift into the ruts. I watched the last miles roll up on the tiny numbers under the speedometer as Dad wrestled the wheel and began his soft Scots cussing: *Snow on a man, will ye? Damn-it-all-to-hell-anyway, git back in those ruts. Damn-such-weather. Hold on, son, there's a ditch here somewhere . . .* The twenty-fifth mile, the last, we bucked down a long slope to the ranch with the heavy wet flakes flying at us like clouds of moths. Dad roared past the lighted windows of the ranch house and spun the pickup inside the shelter of the lambing shed. *Done!* he said out into the storm. *Done, damn ye!*

To my surprise, Battle Creek was not living up to its name, and Dad and Ruth were getting along less edgily there than they ever had. It may have been that there simply was so much cold-weather work to be done, feeding the sheep, carrying in firewood, melting snow for water because the pump had frozen, that they had little stamina left over for argument. Or perhaps they had decided that the winter had to be gotten through, there simply was no route away from one another until spring. Whatever accounted for it, I slipped into its bask and warmed for the days to come.

Each morning, Ruth stood at the window sipping from a white mug of coffee, watching as Dad and the hired man harnessed the team to the hay sled. Then, if Dad had said they needed her that day, she would pull on heavy clothing and go out and take the reins while the men forked hay off to the sheep. Dad helped her in the house, the two of them working better together at the meals and dishes than they had when they were feeding half the town in the Grill. The pair of them even joked about the icy journey to the outhouse which started each day. Whoever went first, the other would demand to know whether the seat had been left good and warm. *It damn well ought to be,* the other would say, *half of my behind is still out on it.* Or: *Sure did, I left it smoking for you.*

The ranch house had been built with its living quarters on the second floor, well above the long snowdrifts which duned against the walls. A railed porch hung out over the snow the full length of the house, and from it the other ranch buildings were in view like a small anchored fleet seen from a ship's deck. The lambing shed, low and cloud-gray and enormously long, seemed to ride full-laden in the white wash of winter. Most of the time, the sheep were corralled on the far side of the shed, their bored bleats coming as far as the house if the wind was down. Not far from the lambing shed stood the barn, dark and bunched into itself, prowing up out of the stillness higher than anything else in sight. A few small sheds lay with their roofs disappearing in drifts, swamped by this cold ocean of a winter. Battle Creek flowed just beyond those sheds, but the only mark of it was a gray skin of ice.

In this snow world, Dad and his hired man skimmed back and forth on the hay sled, a low wide hayrack on a set of runners pulled by a team of plunging workhorses. I rode with the men, hanging tight to the frame of the hayrack prowing above where the horses' hooves chuffed into the snow. When the men talked, their puffs of breath clouded fatly out in front of their faces. Our noses trickled steadily. Dad put a mitten against my face often to see that my cheeks weren't being frostbitten.

The winter fought us again and again. Our dog crashed through the ice of Battle Creek, and the wind carried the sound of his barking away from the house. We found the shatter where he had tried to claw himself out before the creek froze him and then drowned him. A blizzard yammered against the back wall of the house for two days without stop. Outside the snow flew

so thick it seemed there was no space left between the flakes in
the air, just an endless crisscross of flecks the whiteness of goose
down. When Dad and the hired man went to feed the sheep,
they would disappear into the storm, swallowed, thirty feet from
the window where Ruth and I watched.

An afternoon when the weather let up briefly, I climbed the
slope behind the house, to where a long gully troughed toward
Battle Creek. Snow had packed the gulch so full that I could
sled down over its humps and dips for hundreds of feet at a
time. Trying out routes, I flew off a four-foot shale bank and
in the crash sliced my right knee on the end of a sled runner
as if I had fallen against an axe blade.

That moment of recall is dipped in a hot red ooze. The bloody
slash scared out my breath in a long *uhhhhh*. A clench ran
through the inside of me, then the instant heat of tears burned
below my eyes. The climb from the gulch was steep. Now the
burning fell to my leg. Blood sopped out as I hobbled to the
house with both hands clamped over my wound, and Ruth shook
as she snipped away the heavy-stained pants leg. The cut, she
quickly told me, did not live up to its first horrific gush; it was
long but shallow and clean, and dressings easily took care of it.
In a few days, I could swing my leg onto the hay sled and again
ride with the men above the horses' white-frosted heels.

The two weeks passed in surges of that winter weather, like
tides flowing in long and hard. On the last morning, no snow
was falling, but Dad said so much had piled by then that we
could get to town only by team and sled. Ruth said she wanted
to go with us. Dad looked at her once and nodded.

Dad and the hired man lifted the rack off the hay boat and
fixed a seat of planks onto the front pair of sled runners. Inside
that seat, blankets piled thickly onto the heavy coats we wore,
we sat buried in warmth, almost down in the snow as the horses
tugged us along on the running bob. Harness buckles sang a
ching-tink, ching-tink with every step of the horses. Dad slapped
the reins against the team's rumps and headed us toward the
hayfields along Battle Creek. The road would be no help to us,

drift humped onto drift there by now. We would aim through meadows and bottomlands where the snow lay flatter.

The grayness stretching all around us baffled my eyes. Where I knew hills had to be, no hills showed. The sagebrush too had vanished, from a countryside forested with its clumps. One gray sheet over and under and around, the snow and overcast had fused land and sky together. Even our sleigh was gray and half-hidden, weathered ash moving like a pale shadow through ashen weather.

Dad headed the team by the tops of fenceposts, and where the snow had buried even them, by trying to pick out the thin besieged hedge of willows along the creek. I peeked out beside Ruth, the two fogs of our breath blowing back between us as the horses found footing to trot. More often, they lunged at the snow, breaking through halfway up their thick legs. Dad talked to the horses every little while: *Hup there, Luck, get your heft into it. . . . Pull a bit, damn ye, Bess . . . Up this rise, now, get yourself crackin' there . . .* Their ears would jab straight up when they felt the flat soft slap of the reins and heard Dad's voice, and they would pull faster and we would go through the snow as if the sled was a running creature carrying us on its back.

The twin cuts of our sled tracks, the only clear lines the snow had not yet had time to seize and hide, traced away farther and farther behind us. Except for the strides of the horses and Dad's words to them, the country was silent, held so under the weight of the snow. In my memory that day has become a set of instants somewhere between life and death, a kind of eclipse in which hours did not pass and sound did not echo, all color washed to a flannel sameness and distance swelling away beyond any counting of it. We went into that fog-world at one end of Battle Creek and long after came out at the other, but what happened in between was as measureless as a float through space. If it was any portion of existence at all, it did not belong to the three of us, but to that winter which had frozen all time but its own.

After that ghostly trip, I went back to my boarding family and Dad and Ruth went on with the struggle against the winter.

It was another month or so before Dad arrived to take me to
the ranch again. This time, we drove across the drifted world
inside a plowed canyon, the slabs and mounds of frozen snow
wrenched high as walls on either side of the thin route. *We've
had a D-8 'dozer in here, the government sent it out when it looked
like we were all gonna lose the livestock out here. I had to get a
truckload of cottonseed cake sent in for the sheep, the hay's goin' so
damn fast. They put the bumper of that truck right behind the 'dozer
and even so it took 'em sixty-six hours to make it to the ranch and
back, can ye feature that? That load of cottoncake is gonna cost us
$2500 in transportation, but we had to have 'er.* I looked at him as
if he'd said the moon was about to fall on us; $2500 sounded
to me like all the money in the state of Montana. But Dad
grinned and talked on: *You should of been out here to see all the
snowplowin'. After they 'dozed out our haystacks, the crew was supposed to go up and 'doze out Jim Bill Keith's place. I was the guy that
was showin' them the way, ridin' the front end of that Cat. Hell, I
got us lost on the flats up here—same damn country I grew up in, ye
know—and we 'dozed in a big circle before we knew what was goin'
on. Plowed up a quarter of a mile of Jim Bill's fence and didn't even
know it. Blizzardin', boy it's been ablowin' out here, son. They came
out in one of those snow crawlers to change Cat crews—changed 'em
with an airplane when they first started, but the weather got so bad
they couldn't fly—so here they come now in one of these crawlers,
and the guy drivin' is drunker'n eight hundred dollars. I thought he
was gonna bring that damned crawler through the window of the
house . . .* I laughed with him, but must have looked worried.
He grinned again. *We're doin' okay in spite of it all. Haven't lost
any sheep yet, and that high-priced cottoncake gives us plenty of feed.
If this winter don't last into the summer, we're even gonna make some
pretty good money on the deal.*

Then in the next weeks came an afternoon when Dad saddled
a horse and plunged off through the below-zero weather to the
neighboring Keith ranch. *He came up here wanting to borrow some
cigarettes, and some whiskey.* Probably the truce with Ruth was
wearing through by then. Dad idled in the kitchen, talking and

drinking coffee with Mrs. Keith while waiting for Jim Bill and his hired man to come back from feeding their cattle. *I remember, yes, your dad had ridden up on a little sorrel horse and he was sitting in the kitchen with Flossie, and he kept looking out at this kind of a red knob out here on the hill. He looked and he looked, and pretty soon he jumped up and yelled: 'It's broke, it's broke!' and he ran outside. And that winter was broke. The hired man and I came riding home with our earflaps rolled up and our coats off, and our mittens stuck in the fork-hole of the saddle. Just like that.*

The chinook which had begun melting the snowdrifts even as Dad watched did signal the end of that ferocious winter, and somehow too it seemed to bring the end of the long storm within our household. Before, neither Dad nor Ruth had been able to snap off the marriage. Now they seemed in a contest to do it first, like a pair tugging at a stubborn wishbone.

Near the start of summer, Ruth announced she was leaving, this time for all time. Dad declared it the best idea he'd ever heard out of her. Alone with Ruth sometime in the swash and swirl of all this, I asked why she had to go. She gave me her tough grin, shook her head and said: *Your dad and me are never gonna get along together. We're done. We gave it our try.*

Why it was that the two of them had to endure that winter together before Ruth at last could go from Dad, I have never fathomed. Perhaps it was a final show of endurance against one another, some way to say *I can last at this as long as you can.* But that long since had been proved by both, and it is one of the strangenesses of this time that they had to go on and on with the proof of it. A last strangeness came over these years even after Ruth had vanished from us, and the divorce been handed down, one last unrelenting echo of it all. Dad no longer would even refer to Ruth by name. Instead, he took up something provided by one of the onlookers to our household's civil war. Naturally, the valley had not been able to resist choosing up sides in such a squabble, and a woman coming to Dad's defense reached for anything contemptible enough to call Ruth. At last she spluttered: *Why, that . . . that little flip!* For whatever reason,

that Victorian blurt rang perfectly with Dad, put him in the
right in all the arguments he was replaying in his mind. From
the moment the surprising word got back to him, he would talk
of Ruth only as *Flip, that damned Flip.*

Ruth went, and Flip stayed, one single poisoned word which
was all that was left of two persons' misguess about one another.
I have not seen Ruth for twenty years, nor spoken with her for
twenty-five. But for a time after those few warring years with
my father, her life straightened, perhaps like a piece of metal
seethed in fire for the anvil. She married again, there was a
son. And then calamity anew, that marriage in wreckage, and
another after that, the town voice saying more than ever of her
*She thinks everything should come in a cloud for her but she has
hatefulness in herself,* until at last she had gone entirely, *disappeared
somewhere out onto the Coast, nobody's cared to keep track of her.*

The son: I am curious about him. Was he taken by Ruth to
see the grandmother blinking back age and blindness? Did Ruth
stand with him, white mug of coffee in her hand, to watch snow
sift on a winter's wind? But the curiosity at last stops there.
When Dad and Ruth finally pulled apart, the one sentiment I
could recognize within me—have recognized ever since—was
relief that she had gone, and that the two of them could do no
more harm to each other.

Once more Dad had to right our life, and this time he did it
simply by letting the seasons work him up and down the valley.
He went to one ranch as foreman of the haying crew, on to
another to feed cattle during the winter, to a third for spring
and the lambing season.

When school started and I could not be with him, he rented
a cabin in White Sulphur and drove out to his ranch work in
the morning and back at night. During the winter and in spring's
busyness of lambing, I usually boarded with Nellie and his wife
in their fine log house. Nellie's wife was a world of improvement
from Ruth—a quiet approving woman, head up and handsome.
In the pasture behind their house she raised palomino horses,
flowing animals of a rich golden tan and with light blond manes

of silk. The horses seemed to represent her independence, her declaration away from Nellie's life of drinking, and she seemed to think Dad was right in letting me be as free and roaming as I was. It occurs to me now that she would have given me her quiet approving smile if I had come home from a wandering to report that I'd just been down at the Grand Central watching a hayhand knife a sheepherder.

And after her season of calm, Dad began one for us together. When the summer of 1950 came, he bought a herd of cattle, and we moved them and ourselves to a cattle camp along Sixteenmile Creek.

There our life held a simpler pace than I could ever remember. The two of us lived in a small trailer house, the only persons from horizon to horizon and several miles beyond. Dad decided to teach me to shoot a single-shot .22 rifle, using as targets the tan gophers which every horseback man hated for the treacherous little burrows they dug. We shot by the hour, rode into the hills every few days to look at the cattle, caught trout in the creek, watched the Milwaukee Railroad trains clip past four times every day.

Then I had my eleventh birthday—five years since my mother had died—and it seemed to trigger a decision in Dad. Something had been working at him, a mist of despond and unsteady health which would take him off into himself for hours at a time. One evening in the first weeks after my birthday, after he had been silent most of the day, he told me a woman would be coming into our lives again.

His words rolled a new planet under our feet, so astonishing and unlikely was this prospect. Ruth had come and gone without much lasting effect, except for the scalded mood Dad showed whenever he had a reason to mention her. But the person he had in mind now cast a shadowline across everything ahead of us, stood forth as the one apparition I could not imagine into our way of life. My mother's mother.

NORMAN MACLEAN

LOGGING AND PIMPING AND "YOUR PAL, JIM"

The first time I took any real notice of him was on a Sunday afternoon in a bunkhouse in one of the Anaconda Company's logging camps on the Blackfoot River. He and I and some others had been lying on our bunks reading, although it was warm and half-dark in the bunkhouse this summer afternoon. The rest of them had been talking, but to me everything seemed quiet. As events proved in a few minutes, the talking had been about "The Company," and probably the reason I hadn't heard it was that the lumberjacks were registering their customary complaints about the Company—it owned them body and soul; it owned the state of Montana, the press, the preachers, etc.; the grub was lousy and likewise the wages, which the Company took right back from them anyway by overpricing everything at the commissary, and they had to buy from the commissary, out in the woods where else could they buy. It must have been something like this they were saying, because all of a sudden I heard him break the quiet: "Shut up, you incompetent sons of bitches. If it weren't for the Company, you'd all starve to death."

At first, I wasn't sure I had heard it or he had said it, but he had. Everything was really quiet now and everybody was watching his small face and big head and body behind an elbow on his bunk. After a while, there were stirrings and one by one the stirrings disappeared into the sunlight of the door. Not a stirring spoke, and this was a logging camp and they were big men.

Lying there on my bunk, I realized that actually this was not the first time I had noticed him. For instance, I already knew his name, which was Jim Grierson, and I knew he was a socialist who thought Eugene Debs was soft. Probably he hated the Company more than any man in camp, but the men he hated more than the Company. It was also clear I had noticed him before, because when I started to wonder how I would come out with him in a fight, I discovered I already had the answer. I estimated he weighed 185 to 190 pounds and so was at least 35 pounds heavier than I was, but I figured I had been better taught and could reduce him to size if I could last the first ten minutes. I also figured that probably I could not last the first ten minutes.

I didn't go back to my reading but lay there looking for something interesting to think about, and was interested finally in realizing that I had estimated my chances with Jim in a fight even before I thought I had noticed him. Almost from the first moment I saw Jim I must have felt threatened, and others obviously felt the same way—later as I came to know him better all my thinking about him was colored by the question, "Him or me?" He had just taken over the bunkhouse, except for me, and now he was tossing on his bunk to indicate his discomfort at my presence. I stuck it out for a while, just to establish homestead rights to existence, but now that I couldn't read anymore, the bunkhouse seemed hotter than ever, so, after carefully measuring the implications of my not being wanted, I got up and sauntered out the door as he rolled over and sighed.

By the end of the summer, when I had to go back to school, I knew a lot more about Jim, and in fact he and I had made a deal to be partners for the coming summer. It didn't take long to find out that he was the best lumberjack in camp. He was probably the best with the saw and ax, and he worked with a kind of speed that was part ferocity. This was back in 1927, as I remember, and of course there was no such thing as a chain saw then, just as now there is no such thing as a logging camp or a bunkhouse the whole length of the Blackfoot River, although there is still a lot of logging going on there. Now the

saws are one-man chain saws run by light high-speed motors,
and the sawyers are married and live with their families, some
of them as far away as Missoula, and drive more than a hundred
miles a day to get to and from work. But in the days of the
logging camps, the men worked mostly on two-man crosscut
saws that were things of beauty, and the highest paid man in
camp was the man who delicately filed and set them. The two-
man teams who pulled the saws either worked for wages or
"gyppoed." To gyppo, which wasn't meant to be a nice-sounding
word and could be used as either a noun or a verb, was to be
paid by the number of thousands of board feet you cut a day.
Naturally, you chose to gyppo only if you thought you could
beat wages and the men who worked for wages. As I said, Jim
had talked me into being his partner for next summer, and we
were going to gyppo and make big money. You can bet I agreed
to this with some misgivings, but I was in graduate school now
and on my own financially and needed the big money. Besides,
I suppose I was flattered by being asked to be the partner of the
best sawyer in camp. It was a long way, though, from being all
flattery. I also knew I was being challenged. This was the world
of the woods and the working stiff, the logging camp being a
world especially overbearing with challenges, and, if you expected to duck all challenges, you shouldn't have wandered into
the woods in the first place. It is true, too, that up to a point
I liked being around him—he was three years older than I was,
which at times is a lot, and he had seen parts of life with which
I, as the son of a Presbyterian minister, wasn't exactly intimate.

A couple of other things cropped up about him that summer
that had a bearing on the next summer when he and I were to
gyppo together. He told me he was Scotch, which figured, and
that made two of us. He said that he had been brought up in
the Dakotas and that his father (and I quote) was "a Scotch
son of a bitch" who threw him out of the house when he was
fourteen and he had been making his own living ever since. He
explained to me that he made his living only partly by working.
He worked just in the summer, and then this cultural side of

him, as it were, took over. He holed up for the winter in some town that had a good Carnegie Public Library and the first thing he did was take out a library card. Then he went looking for a good whore, and so he spent the winter reading and pimping—or maybe this is stated in reverse order. He said that on the whole he preferred southern whores; southern whores, he said, were generally "more poetical," and later I think I came to know what he meant by this.

So I started graduate school that autumn, and it was tough and not made any easier by the thought of spending all next summer on the end of a saw opposite this direct descendant of a Scotch son of a bitch.

But finally it was late June and there he was, sitting on a log across from me and looking as near like a million dollars as a lumberjack can look. He was dressed all in wool—in a rich Black Watch plaid shirt, gray, short-legged stag pants, and a beautiful new pair of logging boots with an inch or so of white sock showing at the top. The lumberjack and the cowboy followed many of the same basic economic and ecological patterns. They achieved a balance if they were broke at the end of the year. If they were lucky and hadn't been sick or anything like that, they had made enough to get drunk three or four times and to buy their clothes. Their clothes were very expensive; they claimed they were robbed up and down the line and probably they were, but clothes that would stand their work and the weather had to be something special. Central to both the lumberjack's and the cowboy's outfit were the boots, which took several months of savings.

The pair that Jim had on were White Loggers made, as I remember, by a company in Spokane that kept your name and measurements. It was a great shoe, but there were others and they were great, too—they had to be. The Bass, the Bergman, and the Chippewa were all made in different parts of the country, but in the Northwest most of the jacks I remember wore the Spokane shoe.

As the cowboy boot was made all ways for riding horses and

working steers, the logger's boot was made for working on and around logs. Jim's pair had a six-inch top, but there were models with much higher tops—Jim happened to belong to the school that wanted their ankles supported but no tie on their legs. The toe was capless and made soft and somewhat waterproof with neat's-foot oil. The shoe was shaped to walk or "ride" logs. It had a high instep to fit the log, and with a high instep went a high heel, not nearly so high as a cowboy's and much sturdier because these were walking shoes; in fact, very fine walking shoes—the somewhat high heel threw you slightly forward of your normal stance and made you feel you were being helped ahead. Actually, this feeling was their trademark.

Jim was sitting with his right leg rocking on his left knee, and he gestured a good deal with his foot, raking the log I was sitting on for emphasis and leaving behind a gash in its side. The soles of these loggers' boots looked like World War I, with trenches and barbwire highly planned—everything planned, in this case, for riding logs and walking. Central to the grand design were the caulks, or "corks" as the jacks called them; they were long and sharp enough to hold to a heavily barked log or, tougher still, to one that was dead and had no bark on it. But of course caulks would have ripped out at the edges of a shoe and made you stumble and trip at the toes, so the design started with a row of blunt, sturdy hobnails around the edges and maybe four or five rows of them at the toes. Then inside came the battlefield of caulks, the real barbwire, with two rows of caulks coming down each side of the sole and one row on each side continuing into the instep to hold you when you jumped crosswise on a log. Actually, it was a beautiful if somewhat primitive design and had many uses—for instance, when a couple of jacks got into a fight and one went down the other was almost sure to kick and rake him with his boots. This treatment was known as "giving him the leather" and, when a jack got this treatment, he was out of business for a long time and was never very pretty again.

Every time Jim kicked and raked the log beside me for emphasis I wiped small pieces of bark off my face.

In this brief interlude in our relations it seemed to me that
his face had grown a great deal since I first knew him last year.
From last year I remembered big frame, big head, small face,
tight like a fist; I even wondered at times if it wasn't his best
punch. But sitting here relaxed and telling me about pimping
and spraying bark on my face, he looked all big, his nose too
and eyes, and he looked handsome and clearly he liked pimping—at least for four or five months of the year—and he especially liked being bouncer in his own establishment, but even
that, he said, got boring. It was good to be out in the woods
again, he said, and it was good to see me—he also said that;
and it was good to be back to work—he said that several times.

Most of this took place in the first three or four days. We
started in easy, each one admitting to the other that he was soft
from the winter, and, besides, Jim hadn't finished giving me
this course on pimping. Pimping is a little more complicated
than the innocent bystander might think. Besides selecting a
whore (big as well as southern, i.e., "poetical") and keeping
her happy (taking her to the Bijou Theater in the afternoons)
and hustling (rounding up all the Swedes and Finns and French
Canadians you had known in the woods), you also had to be
your own bootlegger (it still being Prohibition) and your own
police fixer (it being then as always) and your own bouncer
(which introduced a kind of sporting element into the game).
But after a few days of resting every hour we had pretty well
covered the subject, and still nobody seemed interested in bringing up socialism.

I suppose that an early stage in coming to hate someone is
just running out of things to talk about. I thought then it didn't
make a damn bit of difference to me that he liked his whores
big as well as southern. Besides, we were getting in shape a
little. We started skipping the rest periods and took only half
an hour at lunch and at lunch we sharpened our axes on our

Carborundum stones. Slowly we became silent, and silence itself
is an enemy to friendship; when we came back to camp each
went his own way, and within a week we weren't speaking to
each other. Well, this in itself needn't have been ominous. Lots
of teams of sawyers work in silence because that is pretty much
the kind of guys they are and of course because no one can talk
and at the same time turn out thousands of board feet. Some
teams of sawyers even hate each other and yet work together
year after year, something like the old New York Celtic basketball team, knowing the other guy's moves without troubling
to look. But our silence was different. It didn't have much to
do with efficiency and big production. When he broke the
silence to ask me if I would like to change from a six- to a seven-
foot saw, I knew I was sawing for survival. A six-foot blade was
plenty long enough for the stuff we were sawing, and the extra
foot would have been only that much more for me to pull.

It was getting hot and I was half-sick when I came back to
camp at the end of the day. I would dig into my duffel bag and
get clean underwear and clean white socks and a bar of soap
and go to the creek. Afterwards, I would sit on the bank until
I was dry. Then I would feel better. It was a rule I had learned
my first year working in the Forest Service—when exhausted
and feeling sorry for yourself, at least change socks. On weekends I spent a lot of time washing my clothes. I washed them
carefully and I expected them to be white, not gray, when they
had dried on the brush. At first, then, I relied on small, home
remedies such as cleanliness.

I had a period, too, when I leaned on proverbs, and tried to
pass the blame back on myself, with some justification. All
winter I had had a fair notion that something like this would
happen. Now I would try to be philosophical by saying to myself,
"Well, pal, if you fool around with the bull, you have to expect
the horn."

But, when you are gored, there is not much comfort in
proverbs.

Gradually, though, I began to fade out of my own picture of

myself and what was happening and it was he who controlled my thoughts. In these dreams, some of which I had during the day, I was always pulling a saw and he was always at the other end of it getting bigger and bigger but his face getting smaller and smaller—and closer—until finally it must have come through the cut in the log, and with no log between us now, it threatened to continue on down the saw until it ran into me. It sometimes came close enough so that I could see how it got smaller—by twisting and contracting itself around its nose—and somewhere along here in my dream I would wake up from the exertion of trying to back away from what I was dreaming about.

In a later stage of my exhaustion, there was no dream—or sleep—just a constant awareness of being thirsty and of a succession of events of such a low biological order that normally they escaped notice. All night sighs succeeded grunts and grumblings of the guts, and about an hour after everyone was in bed and presumably asleep there were attempts at homosexuality, usually unsuccessful if the statistics I started to keep were at all representative. The bunkhouse would become almost silent. Suddenly somebody would jump up in his bed, punch another somebody, and mutter, "You filthy son of a bitch." Then he would punch him four or five times more, fast, hard punches. The other somebody never punched back. Instead, trying to be silent, his grieved footsteps returned to bed. It was still early in the night, too early to start thinking about daybreak. You lay there quietly through the hours, feeling as if you had spent all the previous day drinking out of a galvanized pail—eventually, every thought of water tasted galvanized.

After two or three nights of this you came to know you could not be whipped. Probably you could not win, but you could not be whipped.

I'll try not to get technical about logging, but I have to give you some idea of daylight reality and some notion of what was going on in the woods while I was trying to stay alive. Jim's pace was set to kill me off—it would kill him eventually too, but first me. So the problem, broadly speaking, was how to throw him off this pace and not quite get caught doing it, because after working a week with this Jack Dempsey at the other end of the saw I knew I'd never have a chance if he took a punch at me. Yet I would have taken a punching from him before I would ever have asked him to go easier on the saw. You were no logger if you didn't feel this way. The world of the woods and the working stiff was pretty much made of three things— working, fighting, and dames—and the complete lumberjack had to be handy at all of them. But if it came to the bitter choice, he could not remain a logger and be outworked. If I had ever asked for mercy on the saw I might as well have packed my duffel bag and started down the road.

So I tried to throw Jim off pace even before we began a cut. Often, before beginning to saw, sawyers have to do a certain amount of "brushing out," which means taking an ax and chopping bushes or small jack pines that would interfere with the sawing. I guess that by nature I did more of this than Jim, and now I did as much of it as I dared, and it burned hell out of him, especially since he had yelled at me about it early in the season when we were still speaking to each other, "Jesus," he had said, "you're no gyppo. Any time a guy's not sawing he's not making money. Nobody out here is paying you for trimming a garden." He would walk up to a cut and if there was a small jack pine in the way he would bend it over and hold it with his foot while he sawed and he ripped through the huckleberry bushes. He didn't give a damn if the bushes clogged his saw. He just pulled harder.

As to the big thing, sawing, it is something beautiful when you are working rhythmically together—at times, you forget what you are doing and get lost in abstractions of motion and power. But when sawing isn't rhythmical, even for a short time, it becomes a kind of mental illness—maybe even something more deeply disturbing than that. It is as if your heart isn't working right. Jim, of course, had thrown us off basic rhythm when he started to saw me into the ground by making the stroke too fast and too long, even for himself. Most of the time I followed his stroke; I had to, but I would pick periods when I would not pull the saw to me at quite the speed or distance he was pulling it back to him. Just staying slightly off beat, not being quite so noticeable that he could yell but still letting him know what I was doing. To make sure he knew, I would suddenly go back to his stroke.

I'll mention just one more trick I invented with the hope of weakening Jim by frequent losses of adrenalin. Sawyers have many little but nevertheless almost sacred rules of work in order to function as a team, and every now and then I would almost break one of these but not quite. For instance, if you are making a cut in a fallen tree and it binds, or pinches, and you need a wedge to open the cut and free your saw and the wedge is on Jim's side of the log, then you are not supposed to reach over the log and get the wedge and do the job. Among sawyers, no time is wasted doing Alphonse-Gaston acts; what is on your side is your job—that's the rule. But every now and then I would reach over for his wedge, and when our noses almost bumped, we would freeze and glare. It was like a closeup in an early movie. Finally, I'd look somewhere else as if of all things I had never thought of the wedge, and you can be sure that, though I reached for it, I never got to it first and touched it.

Most of the time I took a lot of comfort from the feeling that some of this was getting to him. Admittedly, there were times when I wondered if I weren't making up a good part of this feeling just to comfort myself, but even then I kept doing things that in my mind were hostile acts. The other lumberjacks, though, helped to make me feel that I was real. They all acknowledged I was in a big fight, and quietly they encouraged me, probably with the hope they wouldn't have to take him on themselves. One of them muttered to me as we started out in the morning, "Some day that son of a bitch go out in the woods, he no come back." By which I assumed he meant I was to drop a tree on him and forget to yell, "Timber!" Actually, though, I had already thought of this.

Another good objective sign was that he got in a big argument with the head cook, demanding pie for breakfast. It sounds crazy, for anybody who knows anything knows that the head cook runs the logging camp. He is, as the jacks say, "the guy with the golden testicles." If he doesn't like a jack because the jack has the bad table manners to talk at meal time, the cook goes to the woods foreman and the jack goes down the road. Just the same, Jim got all the men behind him and then put up his big argument and nobody went down the road and we had pie every morning for breakfast—two or three kinds—and nobody ever ate a piece, nobody, including Jim.

Oddly, after Jim won this pie fight with the cook, things got a little better for me in the woods. We still didn't speak to each other, but we did start sawing in rhythm.

Then, one Sunday afternoon this woman rode into camp, and stopped to talk with the woods foreman and his wife. She was a big woman on a big horse and carried a pail. Nearly every one in camp knew her or of her—she was the wife of a rancher who owned one of the finest ranches in the valley. I had only met her but my family knew her family quite well, my father occasionally coming up the valley to preach to the especially congregated Presbyterians. Anyway, I thought I had better go over and speak to her and maybe do my father's cause some good, but it was a mistake. She was still sitting on her big horse and I had talked to her for just a couple of minutes, when who shows up but Jim and without looking at me says he is my partner and "pal" and asks her about the pail. The woods foreman takes all our parts in reply. First, he answers for her and says she is out to pick huckleberries, and then he speaks as foreman and tells her we are sawyers and know the woods well, and then he replies to himself and speaks for us and assures her that Jim would be glad to show her where the huckleberries are, and it's a cinch he was. In the camp, the men were making verbal bets where nothing changes hands that Jim laid her within two hours. One of the jacks said, "He's as fast with dames as with logs." By late afternoon she rode back into camp. She never stopped. She was hurried and at a distance looked white and didn't have any huckleberries. She didn't even have her empty pail. Who the hell knows what she told her husband?

At first I felt kind of sorry for her because she was so well known in camp and was so much talked about, but she was riding "High, Wide, and Handsome." She was back in camp every Sunday. She always came with a gallon pail and she always left without it. She kept coming long after huckleberry season passed. There wasn't a berry left on a bush, but she came with another big pail.

The pie fight with the cook and the empty huckleberry pail were just what I needed psychologically to last until Labor Day weekend, when, long ago, I had told both Jim and the foreman I was quitting in order to get ready for school. There was no great transformation in either Jim or me. Jim was still about the size of Jack Dempsey. Nothing had happened to reduce this combination of power and speed. It was just that something had happened so that most of the time now we sawed to saw logs. As for me, for the first (and only) time in my life I had spent over a month twenty-four hours a day doing nothing but hating a guy. Now, though, there were times when I thought of other things—it got so that I had to say to myself, "Don't ever get soft and forget to hate this guy for trying to kill you off." It was somewhere along in here, too, when I became confident enough to develop the theory that he wouldn't take a punch at me. I probably was just getting wise to the fact that he ran this camp as if he were the best fighter in it without ever getting into a fight. He had us stiffs intimidated because he made us look bad when it came to work and women, and so we went on to feel that we were also about to take a punching. Fortunately, I guess, I always realized this might be just theory, and I continued to act as if he were the best fighter in camp, as he probably was, but, you know, it still bothers me that maybe he wasn't.

When we quit work at night, though, we still walked to camp alone. He still went first, slipping on his Woolrich shirt over the top piece of his underwear and putting his empty lunch pail under his arm. Like all sawyers, we pulled off our shirts first thing in the morning and worked all day in the tops of our underwear, and in the summer we still wore wool underwear, because we said sweat made cotton stick to us and wool absorbed it. After Jim disappeared for camp, I sat down on a log and waited for the sweat to dry. It still took me a while before I felt steady enough to reach for my Woolrich shirt and pick up my lunch pail and head for camp, but now I knew I could last until I had said I would quit, which sometimes can be a wonderful feeling.

One day toward the end of August he spoke out of the silence and said, "When are you going to quit?" It sounded as if someone had broken the silence before it was broken by Genesis.

I answered and fortunately I had an already-made answer; I said, "As I told you, the Labor Day weekend."

He said, "I may see you in town before you leave for the East. I'm going to quit early this year myself." Then he added, "Last spring I promised a dame I would." I and all the other jacks had already noticed that the rancher's wife hadn't shown up in camp last Sunday, whatever that meant.

The week before I was going to leave for school I ran into him on the main street. He was looking great—a little thin, but just a little. He took me into a speakeasy and bought me a drink of Canadian Club. Since Montana is a northern border state, during Prohibition there was a lot of Canadian whiskey in my town if you knew where and had the price. I bought the second round, and he bought another and said he had enough when I tried to do the same. Then he added, "You know, I have to take care of you." Even after three drinks in the afternoon, I was a little startled, and still am.

Outside, as we stood parting and squinting in the sunlight, he said, "I got a place already for this dame of mine, but we've not yet set up for business." Then he said very formally, "We would appreciate it very much if you would pay us a short visit before you leave town." And he gave me the address and, when

I told him it would have to be soon, we made a date for the next evening.

The address he had given me was on the north side, which is just across the tracks, where most of the railroaders lived. When I was a kid, our town had what was called a red-light district on Front Street adjoining the city dump which was always burning with a fitting smell, but the law had more or less closed it up and scattered the girls around, a fair proportion of whom sprinkled themselves among the railroaders. When I finally found the exact address, I recognized the house next to it. It belonged to a brakeman who married a tramp and thought he was quite a fighter, although he never won many fights. He was more famous in town for the story that he came home one night unexpectedly and captured a guy coming out. He reached in his pocket and pulled out three dollars. "Here," he told the guy, "go and get yourself a good screw."

Jim's place looked on the up-and-up—no shades drawn and the door slightly open and streaming light. Jim answered and was big enough to blot out most of the scenery, but I could see the edge of his dame just behind him. I remembered she was supposed to be southern and could see curls on her one visible shoulder. Jim was talking and never introduced us. Suddenly she swept around him, grabbed me by the hand, and said, "God bless your ol' pee hole; come on in and park your ol' prat on the piano."

Suddenly I think I understood what Jim had meant when he told me early in the summer that he liked his whores southern because they were "poetical." I took a quick look around the "parlor," and, sure enough, there was no piano, so it was pure poetry.

Later, when I found out her name, it was Annabelle, which fitted. After this exuberant outcry, she backed off in silence and sat down, it being evident, as she passed the light from a standing lamp, that she had no clothes on under her dress.

When I glanced around the parlor and did not see a piano I

did, however, notice another woman and the motto of Scotland. The other woman looked older but not so old as she was supposed to be, because when she finally was introduced she was introduced as Annabelle's mother. Naturally, I wondered how she figured in Jim's operation and a few days later I ran into some jacks in town who knew her and said she was still a pretty good whore, although a little sad and flabby. Later that evening I tried talking to her; I don't think there was much left to her inside but it was clear she thought the world of Jim.

I had to take another look to believe it, but there it was on the wall just above the chair Jim was about to sit in—the motto of Scotland, and in Latin, too—*Nemo me impune lacesset.* Supposedly, only Jim would know what it meant. The whores wouldn't know and it's for sure his trade, who were Scandinavian and French-Canadian lumberjacks, wouldn't. So he sat on his leather throne, owner and chief bouncer of the establishment, believing only he knew that over his head it said: "No one will touch me with impunity."

But there was one exception. I knew what it meant, having been brought up under the same plaque, in fact an even tougher-looking version that had Scotch thistles engraved around the motto. My father had it hung in the front hall where it would be the first thing seen at all times by anyone entering the manse—and in the early mornings on her way to the kitchen by my mother who inherited the unmentioned infirmity of being part English.

Jim did most of the talking, and the rest of us listened and sometimes I just watched. He sure as hell was a good-looking guy, and now he was all dressed up, conservatively in a dark gray herringbone suit and a blue or black tie. But no matter the clothes, he always looked like a lumberjack to me. Why not? He was the best logger I ever worked with, and I barely lived to say so.

Jim talked mostly about sawing and college. He and I had talked about almost nothing during the summer, least of all about college. Now, he asked me a lot of questions about college, but

it just wasn't the case that they were asked out of envy or regret.
He didn't look at me as a Scotch boy like himself, not so good
with the ax and saw but luckier. He looked at himself, at least
as he sat there that night, as a successful young businessman,
and he certainly didn't think I was ever going to do anything
that he wanted to do. What his being a socialist meant to him
I was never to figure out. To me, he emerged as all laissez-
faire. He was one of those people who turn out not to have
some characteristic that you thought was a prominent one when
you first met them. Maybe you only thought they had it because
what you first saw or heard was at acute angle, or maybe they
have it in some form but your personality makes it recessive.
Anyway, he and I never talked politics (admitting that most of
the time we never talked at all). I heard him talking socialism
to the other jacks—yelling it at them would be more exact, as
if they didn't know how to saw. Coming out the back door of
the Dakotas in the twenties he had to be a dispossessed socialist
of some sort, but his talk to me about graduate school was
concerned mostly with the question of whether, if hypotheti-
cally he decided to take it on, he could reduce graduate study
to sawdust, certainly a fundamental capitalistic question. His
educational experiences in the Dakotas had had a lasting effect.
He had gone as far as the seventh grade, and his teachers in
the Dakotas had been big and tough and had licked him. What
he was wondering was whether between seventh grade and
graduate school the teachers kept pace with their students and
could still lick him. I cheered him up a lot when I told him,
"No, last winter wasn't as tough as this summer." He brought
us all another drink of Canadian Club, and, while drinking this
one, it occurred to me that maybe what he had been doing this
summer was giving me his version of graduate school. If so, he
wasn't far wrong.

Nearly all our talk, though, was about logging, because logging was what loggers talked about. They mixed it into everything. For instance, loggers celebrated the Fourth of July—the
only sacred holiday in those times except Christmas—by con-

tests in logrolling, sawing, and swinging the ax. Their work was
their world, which included their games and their women, and
the women at least had to talk like loggers, especially when they
swore. Annabelle would occasionally come up with such a line
as, "Somebody ought to drop the boom on that bastard," but
when I started fooling around to find out whether she knew
what a boom was, she switched back to pure southern poetry.
A whore has to swear like her working men and in addition she
has to have pretty talk.

I was interested, too, in the way Jim pictured himself and me
to his women—always as friendly working partners talking over
some technical sawing problem. In his creations we engaged in
such technical dialogue as this: " 'How much are you holding
there?' I'd ask; 'I'm holding an inch and a half,' he'd say; and
I'd say, 'God, I'm holding two and a half inches.' " I can tell
you that outside of the first few days of the summer we didn't
engage in any such friendly talk, and any sawyer can tell you
that the technical stuff he had us saying about sawing may sound
impressive to whores but doesn't make any sense to sawyers
and had to be invented by him. He was a great sawyer, and
didn't need to make up anything, but it seemed as if every time
he made us friends he had to make up lies about sawing to go
with us.

I wanted to talk a little to the women before I left, but when
I turned to Annabelle she almost finished me off before I got
started by saying, "So you and I are partners of Jim?" Seeing
that she had made such a big start with this, she was off in
another minute trying to persuade me she was Scotch, but I
told her, "Try that on some Swede."

Her style was to be everything you wished she were except
what you knew she wasn't. I didn't have to listen long before
I was fairly sure she wasn't southern. Neither was the other
one. They said "you all" and "ol' " and had curls and that was
about it, all of which they probably did for Jim from the Dakotas.
Every now and then Annabelle would become slightly hysterical, at least suddenly exuberant, and speak a line of something

like "poetry"—an alliterative toast or rune or foreign expression. Then she would go back to her quiet game of trying to figure out something besides Scotch that she might persuade me she was that I would like but wouldn't know much about.

Earlier in the evening I realized that the two women were not mother and daughter or related in any way. Probably all three of them got strange pleasures from the notion they were a family. Both women, of course, dressed alike and had curls and did the southern bit, but fundamentally they were not alike in bone or body structure, except that they were both big women.

So all three of them created a warm family circle of lies.

The lumberjack in herringbone and his two big women in only dresses blocked the door as we said good-bye. "So long," I said from outside. "Au revoir," Annabelle said. "So long," Jim said, and then he added, "I'll be writing you."

And he did, but not until late in autumn. By then probably all the Swedish and Finnish loggers knew his north-side place and he had drawn out his card from the Missoula Public Library and was rereading Jack London, omitting the dog stories. Since my address on the envelope was exact, he must have called my home to get it. The envelope was large and square; the paper was small, ruled, and had glue on the top edge, so it was pulled off some writing pad. His handwriting was large but grew smaller at the end of each word.

I received three other letters from him before the school year was out. His letters were only a sentence or two long. The one- or two-sentence literary form, when used by a master, is designed not to pass on some slight matter but to put the world in a nutshell. Jim was my first acquaintance with a master of this form.

His letters always began, "Dear partner," and always ended, "Your pal, Jim."

You can be sure I ignored any shadow of suggestion that I work with him the coming summer, and he never openly made the suggestion. I had decided that I had only a part of my life to give to gyppoing and that I had already given generously. I went back to the United States Forest Service and fought fires, which to Jim was like declaring myself a charity case and taking the rest cure.

So naturally I didn't hear from him that summer—undoubtedly, he had some other sawyer at the end of the saw whom he was reducing to sawdust. But come autumn and there was a big square envelope with the big handwriting that grew smaller at the end of each word. Since it was early autumn, he couldn't have been set up in business yet. Probably he had just quit the woods and was in town still looking things over. It could be he hadn't even drawn a library card yet. Anyway, this was the letter:

Dear partner,
    Just to let you know I have screwed a dame that weighs 300 lbs.
                                      Your pal,
                                          Jim

A good many years have passed since I received that letter, and I have never heard from or about Jim since. Maybe at three hundred pounds the son of a bitch was finally overpowered.

JOHN NICHOLS

FROM

THE MILAGRO BEANFIELD WAR

There were no windows in Amarante Córdova's remaining one room: long ago he had adobed them up solid to preserve heat. All the same, he awoke on this morning, as he did every morning, at first daylight and slowly commenced his day, climbing out from under about twenty-five pounds of crazy quilts and old army blankets and hastily drawing on his sloppy old suit over his patched, foul-smelling long underwear. Then he took a shot from a half-pint brandy bottle, and before rolling a cigarette, hefted a couple of piñon logs from a corner stack and stuffed them into his twelve-dollar Sears tin heater. Usually the coals from the night before were still so hot in the heater that after a minute, if he just dropped a lit kitchen match in there—which he now did—the logs burst into flame.

This accomplished, he swung the circular cover back on the stove, unbolted and opened his door, and stood in the doorway a moment assessing the day. The view from this one opening into his room was a view like many another in Milagro. A well housing in the front dirt yard, a rusty 1949 Oldsmobile with bullet holes across the windshield sinking on its rims nearby, big yellow tumbleweed skeletons scattered among a few sunflowers, then the raggedy cottonwoods along the creekbed across the road and the majestic snow-capped Midnight Mountains beyond.

The old man coughed, scratched his balls, snagged a coffeepot with one arthritic paw, and shuffled over to the hand-dug well. Letting the bucket drop slowly to the water thirty feet below, he only a quarter filled it, then slowly, resting after each tug, pulled the bucket up and tipped some water into the coffeepot, which he carried back and set atop the heater.

Next, he proceeded cautiously around his dwelling to the backyard outhouse. And while he camped there with the door open so he could watch the turquoise-silver bluebirds flying about his crumbling farmhouse, he also slowly and shakily, though in the end expertly, rolled a cigarette and lit it, contentedly puffing away as he crapped.

After that, Amarante creaked around to his room again and made a cup of instant coffee, poured some brandy into it, and for almost an hour, while the day began, he sat on a white stump next to his front door, bathed in the early sharp sunlight, letting his eyes go bleary as he sipped the piping hot, spiked coffee and rolled and smoked another cigarette. During this time he talked to himself about his wife, his children—those still living and others dead and gone. He also carried on long, intricate, nonsensical dialogues with his good friend Tranquilino Jeantete, and with God, a number of devils, a few saints, and the Virgin Mary. And another thing during this quiet breakfast time: he had the habit of remembering scenes, moods, geography, little moments—memory blips—that had occurred yesterday or maybe fifty years ago. And so he would picture green fields full of confused and immobile meadowlarks during a late May snowstorm; or he would recall the way lightning had exploded jaggedly all around the Chamisaville drive-in theater when his daughter Sally had taken him to a John Wayne movie fifteen years ago; or maybe he would see his wife, Betita, straining, holding his hands, turning purple and howling with her legs spread wide, crushing his hands (she broke his finger once) during the birth of a child. . . .

And on this morning, as on other recent mornings after he had put on his thick-lensed eyeglasses, Amarante also observed Joe Mondragón several fields away, irrigating his bean plants.

The old man watched Joe's work with interest, with a certain feeling of pride, even with a kind of reverence. Amarante had been born on Milagro's west side, in this same house when it was intact; he had worked the fields that now lay fallow about him, and someday he would die on the west side, in his room, or from a heart attack while splitting wood, or maybe he would freeze to death in a ditch some sparkling winter night on his way back from the Frontier Bar—but whatever, Amarante had stuck with the west side through all the thick shit and all the thin shit, saying good-bye to his neighbors one by one while refusing to budge himself, until he had wound up alone with the swallows and the bluebirds and the crumbling houses whose rooms were full of tumbleweeds. Then here, suddenly, was a stubborn, ornery little bastard who had decided to put some life back into the west side. And as Joe Mondragón's bean plants started to grow, Amarante fixed his eyes on that patch of green, feeling excited and warm and a lot less lonely, too.

It hadn't taken long, though, for Amarante to realize that Joe's beansprouts were really going to stir up something in Milagro.

And so on this morning Amarante had a special plan. Spending less time than usual on the stump beside the front door, he drank only one cup of coffee and forewent his customary wood-chopping session. In its stead he hastily gummed down two Piggly-Wiggly tortillas wrapped around some tiny Vienna sausages, made sure a full book of food stamps was stashed safely in his inside breast pocket, and then from a peg driven into the mud wall over his bed he removed a cracked leather gun belt and holster, which he buckled around his skinny waist.

From a tin box on whose cover fading blue asters had been painted Amarante then removed a well-oiled revolver, an old, very heavy Colt Peacemaker. His father had given him the gun eighty years ago: it was the weapon he'd carried as sheriff of Milagro. Amarante had never discharged it at anybody; in fact, the gun had rarely been used, even for target practice. But it had always been, and yet remained, his most cherished possession.

The old man fitted this monumental weapon into the holster,

made certain his sheriff's badge was pinned correctly to his suit lapel, and hit the road.

Shoulders hunched, leaning way forward, Amarante stomped with a rickety bowlegged gait along the pot-holed dirt path, eyes fixed straight ahead, absolutely determined—once in motion—to let nothing break his feeble rhythms until he had arrived where he planned to go.

He stopped once, however, near Joe's beanfield, swayed uncertainly for a moment before leaving the road, climbed up the Roybal ditch bank, and carefully picked his way over stones and dry weeds to where water left the ditch and entered the field.

He waved at Joe, who was leaning against his shovel, and Joe called, "Howdy, Chief. What's with the pistol this morning?"

Grinning toothlessly and gesturing with his hand, Amarante offered Joe a shot of cheap brandy. So Joe splashed over and fastened onto the bottle, tipping it to his lips while the old man squinted his eyes and watched eagerly, nodding happily as the young man drank.

"*Ai, Chihuahua!*" Joe said. "What is this crap, burro piss?"

Amarante cackled and sucked off a swallow for himself, then patted his gut. "It's good for you," he said. "Keeps you warm."

"So how come the hardware?" Joe asked again.

Winking conspiratorially, Amarante put his bottle away and laid a hand on Joe's shoulder. "I'll be back soon," he said. "I'll take care of you. I'll take care of this field."

"Sure, you do that for me, Chief." Gently, Joe cuffed the old man's face. "You and me together, friend, we'll keep those bastards at bay, qué no?"

Abruptly, Amarante plunged toward the road. But he halted a couple of times, and, looking back, muttered, "I'll be right back . . ."

In town a few minutes later, instead of heading as usual for the bar, he hoofed it directly into Rael's General Store and, pulling the gun from its holster, laid the weapon atop the rubber change mat on the counter in front of Nick Rael.

"Hello, Pop," Nick said, wondering, what in hell is this old looney up to now?

"What kind of bullets does this take?" Amarante asked. "I forget."

After Nick had turned the gun admiringly over in his hands once or twice, he set it back on the rubber mat again.

"Why buy bullets?"

Amarante was a little confused; he could hardly hear anyway. "What kind of cartucho?" he asked again. "I want to buy some shells."

"Sure." Nick swung out from behind the counter, ambling across the store to his ammo shelves. "But what for?"

Following Nick, the old man watched with interest as the storekeeper, after searching among the ammunition for a moment, selected a box of .45 shells, which he slapped into Amarante's hands. Back at the counter the old man asked, "How much?"

"Three dollars and twenty-nine cents, plus fourteen pennies for the governor, equals three-forty-three altogether," Nick said bemusedly. "What are you gonna do, Pop, go hunting for bear?"

"How much?"

"Three-forty-three!" Nick fairly shouted into his ear.

Grinning, Amarante produced the food stamp book and, while Nick looked on incredulously, painstakingly tore out four one-dollar stamps which he laid carefully on the counter.

Nick pushed them back toward the old geezer, shaking his head. "Hey, Grandpa," he explained. "You can't buy bullets with food stamps. You got to pay me money."

Puzzled, Amarante held up the stamps. "What's the matter with these? They're no good?"

"They're for buying *food*," Nick rasped. "You can't use food stamps for bullets. You need *money*. Real dollars."

Amarante scrutinized the pieces of paper in his hand. At length he said, "This is money."

"For food, yeah," Nick sighed. "They're only good for food, man."

"I don't want food. Only these bullets."

"Then put those food stamps away and gimme three dollars and forty-three cents," the storekeeper said.

The old man laid the food stamps on the counter again. "This is the same as money," he explained.

"Aw, come on, Pop. You know as well as I know that there's some things you can't buy with food stamps. You can't buy dog food or beer or nonedible stuff like shampoo or toothpaste or razor blades."

Smiling, Amarante picked up the shells and dropped the box in his pocket.

"Hey wait a minute—" Nick started to grab the old man's arm, but let go quickly. "Money," he said, moving his lips exaggeratedly as if talking to a lip reader. "Not food stamps, you dumb old coot—money. I need *money* for those shells."

Once again, Amarante nodded toward the food stamps on the counter, hoisted his gun and jammed it carefully into the holster, touched the front brim of his rumpled hat by way of saying good day, and lurched off.

Cursing as he did so, Nick snatched up the food stamps and slapped them into the space under the black plastic cash pan in the till.

Amarante teetered into the Frontier Bar, saluted his comrade, Tranquilino Jeantete, tugged himself onto a stool, placed the pistol and the box of shells on the bar, and, while Tranquilino watched, he slowly and very carefully loaded the gun.

"What do you want to load a gun for?" the bartender asked. "Life isn't hard enough, you're out looking for more trouble?"

His feeble hand resting lightly atop the mammoth gun lying on the bar, Amarante said, "Sometimes it's necessary to carry a gun."

"I bet you can't even pull the trigger," Tranquilino replied petulantly. "You're not even as heavy as a little bag of dried-up aspen leaves."

"I can shoot this gun."

"And what could you hit—a dead elephant from two feet away?"

"I can shoot this gun."

"Your brains are scrambled," Tranquilino said. "The defunct ones from the camposanto must be dancing around in there. You're going to give all us rotten old bastards a bad name."

"Sometimes a man should carry a gun."

"Who do you think you are?" the bartender accused. "Pancho Villa? The Lone Ranger?"

Offended by his friend's bad taste, Amarante looked stonily straight ahead, his wrinkled old hand still lying firmly atop the gun.

"Put the safety on, at least," Tranquilino finally grumbled in a more gentle, friendlier tone. "I don't want any bullets flying around my bar."

Refusing even to acknowledge that he'd heard, Amarante remained stiff backed, his shriveled sunken lips as tight as he could make them.

After a long silence, Tranquilino creaked onto his feet and fetched two glasses, filling both a third full of cheap bourbon. Placing one glass next to Amarante's gun hand, he said, "Let's both have a drink to your stupid gun."

Amarante cracked no smile, but he did move his hand from the gun to the glass, and the two old-timers drank.

About half an hour later, as his friend left the bar, Tranquilino called, "Hey, Pancho Villa, you forgot your cannon!"

Amarante returned, almost daintily lifted the weapon off the bar and stuck it in the holster, and then suddenly they both started to laugh.

"Shit," Tranquilino cackled after they had each survived minor coughing jags brought on by their laughter. "Carrying around all that extra weight I bet you get a heart attack!"

Out in the sunshine Amarante swayed and blinked. The road was littered with squashed grasshoppers; and, their wings crackling, a number of live grasshoppers sailed through the air back

and forth across the road as if the summer sun, having thawed
out their nearly frosted bodies, had set them abruptly to siz-
zling. A pickup carrying plumbing for a frame house being built
by a Texas couple in the canyon slowed down and stopped,
and the woman from the Strawberry Mesa Body Shop and Pipe
Queen, Ruby Archuleta, poked her red bandannaed head out
the window.

"Hey Amarante. What are you going to do with that gun?"
she asked.

He grinned, tipping his hat to her. "Hello," he said. "How
are you today, Mrs. Archuleta?"

She pointed. "How come the hardware, cousin? Who you
gonna plug?"

"A Thanksgiving turkey," the old man suddenly barked. "A
big Thanksgiving turkey."

Ruby arched her eyebrows, laughing again, ground the stick-
shift into first, and, with the admonition "Make sure it's pointed
in the right direction before you squeeze the trigger!" she bolted
her truck away.

Whereupon Amarante Córdova, shining in a triumphal light,
pirouetted clumsily in the middle of the plaza area to acknowledge the attention and admiration of any other onlookers. But
at this moment the heart of town, such as it was, was deserted.
Disappointed, the old man toppled painfully into gear, bumping
into Seferino Pacheco, who had tears in his eyes.

"My pig is gone again," Pacheco moaned.

"Fuck your pig! Fie on your pig! Death to your voracious
pig!" the old man spat, circling huffily around the stunned,
slope-shouldered Pacheco.

"She was in her pen just this morning," Pacheco called. But
Amarante couldn't have cared less—he was heading home.

The old man reached the highway just as the sheriff was
turning in. Bernabé Montoya's pickup coasted a little past him,
and, without even looking around, Amarante could tell the truck
had stopped. Guiltily, he waddled across the highway.

Bernabé negotiated a tight U-turn, paused to let a two-ton flatbed, piled high with hay bales from Colorado, zoom down the highway, then crossed the road and pulled over slightly ahead of Amarante.

The old man halted. For effect, Bernabé took his time slouching out of the cab.

"Uh, how come you're wearing that antique buffalo gun?" the sheriff wanted to know.

Unable to think of answers, Amarante just stood still, his hat off in the presence of the law, grinning and wheezing laboriously, playing the fool.

"Excuse me," Bernabé said, gently lifting the pistol from its holster. When he'd ascertained that it was loaded he rolled his eyes wearily to the sky, moaning uphappily. "What's happening all of a sudden that this town is filling up with troublemakers? What kind of charge does a wrinkled little old prune like you, Mr. Córdova, get out of walking around with a two-thousand-year-old shooting iron on your hip and your pockets full of bullets? What do you want to do, incite this poor town into another Smokey the Bear santo riot or something? Take the bullets out of the gun, Mr. Córdova—" And here the sheriff actually removed the cartridges himself, plip-plopping them into the old man's palm.

"If it's loaded," he explained sorrowfully, shoving the gun carefully back into its holster, "it can go off. Hang it back on the wall where it belongs, Mr. Córdova. Please, huh? Nobody wants violence."

Amarante said, "I can go home now?"

"Yeah, sure. Whatever you want . . ." Bernabé backed up, hesitating momentarily at the door of his truck, disturbed by the old man who was grinning absurdly in his direction. But finally, with a shrug and a worried "Ai, Chihuahua," he climbed behind the wheel and effected another U-turn.

Amarante waited until the sheriff was gone before moving on. Slowly he rattled along the dusty road to where he had to climb the Roybal ditch bank, and once he had accomplished that he teetered along the bank to the field.

Joe was gone. Amarante surveyed the damp earth, the glistening green bean plants, the faint yellow irrigation foam left around the stalks, the mud cracking softly in some freshly watered rows. A few robins, starlings, and blackbirds were still scavenging. The old man trundled off a ways into the shade afforded by dusty, silver-leafed cottonwoods and sat down on a log.

Spastically, dropping a half-dozen bullets, he reloaded the gun, placing it on the log beside him. Next he rolled a cigarette, and, quietly smoking, he listened woozily to faint meadowlark songs drifting melodically on the clear summer air.

From here on in, he thought, if anybody like Eusebio Lavadie or Zopi Devine tried to mess with José Mondragón's beanfield, they would have to reckon with Amarante Córdova first.

But he was sleepy, his head buzzed drowsily. Grasshoppers crackled, a locust buzzed, a woodpecker blammed against a faraway hollow tree. Somewhere, too, a chain saw was droning.

Amarante lowered himself so that his back pressed against the log on which he'd been sitting. The gun he laid carefully in his lap. His eyes flickered and were about to close when he noticed something odd hovering over town. For a moment the thing was so out of place that his mind could not translate what it saw. Then he realized that, even though no rain had fallen at all for the past few days, the arching vision, shining faintly but unmistakably over Milagro, was a rainbow.

Too tired to worry about such a sight, Amarante fell asleep. But no sooner had he begun to snore than that queer rainbow appeared in his dream, shimmering faintly in the hot dry air muffling Milagro, and a few minutes later an angel showed up to complicate the miracle.

No shining angel with a golden halo straight from Tiffany's, a French horn, and wings fabricated out of pristine Chinese swansdown arrived to bless Amarante's fertile imagination; rather, a half-toothless, one-eyed bum sort of coyote dressed in tattered blue jeans and sandals, and sporting a pair of drab motheaten

wings that looked as if they had come off the remainder shelves
of a disreputable cut-rate discount store during a fire-damage
sale, appeared.

This grisly sight limped along the Milagro—García spur paus-
ing every now and again to blow its bulbous gray nose onto a
greasy unhallowed sleeve, after which it rumbled and choked
for a while like an old crone dying of TB.

"Hey, Angel," Amarante called out in his dream. "What's
a rainbow doing over our town on a sunny day like today?"

The angel, startled by Amarante's voice, froze stiff with its
ears lying back flat; and then, realizing there was no immediate
danger, it turned to observe the puzzling natural phenomenon.

"Who knows, cousin," the coyote apparition mumbled at last.
"Maybe it's because for once in your lives you people are trying
to do something right."

Abruptly, then, the angel disappeared. And Amarante went
on to dream he was on a horse, carrying a rifle across the pommel
of his saddle, tracking a deer through snow in the high open
country around the Little Baldy Bear Lakes. . . .

When Amarante Córdova was young he used to throw stones
at birds in flight. Of course he never hit a bird with one of those
stones, and that was probably why it was fun to throw them—
knowing absolutely that the birds would always dodge, or be
going too fast for either his pitching arm or the missiles it
released. In fact, as he remembered it, there had always been a
kind of joy in attacking a thing that could not be hurt, a kind
of satisfaction to be derived by all parties involved.

Amarante had stopped chucking rocks at little birds around
the time he became sheriff, but in an old age that might be called
a reversion to his childhood, he suddenly returned to a variation
of his former pastime. The precise moment that he reverted
into his former self occurred during one of the old man's daily
jaunts into town, when he spied a redwing blackbird drinking
from a small rain puddle in the Milagro—García spur and for
some reason decided to throw a stone at it. With considerable

effort he stooped over and selected a golf ball–sized weapon, straightened up, tiptoed a little closer, and then flung the rock at his target. But as his skinny, bent fingers could not release the projectile in time, he wound up drilling it against his own foot instead of at the bird. This smarted a little, and Amarante croaked a string of feeble curses as he limped around in the road, amazed by what a flabby uncoordinated old geezer he had become.

And then the butt of his mammoth, archaic six-gun collided with his wandering gaze; abruptly he quit stumbling around.

Obviously unafraid of such a decrepit old fart, the redwing blackbird was still dawdling around down by the puddle, nailing whatever insect tidbits had drifted close to shore.

Moving—now that he'd decided to hunt the bird—with a deliberate and cunning dexterity, Amarante removed his huge Peacemaker from its scabbard, and, holding it in both hands after laboriously cocking the hammer, he aimed for almost a minute at the blackbird, then pulled the trigger. By some sort of miracle the bullet, which was immediately projected forth at a high rate of speed amid a flash of fire, a boom of noise, and a spurt of smoke, drilled the bird squarely amidships, causing it to disintegrate in a great puff of black and yellow and red feathers, some of which—as the smoke cleared—floated tenderly back down like autumn leaves, alighting delicately on the puddle.

Well, at first Amarante was shocked, because he had not intended to kill the bird, just as he had never intended to kill the little feathered creatures when he'd been a kid hurling stones at them.

But then it occurred to him that this was a sign, a message, an omen—maybe even from God himself: Amarante Córdova, useless old man, protector of Joe's beanfield, had been blessed with an aim that was accurate and true, the better to defend the beanfield, to save Milagro, to conquer the forces of evil and Ladd Devine—

Amarante gathered up some feathers and waddled into town as fast as his bowed arthritic legs could carry him. Plunking onto a stool at the Frontier, he jubilantly splashed the feathers across the bar, then banged down his six-gun on the hard mahogany top.

"A rat killed a blackbird out at your place?" Tranquilino Jeantete asked, adjusting his hearing aid and popping them both a beer.

"*I* shot a blackbird from a hundred paces," Amarante bragged lying through his teeth because the bird had only been about twenty feet away.

"Sure. And I strangled a wolf bare-handed last night," the crusty old bartender retorted, sucking on his thumb because he had cut it a little on the second poptop.

"You make fun of me," Amarante complained. "Everybody makes fun of me. But then . . . everybody made fun of Jesus Christ himself."

"If Jesus Christ himself walked into my bar and ordered a shot of blackberry brandy or tequila, I wouldn't make fun of him," Tranquilino said. "But when Amarante Córdova walks into my bar telling me that with his lousy eyesight he could even see, let alone kill with a pistol that weighs a ton, a blackbird at one hundred paces, then I got a right to mock, because somebody is lying through their teeth, what's left of them."

Amarante was hurt. "But I did," he protested. "You can walk back over to the Milagro–García spur and see for yourself the rest of the feathers and all the blood and gore."

"No thanks, cousin. Every morning I walk a hundred yards to the bar, I'm out of breath all morning. But I'm a fair man, my friend—" And so saying he tottered around the bar and lugged a wooden stool over to the far end of the room and set an almost-empty sherry bottle atop the stool. Then, plugging in the jukebox so that its internal gleam would shed some garish blue light on the target, he said, "Okay, you go ahead and prove to me you killed a blackbird at one hundred paces."

"In the bar?" Amarante was astonished.

"In the bar," Tranquilino insisted firmly. "It won't be the first time somebody discharged a firearm in here."

Amarante scrutinized Tranquilino to see if his old friend had gone off his rocker, but the bartender had his eyes sarcastically trained on the bottle and his hearing aid turned off, so how could a Gunfighter Supreme by recent Order of the Lord refuse to accept the challenge?

Amarante creaked gingerly off his stool, took forever to sight in his blunderbuss—and, along with a million painful fragments of gunshot echo, a thousand pieces of amber-colored glass ricocheted off the wall and sprinkled across the floor like stars during the creation of a small universe.

"Hijo, Madre, puto, cabrón!" Tranquilino Jeantete commented.

Then he located another almost-empty bottle and set it up on the stool and retreated behind the bar, saying "Whenever you're ready, maestro."

Ignoring the sarcasm in his lifelong friend's voice, Amarante thumbed back the hammer, took careful aim . . . and blew the second bottle into just as spectacular smithereens.

The glass had barely tinkled to rest around their feet when Harlan Betchel, Nick Rael, Ray Gusdorf, Bernabé Montoya, Betty Apodaca, Carl Abeyta and Floyd Cowlie, and Sparky Pacheco and Tobías Mondragón careened into the bar to see who was getting laid out. Naturally, when they saw the two old men, or more specifically, when they saw Amarante's huge six-iron, all of them ground to a halt; but before anybody could speak, Tranquilino said matter-of-factly, "Watch this, friends," and he carted another bottle over to the stool.

Bernabé Montoya knew he should have called a halt to the target practice right then and there, but like everyone else he was curious, so instead of saying no he said nothing, and, of course, having condoned the first demonstration, which ended with bottle fragments no bigger than BBs falling on all their heads like rain, he was powerless to stop the subsequent carnage.

By the time Tranquilino had begun setting up half-full liquor bottles, at least four dozen people were gathered in the back and in the doorway of the Frontier; Nick Rael had already donated a box of .45 shells free, and Amarante Córdova was so drunk with his own power and accuracy that he could hardly stand up straight, let alone focus on what he was trying to hit . . . and yet, thus far he had not missed a single bottle. So incredible was this feat that everyone present had become hushed, reverent, awestruck, aware they were probably witnessing a miracle. In fact, the tension among the onlookers had grown almost unbearable. Also, the slugs from Amarante's Peacemaker had almost dug a small round hole in the bar's adobe wall.

Suddenly, however, Amarante felt a nerve somewhere deep inside his body: he held his fire, blinked his eyes, and then lowered the gun.

Nobody said anything. Finally Amarante announced, "That's enough."

"Whatta you mean, that's enough?" a handful of people complained.

"That's just enough," Amarante said complacently, because he knew—quite simply—that if he fired again he would miss.

He holstered the gun, and, shooting his three brown teeth at everyone from a wide grin as he politely tipped his hat to the onlookers, he walked outside and headed home.

Amarante veered off the road at Joe's beanfield, however, having decided it wouldn't hurt to stand watch for an hour or two; and he was almost asleep, with his back to a bleached cottonwood log, when he realized a plane was coming up from the south.

Now normally there would be nothing unusual in a plane coming up from the south. But today was a strange day. Amarante's eyes popped open, and he fumbled in his suit pockets for his glasses, which he finally located and lodged in front of his eyes so as to identify the oncoming aircraft. Pretty soon he could begin to make out the markings on the plane. By the time the small Cessna reached Milagro he knew it belonged to Ladd

Devine, and he had already unconsciously cocked the hammer
on his Peacemaker while waiting eagerly for whoever was at
the controls to guide that Cessna within pistol range.

Amarante did not know it, of course, but there were four
men in the plane: Ladd Devine, Bud Gleason, the state engineer,
Nelson Bookman, and the governor. They were all guests at a
real estate conference slated to begin in Chamisaville that noon;
the governor would give a keynote address, opening the two-
day festivities. They were all taking an opportunity to become
a little more familiar with the situation in Milagro, and for this
reason they had decided to make a pass over the scene while
Ladd Devine and Bud Gleason ran down the various Miracle
Valley enterprise facts and figures, and also offered off-the-cuff
comments on the local flora, fauna, and fulleros.

Down below, Amarante wasn't thinking much about the consequences of shooting Ladd Devine's plane from the sky, he was
more or less allowing himself to be led by divine guidance, as
it were. And so, as the little plane buzzed closer, he raised the
pistol, and, overcome with a great calmness inside, he began to
sight on the merrily droning target, waiting for it to approach
a little closer so that God could pull the trigger.

"There's the beanfield," Bud Gleason said, and all eyes in
the plane turned left and downward to take in, almost with
respect if not awe, the tiny green plot among those barren west
side fields that was causing such a hoopla.

And as Ladd Devine tilted the plane slightly to give them a
better view, Amarante pulled the trigger, causing the hammer
to snap forward driving the firing pin into the center of the .45
cartridge aimed at the slowly turning plane.

Nothing happened, however.

The cartridge was a dud. . . .

At about noon that day a backhoe driven by Jerry Grindstaff
emerged from the Dancing Trout's white gravel drive, turned
right, and descended the bumpy road past thick pastures in
which Morgan horses grazed, and past tennis courts where Bos-

tonians and Dallasites, clad in snowy white, exercised. Then it chugged slowly past orchards that eventually gave way to the valley's overgrazed fields, which were pocked with animal shit and smelled strongly of ammonia, and the backhoe continued on through the tightly clustered houses at the heart of town, past Rael's, the Frontier, the Forest Service headquarters, and the Pilar, and across the highway onto the Milagro–García spur. Jerry G. braked at Joe Mondragón's beanfield and, as he surveyed the scene, motor idling, he lit a cigarette.

There was nobody around. Jerry G. had come on orders from the boss, who felt that policies so far had only led to more trouble than might have occurred had the beanfield been leveled long ago, Joe Mondragón arrested, and the matter fought out then and there, perhaps savagely—but at least it would have ended quickly, and by now would have been all but forgotten. As it was, things had gone much too far. A hands-off policy had backfired, the insurgents had gathered strength. And so, with Joe on the run and half the town chasing him, and with the rest of the town hiding behind barricades (and having consulted neither the state engineer nor the state police nor his own partner, Jim Hirsshorn, nor Horsethief Shorty), Ladd Devine had decided to kill the heart of the controversy, namely Joe's tiny beanfield.

Letting his eyes laze around, Jerry G. took his time with the cigarette. Wind puffs rattled the cottonwoods, dust swirled in the road stirring grasshoppers up into their crackling, chili-red flights. A dust devil twirled eastward from the sage across the flat deserted fields, catching tumbleweeds, bouncing them along and letting them go, weaving among the crumbled houses and rusty car hulks—a truly desolate scene.

Increasingly, Joe's beanfield had made Jerry G. mad. He hadn't gone into exactly why, but the damn field threatened everything he had worked for all his life, it was holding a knife to the throat of the established order. Somehow just a few lousy green plants that wouldn't bring a plug nickel on anyone's market were a menace to Jerry G.'s future. So he sure hadn't balked (as he never balked) when Ladd Devine told him to have at it. In fact, for the first time in almost a week, he had smiled.

Flipping the cigarette, Jerry G. shifted into gear, climbed off the roadbank, chugged along the flatland beside the Roybal ditch, and hopped off the machine to open the barbed wire gate into Joe's beanfield.

But when he swung the gate open and turned around, a little old bespectacled man whom Jerry G. had seen often around town (usually drunk), but whose name escaped the foreman just now, was standing beside the backhoe's rear wheel, aiming the biggest goddam shooting iron Jerry G. had ever seen directly at his heart.

"Hey . . . what—?"

"You come a step closer," Amarante Córdova said in Spanish, "and I'll blow your head into pieces like it was a rotten pumpkin."

Now the foreman did not understand these words, but there was enough unmistakable authority in the ninety-three-year-old voice and also in the size of his Colt Peacemaker's snout to make Jerry G. freeze.

"Put the gate back up," Amarante ordered. "You put it back up right now." He gestured slightly with the gun, and Jerry G. savvied; he hopped to do as he was bid.

"Okay, go home," Amarante said. "Or I'll make a hole big enough for an owl to nest in in your chest."

The drift of this, too, Jerry G. managed to grasp perfectly. Hands awkwardly raised, he circled warily around the old man, backed up to the ditch bank, and walked sideways along the bank to the road. At the road he halted, briefly apprehensive about the backhoe, but he recommenced his hasty retreat with a jump as the old man bleated, "Get going! Beat it! Go home!" On the double, Jerry G. hightailed it for the highway.

Amarante grinned, giggled, holstered his oversized blunder-buss, and, grimacing awkwardly, trembling from the effort, claw-ing a bit like a man falling off a cliff, he somehow managed to haul his ancient bones up into the driver's seat of the powerful yellow machine.

In his younger days Amarante had often run a backhoe, but now he had trouble holding the clutch down long enough to push the shifting lever into gear. In the end, though, cursing his old bones and grunting like a hungry pig, he succeeded; the backhoe lurched forward, and as it did Amarante's floppy hat jolted off his head.

It was no picnic for a derelict that old to wrestle with the wheel, guiding the heavy machine, but the angels were on his side, saluting him, no doubt, with heavenly laughter as they gave strength to his feeble hands and as they gave the joyful determination of all legendary heroes from John Henry through Emiliano Zapata to his tenacious heart. Amarante cackled, hugging the wheel with all his might, aiming the backhoe westward. Fences snapped with melodious twangs as he plowed through, the strands sometimes whizzing past his ears. The machine jolted into gullies, lurched and coughed; Amarante bounced out of his seat, clinging for dear life; fence posts splintered. An adobe wall crumbled like stale cookies; the backhoe punched aside a wrecked car, then chewed mighty tracks through flat empty field after flat empty field, bursting at last through a final fence into the purple sage.

Bouncing, rocking, tipping, Amarante rode his mammoth mechanical bronco across the wide and lovely mesa—jackrabbits fled for their lives. The old man's chin hit against the wheel, the blow almost knocking him out. Yet he had determined to do this thing; his ninety-three-year-old pride would not allow him to fail. His fingers felt broken, his ribs and shoulders were certainly smashed, his head ached from the beating and from the noonday summer sun also, but he refused to die. His father's huge gun popped out of the holster, disappearing forever into the sage—Amarante did not notice. His final three teeth (though not—miraculously—his glasses) were jarred loose—he swallowed one and the other two fell to the ground . . . then he pissed in his britches. But he whooped also, croaking hoarsely, glutinous, joyful sounds, riding that bright yellow Ladd Devine backhoe westward, ever westward—

Toward the gorge.

And he could see it now, the break in the earth, faintly ahead, and then more clearly, and then he could make out a far sunny wall dropping sheerly; with the gorge in sight he stepped on the gas and all hell broke loose. What a way, he thought, his wrinkled lips flapping as he laughed and sputtered: *What a glorious way to go!*

The split in the earth widened, became immense. The ground sloped more, became smoother. Around here somewhere was a path down to the hot springs where Amarante had gone many years ago, courting, drinking, swimming, fishing sometimes, and he'd driven sheep up that path after taking them to graze on the rich bottomland beside the river. . . .

Betita's death—he suddenly remembered, then just as suddenly forgot as the backhoe glanced off a boulder, and he was thrown from the yellow machine, crashing atop a sagebush and bouncing from it into a small cholla cactus, and with that, abruptly—incredibly—the violence and the noise, the jerking and the bolting and the chugging were gone, and Amarante, on his feet for this sensational and emotional good-bye, saw the backhoe nose out into space and then keel over, diving from sight. Summoning his last reserve of strength, the old man limped to the edge in order to watch it fall.

Sideways it skidded through the air, hit an outcropping and flipped; turning several somersaults and bursting into flame, the backhoe sailed down trailing a brilliant fantail of sparks. Then, hitting a slope, it continued to roll, or rather to lope toward the river, and the fireball struck sandy earth a few yards south of the largest hot spring, where, overturning five or six times, it then leaped ten feet over Snuffy Ledoux, who was still lounging in the bathtub-sized hot spring putting the finishing touches on his last tallboy, and with a stupendous sizzle splashed into the Rio Grande, sinking instantly, leaving a fat greasy smoke ball hovering like a concerned mother over the bubbling spot where it had disappeared.

Snuffy Ledoux splashed to his feet. Screaming, *"You son of a bitch, I'll get you!''* he scrambled to his clothes, tugged them on in fifteen seconds, jammed his feet into the wrong boots, and hit the narrow path out bent on revenge.

Nobody in Milagro had ever made it up that gorge trail in even triple the time it took Snuffy Ledoux—who'd been at peace with the world for the first moment in ten years when that fireball thundered over his head—to make it. And nobody in Milagro had ever been even one-half as surprised as was Snuffy when he panted over the gorge rim to discover, not a sly, conniving villain with handlebar moustaches and shifty eyes who'd attempted to end his life, but rather the old man, Amarante Córdova, looking like a thing that had just gone sixty-three rounds with seven bald eagles, staggering in zigzagging circles, gasping and bubbling out ding-y sounds, with nobody else around.

Snuffy hobbled over to Amarante, waved hi, and collapsed. The old man sat down. They gaped at each other, unable to talk, huffing and puffing.

It was Amarante who spoke first. "I can't walk back," he croaked. "I'll have a heart attack. I'll drop dead. I'm an old man."

Without thinking, Snuffy said, "I'll carry you on my back."

"Thanks," Amarante gasped. "You're a good boy. When did you return from the capital?"

"Just this morning. I saw you. What was that thing you tried to kill me with?"

"I wasn't trying to kill you. Nobody told me you were there."

Snuffy held his hands apart like a man describing a four-inch fish: "You missed me by that much."

"I apologize."

"What was that thing?" Snuffy insisted.

"A backhoe."

"Ai, Chihuahua!"

They sat there a while, not speaking, awaiting heart attacks. But nothing happened. The sun traveled farther westward; sage and cholla shadows shifted slightly; some ants crawled up their pant legs.

"I guess we might as well begin," Snuffy said, slowly un-bending his aching limbs, arising. He pulled Amarante onto his feet, then turned around, squatting down, and hoisted the old man piggyback.

Lurching to the right, to the left, halting, leaning forward, taking a step, they began. Amarante held onto Snuffy Ledoux, smiling with a mouth that had no teeth now, and Snuffy's head began throbbing. He bit his lower lip until the blood flowed, carrying the old man a hundred yards, then halting to rest for five minutes, then starting off again.

In this way they progressed across the mesa, through the pale lavender sageland. Amarante began to sing in a high hoarse voice, a song with no notes, really, it was more of an Indian-style chant, high and sing-song wonderful, with no words any-one could understand, his radiant face tilted to the blue sky, shining like the face of a little boy or of an old old being as powerful as God, and his eyes were fixed on the permanent rainbow he could still see arching delicately over his hometown. And although blisters formed on Snuffy's feet, and although they began to bleed, he found himself marching farther between rests, the old man growing lighter with this triumphant out-pouring of song; and by the time they reached the deserted west side beanfields the sun was hanging like a fiery orange in the west, and Snuffy Ledoux had also broken out into victorious song. . . .

RUDOLFO ANAYA

FROM

BLESS ME, ULTIMA

"Hey Toni-eeeeee. Huloooooo Antonioforous!"

A voice called.

At first I thought I was dreaming. I was fishing, and sitting on a rock; the sun beating on my back had made me sleepy. I had been thinking how Ultima's medicine had cured my uncle and how he was well and could work again. I had been thinking how the medicine of the doctors and of the priest had failed. In my mind I could not understand how the power of God could fail. But it had.

"Toni-eeeeee!" the voice called again.

I opened my eyes and peered into the green brush of the river. Silently, like a deer, the figure of Cico emerged. He was barefoot, he made no noise. He moved to the rock and squatted in front of me. I guess it was then that he decided to trust me with the secret of the golden carp.

"Cico?" I said. He nodded his dark, freckled face.

"Samuel told you about the golden carp," he said.

"Yes," I replied.

"Have you ever fished for carp?" he asked. "Here in the river, or anywhere?"

"No," I shook my head. I felt as if I was making a solemn oath.

"Do you want to see the golden carp?" he whispered.

"I have hoped to see him all summer," I said breathlessly.

"Do you believe the golden carp is a god?" he asked.

The commandment of the Lord said, Thou shalt have no
other gods before me . . .

I could not lie. I knew he would find the lie in my eyes if I
did. But maybe there were other gods? Why had the power of
God failed to cure my uncle?

"I am a Catholic," I stuttered, "I can believe only in the
God of the churchs2—" I looked down. I was sorry because now
he would not take me to see the golden carp. For a long time
Cico did not speak.

"At least you are truthful, Tony," he said. He stood up. The
quiet waters of the river washed gently southward. "We have
never taken a non-believer to see him," he said solemnly.

"But I want to believe," I looked up and pleaded, "it's just
that I have to believe in Him?" I pointed across the river to
where the cross of the church showed above the tree tops.

"Perhaps—" he mused for a long time. "Will you make an
oath?" he asked.

"Yes," I answered. But the commandment said, Thou shalt
not take the Lord's name in vain.

"Swear by the cross of the church that you will never hunt
or kill a carp." He pointed to the cross. I had never sworn on
the cross before. I knew that if you broke your oath it was the
biggest sin a man could commit, because God was witness to
the swearing on his name. But I would keep my promise! I
would never break my oath!

"I swear," I said.

"Come!" Cico was off, wading across the river. I followed.
I had waded across that river many times, but I never felt an
urgency like today. I was excited about seeing the magical golden
carp.

"The golden carp will be swimming down the creek today,"
Cico whispered. We scrambled up the bank and through the
thick brush. We climbed the steep hill to the town and headed
towards the school. I never came up this street to go to school
and so the houses were not familiar to me. We paused at one
place.

"Do you know who lives there?" Cico pointed at a green arbor. There was a fence with green vines on it, and many trees. Every house in town had trees but I had never seen a place so green. It was thick like some of the jungles I saw in the movies in town.

"No," I said. We drew closer and peered through the dense curtain of green that surrounded a small adobe hut.

"Narciso," Cico whispered.

Narciso had been on the bridge the night Lupito was murdered. He had tried to reason with the men, he had tried to save Lupito's life. He had been called a drunk.

"My father and my mother know him," I said. I could not take my eyes from the garden that surrounded the small house. Every kind of fruit and vegetable I knew seemed to grow in the garden, and there was even more abundance here than on my uncles' farms.

"I know," Cico said, "they are from the llano—"

"I have never seen such a place," I whispered. Even the air of the garden was sweet to smell.

"The garden of Narciso," Cico said with reverence, "is envied by all— Would you like to taste its fruits?"

"We can't," I said. It was a sin to take anything without permission.

"Narciso is my friend," Cico said. He reached through the green wall and a secret latch opened an ivy-laden door. We walked into the garden. Cico closed the door behind him and said, "Narciso is in jail. The sheriff found him drunk."

I was fascinated by the garden. I forgot about seeing the golden carp. The air was cool and clear, not dusty and hot like the street. Somewhere I heard the sound of gurgling water.

"Somewhere here there is a spring," Cico said, "I don't know where. That is what makes the garden so green. That and the magic of Narciso—"

I was bewildered by the garden. Everywhere I looked there were fruit-laden trees and rows and rows of vegetables. I knew the earth was fruitful because I had seen my uncles make it bear in abundance; but I never realized it could be like this! The ground was soft to walk on. The fragrance of sun-dazzling flowers was deep, and soft, and beautiful.

"The garden of Narciso," I whispered.

"Narciso is my friend," Cico intoned. He pulled some carrots from the soft, dark earth and we sat down to eat.

"I cannot," I said. It was silent and peaceful in the garden. I felt that someone was watching us.

"It is all right," Cico said.

And although I did not feel good about it, I ate the golden carrot. I had never eaten anything sweeter or juicier in my life.

"Why does Narciso drink?" I asked.

"To forget," Cico answered.

"Does he know about the golden carp?" I asked.

"The magic people all know about the coming day of the golden carp," Cico answered. His bright eyes twinkled. "Do you know how Narciso plants?" he asked.

"No," I answered. I had always thought farmers were sober men. I could not imagine a drunk man planting and reaping such fruits!

"By the light of the moon," Cico whispered.

"Like my uncles, the Lunas—"

"In the spring Narciso gets drunk," Cico continued. "He stays drunk until the bad blood of spring is washed away. Then the moon of planting comes over the elm trees and shines on the horde of last year's seeds— It is then that he gathers the seeds and plants. He dances as he plants, and he sings. He scatters the seeds by moonlight, and they fall and grow— The garden is like Narciso, it is drunk."

"My father knows Narciso," I said. The story Cico had told me was fascinating. It seemed that the more I knew about people the more I knew about the strange magic hidden in their hearts.

"In this town, everybody knows everybody," Cico said.

"Do you know everyone?" I asked.

"Uh-huh," he nodded.

"You know Jasón's Indian?"

"Yes."

"Do you know Ultima?" I asked.

"I know about her cure," he said. "It was good. Come on now, let's be on our way. The golden carp will be swimming soon—"

We slipped out of the coolness of the garden into the hot, dusty street. On the east side of the school building was a barren playground with a basketball goal. The gang was playing basketball in the hot sun.

"Does the gang know about the golden carp?" I asked as we approached the group.

"Only Samuel," Cico said, "only Samuel can be trusted."

"Why do you trust me?" I asked. He paused and looked at me.

"Because you are a fisherman," he said. "There are no rules on who we trust, Tony, there is just a feeling. The Indian told Samuel the story; Narciso told me; now we tell you. I have a feeling someone, maybe Ultima, would have told you. We all share—"

"Hey!" Ernie called, "you guys want to play!" They ran towards us.

"Nah," Cico said. He turned away. He did not face them.

"Hi, Tony," they greeted me.

"Hey, you guys headed for Blue Lake? Let's go swimming," Florence suggested.

"It's too hot to play," Horse griped. He was dripping with sweat.

"Hey, Tony, is it true what they say? Is there a bruja at your house?" Ernie asked.

"¡A bruja!" "¡Chingada!" "¡A la veca!"

"No," I said simply.

"My father said she cursed someone and three days later that person changed into a frog—"

"Hey! Is that the old lady that goes to church with your family!" Bones shrieked.

"Let's go," Cico said.

"Knock it off, you guys, are we going to play or not!" Red

pleaded. Ernie spun the basketball on his finger. He was standing close to me and grinning as the ball spun.

"Hey, Tony, can you make the ball disappear?" He laughed. The others laughed too.

"Hey, Tony, do some magic!" Horse threw a hold around my neck and locked me into his half-nelson.

"Yeah!" Ernie shouted in my face. I did not know why he hated me.

"Leave him alone, Horse," Red said.

"Stay out of it, Red," Ernie shouted, "you're a Protestant. You don't know about the brujas!"

"They turn to owls and fly at night," Abel shouted.

"You have to kill them with a bullet marked with a cross," Lloyd added. "It's the law."

"Do magic," Horse grunted in my ear. His half-nelson was tight now. My stomach felt sick.

"Voodoo!" Ernie spun the ball in my face.

"Okay!" I cried. It must have scared Horse because he let loose and jumped back. They were all still, watching me.

The heat and what I had heard made me sick. I bent over, wretched and vomited. The yellow froth and juice of the carrots splattered at their feet.

"Jesuschriss!" "¡Chingada!" "¡Puta!" "¡A la madre!"

"Come on," Cico said. We took advantage of their surprise and ran. We were over the hill, past the last few houses, and at Blue Lake before they recovered from the astonishment I saw in their faces. We stopped to rest and laugh.

"That was great, Tony," Cico gasped, "that really put Ernie in his place—"

"Yeah," I nodded. I felt better after vomiting and running. I felt better about taking the carrots, but I did not feel good about what they had said about Ultima.

"Why are they like that?" I asked Cico. We skirted Blue Lake and worked our way through the tall, golden grass to the creek.

"I don't know," Cico answered, "except that people, grown-ups and kids, seem to want to hurt each other—and it's worse when they're in a group."

We walked on in silence. I had never been this far before so the land interested me. I knew that the waters of el Rito flowed from springs in the dark hills. I knew that those hills cradled the mysterious Hidden Lakes, but I had never been there. The creek flowed around the town, crossed beneath the bridge to El Puerto, then turned towards the river. There was a small reservoir there, and where the water emptied into the river the watercress grew thick and green. Ultima and I had visited the place in search of roots and herbs.

The water of el Rito was clear and clean. It was not muddy like the water of the river. We followed the footpath along the creek until we came to a thicket of brush and trees. The trail skirted around the bosque.

Cico paused and looked around. He pretended to be removing a splinter from his foot, but he was cautiously scanning the trail and the grass around us. I was sure we were alone; the last people we had seen were the swimmers at the Blue Lake a few miles back. Cico pointed to the path.

"The fishermen follow the trail around the brush," he whispered, "they hit the creek again just below the pond that's hidden in here." He squirmed into the thicket on hands and knees, and I followed. After a while we could stand up again and follow the creek to a place where an old beaver dam made a large pond.

It was a beautiful spot. The pond was dark and clear, and the water trickled and gurgled over the top of the dam. There was plenty of grass along the bank, and on all sides the tall brush and trees rose to shut off the world.

Cico pointed. "The golden carp will come through there." The cool waters of the creek came out of a dark, shadowy grotto of overhanging thicket, then flowed about thirty feet before they entered the large pond. Cico reached into a clump of grass and

brought out a long, thin salt cedar branch with a spear at the
end. The razor-sharp steel glistened in the sun. The other end
of the spear had a nylon cord attached to it for retrieving.

"I fish for the black bass of the pond," Cico said. He took
a position on a high clump of grass at the edge of the bank and
motioned for me to sit by the bank, but away from him.

"How can you see him?" I asked. The waters of the pool
were clear and pure, but dark from their depth and shadows of
the surrounding brush. The sun was crystaline white in the
clear, blue sky, but still there was the darkness of shadows in
this sacred spot.

"The golden carp will scare him up," Cico whispered. "The
black bass thinks he can be king of the fish, but all he wants
is to eat them. The black bass is a killer. But the real king is
the golden carp, Tony. He does not eat his own kind—"

Cico's eyes remained glued on the dark waters. His body was
motionless, like a spring awaiting release. We had been whispering since we arrived at the pond, why I didn't know, except
that it was just one of those places where one can communicate
only in whispers, like church.

We sat for a long time, waiting for the golden carp. It was
very pleasant to sit in the warm sunshine and watch the pure
waters drift by. The drone of the summer insects and grasshoppers made me sleepy. The lush green of the grass was cool,
and beneath the grass was the dark earth, patient, waiting . . .

To the northeast two hawks circled endlessly in the clear
sky. There must be something dead on the road to Tucumcari,
I thought.

Then the golden carp came. Cico pointed and I turned to
where the stream came out of the dark grotto of overhanging
tree branches. At first I thought I must be dreaming. I had
expected to see a carp the size of a river carp, perhaps a little
bigger and slightly orange instead of brown. I rubbed my eyes
and watched in astonishment.

"Behold the golden carp, Lord of the waters—" I turned and

saw Cico standing, his spear held across his chest as if in acknowledgement of the presence of a ruler.

The huge, beautiful form glided through the blue waters. I could not believe its size. It was bigger than me! And bright orange! The sunlight glistened off his golden scales. He glided down the creek with a couple of smaller carp following, but they were like minnows compared to him.

"The golden carp," I whispered in awe. I could not have been more entranced if I had seen the Virgin, or God Himself. The golden carp had seen me. It made a wide sweep, its back making ripples in the dark water. I could have reached out into the water and touched the holy fish!

"He knows you are a friend," Cico whispered.

Then the golden carp swam by Cico and disappeared into the darkness of the pond. I felt my body trembling as I saw the bright golden form disappear. I knew I had witnessed a miraculous thing, the appearance of a pagan god, a thing as miraculous as the curing of my uncle Lucas. And I thought, the power of God failed where Ultima's worked; and then a sudden illumination of beauty and understanding flashed through my mind. This is what I had expected God to do at my first holy communion! If God was witness to my beholding of the golden carp then I had sinned! I clasped my hands and was about to pray to the heavens when the waters of the pond exploded.

I turned in time to see Cico hurl his spear at the monstrous black bass that had broken the surface of the waters. The evil mouth of the black bass was open and red. Its eyes were glazed with hate as it hung in the air surrounded by churning water and a million diamond droplets of water. The spear whistled through the air, but the aim was low. The huge tail swished and contemptuously flipped it aside. Then the black form dropped into the foaming waters.

"Missed," Cico groaned. He retrieved his line slowly.

I nodded my head. "I can't believe what I have seen," I heard myself say, "are all the fish that big here—"

"No," Cico smiled, "they catch two and three pounders below
the beaver dam, the black bass must weigh close to twenty—"
He threw his spear and line behind the clump of grass and came
to sit by me. "Come on, let's put our feet in the water. The
golden carp will be returning—"

"Are you sorry you missed?" I asked as we slid our feet into
the cool water.

"No," Cico said, "it's just a game."

The orange of the golden carp appeared at the edge of the
pond. As he came out of the darkness of the pond the sun caught
his shiny scales and the light reflected orange and yellow and
red. He swam very close to our feet. His body was round and
smooth in the clear water. We watched in silence at the beauty
and grandeur of the great fish. Out of the corners of my eyes
I saw Cico hold his hand to his breast as the golden carp glided
by. Then with a switch of his powerful tail the golden carp
disappeared into the shadowy water under the thicket.

I shook my head. "What will happen to the golden carp?"

"What do you mean?" Cico asked.

"There are many men who fish here—"

Cico smiled. "They can't see him, Tony, they can't see him.
I know every man from Guadalupe who fishes, and there ain't
a one who has ever mentioned seeing the golden carp. So I guess
the grown-ups can't see him—"

"The Indian, Narciso, Ultima—"

"They're different, Tony. Like Samuel, and me, and you—"

"I see," I said. I did not know what that difference was, but
I did feel a strange brotherhood with Cico. We shared a secret
that would always bind us.

"Where does the golden carp go?" I asked and nodded upstream.

"He swims upstream to the lakes of the mermaid, the Hidden
Lakes—"

"The mermaid?" I questioned him.

"There are two deep, hidden lakes up in the hills," he continued, "they feed the creek. Some people say those lakes have

no bottom. There's good fishing, but very few people go there. There's something strange about those lakes, like they are haunted. There's a strange power, it seems to watch you—"

"Like the *presence* of the river?" I asked softly. Cico looked at me and nodded.

"You've felt it," he said.

"Yes."

"Then you understand. But this thing at the lakes is stronger, or maybe not stronger, it just seems to want you more. The time I was there—I climbed to one of the overhanging cliffs, and I just sat there, watching the fish in the clear water—I didn't know about the power then, I was just thinking how good the fishing could be, when I began to hear strange music. It came from far away. It was a low, lonely murmuring, maybe like something a sad girl would sing. I looked around, but I was alone. I looked over the ledge of the cliff and the singing seemed to be coming from the water, and it seemed to be calling me—"

I was spellbound with Cico's whispered story. If I had not seen the golden carp perhaps I would not have believed him. But I had seen too much today to doubt him.

"I swear, Tony, the music was pulling me into the dark waters below! The only thing that saved me from plunging into the lake was the golden carp. He appeared and the music stopped. Only then could I tear myself away from that place. Man, I ran! Oh how I ran! I had never been afraid before, but I was afraid then. And it wasn't that the singing was evil, it was just that it called for me to join it. One more step and I'da stepped over the ledge and drowned in the waters of the lake—"

I waited a long time before I asked the next question. I waited for him to finish reliving his experience. "Did you see the mermaid?"

"No," he answered.

"Who is she?" I whispered.

"No one knows. A deserted woman—or just the wind singing around the edges of those cliffs. No one really knows. It just calls people to it—"

"Who?"

He looked at me carefully. His eyes were clear and bright, like Ultima's, and there were lines of age already showing.

"Last summer the mermaid took a shepherd. He was a man from Méjico, new here and working for a ranch beyond the hills. He had not heard the story about the lakes. He brought his sheep to water there, and he heard the singing. He made it back to town and even swore that he had seen the mermaid. He said it was a woman, resting on the water and singing a lonely song. She was half woman and half fish— He said the song made him want to wade out to the middle of the lake to help her, but his fear had made him run. He told everyone the story, but no one believed him. He ended up getting drunk in town and swearing he would prove his story by going back to the lakes and bringing back the mer-woman. He never returned. A week later the flock was found near the lakes. He had vanished—"

"Do you think the mermaid took him?" I asked.

"I don't know, Tony," Cico said and knit his brow, "there's a lot of things I don't know. But never go to the Hidden Lakes alone, Tony, never. It's not safe."

I nodded that I would honor his warning. "It is so strange," I said, "the things that happen. The things that I have seen, or heard about."

"Yes," he agreed.

"These things of the water, the mermaid, the golden carp. They are strange. There is so much water around the town, the river, the creek, the lakes—"

Cico leaned back and stared into the bright sky. "This whole land was once covered by a sea, a long time ago—"

"My name means sea," I pondered aloud.

"Hey, that's right," he said, "Márez means sea, it means you came from the ocean, Tony Márez arisen from the sea—"

"My father says our blood is restless, like the sea—"

"That is beautiful," he said. He laughed. "You know, this land belonged to the fish before it belonged to us. I have no doubt about the prophecy of the golden carp. He will come to rule again!"

"What do you mean?" I asked.

"What do I mean?" Cico asked quizzically, "I mean that the golden carp will come to rule again. Didn't Samuel tell you?"

"No," I shook my head.

"Well he told you about the people who killed the carp of the river and were punished by being turned into fish themselves. After that happened, many years later, a new people came to live in this valley. And they were no better than the first inhabitants, in fact they were worse. They sinned a lot, they sinned against each other, and they sinned against the legends they knew. And so the golden carp sent them a prophecy. He said that the sins of the people would weigh so heavy upon the land that in the end the whole town would collapse and be swallowed by water—"

I must have whistled in exclamation and sighed.

"Tony," Cico said, "this whole town is sitting over a deep, underground lake! Everybody knows that. Look." He drew on the sand with a stick. "Here's the river. The creek flows up here and curves into the river. The Hidden Lakes complete the other border. See?"

I nodded. The town was surrounded by water. It was frightening to know that! "The whole town!" I whispered in amazement.

"Yup," Cico said, "the whole town. The golden carp has warned us that the land cannot take the weight of the sins— the land will finally sink!"

"But you live in town!" I exclaimed.

He smiled and stood up. "The golden carp is my god, Tony. He will rule the new waters. I will be happy to be with my god—"

It was unbelievable, and yet it made a wild kind of sense! All the pieces fitted!

"Do the people of the town know?" I asked anxiously.

"They know," he nodded, "and they keep on sinning."

"But it's not fair to those who don't sin!" I countered.

"Tony," Cico said softly, "all men sin."

I had no answer to that. My own mother had said that losing your innocence and becoming a man was learning to sin. I felt weak and powerless in the knowledge of the impending doom.

"When will it happen?" I asked.

"No one knows," Cico answered. "It could be today, tomorrow, a week, a hundred years—but it will happen."

"What can we do?" I asked. I heard my voice tremble.

"Sin against no one," Cico answered.

I walked away from that haven which held the pond and the swimming waters of the golden carp feeling a great weight in my heart. I was saddened by what I had learned. I had seen beauty, but the beauty had burdened me with responsibility. Cico wanted to fish at the dam, but I was not in the mood for it. I thanked him for letting me see the golden carp, crossed the river, and trudged up the hill homeward.

I thought about telling everyone in town to stop their sinning, or drown and die. But they would not believe me. How could I preach to the whole town, I was only a boy. They would not listen. They would say I was crazy, or bewitched by Ultima's magic.

I went home and thought about what I had seen and the story Cico told. I went to Ultima and told her the story. She said nothing. She only smiled. It was as if she knew the story and found nothing fantastic or impending in it. "I would have told you the story myself," she nodded wisely, "but it is better that you hear the legend from someone your own age . . ."

"Am I to believe the story?" I asked. I was worried.

"Antonio," she said calmly and placed her hand on my shoulder, "I cannot tell you what to believe. Your father and your mother can tell you, because you are their blood, but I cannot. As you grow into manhood you must find your own truths—"

That night in my dreams I walked by the shore of a great lake. A bewitching melody filled the air. It was the song of the mer-woman!

I looked into the dark depths of the lake and saw the golden carp, and all around him were the people he had saved. On the bleached shores of the lake the carcasses of sinners rotted.

Then a huge golden moon came down from the heavens and settled on the surface of the calm waters. I looked towards the enchanting light, expecting to see the Virgin of Guadalupe, but in her place I saw my mother!

Mother, I cried, you are saved! We are all saved!

Yes, my Antonio, she smiled, we who were baptized in the water of the moon which was made holy by our Holy Mother the Church are saved.

Lies! my father shouted, Antonio was not baptized in the holy water of the moon, but in the salt water of the sea!

I turned and saw him standing on the corpse-strewn shore. I felt a searing pain spread through my body.

Oh please tell me which is the water that runs through my veins, I moaned; oh please tell me which is the water that washes my burning eyes!

It is the sweet water of the moon, my mother crooned softly, it is the water the Church chooses to make holy and place in its font. It is the water of your baptism.

Lies, lies, my father laughed, through your body runs the salt water of the oceans. It is that water which makes you Márez and not Luna. It is the water that binds you to the pagan god of Cico, the golden carp!

Oh, I cried, please tell me. The agony of pain was more than I could bear. The excruciating pain broke and I sweated blood.

There was a howling wind as the moon rose and its powers pulled at the still waters of the lake. Thunder split the air and the lightning bursts illuminated the churning, frothy tempest. The ghosts stood and walked upon the shore.

The lake seemed to respond with rage and fury. It cracked with the laughter of madness as it inflicted death upon the people. I thought the end had come to everything. The cosmic struggle of the two forces would destroy everything!

The doom which Cico had predicted was upon us! I clasped my

hands and knelt to pray. The terrifying end was near. Then I heard a voice speak above the sound of the storm. I looked up and saw Ultima.

Cease! she cried to the raging powers, and the power from the heavens and the power from the earth obeyed her. The storm abated.

Stand, Antonio, she commanded, and I stood. You both know, she spoke to my father and my mother, that the sweet water of the moon which falls as rain is the same water that gathers into rivers and flows to fill the seas. Without the waters of the moon to replenish the oceans there would be no oceans. And the same salt waters of the oceans are drawn by the sun to the heavens, and in turn become again the waters of the moon. Without the sun there would be no waters formed to slake the dark earth's thirst.

The waters are one, Antonio. I looked into her bright, clear eyes and understood her truth.

You have been seeing only parts, she finished, and not looking beyond into the great cycle that binds us all.

Then there was peace in my dreams and I could rest.

DAVID QUAMMEN

WALKING OUT

As the train rocked dead at Livingston he saw the man, in a worn khaki shirt with button flaps buttoned, arms crossed. The boy's hand sprang up by reflex, and his face broke into a smile. The man smiled back gravely, and nodded. He did not otherwise move. The boy turned from the window and, with the awesome deliberateness of a fat child harboring reluctance, began struggling to pull down his bag. His father would wait on the platform. First sight of him had reminded the boy that nothing was simple enough now for hurrying.

They drove in the old open Willys toward the cabin beyond town. The windshield of the Willys was up, but the fine cold sharp rain came into their faces, and the boy could not raise his eyes to look at the road. He wore a rain parka his father had handed him at the station. The man, protected by only the khaki, held his lips strung in a firm silent line that seemed more grin than wince. Riding through town in the cold rain, open topped and jaunty, getting drenched as though by necessity, was—the boy understood vaguely—somehow in the spirit of this season.

"We have a moose tag," his father shouted.

The boy said nothing. He refused to care what it meant, that they had a moose tag.

"I've got one picked out. A bull. I've stalked him for two weeks. Up in the Crazies. When we get to the cabin, we'll build a good roaring fire." With only the charade of a pause, he added, "Your mother." It was said like a question. The boy waited. "How is she?"

"All right, I guess." Over the jeep's howl, with the wind stealing his voice, the boy too had to shout.

"Are you friends with her?"

"I guess so."

"Is she still a beautiful lady?"

"I don't know. I guess so. I don't know that."

"You must know that. Is she starting to get wrinkled like me? Does she seem worried and sad? Or is she just still a fine beautiful lady? You must know that."

"She's still a beautiful lady, I guess."

"Did she tell you any messages for me?"

"She said . . . she said I should give you her love," the boy lied, impulsively and clumsily. He was at once embarrassed that he had done it.

"Oh," his father said. "Thank you, David."

They reached the cabin on a mile of dirt road winding through meadow to a spruce grove. Inside, the boy was enwrapped in the strong syncretic smell of all seasonal mountain cabins: pine resin and insect repellent and a mustiness suggesting damp bathing trunks stored in a drawer. There were yellow pine floors and rope-work throw rugs and a bead curtain to the bedroom and a cast-iron cook stove with none of the lids or handles missing and a pump in the kitchen sink and old issues of *Field and Stream,* and on the mantel above where a fire now finally burned was a picture of the boy's grandfather, the railroad telegrapher, who had once owned the cabin. The boy's father cooked a dinner of fried ham, and though the boy did not like ham he had expected his father to cook canned stew or Spam, so he said nothing. His father asked him about school and the boy talked and his father seemed to be interested. Warm and dry, the boy began to feel safe from his own anguish. Then his father said:

"We'll leave tomorrow around ten."

Last year on the boy's visit they had hunted birds. They had lived in the cabin for six nights, and each day they had hunted pheasant in the wheat stubble, or blue grouse in the woods, or ducks along the irrigation slews. The boy had been wet and cold and miserable at times, but each evening they returned to the cabin and to the boy's suitcase of dry clothes. They had eaten hot food cooked on a stove, and had smelled the cabin smell, and had slept together in a bed. In six days of hunting, the boy had not managed to kill a single bird. Yet last year he had known that, at least once a day, he would be comfortable, if not happy. This year his father planned that he should not even be comfortable. He had said in his last letter to Evergreen Park, before the boy left Chicago but when it was too late for him not to leave, that he would take the boy camping in the mountains, after big game. He had pretended to believe that the boy would be glad.

The Willys was loaded and moving by ten minutes to ten. For three hours they drove, through Big Timber, and then north on the highway, and then back west again on a logging road that took them winding and bouncing higher into the mountains. Thick cottony streaks of white cloud hung in among the mountaintop trees, light and dense dollops against the bulking sharp dark olive, as though in a black-and-white photograph. They followed the gravel road for an hour, and the boy thought they would soon have a flat tire or break an axle. If they had a flat, the boy knew, his father would only change it and drive on until they had the second, farther from the highway. Finally they crossed a creek and his father plunged the Willys off into a bed of weeds.

His father said, "Here."

The boy said, "Where?"

"Up that little drainage. At the head of the creek."

"How far is it?"

"Two or three miles."

"Is that where you saw the moose?"

"No. That's where I saw the sheepman's hut. The moose is farther. On top."

"Are we going to sleep in a hut? I thought we were going to sleep in a tent."

"No. Why should we carry a tent up there when we have a perfectly good hut?"

The boy couldn't answer that question. He thought now that this might be the time when he would cry. He had known it was coming.

"I don't much want to sleep in a hut," he said, and his voice broke with the simple honesty of it, and his eyes glazed. He held his mouth tight against the trembling.

As though something had broken in him too, the boy's father laid his forehead down on the steering wheel, against his knuckles. For a moment he remained bowed, breathing exhaustedly. But he looked up again before speaking.

"Well, we don't have to, David."

The boy said nothing.

"It's an old sheepman's hut made of logs, and it's near where we're going to hunt, and we can fix it dry and good. I thought you might like that. I thought it might be more fun than a tent. But we don't have to do it. We can drive back to Big Timber and buy a tent, or we can drive back to the cabin and hunt birds, like last year. Whatever you want to do. You have to forgive me the kind of ideas I get. I hope you will. We don't have to do anything that you don't want to do."

"No," the boy said. "I want to."

"Are you sure?"

"No," the boy said. "But I just want to."

They bushwhacked along the creek, treading a thick soft mixture of moss and humus and needles, climbing upward through brush. Then the brush thinned and they were ascending an open creek bottom, thirty yards wide, darkened by fir and cedar. Farther, and they struck a trail, which led them upward along the creek. Farther still, and the trail received a branch, then another, then forked.

"Who made this trail? Did the sheepman?"

"No," his father said. "Deer and elk."

Gradually the creek's little canyon narrowed, steep wooded shoulders funneling closer on each side. For a while the game trails forked and converged like a maze, but soon again there were only two branches, and finally one, heavily worn. It dodged through alder and willow, skirting tangles of browned raspberry, so that the boy and his father could never see more than twenty feet ahead. When they stopped to rest, the boy's father unstrapped the .270 from his pack and loaded it.

"We have to be careful now," he explained. "We may surprise a bear."

Under the cedars, the creek bottom held a cool dampness that seemed to be stored from one winter to the next. The boy began at once to feel chilled. He put on his jacket, and they continued climbing. Soon he was sweating again in the cold.

On a small flat where the alder drew back from the creek, the hut was built into one bank of the canyon, with the sod of the hillside lapping out over its roof. The door was a low dark opening. Forty or fifty years ago, the boy's father explained, this hut had been built and used by a Basque shepherd. At that time there had been many Basques in Montana, and they had run sheep all across this ridge of the Crazies. His father forgot to explain what a Basque was, and the boy didn't remind him.

They built a fire. His father had brought sirloin steaks and an onion for dinner, and the boy was happy with him about that. As they ate, it grew dark, but the boy and his father had stocked a large comforting pile of naked deadfall. In the darkness, by firelight, his father made chocolate pudding. The pudding had been his father's surprise. The boy sat on a piece of canvas and added logs to the fire while his father drank coffee. Sparks rose on the heat and the boy watched them climb toward the cedar limbs and the black pools of sky. The pudding did not set.

"Do you remember your grandfather, David?"

"Yes," the boy said, and wished it were true. He remembered a funeral when he was three.

"Your grandfather brought me up on this mountain when I

was seventeen. That was the last year he hunted." The boy knew what sort of thoughts his father was having. But he knew also that his own home was in Evergreen Park, and that he was another man's boy now, with another man's name, though this indeed was his father. "Your grandfather was fifty years older than me."

The boy said nothing.

"And I'm thirty-four years older than you."

"And I'm only eleven," the boy cautioned him.

"Yes," said his father. "And someday you'll have a son and you'll be forty years older than him, and you'll want so badly for him to know who you are that you could cry."

The boy was embarrassed.

"And that's called the cycle of life's infinite wisdom," his father said, and laughed at himself unpleasantly.

"What did he die of?" the boy asked, desperate to escape the focus of his father's rumination.

"He was eighty-seven then. Christ. He was tired." The boy's father went silent. Then he shook his head, and poured himself the remaining coffee.

Through that night the boy was never quite warm. He slept on his side with his knees drawn up, and this was uncomfortable but his body seemed to demand it for warmth. The hard cold mountain earth pressed upward through the mat of fir boughs his father had laid, and drew heat from the boy's body like a pallet of leeches. He clutched the bedroll around his neck and folded the empty part at the bottom back under his legs. Once he woke to a noise. Though his father was sleeping between him and the door of the hut, for a while the boy lay awake, listening worriedly, and then woke again on his back to realize time had passed. He heard droplets begin to hit the canvas his father had spread over the sod roof of the hut. But he remained dry.

He rose to the smell of a fire. The tarp was rigid with sleet and frost. The firewood and the knapsacks were frosted. It was that gray time of dawn before any blue and, through the branches above, the boy was unable to tell whether the sky was murky or clear. Delicate sheet ice hung on everything, but there was no wetness. The rain seemed to have been hushed by the cold.

"What time is it?"

"Early yet."

"How early?" the boy was thinking about the cold at home as he waited outside on 96th Street for his school bus. That was the cruelest moment of his day, but it seemed a benign and familiar part of him compared to this.

"Early. I don't have a watch. What difference does it make, David?"

"Not any."

After breakfast they began walking up the valley. His father had the .270 and the boy carried an old Winchester .30–30, with open sights. The walking was not hard, and with this gentle exercise in the cold morning the boy soon felt fresh and fine. Now I'm hunting for moose with my father, he told himself. That's just what I'm doing. Few boys in Evergreen Park had ever been moose hunting with their fathers in Montana, he knew. I'm doing it now, the boy told himself.

Reaching the lip of a high meadow, a mile above the shepherd's hut, they had not seen so much as a magpie.

Before them, across hundreds of yards, opened a smooth lake of tall lifeless grass, browned by September drought and killed by the frosts and beginning to rot with November's rain. The creek was here a deep quiet channel of smooth curves overhung by the grass, with a dark surface like heavy oil. When they had come fifty yards into the meadow, his father turned and pointed out to the boy a large ponderosa pine with a forked crown that marked the head of their creek valley. He showed the boy a small aspen grove midway across the meadow, toward which they were aligning themselves.

"Near the far woods is a beaver pond. The moose waters there. We can wait in the aspens and watch the whole meadow without being seen. If he doesn't come, we'll go up another canyon, and check again on the way back."

For an hour, and another, they waited. The boy sat with his hands in his jacket pockets, bunching the jacket tighter around him, and his buttocks drew cold moisture from the ground. His father squatted on his heels like a country man, rising periodically to inspect the meadow in all directions. Finally he stood up; he fixed his stare on the distant fringe of woods and, like a retriever, did not move. He said, "David."

The boy stood beside him. His father placed a hand on the boy's shoulder. The boy saw a large dark form rolling toward them like a great slug in the grass.

"Is it the moose?"

"No," said his father. "That is a grizzly bear, David. An old male grizzly."

The boy was impressed. He sensed an aura of power and terror and authority about the husky shape, even at two hundred yards.

"Are we going to shoot him?"

"No."

"Why not?"

"We don't have a permit," his father whispered. "And because we don't want to."

The bear plowed on toward the beaver pond for a while, then stopped. It froze in the grass and seemed to be listening. The boy's father added: "That's not hunting for the meat. That's hunting for the fear. I don't need the fear. I've got enough in my life already."

The bear turned and moiled off quickly through the grass. It disappeared back into the far woods.

"He heard us."

"Maybe," the boy's father said. "Let's go have a look at that beaver pond."

A sleek furred carcass lay low in the water, swollen grotesquely with putrescence and coated with glistening blowflies. Four days, the boy's father guessed. The moose had been shot at least eighteen times with a .22 pistol. One of its eyes had been shot out; it had been shot twice in the jaw; and both quarters on the side that lay upward were ruined with shots. Standing up to his knees in the sump, the boy's father took the trouble of counting the holes, and probing one of the slugs out with his knife. That only made him angrier. He flung the lead away.

For the next three hours, with his father withdrawn into a solitary and characteristic bitterness, the boy felt abandoned. He did not understand why a moose would be slaughtered with a light pistol and left to rot. His father did not bother to explain; like the bear, he seemed to understand it as well as he needed to. They walked on, but they did not really hunt.

They left the meadow for more pine, and now tamarack, naked tamarack, the yellow needles nearly all down and going ginger where they coated the trail. The boy and his father hiked along a level path into another canyon, this one vast at the mouth and narrowing between high ridges of bare rock. They crossed and recrossed the shepherd's creek, which in this canyon was a tumbling free-stone brook. Following five yards behind his father, watching the cold, unapproachable rage that shaped the line of the man's shoulders, the boy was miserably uneasy because his father had grown so distant and quiet. They climbed over deadfalls blocking the trail, skirted one boulder large as a cabin, and blundered into a garden of nettles that stung them fiercely through their trousers. They saw fresh elk scat, and they saw bear, diarrhetic with late berries. The boy's father eventually grew bored with brooding, and showed the boy how to stalk. Before dusk that day they had shot an elk.

An open and gently sloped hillside, almost a meadow, ran for a quarter mile in quaking aspen, none over fifteen feet tall. The elk was above. The boy's father had the boy brace his gun in the notch of an aspen and take the first shot. The boy missed. The elk reeled and bolted down and his father killed it before it made cover. It was a five-point bull. They dressed the elk out and dragged it down to the cover of large pines, near the stream, where they would quarter it tomorrow, and then they returned under twilight to the hut.

That night even the fetal position could not keep the boy warm. He shivered wakefully for hours. He was glad that the following day, though full of walking and butchery and oppressive burdens, would be their last in the woods. He heard nothing. When he woke, through the door of the hut he saw whiteness like bone.

Six inches had fallen, and it was still snowing. The boy stood about in the campsite, amazed. When it snowed three inches in Evergreen Park, the boy would wake before dawn to the hiss of sand trucks and the ratchet of chains. Here there had been no warning. The boy was not much colder than he had been yesterday, and the transformation of the woods seemed mysterious and benign and somehow comic. He thought of Christmas. Then his father barked at him.

His father's mood had also changed, but in a different way; he seemed serious and hurried. As he wiped the breakfast pots clean with snow, he gave the boy orders for other chores. They left camp with two empty pack frames, both rifles, and a handsaw and rope. The boy soon understood why his father felt pressure of time: it took them an hour to climb the mile to the meadow. The snow continued. They did not rest until they reached the aspens.

"I had half a mind at breakfast to let the bull lie and pack us straight down out of here," his father admitted. "Probably smarter and less trouble in the long run. I could have come back on snowshoes next week. But by then it might be three feet deep and starting to drift. We can get two quarters out today. That will make it easier for me later." The boy was surprised by two things: that his father would be so wary in the face of a gentle snowfall and that he himself would have felt disappointed to be taken out of the woods that morning. The air of the meadow teemed with white.

"If it stops soon, we're fine," said his father.

It continued.

The path up the far canyon was hard climbing in eight inches of snow. The boy fell once, filling his collar and sleeves, and the gun-sight put a small gouge in his chin. But he was not discouraged. That night they would be warm and dry at the cabin. A half mile on and he came up beside his father, who had stopped to stare down at dark splashes of blood.

Heavy tracks and a dragging belly mark led up to the scramble of deepening red, and away. The tracks were nine inches long and showed claws. The boy's father knelt. As the boy watched, one shining maroon splotch the size of a saucer sank slowly beyond sight into the snow. The blood was warm.

Inspecting the tracks carefully, his father said, "She's got a cub with her."

"What happened?"

"Just a kill. Seems to have been a bird. That's too much blood for a grouse, but I don't see signs of any four-footed creature. Maybe a turkey." He frowned thoughtfully. "A turkey without feathers. I don't know. What I dislike is coming up on her with a cub." He drove a round into the chamber of the .270.

Trailing red smears, the tracks preceded them. Within fifty feet they found the body. It was half-buried. The top of its head had been shorn away, and the cub's brains had been licked out.

His father said "Christ," and plunged off the trail. He snapped at the boy to follow closely.

They made a wide crescent through brush and struck back after a quarter mile. His father slogged ahead in the snow, stopping often to stand holding his gun ready and glancing around while the boy caught up and passed him. The boy was confused. He knew his father was worried, but he did not feel any danger himself. They met the trail again, and went on to the aspen hillside before his father allowed them to rest. The boy spat on the snow. His lungs ached badly.

"Why did she do that?"

"She didn't. Another bear got her cub. A male. Maybe the one we saw yesterday. Then she fought him for the body, and she won. We didn't miss them by much. She may even have been watching. Nothing could put her in a worse frame of mind."

He added: "If we so much as see her, I want you to pick the nearest big tree and start climbing. Don't stop till you're twenty feet off the ground. I'll stay down and decide whether we have to shoot her. Is your rifle cocked?"

"No."

"Cock it, and put on the safety. She may be a black bear and black bears can climb. If she comes up after you, lean down and stick your gun in her mouth and fire. You can't miss."

He cocked the Winchester, as his father had said.

They angled downhill to the stream, and on to the mound of their dead elk. Snow filtered down steadily in purposeful silence. The boy was thirsty. It could not be much below freezing, he was aware, because with the exercise his bare hands were comfortable, even sweating between the fingers.

"Can I get a drink?"

"Yes. Be careful you don't wet your feet. And don't wander anywhere. We're going to get this done quickly."

He walked the few yards, ducked through the brush at streamside, and knelt in the snow to drink. The water was painful to his sinuses and bitterly cold on his hands. Standing again, he noticed an animal body ahead near the stream bank. For a moment he felt sure it was another dead cub. During that moment his father called:

"David! Get up here right now!"

The boy meant to call back. First he stepped closer to turn the cub with his foot. The touch brought it alive. It rose suddenly with a high squealing growl and whirled its head like a snake and snapped. The boy shrieked. The cub had his right hand in its jaws. It would not release.

It thrashed senselessly, working its teeth deeper and tearing flesh with each movement. The boy felt no pain. He knew his hand was being damaged and that realization terrified him and he was desperate to get the hand back before it was ruined. But he was helpless. He sensed the same furious terror racking the cub that he felt in himself, and he screamed at the cub almost reasoningly to let him go. His screams scared the cub more. Its head snatched back and forth. The boy did not think to shout for his father. He did not see him or hear him coming.

His father moved at full stride in a slowed laboring run through the snow, saying nothing and holding the rifle he did not use, crossed the last six feet still gathering speed, and brought his right boot up into the cub's belly. That kick seemed to lift the cub clear of the snow. It opened its jaws to another shrill piggish squeal, and the boy felt dull relief on his hand, as though his father had pressed open the blades of a spring trap with his foot. The cub tumbled once and disappeared over the stream bank, then surfaced downstream, squalling and paddling. The boy looked at his hand and was horrified. He still had no pain, but the hand was unrecognizable. His fingers had been peeled down through the palm like flaps on a banana. Glands at the sides of his jaw threatened that he would vomit, and he might have stood stupidly watching the hand bleed if his father had not grabbed him.

He snatched the boy by the arm and dragged him toward a tree without even looking at the boy's hand. The boy jerked back in angry resistance as though he had been struck. He screamed at his father. He screamed that his hand was cut, believing his father did not know, and as he screamed he began to cry. He began to feel hot throbbing pain. He began to worry about the blood he was losing. He could imagine his blood melting red holes in the snow behind him and he did not want to look. He did not want to do anything until he had taken care of his hand. At that instant he hated his father. But his father was stronger. He all but carried the boy to a tree.

He lifted the boy. In a voice that was quiet and hurried and very unlike the harsh grip with which he had taken the boy's arm, he said:

"Grab hold and climb up a few branches as best you can. Sit on a limb and hold tight and clamp the hand under your other armpit, if you can do that. I'll be right back to you. Hold tight because you're going to get dizzy." The boy groped desperately for a branch. His father supported him from beneath, and waited.

The boy clambered. His feet scraped at the trunk. Then he was in the tree. Bark flakes and resin were stuck to the raw naked meat of his right hand. His father said:

"Now here, take this. Hurry."

The boy never knew whether his father himself had been frightened enough to forget for that moment about the boy's hand, or whether his father was still thinking quite clearly. His father may have expected that much. By the merciless clarity of his own standards, he may have expected that the boy should be able to hold onto a tree, and a wound, and a rifle, all with one hand. He extended the stock of the Winchester toward the boy.

The boy wanted to say something, but his tears and his fright would not let him gather a breath. He shuddered, and could not speak. "David," his father urged. The boy reached for the stock and faltered and clutched at the trunk with his good arm. He was crying and gasping, and he wanted to speak. He was afraid he would fall out of the tree. He released his grip once again, and felt himself tip. His father extended the gun higher, holding the barrel. The boy swung out his injured hand, spraying his father's face with blood. He reached and he tried to close torn dangling fingers around the stock and he pulled the trigger.

The bullet entered low on his father's thigh and shattered the knee and traveled down the shin bone and into the ground through his father's heel.

His father fell, and the rifle fell with him. He lay in the snow without moving. The boy thought he was dead. Then the boy saw him grope for the rifle. He found it and rolled onto his stomach, taking aim at the sow grizzly. Forty feet up the hill, towering on hind legs, she canted her head to one side, indecisive. When the cub pulled itself up a snowbank from the stream, she coughed at it sternly. The cub trotted straight to her with its head low. She knocked it off its feet with a huge paw, and it yelped. Then she turned quickly. The cub followed.

The woods were silent. The gunshot still echoed awesomely

back to the boy but it was an echo of memory, not sound. He felt nothing. He saw his father's body stretched on the snow and he did not really believe he was where he was. He did not want to move: he wanted to wake. He sat in the tree and waited. The snow fell as gracefully as before.

His father rolled onto his back. The boy saw him raise himself to a sitting position and look down at the leg and betray no expression, and then slump back. He blinked slowly and lifted his eyes to meet the boy's eyes. The boy waited. He expected his father to speak. He expected his father to say *Shinny down using your elbows and knees and get the first-aid kit and boil water and phone the doctor. The number is taped to the dial.* His father stared. The boy could see the flicker of thoughts behind his father's eyes. His father said nothing. He raised his arms slowly and crossed them over his face, as though to nap in the sun.

The boy jumped. He landed hard on his feet and fell onto his back. He stood over his father. His hand dripped quietly onto the snow. He was afraid that his father was deciding to die. He wanted to beg him to reconsider. The boy had never before seen his father hopeless. He was afraid.

But he was no longer afraid of his father.

Then his father uncovered his face and said, "Let me see it."

They bandaged the boy's hand with a sleeve cut from the other arm of his shirt. His father wrapped the hand firmly and split the sleeve end with his deer knife and tied it neatly in two places. The boy now felt searing pain in his torn palm, and his stomach lifted when he thought of the damage, but at least he did not have to look at it. Quickly the plaid flannel bandage began to soak through maroon. They cut a sleeve from his father's shirt to tie over the wound in his thigh. They raised the trouser leg to see the long swelling bruise down the calf where he was hemorrhaging into the bullet's tunnel. Only then did his father realize that he was bleeding also from the heel. The boy took off his father's boot and placed a half-clean hand-kerchief on the insole where the bullet had exited, as his father instructed him. Then his father laced the boot on again tightly.

The boy helped his father to stand. His father tried a step, then collapsed in the snow with a blasphemous howl of pain. They had not known that the knee was shattered.

The boy watched his father's chest heave with the forced sighs of suffocating frustration, and heard the air wheeze through his nostrils. His father relaxed himself with the breathing, and seemed to be thinking. He said,

"You can find your way back to the hut."

The boy held his own breath and did not move.

"You can, can't you?"

"But I'm not. I'm not going alone. I'm only going with you."

"All right, David, listen carefully," his father said. "We don't have to worry about freezing. I'm not worried about either of us freezing to death. No one is going to freeze in the woods in November, if he looks after himself. Not even in Montana. It just isn't that cold. I have matches and I have a fresh elk. And I don't think this weather is going to get any worse. It may be raining again by morning. What I'm concerned about is the bleeding. If I spend too much time and effort trying to walk out of here, I could bleed to death.

"I think your hand is going to be all right. It's a bad wound, but the doctors will be able to fix it as good as new. I can see that. I promise you that. You'll be bleeding some too, but if you take care of that hand; it won't bleed any more walking than if you were standing still. Then you'll be at the doctor's tonight. But if I try to walk out on this leg it's going to bleed and keep bleeding and I'll lose too much blood. So I'm staying here and bundling up warm and you're walking out to get help. I'm sorry about this. It's what we have to do.

"You can't possibly get lost. You'll just follow this trail straight down the canyon the way we came up, and then you'll come to the meadow. Point yourself toward the big pine tree with the forked crown. When you get to that tree you'll find the creek again. You may not be able to see it, but make yourself quiet and listen for it. You'll hear it. Follow that down off the mountain and past the hut till you get to the jeep."

He struggled a hand into his pocket. "You've never driven a car, have you?"

The boy's lips were pinched. Muscles in his cheeks ached from clenching his jaws. He shook his head.

"You can do it. It isn't difficult." His father held up a single key and began telling the boy how to start the jeep, how to work the clutch, how to find reverse and then first and then second. As his father described the positions on the floor shift the boy raised his swaddled right hand. His father stopped. He rubbed at his eye sockets, like a man waking.

"Of course," he said. "All right. You'll have to help me."

Using the saw with his left hand, the boy cut a small forked aspen. His father showed the boy where to trim it so that the fork would reach just to his armpit. Then they lifted him to his feet. But the crutch was useless on a steep hillside of deep grass and snow. His father leaned over the boy's shoulders and they fought the slope for an hour.

When the boy stepped in a hole and they fell, his father made no exclamation of pain. The boy wondered whether his father's knee hurt as badly as his own hand. He suspected it hurt worse. He said nothing about his hand, though several times in their climb it was twisted or crushed. They reached the trail. The snow had not stopped, and their tracks were veiled. His father said:

"We need one of the guns. I forgot. It's my fault. But you'll have to go back down and get it."

The boy could not find the tree against which his father said he had leaned the .270, so he went toward the stream and looked for blood. He saw none. The imprint of his father's body was already softened beneath an inch of fresh silence. He scooped his good hand through the snowy depression and was startled by cool slimy blood, smearing his fingers like phlegm. Nearby he found the Winchester.

"The lucky one," his father said. "That's all right. Here." He snapped open the breach and a shell flew and he caught it in the air. He glanced dourly at the casing, then cast it aside in the snow. He held the gun out for the boy to see, and with his thumb let the hammer down one notch.

"Remember?" he said. "The safety."

The boy knew he was supposed to feel great shame, but he felt little. His father could no longer hurt him as he once could, because the boy was coming to understand him. His father could not help himself. He did not want the boy to feel contemptible, but he needed him to, because of the loneliness and the bitterness and the boy's mother; and he could not help himself.

After another hour they had barely traversed the aspen hillside. Pushing the crutch away in angry frustration, his father sat in the snow. The boy did not know whether he was thinking carefully of how they might get him out, or still laboring with the choice against despair. The light had wilted to something more like moonlight than afternoon. The sweep of snow had gone gray, depthless, flat, and the sky warned sullenly of night. The boy grew restless. Then it was decided. His father hung himself piggyback over the boy's shoulders, holding the rifle. The boy supported him with elbows crooked under his father's knees. The boy was tall for eleven years old, and heavy. The boy's father weighed 164 pounds.

The boy walked.

He moved as slowly as drifting snow: a step, then time, then another step. The burden at first seemed to him overwhelming. He did not think he would be able to carry his father far.

He took the first few paces expecting to fall. He did not fall, so he kept walking. His arms and shoulders were not exhausted as quickly as he had thought they would be, so he kept walking. Shuffling ahead in the deep powder was like carrying one end of an oak bureau up stairs. But for a surprisingly long time the burden did not grow any worse. He found balance. He found rhythm. He was moving.

Dark blurred the woods, but the snow was luminous. He could see the trail well. He walked.

"How are you, David? How are you holding up?"

"All right."

"We'll stop for a while and let you rest. You can set me down here." The boy kept walking. He moved so ponderously, it seemed after each step that he had stopped. But he kept walking.

"You can set me down. Don't you want to rest?"

The boy did not answer. He wished that his father would not make him talk. At the start he had gulped for air. Now he was breathing low and regularly. He was watching his thighs slice through the snow. He did not want to be disturbed. After a moment he said, "No."

He walked. He came to the cub, shrouded beneath new snow, and did not see it, and fell over it. His face was smashed deep into the snow by his father's weight. He could not move. But he could breathe. He rested. When he felt his father's thigh roll across his right hand, he remembered the wound. He was lucky his arms had been pinned to his sides, or the hand might have taken the force of their fall. As he waited for his father to roll himself clear, the boy noticed the change in temperature. His sweat chilled him quickly. He began shivering.

His father had again fallen in silence. The boy knew that he would not call out or even mention the pain in his leg. The boy realized that he did not want to mention his hand. The blood soaking the outside of his flannel bandage had grown sticky. He did not want to think of the alien tangle of flesh and tendons and bones wrapped inside. There was pain, but he kept the pain at a distance. It was not *his* hand any more. He was not counting on ever having it back. If he was resolved about that, then the pain was not his either. It was merely pain of which he was aware. His good hand was numb.

"We'll rest now."

"I'm not tired," the boy said. "I'm just getting cold."

"We'll rest," said his father. "I'm tired."

Under his father's knee, the boy noticed, was a cavity in the snow, already melted away by fresh blood. The dark flannel around his father's thigh did not appear sticky. It gleamed.

His father instructed the boy how to open the cub with the deer knife. His father stood on one leg against a deadfall, holding

the Winchester ready, and glanced around on all sides as he
spoke. The boy used his left hand and both his knees. He
punctured the cub low in the belly, to a soft squirting sound,
and sliced upward easily. He did not gut the cub. He merely
cut out a large square of belly meat. He handed it to his father,
in exchange for the rifle.

His father peeled off the hide and left the fat. He sawed the
meat in half. One piece he rolled up and put in his jacket pocket.
The other he divided again. He gave the boy a square thick
with glistening raw fat.

"Eat it. The fat too. Especially the fat. We'll cook the rest
farther on. I don't want to build a fire here and taunt Momma."

The meat was chewy. The boy did not find it disgusting. He
was hungry.

His father sat back on the ground and unlaced the boot from
his good foot. Before the boy understood what he was doing,
he had relaced the boot. He was holding a damp wool sock.

"Give me your left hand." The boy held out his good hand,
and his father pulled the sock down over it. "It's getting a lot
colder. And we need that hand."

"What about yours? We need your hands too. I'll give you
my—"

"No, you won't. We need your feet more than anything. It's
all right. I'll put mine inside your shirt."

He lifted his father, and they went on. The boy walked.

He moved steadily through cold darkness. Soon he was sweating again, down his ribs and inside his boots. Only his hands
and ears felt as though crushed in a cold metal vise. But his
father was shuddering. The boy stopped.

His father did not put down his legs. The boy stood on the
trail and waited. Slowly he released his wrist holds. His father's
thighs slumped. The boy was careful about the wounded leg.
His father's grip over the boy's neck did not loosen. His fingers
were cold against the boy's bare skin.

"Are we at the hut?"

"No. We're not even to the meadow."

"Why did you stop?" his father asked.

"It's so cold. You're shivering. Can we build a fire?"

"Yes," his father said hazily. "We'll rest. What time is it?"

"We don't know," the boy said. "We don't have a watch."

The boy gathered small deadwood. His father used the Winchester stock to scoop snow away from a boulder, and they placed the fire at the boulder's base. His father broke up pine twigs and fumbled dry toilet paper from his breast pocket and arranged the wood, but by then his fingers were shaking too badly to strike a match. The boy lit the fire. The boy stamped down the snow, as his father instructed, to make a small ovenlike recess before the fire boulder. He cut fir boughs to floor the recess. He added more deadwood. Beyond the invisible clouds there seemed to be part of a moon.

"It stopped snowing," the boy said.

"Why?"

The boy did not speak. His father's voice had sounded unnatural. After a moment his father said:

"Yes, indeed. It stopped."

They roasted pieces of cub meat skewered on a green stick. Dripping fat made the fire spatter and flare. The meat was scorched on the outside and raw within. It tasted as good as any meat the boy had ever eaten. They burned their palates on hot fat. The second stick smoldered through before they had noticed, and that batch of meat fell in the fire. The boy's father cursed once and reached into the flame for it and dropped it and clawed it out, and then put his hand in the snow. He did not look at the blistered fingers. They ate. The boy saw that both his father's hands had gone clumsy and almost useless.

The boy went for more wood. He found a bleached deadfall not far off the trail, but with one arm he could only break up and carry small loads. They lay down in the recess together like spoons, the boy nearer the fire. They pulled fir boughs into place above them, resting across the snow. They pressed close together. The boy's father was shivering spastically now, and he clenched the boy in a fierce hug. The boy put his father's hands back inside his own shirt. The boy slept. He woke when the fire faded and added more wood and slept. He woke again and tended the fire and changed places with his father and slept. He slept less soundly with his father between him and the fire. He woke again when his father began to vomit.

The boy was terrified. His father wrenched with sudden vomiting that brought up cub meat and yellow liquid and blood and sprayed them across the snow by the grayish-red glow of the fire and emptied his stomach dry and then would not release him. He heaved on pathetically. The boy pleaded to be told what was wrong. His father could not or would not answer. The spasms seized him at the stomach and twisted the rest of his body taut in ugly jerks. Between the attacks he breathed with a wet rumbling sound deep in his chest, and did not speak. When the vomiting subsided, his breathing stretched itself out into long bubbling sighs, then shallow gasps, then more liquidy sighs. His breath caught and froth rose in his throat and into his mouth and he gagged on it and began vomiting again. The boy thought his father would choke. He knelt beside him and held him and cried. He could not see his father's face well and he did not want to look closely while the sounds that were coming from inside his father's body seemed so unhuman. The boy had never been more frightened. He wept for himself, and for his father. He knew from the noises and movements that his father must die. He did not think his father could ever be human again.

When his father was quiet, he went for more wood. He broke limbs from the deadfall with fanatic persistence and brought them back in bundles and built the fire up bigger. He nestled his father close to it and held him from behind. He did not sleep, though he was not awake. He waited. Finally he opened his eyes on the beginnings of dawn. His father sat up and began to spit.

"One more load of wood and you keep me warm from behind and then we'll go."

The boy obeyed. He was surprised that his father could speak.

He thought it strange now that his father was so concerned for himself and so little concerned for the boy. His father had not even asked how he was.

The boy lifted his father, and walked.

Sometime while dawn was completing itself, the snow had resumed. It did not filter down soundlessly. It came on a slight wind at the boy's back, blowing down the canyon. He felt as though he were tumbling forward with the snow into a long vertical shaft. He tumbled slowly. His father's body protected the boy's back from being chilled by the wind. They were both soaked through their clothes. His father was soon shuddering again.

The boy walked. Muscles down the back of his neck were sore from yesterday. His arms ached, and his shoulders and thighs, but his neck hurt him most. He bent his head forward against the weight and the pain, and he watched his legs surge through the snow. At his stomach he felt the dull ache of hunger, not as an appetite but as an affliction. He thought of the jeep. He walked.

He recognized the edge of the meadow but through the snow-laden wind he could not see the cluster of aspens. The snow became deeper where he left the wooded trail. The direction of the wind was now variable, sometimes driving snow into his face, sometimes whipping across him from the right. The grass and snow dragged at his thighs, and he moved by stumbling forward and then catching himself back. Twice he stepped into small overhung fingerlets of the stream, and fell violently, shocking the air from his lungs and once nearly spraining an ankle. Farther out into the meadow, he saw the aspens. They were a hundred yards off to his right. He did not turn directly toward them. He was afraid of crossing more hidden creeks on the intervening ground. He was not certain now whether the main channel was between him and the aspen grove or behind him to the left. He tried to project from the canyon trail to the aspens and on to the forked pine on the far side of the meadow, along what he remembered as almost a straight line. He pointed himself toward the far edge, where the pine should have been. He could not see a forked crown. He could not even see trees. He could see only a vague darker corona above the curve of white. He walked.

He passed the aspens and left them behind. He stopped several times with the wind rasping against him in the open meadow, and rested. He did not set his father down. His father was trembling uncontrollably. He had not spoken for a long time. The boy wanted badly to reach the far side of the meadow. His socks were soaked and his boots and cuffs were glazed with ice. The wind was chafing his face and making him dizzy. His thighs felt as if they had been bruised with a club. The boy wanted to give up and set his father down and whimper that this had gotten to be very unfair; and he wanted to reach the far trees. He did not doubt which he would do. He walked.

He saw trees. Raising his head painfully, he squinted against the rushing flakes. He did not see the forked crown. He went on, and stopped again, and craned his neck, and squinted. He scanned a wide angle of pines, back and forth. He did not see it. He turned his body and his burden to look back. The snow blew across the meadow and seemed, whichever way he turned, to be streaking into his face. He pinched his eyes tighter. He could still see the aspens. But he could not judge where the canyon trail met the meadow. He did not know from just where he had come. He looked again at the aspens, and then ahead to the pines. He considered the problem carefully. He was irritated that the forked ponderosa did not show itself yet, but not worried. He was forced to estimate. He estimated, and went on in that direction.

When he saw a forked pine it was far off to the left of his course. He turned and marched toward it gratefully. As he came nearer, he bent his head up to look. He stopped. The boy was not sure that this was the right tree. Nothing about it looked different, except the thick cakes of snow weighting its limbs, and nothing about it looked especially familiar. He had seen thousands of pine trees in the last few days. This was one like the others. It definitely had a forked crown. He entered the woods at its base.

He had vaguely expected to join a trail. There was no trail. After two hundred yards he was still picking his way among trees and deadfalls and brush. He remembered the shepherd's creek that fell off the lip of the meadow and led down the first canyon. He turned and retraced his tracks to the forked pine.

He looked for the creek. He did not see it anywhere near the tree. He made himself quiet, and listened. He heard nothing but wind, and his father's tremulous breathing.

"Where is the creek?"

His father did not respond. The boy bounced gently up and down, hoping to jar him alert.

"Where is the creek? I can't find it."

"What?"

"We crossed the meadow and I found the tree but I can't find the creek. I need you to help."

"The compass is in my pocket," his father said.

He lowered his father into the snow. He found the compass in his father's breast pocket, and opened the flap, and held it level. The boy noticed with a flinch that his right thigh was smeared with fresh blood. For an instant he thought he had a new wound. Then he realized that the blood was his father's. The compass needle quieted.

"What do I do?"

His father did not respond. The boy asked again. His father said nothing. He sat in the snow and shivered.

The boy left his father and made random arcs within sight of the forked tree until he found a creek. They followed it onward along the flat and then where it gradually began sloping away. The boy did not see what else he could do. He knew that this was the wrong creek. He hoped that it would flow into the shepherd's creek, or at least bring them out on the same road where they had left the jeep. He was very tired. He did not want to stop. He did not care any more about being warm. He wanted only to reach the jeep, and to save his father's life.

He wondered whether his father would love him more generously for having done it. He wondered whether his father
would ever forgive him for having done it.

If he failed, his father could never again make him feel shame,
the boy thought naively. So he did not worry about failing. He
did not worry about dying. His hand was not bleeding, and he
felt strong. The creek swung off and down to the left. He followed it, knowing that he was lost. He did not want to reverse
himself. He knew that turning back would make him feel confused and desperate and frightened. As long as he was following
some pathway, walking, going down, he felt strong.

That afternoon he killed a grouse. He knocked it off a low
branch with a heavy short stick that he threw like a boomerang.
The grouse fell in the snow and floundered and the boy ran up
and plunged on it. He felt it thrashing against his chest. He
reached in and it nipped him and he caught it by the neck and
squeezed and wrenched mercilessly until long after it stopped
writhing. He cleaned it as he had seen his father clean grouse
and built a small fire with matches from his father's breast
pocket and seared the grouse on a stick. He fed his father. His
father could not chew. The boy chewed mouthfuls of grouse,
and took the chewed gobbets in his hand, and put them into
his father's mouth. His father could swallow. His father could
no longer speak.

The boy walked. He thought of his mother in Evergreen Park,
and at once he felt queasy and weak. He thought of his mother's
face and her voice as she was told that her son was lost in the
woods in Montana with a damaged hand that would never be
right, and with his father, who had been shot and was unconscious and dying. He pictured his mother receiving the news
that her son might die himself, unless he could carry his father
out of the woods and find his way to the jeep. He saw her face
change. He heard her voice. The boy had to stop. He was crying.
He could not control the shape of his mouth. He was not crying
with true sorrow, as he had in the night when he held his father

and thought his father would die; he was crying in sentimental self-pity. He sensed the difference. Still he cried.

He must not think of his mother, the boy realized. Thinking of her could only weaken him. If she knew where he was, what he had to do, she could only make it impossible for him to do it. He was lucky that she knew nothing, the boy thought.

No one knew what the boy was doing, or what he had yet to do. Even the boy's father no longer knew. The boy was lucky. No one was watching, no one knew, and he was free to be capable.

The boy imagined himself alone at his father's grave. The grave was open. His father's casket had already been lowered. The boy stood at the foot in his black Christmas suit, and his hands were crossed at his groin, and he was not crying. Men with shovels stood back from the grave, waiting for the boy's order for them to begin filling it. The boy felt a horrible swelling sense of joy. The men watched him, and he stared down into the hole. He knew it was a lie. If his father died, the boy's mother would rush out to Livingston and have him buried and stand at the grave in a black dress and veil squeezing the boy to her side like he was a child. There was nothing the boy could do about that. All the more reason he must keep walking.

Then she would tow the boy back with her to Evergreen Park. And he would be standing on 96th Street in the morning dark before his father's cold body had even begun to grow alien and decayed in the buried box. She would drag him back, and there would be nothing the boy could do. And he realized that if he returned with his mother after the burial, he would never again see the cabin outside Livingston. He would have no more summers and no more Novembers anywhere but in Evergreen Park.

The cabin now seemed to be at the center of the boy's life. It seemed to stand halfway between this snowbound creek valley and the train station in Chicago. It would be his cabin soon.

The boy knew nothing about his father's will, and he had

never been told that legal ownership of the cabin was destined for him. Legal ownership did not matter. The cabin might be owned by his mother, or sold to pay his father's debts, or taken away by the state, but it would still be the boy's cabin. It could only forever belong to him. His father had been telling him *Here, this is yours. Prepare to receive it.* The boy had sensed that much. But he had been threatened, and unwilling. The boy realized now that he might be resting warm in the cabin in a matter of hours, or he might never see it again. He could appreciate the justice of that. He walked.

He thought of his father as though his father were far away from him. He saw himself in the black suit at the grave, and he heard his father speak to him from aside: *That's good. Now raise your eyes and tell them in a man's voice to begin shoveling. Then turn away and walk slowly back down the hill. Be sure you don't cry. That's good.* The boy stopped. He felt his glands quiver, full of new tears. He knew that it was a lie. His father would never be there to congratulate him. His father would never know how well the boy had done.

He took deep breaths. He settled himself. Yes, his father would know somehow, the boy believed. His father had known all along. His father knew.

He built the recess just as they had the night before, except this time he found flat space between a stone bank and a large fallen cottonwood trunk. He scooped out the snow, he laid boughs, and he made a fire against each reflector. At first the bed was quite warm. Then the melt from the fires began to run down and collect in the middle, forming a puddle of wet boughs under them. The boy got up and carved runnels across the packed snow to drain the fires. He went back to sleep and slept warm, holding his father. He rose again each half hour to feed the fires.

The snow stopped in the night, and did not resume. The woods seemed to grow quieter, settling, sighing beneath the new weight. What was going to come had come.

The boy grew tired of breaking deadwood and began walking

again before dawn and walked for five more hours. He did not try to kill the grouse that he saw because he did not want to spend time cleaning and cooking it. He was hurrying now. He drank from the creek. At one point he found small black insects like winged ants crawling in great numbers across the snow near the creek. He stopped to pinch up and eat thirty or forty of them. They were tasteless. He did not bother to feed any to his father. He felt he had come a long way down the mountain. He thought he was reaching the level now where there might be roads. He followed the creek, which had received other branches and grown to a stream. The ground was flattening again and the drainage was widening, opening to daylight. As he carried his father, his head ached. He had stopped noticing most of his other pains. About noon of that day he came to the fence.

It startled him. He glanced around, his pulse drumming suddenly, preparing himself at once to see the long empty sweep of snow and broken fence posts and thinking of Basque shepherds fifty years gone. He saw the cabin and the smoke. He relaxed, trembling helplessly into the laughter. He relaxed, and was unable to move. Then he cried, still laughing. He cried shamelessly with relief and dull joy and wonder, for as long as he wanted. He held his father, and cried. But he set his father down and washed his own face with snow before he went to the door.

He crossed the lot walking slowly, carrying his father. He did not now feel tired.

The young woman's face was drawn down in shock and revealed at first nothing of friendliness.

"We had a jeep parked somewhere, but I can't find it," the boy said. "This is my father."

They would not talk to him. They stripped him and put him before the fire wrapped in blankets and started tea and made him wait. He wanted to talk. He wished they would ask him a lot of questions. But they went about quickly and quietly, making things warm. His father was in the bedroom.

The man with the face full of dark beard had telephoned for a doctor. He went back into the bedroom with more blankets, and stayed. His wife went from room to room with hot tea. She rubbed the boy's naked shoulders through the blanket, and held a cup to his mouth, but she would not talk to him. He did not know what to say to her, and he could not move his lips very well. But he wished she would ask him some questions. He was restless, thawing in silence before the hearth.

He thought about going back to their own cabin soon. In his mind he gave the bearded man directions to take him and his father home. It wasn't far. It would not require much of the man's time. They would thank him, and give him an elk steak. Later he and his father would come back for the jeep. He could keep his father warm at the cabin as well as they were doing here, the boy knew.

While the woman was in the bedroom, the boy overheard the bearded man raise his voice:

"He what?"

"He carried him out," the woman whispered.

"What do you mean, carried him?"

"Carried him. On his back. I saw."

"Carried him from where?"

"Where it happened. Somewhere on Sheep Creek, maybe."

"Eight miles?"

"I know."

"*Eight miles?* How could he do that?"

"I don't know. I suppose he couldn't. But he did."

The doctor arrived in half an hour, as the boy was just starting to shiver. The doctor went into the bedroom and stayed five minutes. The woman poured the boy more tea and knelt beside him and hugged him around the shoulders.

When the doctor came out, he examined the boy without speaking. The boy wished the doctor would ask him some questions, but he was afraid he might be shivering too hard to answer in a man's voice. While the doctor touched him and probed him and took his temperature, the boy looked the doctor directly in the eye, as though to show him he was really all right.

The doctor said:

"David, your father is dead. He has been dead for a long time. Probably since yesterday."

"I know that," the boy said.

GRETEL EHRLICH

THE SOLACE OF OPEN SPACES

It's May, and I've just awakened from a nap, curled against sagebrush the way my dog taught me to sleep—sheltered from wind. A front is pulling the huge sky over me, and from the dark a hailstone has hit me on the head. I'm trailing a band of 2000 sheep across a stretch of Wyoming badland, a fifty-mile trip that takes five days because sheep shade up in hot sun and won't budge until it cools. Bunched together now, and excited into a run by the storm, they drift across dry land, tumbling into draws like water and surging out again onto the rugged, choppy plateaus that are the building blocks of this state.

The name Wyoming comes from an Indian word meaning "at the great plains," but the plains are really valleys, great arid valleys, 1600 square miles, with the horizon bending up on all sides into mountain ranges. This gives the vastness a sheltering look.

Winter lasts six months here. Prevailing winds spill snowdrifts to the east, and new storms from the northwest replenish them. This white bulk is sometimes dizzying, even nauseating, to look at. At twenty, thirty, and forty degrees below zero, not only does your car not work but neither do your mind and body. The landscape hardens into a dungeon of space. During the winter, while I was riding to find a new calf, my legs froze to the saddle, and in the silence that such cold creates I felt like the first person on earth, or the last.

Today the sun is out—only a few clouds billowing. In the east, where the sheep have started off without me, the benchland tilts up in a series of red-earthed, eroded mesas, planed flat on top by a million years of water; behind them, a bold line of muscular scarps rears up 10,000 feet to become the Big Horn Mountains. A tidal pattern is engraved into the ground, as if left by the sea that once covered this state. Canyons curve down like galaxies to meet the oncoming rush of flat land.

To live and work in this kind of open country, with its hundred-mile views, is to lose the distinction between background and foreground. When I asked an older ranch hand to describe Wyoming's openness, he said, "It's all a bunch of nothing—wind and rattlesnakes—and so much of it you can't tell where you're going or where you've been and it don't make much difference." John, a sheepman I know, is tall and handsome and has an explosive temperament. He has a perfect intuition about people and sheep. They call him "Highpockets," because he's so long-legged; his graceful stride matches the distances he has to cover. He says, "Open space hasn't affected me at all. It's all the people moving in on it." The huge ranch he was born on takes up much of one county and spreads into another state; to put 100,000 miles on his pickup in three years and never leave home is not unusual. A friend of mine has an aunt who ranched on Powder River and didn't go off her place for eleven years. When her husband died, she quickly moved to town, bought a car, and drove around the States to see what she'd been missing.

Most people tell me they've simply driven through Wyoming, as if there were nothing to stop for. Or else they've skied in Jackson Hole, a place Wyomingites acknowledge uncomfortably, because its green beauty and chic affluence are mismatched with the rest of the state. Most of Wyoming has a "lean-to" look. Instead of big, roomy barns and Victorian houses, there are dugouts, low sheds, log cabins, sheep camps, and fence lines that look like driftwood blown haphazardly into place. People here still feel pride because they live in such a harsh place, part of the glamorous cowboy past, and they are determined not to be the victims of a mining-dominated future.

Most characteristic of the state's landscape is what a developer euphemistically describes as "indigenous growth right up to your front door"—a reference to waterless stands of salt sage, snakes, jackrabbits, deerflies, red dust, a brief respite of wild-flowers, dry washes, and no trees. In the Great Plains, the vistas look like music, like kyries of grass, but Wyoming seems to be the doing of a mad architect—tumbled and twisted, ribboned with faded, deathbed colors, thrust up and pulled down as if the place had been startled out of a deep sleep and thrown into a pure light.

I came here four years ago. I had not planned to stay, but I couldn't make myself leave. John, the sheepman, put me to work immediately. It was spring, and shearing time. For fourteen days of fourteen hours each, we moved thousands of sheep through sorting corrals to be sheared, branded, and deloused. I suspect that my original motive for coming here was to "lose myself" in new and unpopulated territory. Instead of producing the numbness I thought I wanted, life on the sheep ranch woke me up. The vitality of the people I was working with flushed out what had become a hallucinatory rawness inside me. I threw away my clothes and bought new ones; I cut my hair. The arid country was a clean slate. Its absolute indifference steadied me.

Sagebrush covers 58,000 square miles of Wyoming. The big-gest city has a population of 50,000, and there are only five settlements that could be called cities in the whole state. The rest are towns, scattered across the expanse with as much as sixty miles between them, their populations 2000, fifty, or ten. They are fugitive-looking, perched on a barren, windblown bench, or tagged onto a river or a railroad, or laid out straight in a farming valley with implement stores and a block-long Mormon church. In the eastern part of the state, which slides down into the Great Plains, the new mining settlements are boomtowns, trailer cities, metal knots on flat land.

Despite the desolate look, there's a coziness to living in this state. There are so few people (only 470,000) that ranchers who buy and sell cattle know each other statewide; the kids who choose to go to college usually go to the state's one university, in Laramie; hired hands work their way around Wyoming in a lifetime of hirings and firings. And, despite the physical separation, people stay in touch, often driving two or three hours to another ranch for dinner.

Seventy-five years ago, when travel was by buckboard or horseback, cowboys who were temporarily out of work rode the grub line—drifting from ranch to ranch, mending fences or milking cows, and receiving in exchange a bed and meals. Gossip and messages traveled this slow circuit with them, creating an intimacy between ranchers who were three and four weeks' ride apart. One old-time couple I know, whose turn-of-the-century homestead was used by an outlaw gang as a relay station for stolen horses, recall that if you were traveling, desperado or not, any lighted ranch house was a welcome sign. Even now, for someone who lives in a remote spot, arriving at a ranch or coming to town for supplies is cause for celebration. To emerge from isolation can be disorienting. Everything looks bright, new, vivid. After I had been herding sheep for only three days, the sound of the camp tender's pickup flustered me. Longing for human company, I felt a foolish grin take over my face, yet I had to resist an urgent temptation to run and hide.

Things happen suddenly in Wyoming: the change of seasons and weather; for people, the violent swings in and out of isolation. But goodnaturedness is concomitant with severity. Friendliness is a tradition. Strangers passing on the road wave hello. A common sight is two pickups stopped side by side far out on a range, on a dirt track winding through the sage. The drivers will share a cigarette, uncap their thermos bottles, and pass a battered cup, steaming with coffee, between windows. These meetings summon up the details of several generations, because in Wyoming, private histories are largely public knowledge.

Because ranch work is a physical and, these days, economic strain, being "at home on the range" is a matter of vigor, self-reliance, and common sense. A person's life is not a series of dramatic events for which he or she is applauded or exiled but a slow accumulation of days, seasons, years, fleshed out by the generational weight of one's family and anchored by a land-bound sense of place.

In most parts of Wyoming, the human population is visibly outnumbered by the animal. Not far from my town of fifty, I rode into a narrow valley and startled a herd of 200 elk. Eagles look like small people as they eat car-killed deer by the road. Antelope, moving in small, graceful bands, travel at 60 miles an hour, their mouths open as if drinking in the space.

The solitude in which westerners live makes them quiet. They telegraph thoughts and feelings by the way they tilt their heads and listen; pulling their Stetsons into a steep dive over their eyes, or pigeon-toeing one boot over the other, they lean against a fence with a fat wedge of snoose beneath their lower lips and take the whole scene in. These detached looks of quiet amusement are sometimes cynical, but they can also come from a dry-eyed humility as lucid as the air is clear.

Conversation goes on in what sounds like a private code; a few phrases imply a complex of meanings. Asking directions, you get a curious list of details. While trailing sheep, I was told to "ride up to that kinda upturned rock, follow the pink wash, turn left at the dump, and then you'll see the waterhole." One friend told his wife on roundup to "turn at the salt lick and the dead cow," which turned out to be a scattering of bones and no salt lick at all.

Sentence structure is shortened to the skin and bones of a thought. Descriptive words are dropped, even verbs; a cowboy looking over a corral full of horses will say to a wrangler, "Which one needs rode?" People hold back their thoughts in what seems to be a dumbfounded silence, then erupt with an excoriating, perceptive remark. Language, so compressed, becomes meta-phorical. A rancher ended a relationship with one remark: "You're a bad check," meaning bouncing in and out was intolerable, and even coming back would be no good.

What's behind this laconic style is shyness. There is no vocabulary for the subject of feelings. It's not a hangdog shyness, or anything coy—always there's a robust spirit in evidence behind the restraint, as if the earth-dredging wind that pulls across Wyoming had carried its people's voices away but everything else in them had shouldered confidently into the breeze.

I've spent hours riding to sheep camp at dawn in a pickup when nothing was said; eaten meals in the cookhouse when the only words spoken were a mumbled "Thank you, ma'am" at the end of dinner. The silence is profound. Instead of talking, we seem to share one eye. Keenly observed, the world is transformed. The landscape is engorged with detail, every movement on it chillingly sharp. The air between people is charged. Days unfold, bathed in their own music. Nights become hallucinatory; dreams, prescient.

Spring weather is capricious and mean. It snows, then blisters with heat. There have been tornadoes. They lay their elephant trunks out in the sage until they find houses, then slurp everything up and leave. I've noticed that melting snowbanks hiss and rot, viperous, then drip into calm pools where ducklings hatch and livestock, being trailed to summer range, drink. With the ice cover gone, rivers churn a milkshake brown, taking culverts and small bridges with them. Water in such an arid place (the average annual rainfall where I live is less than eight inches) is like blood. It festoons drab land with green veins: a line of cottonwoods following a stream; a strip of alfalfa; and on ditchbanks, wild asparagus growing.

I've moved to a small cattle ranch owned by friends. It's at the foot of the Big Horn Mountains. A few weeks ago, I helped them deliver a calf who was stuck halfway out of his mother's body. By the time he was freed, we could see a heartbeat, but he was straining against a swollen tongue for air. Mary and I

held him upside down by his back feet, while Stan, on his hands
and knees in the blood, gave the calf mouth-to-mouth resus-
citation. I have a vague memory of being pneumonia-choked as
a child, my mother giving me her air, which may account for
my romance with this windswept state.

If anything is endemic to Wyoming, it is wind. This big room
of space is swept out daily, leaving a boneyard of fossils, agates,
and carcasses in every stage of decay. Though it was water that
initially shaped the state, wind is the meticulous gardener, raising dust and pruning the sage.

I try to imagine a world of uncharted land, in which one could
look over an uncompleted map and ride a horse past where all
the lines have stopped. There is no wilderness left; wildness,
yes, but true wilderness has been gone on this continent since
the time of Lewis and Clark's overland journey.

Two hundred years ago, the Crow, Shoshone, Arapaho,
Cheyenne, and Sioux roamed the intermountain West, orches-
trating their movements according to hunger, season, and warfare. Once they acquired horses, they traversed the spines of
all the big Wyoming ranges—the Absarokas, the Wind Rivers,
the Tetons, the Big Horns—and wintered on the unprotected
plains that fan out from them. Space was life. The world was
their home.

What was life-giving to native Americans was often night-
marish to sodbusters who arrived encumbered with families and
ethnic pasts to be transplanted in nearly uninhabitable land.
The great distances, the shortage of water and trees, and the
loneliness created unexpected hardships for them. In her book
O Pioneers!, Willa Cather gives a settler's version of the bleak
landscape:

> The little town behind them had vanished as if it had never
> been, had fallen behind the swell of the prairie, and the
> stern frozen country received them into its bosom. The
> homesteads were few and far apart; here and there a wind-

mill gaunt against the sky, a sod house crouching in a hollow.

The emptiness of the West was for others a geography of possibility. Men and women who amassed great chunks of land and struggled to preserve unfenced empires were, despite their self-serving motives, unwitting geographers. They understood the lay of the land. But by the 1850s, the Oregon and Mormon trails sported bumper-to-bumper traffic. Wealthy landowners, many of them aristocratic absentee landlords, known as remittance men because they were paid to come West and get out of their families' hair, overstocked the range with more than a million head of cattle. By 1885, the feed and water were desperately short, and the winter of 1886 laid out the gaunt bodies of dead animals so closely together that when the thaw came, one rancher from Kaycee claimed to have walked on cowhide all the way to Crazy Woman Creek, twenty miles away.

Territorial Wyoming was a boy's world. The land was generous with everything but water. At first there was room enough, food enough, for everyone. And, as with all beginnings an expansive mood set in. The young cowboys, drifters, shopkeepers, schoolteachers, were heroic, lawless, generous, rowdy, and tenacious. The individualism and optimism generated during those times have endured.

John Tisdale rode north with the trail herds from Texas. He was a college-educated man with enough money to buy a small outfit near the Powder River. While driving home from the town of Buffalo with a buckboard full of Christmas toys for his family and a winter's supply of food, he was shot in the back by an agent of the cattle barons who resented the encroachment of small-time stockmen like him. The wealthy cattlemen tried to control all the public grazing land by restricting membership in the Wyoming Stock Growers Association, as if it were a country club. They ostracized from roundups and brandings cowboys and ranchers who were not members, then denounced them as rustlers. Tisdale's death, the second such cold-blooded

murder, kicked off the Johnson County cattle war, which was
no simple good-guy-bad-guy shoot-out but a complicated class
struggle between landed gentry and less affluent settlers—a
shocking reminder that the West was not an egalitarian sanc-
tuary after all.

Fencing ultimately enforced boundaries, but barbed wire ab-
rogated space. It was stretched across the beautiful valleys, into
the mountains, over desert badlands, through buffalo grass. The
"anything is possible" fever—the lure of any new place—was
constricted. The integrity of the land as a geographical body,
and the freedom to ride anywhere on it, was lost.

I punched cows with a young man named Martin, who is the
great-grandson of John Tisdale. His inheritance is not the open
land that Tisdale knew and prematurely lost but a rage against
restraint.

Wyoming tips down as you head northeast; the highest ground—
the Laramie Plains—is on the Colorado border. Up where I
live, the Big Horn River leaks into difficult, arid terrain. In
the basin where it's dammed, sandhill cranes gather and, with
delicate legwork, slice through the stilled water. I was driving
by with a rancher one morning when he commented that cranes
are "old-fashioned." When I asked why, he said, "Because they
mate for life." Then he looked at me with a twinkle in his eyes,
as if to say he really did believe in such things but also understood why we break our own rules.

In all this open space, values crystallize quickly. People are
strong on scruples but tenderhearted about quirky behavior. A
friend and I found one ranch hand, who's "not quite right in
the head," sitting in front of the badly decayed carcass of a cow,
shaking his finger and saying, "Now, I don't want you to do
this ever again!" When I asked what was wrong with him, I
was told, "He's goofier than hell, just like the rest of us."
Perhaps because the West is historically new, conventional morality is still felt to be less important than rock-bottom truths.
Though there's always a lot of teasing and sparring around,

people are blunt with each other, sometimes even cruel, believing honesty is stronger medicine than sympathy, which may
console but often conceals.

The formality that goes hand in hand with the rowdiness is
known as "the Western Code." It's a list of practical dos and
don'ts, faithfully observed. A friend, Cliff, who runs a trapline
in the winter, cut off half his foot while axing a hole in the ice.
Alone, he dragged himself to his pickup and headed for town,
stopping to open the ranch gate as he left, and getting out to
close it again, thus losing, in his observance of rules, precious
time and blood. Later, he commented, "How would it look,
them having to come to the hospital to tell me their cows had
gotten out?"

Accustomed to emergencies, my friends doctor each other
from the vet's bag with relish. When one old-timer suffered a
heart attack in hunting camp, his partner quickly stirred up a
brew of red horse liniment and hot water and made the half-
conscious victim drink it, then tied him onto a horse and led
him twenty miles to town. He regained consciousness and lived.

The roominess of the state has affected political attitudes as
well. Ranchers keep up with world politics and the convulsions
of the economy but are basically isolationists. Being used to
running their own small empires of land and livestock, they're
suspicious of big government. It's a "don't fence me in" hold-
over from a century ago. They still want the elbow room their
grandfathers had, so they're strongly conservative, but with a
populist twist.

Summer is the season when we get our "cowboy tans"—on
the lower parts of our faces and on three fourths of our arms.
Excessive heat, in the nineties and higher, sends us outside with
the mosquitoes. In winter, we're tucked inside our houses, and
the white wasteland outside appears to be expanding, but in
summer, all the greenery abridges space. Summer is a go-ahead
season. Every living thing is off the block and in the race:
battalions of bugs in flight and biting; bats swinging around my

log cabin as if the bases were loaded and someone had hit a
home run. Some of summer's high-speed growth is ominous:
larkspur, death camas, and green greasewood can kill sheep—
an ironic idea, dying in this desert from eating what is too
verdant. With sixteen hours of daylight, farmers and ranchers
irrigate feverishly. There are first, second, and third cuttings
of hay, some crews averaging only four hours of sleep a night
for weeks. And, like the cowboys who in summer ride the night
rodeo circuit, nighthawks make daredevil dives at dusk with an
eerie whirring that sounds like a plane going down on the shimmering horizon.

In the town where I live, they've had to board up the dancehall windows because there have been so many fights. There's
so little to do except work that people wind up in a state of idle
agitation that becomes fatalistic, as if there were nothing to be
done about all this untapped energy. So the dark side to the
grandeur of these spaces is the small-mindedness that seals people in. Men become hermits; women go mad. Cabin fever ex-
plodes into suicides, or into grudges and lifelong family feuds.
Two sisters in my area inherited a ranch but found they couldn't
get along. They fenced the place in half. When one's cows got
out and mixed with the other's, the women went at each other
with shovels. They ended up in the same hospital room, but
never spoke a word to each other for the rest of their lives.

Eccentricity ritualizes behavior. It's a shortcut through un-
manageable emotions and strict social conventions. I knew a
sheepherder named Fred who, at seventy-eight, still had a handsome face, which he kept smooth by plastering it each day with
bag balm and Vaseline. He was curious, well-read, and had a
fact-keeping mind to go along with his penchant for hoarding.
His reliquary of gunnysacks, fence wire, wood, canned food,
unopened Christmas presents, and magazines matched his odd
collages of meals: sardines with maple syrup; vegetable soup
garnished with Fig Newtons. His wagon was so overloaded that
he had to sleep sitting up because there was no room on the
bed. Despite his love of up-to-date information, Fred died from

gangrene when an old-timer's remedy of fresh sheep manure, applied as a poultice to a bad cut, failed to save him.

After the brief lushness of summer, the sun moves south. The range grass is brown. Livestock has been trailed back down from the mountains. Waterholes begin to frost over at night. Last fall Martin asked me to accompany him on a pack trip. With five horses, we followed a river into the mountains behind the tiny Wyoming town of Meeteetse. Groves of aspen, red and orange, gave off a light that made us look toasted. Our hunting camp was so high that clouds skidded across our foreheads, then slowed to sail out across the warm valleys. Except for a bull moose who wandered into our camp and mistook our black gelding for a rival, we shot at nothing.

One of our evening entertainments was to watch the night sky. My dog, who also came on the trip, a dingo bred to herd sheep, is so used to the silence and empty skies that when an airplane flies over he always looks up and eyes the distant intruder quizzically. The sky, lately, seems to be much more crowded than it used to be. Satellites make their silent passes in the dark with great regularity. We counted eighteen in one hour's viewing. How odd to think that while they circumnavigated the planet, Martin and I had moved only six miles into our local wilderness, and had seen no other human for the two weeks we stayed there.

At night, by moonlight, the land is whittled to slivers—a ridge, a river, a strip of grassland stretching to the mountains, then the huge sky. One morning a full moon was setting in the west just as the sun was rising. I felt precariously balanced between the two as I loped across a meadow. For a moment, I could believe that the stars, which were still visible, work like cooper's bands, holding everything above Wyoming together.

Space has a spiritual equivalent, and can heal what is divided and burdensome in us. My grandchildren will probably use space shuttles for a honeymoon trip or to recover from heart attacks, but closer to home we might also learn how to carry space inside ourselves in the effortless way we carry our skins. Space represents sanity, not a life purified, dull, or "spaced out" but one that might accommodate intelligently any idea or situation.

From the clayey soil of northern Wyoming is mined bentonite, which is used as a filler in candy, gum, and lipstick. We Americans are great on fillers, as if what we have, what we are, is not enough. We have a cultural tendency toward denial, but, being affluent, we strangle ourselves with what we can buy. We have only to look at the houses we build to see how we build *against* space, the way we drink against pain and loneliness. We fill up space as if it were a pie shell, with things whose opacity further obstructs our ability to see what is already there.

EDWARD ABBEY

CAPE SOLITUDE

There comes a day when a man must hide. Must slip away from the human world and its clutching, insane, insatiable demands.

For nearly a month I'd been in the air and on the road. Doing the college lecture bit from Pennsylvania to Wisconsin, from Arizona to Alaska to the Wabash. (Why do I do it? Not for the money—those insincere paper checks from boards of regents. For the ego massage, that's what for. To spread the message. To meet the audience face to face. To meet those lovely girls, "My name's Sharon," she says. Or Susan. Or Kathy. Or Pamela. Or Tammy. And, "Oh Mister Abbey, I've been wanting to meet you for years!" "That's funny," I reply, "I've been wanting to meet you too; how about a drink as soon as we can sneak away from this mob?" "Oh, I'd *love* to." she says, "and"—she tugs at the arm of a shy, pimply, long-haired, very tall and thin young lad standing a bit to her rear—"and this is my boy friend George." Jack. Henry. Willy. "He wants to meet you too.") And going to hearings, reading prepared statements before bored bureaucrats in business suits. Wearisome interviews. Writing letters to hostile congressmen, editors, tycoons. Trying to save the world, that's all. A piece of the West at least. Something. Useless stuff.

Tales of the Western lecture circuit. Marge Piercy, feminist novelist, doing her best for women's liberation in a sophomore seminar at the University of Colorado. "But *I like* being a girl," says one of those mountain coeds, wiggling on her seat. The decadent West. Amazing Grace Lichtenstein, Denver-based reporter for the *New York Times,* accused me—when I told her this story—of being thirty years behind the times. "Thirty years?" I said, insulted. "I'm a hundred years behind the times."

Weary, discouraged, still smelling of nervous sweat, I pointed the old Dodge carryall south by east, heading for a place I know. Call it—Cape Solitude. I like the name. A fictitious name, of course, but the place is real. Or a real name for an impossible place. A high, open, uncrowded point on the rim of the canyon, on the edge of the world, fifty miles by wagon trail from the nearest paved road, twenty miles from the last Navajo hogan, sixty from the nearest white man's house. I was going there alone—alone!—and I was going to stay there, hardly moving, until I felt ready to return to human society. Whether it took twenty-four hours or forty days. Or longer. I had plenty of dried beans and green chili and canned corn in the truck, and enough water for a while—if the rains failed and the potholes were dry.

We came down through the valley, me and the truck, across the river, up past the Echo Cliffs, down to the Little Colorado, west on the highway to the turnoff. Two hundred miles. I opened a wire gate in the fence, drove through, closed the gate, locking it shut with a Gordian knot of rusty barbed wire. This route is seldom used. Now it'll be used less. I took a broom and swept away my tire tracks, then drove north on the dirt road until I was beyond sight and sound of the highway, stopped, shut off the throbbing engine, sat up front on the hood with a bottle of wine and listened to the silence. Each time I come here, I wonder why I ever go back. Every time I go anywhere out in the desert or mountains, I wonder why I should return. Someday I won't.

Nerves, nerves. I held my right hand straight out, palm down. The hand trembled. I brought it back to the bottle where it closed at once—the sensitive plant—around the cool smooth glass. Hold on to something steady, solid, secure. You can count on us, say the Christian Brothers. We'll not fail you, old buddy, says Gallo's Hearty Burgundy. I'll stick by you to the end, says

Almandén. No doubt. The day he stopped drinking was the day that Mulligan died.

The high plateau stands on my left, a forest of jackpine on the horizon. Ahead lies a rolling, sandy plain and a scatter of juniper and scrubby little piñon pine stretching toward infinity. On the east, below, the Painted Desert shimmers in the afternoon sun—lavender hills, burnt cliffs, rosy pinnacles of mud and clay.

> Oh that the desert were my dwelling place,
> With one fair Spirit for my minister,
> That I might all forget the human race,
> And, hating no one, love but only her.

I don't even want her right now. Right now I want no one, least of all myself. All my life a loner, an outsider, a barbarian from the steppes, the wolf on the snow-covered hill looking down at the lights of the village, I think I've never been accepted by my fellow men, fellow women, never been a bona fide member of the club. And looking back at the human race, feeling I never belonged, my first thought, right now, is—thank God. Or Whatever.

The wine sings in my blood. Blood and wine, wine and bread, bread and love and music. The full circle. Back to the flesh. Getting nowhere. Going home. The sky hangs over me, that delirious dome of burning blue, where white, woolly, quiet clouds drift slowly eastward like a herd of grazing sheep. Who or what is the herdsman of that flock? The sun? But the sun is going the other way.

I discover, to my surprise, that the bottle is nearly empty. I finish it off, take a hearty burgundy piss on the sand, crank up the engine, and drive on. The truck bumps over the stones, thrashes in low through a stretch of soft sand, brushes over the sage and prickly pear and spiny yucca growing in the high center of the road. I shift down into compound low, climbing the sandstone ledges up and around a hill. The rear wheels spin, I have to stop and pile rocks in the back to gain sufficient traction. We go on, passing an empty hogan of cedar logs chinked with mud. The blank, black, open doorway, facing the east as a proper hogan doorway should, has a long-abandoned look.

I stop to contemplate. The wooden bed of a buckboard wagon, *sans* wheels, rests half-buried in the sand; the tongue of the wagon rests in the crotch of a juniper. No sign of recent occupancy. The few tin cans strewn about are well rusted, the old tokay bottles blue from sunlight. No plastic, paper, or aluminum anywhere in sight. Somebody died here long ago, but the ghost still lingers; that is why, according to Navajo theology, the place cannot be used. I'm not afraid of ghosts, being chiefly a ghost myself, and for a moment I'm tempted to pause here, stay a few days before going on to the cape. I decide against it; the attraction of the abyss is too strong.

We drive on.

The going is good, gets better all the time, rougher and rockier, more brush, more sand, more cactus. The parallel tracks meander like snakes toward the unimaginable goal. I follow with caution, nursing the motor to keep it cool, babying the old, loose transmission (this truck was born in 1962), watching for oil-pan-ripping stones in the high center.

One mile short of my destination I turn off the trail and hide the truck under, or rather within, the sheltering branches of the biggest juniper nearby. It is possible to drive a motor vehicle to the very rim of Cape Solitude, but that seems disrespectful. And unnecessary. I load my backpack and walk the final distance.

The land tilts upward, stony and harsh. The long shadows of yucca, the cliff rose, the squawbush, the scrubby juniper stretch across basins of sand, the humps and hollows of monolithic sandstone—golden in the evening sun. I sense an emptiness ahead.

I come to the edge. The verge of the abyss. Three thousand feet below and little more than a mile away, as a hang glider might descend, is the river. The Grand River, as it once was known. Not far, but inaccessible from here. On my right is the dark, narrow, snaky gorge of the Little Colorado, the bottom of it out of sight, concealed in depth and shadow.

On this point I halt. One step further would take me into another world, the next world, the ultimate world. The longest journey begins with a single step. But I pause, hesitate, defer that step, as always. Not out of fear—I'm afraid of dying but not of death—but again, from respect. Respect for my obligations to others, respect for the work I still hope to do, respect for myself. The despair that haunts the background of our lives, sometimes obtruding itself into consciousness, can still be modulated, as I know from experience, into a comfortable melancholia and from there to defiance, delight, a roaring affirmation of self-existence. Even, at times, into a quiet and blessedly self-forgetful peace, a modest joy.

We are more than 6,000 feet above sea level, but the warm air rising from the canyon, flowing over the rimrock, supports desert plants like cactus and cliff rose that flourish here a thousand feet above their usual habitat. Standing in the balmy, blessed flow, I drop the pack, shed my clothes, even, even hat and boots, kneel down naked on the stone and build a little fire of juniper twigs. I want incense and ceremony and there is no incense finer, no ceremony more fitting—for my soul and this place—than the cedarlike aroma and smokeless flame of burning juniper.

I add larger sticks to the fire, take my flute from the pack, stand, and play a little desert music. Improvised music: a song for any coyotes that may be listening, a song for the river and the great canyon, a song for the sky, a song for the setting sun. Doing only what is proper and necessary. I stop; we listen to the echoes floating back. I write "we" because, in the company of other nearby living things—lizards, ravens, snakes, bushes, grass, weeds—I do not feel myself to be alone.

The desert world accepts my homage with its customary silence. The grand indifference. As any man of sense would want it. If a voice from the clouds suddenly addressed me, speaking my name in trombone tones, or some angel in an aura of blue flame came floating toward me along the canyon rim, I think I would be more embarrassed than frightened—embarrassed by the vulgarity of such display. That is what depresses in the mysticism of Carlos Castaneda and his like: their poverty of imagination. As any honest magician knows, true magic inheres in the ordinary, the commonplace, the everyday, the mystery of the obvious. Only petty minds and trivial souls yearn for supernatural events, incapable of perceiving that everything—everything!—within and around them is pure miracle.

Or so I say. So I have always thought. But I am willing to see my whole world splintered by a sword of light, if such can happen. What choice would I have? Let it come down. Let God speak, here and now, plain and honest and once and for all, or forever hold His peace. Enough of this muttering in the distance, that awkward blundering behind the scenes. Come on out, whatever You are, show me Your face, kiss me, embrace me, enslave me in bliss. Or else shut up.

The silent desert makes no reply. I put the flute aside and urinate on Mother Earth, respectfully, as always, taking care to avoid the little living things, the sand verbena, the phacelia, the dry, tawny bunches of grass. Letting the fire die to a bed of coals, I sit on the edge of the rock, my feet dangling over a 1,500-foot drop-off, and try not to think about what I know I am going to think about.

(I enjoy the feel of the stone on my bare skin; I find pleasure in the rock's abrasiveness, its staunch solidity, its purchase on the cliff's rim—which might, who knows, give way at any moment.)

I came here to forget some things, at least for a while, but in order to forget I must first remember what I wish to forget, the confused scene presented by my country, the only one I've got, in this summer of the year. Which year? It makes little difference.

My country? *Our* country? The U.S. of A.? Whose country,

indeed? Everywhere I went in my little tour of the American campus I found majority support for the idea that we must bring the growth machine to a halt; that we must change our collective way of life; that we must conserve, not waste, energy and other resources; save, not destroy, the family farm, the small enterprise and independent business—that we must preserve, not obliterate, what still remains of the American wilderness, the American hope, the American adventure.

Overwhelming support—for if anyone objected to the thesis I was promoting in my slapstick, slapdash, sex-crazed manner, they failed to speak up. Indeed, the only objections I had to deal with were accusations that I myself was exploiting the land, the wild, the agrarian life by writing about it. A charge to which I pled guilty; for it's true, I've made a stack of easy money praising country life and attacking the greedheads (as Hunter Thompson calls them) who own and operate America. Nothing easier.

My defense, as I pointed out, consists solely in this, that I give a tenth of my income (as a good Mormon should) to the conservation cause. While the other ninety percent goes to support my family, myself, and the useless federal government.

Some of us are beginning to catch on to something. Government does not exist to ease, facilitate, moderate, and preside over necessary social change. On the contrary, the purpose of government is to prevent change. At all costs. By any means. That is why government reserves to itself the monopoly of coercion, of organized, large-scale violence.

Take this job and shove it.

Too much, to much. Too much is enough. I get up from the cold rimrock, pull on my pants, a shirt, a vest. Sun long down and the air is chilling fast. Let somebody else save the world for a while; I'm tired of even thinking about it. Not that I seriously imagine myself a thinker. I am a feeler, not a thinker, and proud of it. An extremist? Yes. And a revolutionist? Naturally. Do I advocate another revolution? What do you mean, *another*? We have yet to see the first. But it's coming.

Take a look in your local disco this coming Saturday night. Observe that jampacked multitude of solitary dancers, the critical mass, the unquiet desperation. Hear the urgency, feel the murderous beat, of that deafening, tremendous, overpowering sound. (Not music—*sound.*) Some day that energy is going to discover its secret meaning, find the hidden door, burst out into the night, go blazing up the avenue toward those dark towers of glass and aluminum that dominate our lives—and shatter them to bits.

Take this job . . . and shove it!

There is a little town in Arizona called Why. (Why is a good name for any town.) But in the America of my dreams there is a city called Why Not.

I restoke the fire, warm hands and kneecaps, scratch my itchy shanks, and think of supper. But we're fasting tonight. I open another bottle from my Christian Brothers. Vintage '77, California Red. Seventy-seven—double good luck. Here's to you, my brothers, my sisters. To us, the green elves. We are everywhere. Nothing is more subversive than grass. Joy, shipmates, joy.

But as I was saying, let others save the world for the time being. Tonight and tomorrow and for the next few days I am going to walk the rim of Cape Solitude, along the palisades of the desert, and save myself. Without half trying.

When the dawn comes I'll crawl from my sack, naked as the snake in my hand, face the east, kneel on the bare rock, and make an offering for Mother. Then stand and face my god, that savage and merciless deity, brazen with fire, as he rises from beyond Shinumo Altar, the Painted Desert, the Echo Cliffs. Shall I pray for justice? Mercy? Eternal life? I think not. For what then? For nothing. There is nothing to pray for. Let us pray.

>   *Black sun*
>   *Heart's sun*
>   *Black raging sun of my heart*

Burn me pure as the flame
Burn me and take me
And let me sleep
Down by a river I know
In the land of stone and sky
Until we wake again
In a new and bolder dawn.

RICK DeMARINIS

WEEDS

A black helicopter flapped out of the morning sun and dumped its sweet orange mist on our land instead of the Parley farm where it was intended. It was weedkiller, something strong enough to wipe out leafy spurge, knapweed, and Canadian thistle, but it made us sick.

My father had a fatal stroke a week after that first spraying. I couldn't hold down solid food for nearly a month and went from 200 pounds to 170 in that time. Mama went to bed and slept for two days, and when she woke up she was not the same. She'd lost something of herself in that long sleep, and something that wasn't herself had replaced it.

Then it hit the animals. We didn't have much in the way of animals, but one by one they dropped. The chickens, the geese, the two old mules—Doc and Rex—and last of all, our only cow, Miss Milky, who was more or less the family pet.

Miss Milky was the only animal that didn't outright up and die. She just got sick. There was blood in her milk and her milk was thin. Her teats got so tender and brittle that she would try to mash me against the milk-stall wall when I pulled them. The white part of her eyes looked like fresh red meat. Her piss was so strong that the green grass wherever she stood died off. She got so bound up that when she'd lift her tail and bend with strain, only one black apple would drop. Her breath took on a burning sulfurous stink that would make you step back.

She also went crazy. She'd stare at me like she all at once

150

had a desperate human mind and had never seen me before. Then she'd act as if she wanted to slip a horn under my ribs and peg me to the barn. She would drop her head and charge, blowing like a randy bull, and I would have to scramble out of the way. Several times I saw her gnaw on her hooves or stand stock-still in water up to her blistered teats. Or she would walk backwards all day long, mewling like a lost cat that had been dropped off in a strange place. That mewling was enough to make you clap a set of noise dampers on your ears. The awful sound led Mama to say this: "It's the death song of the land, mark my words."

Mama never talked like that before in her life. She'd always been a cheerful woman who could never see the bad part of anything. But now she was dark and strange as a gypsy, and she would have spells of sheer derangement during which she'd make noises like a wild animal, or she'd play the part of another person—the sort of person she'd normally have nothing to do with at all. At Daddy's funeral, she got dressed in an old and tattered evening gown the color of beet juice, her face painted and powdered like that of a barfly. And while the preacher told the onlookers what a fine man Daddy had been, Mama made little night-animal sounds that kept heads turning our way. "Loo, loo, loo," she said, and, "kuk-a-kuk," her scared eyes scanning the trees for owls.

I was 28 years old and my life had come to nothing. I'd had a girl but I'd lost her through neglect and a careless attitude that had spilled over into my personal life, souring it. I had no ambition to make something worthwhile of myself, and it nettled her. Toward the end, she began to parrot her mother: "You need to get yourself *established*, Jack," she would say. But I didn't want to get myself established. I was getting poorer and more aimless day by day, and I supposed she believed that "getting established" would stop the downhill slide, but I had no desire to do whatever it took to accomplish that.

— — —

Shortly after Daddy died, the tax man came to our door with
a paper in his hand. "Inheritance tax," he said, handing me the
paper.

"What do you mean?" I asked.

"It's the law," he said. "Your father died, you see. And that's
going to cost you some. You should have made better plans."
He had a way of expressing himself that made me think he was
country born and raised but wanted to seem citified. Or maybe
it was the other way around.

"I don't understand this," I mumbled. I felt the weight of a
world I'd so far been able to avoid. It was out there, tight-assed
and squinty-eyed, and it knew to the dollar and dime what it
needed to keep itself in business.

"Simple," he said. "Pay or move off. The government is the
government, and it can't bend a rule to accommodate the confused. It's your decision. Pay, or the next step is litigation."

He smiled when he said goodbye. I closed the door against
the weight of his smile, which was the weight of the world. I
went to a window and watched him head back to his green
government car. The window was open and I could hear him.
He was singing loudly in a fine tenor voice. He raised his right
hand to hush an invisible audience that had broken into un-
controlled applause. I could still hear him singing as he slipped
the car into gear and idled away. He was singing "Red River
Valley."

Even though the farm was all ours, paid up in full, we had
to give the government $7000 for the right to stay on it. The
singing tax man said we had inherited the land from my father,
and the law was sharp on the subject.

I didn't know where the money was going to come from. I
didn't talk it over with Mama because even in her better moments she would talk in riddles. To a simple question such as,
"Should I paint the barns this year, Mama?" she might answer,
"I've got no eyes for glitter, nor ears for ridicule."

— — —

One day I decided to load Miss Milky into the stock trailer and
haul her into Saddle Butte where the vet, Doc Nevers, had his
office. Normally, Doc Nevers would come out to your place,
but he'd heard about the spraying that was going on and said
he wouldn't come within three miles of our property until they
were done.

The Parley farm was being sprayed regularly, for they grew
an awful lot of wheat and almost as much corn, and they had
the biggest haying operation in the country. Often, the helicopters they used were upwind from us and we were sprayed
too. ("Don't complain," said Big Pete Parley when I called him
up about it. "Think of it this way—you're getting your place
weeded for *free!* When I said I might have to dynamite some
stumps on the property line and that he might get a barn or
two blown away for free, he just laughed like hell, as if I had
told one of the funniest jokes he'd ever heard.)

There was a good windbreak between our places, a thick grove
of Lombardy poplars, but the orange mist, sweet as a flower
garden in full bloom, sifted through the trees and settled on our
fields. Soon the poplars were mottled and dying. Some branches
curled in an upward twist, as if flexed in pain, and others became
soft and fibrous as if the wood were trying to turn itself into
sponge.

With Miss Milky in the trailer, I sat in the truck sipping on
a pint of Lewis and Clark bourbon and looking out across our
unplanted fields. It was late—almost too late—to plant anything. Mama, in the state she was in, hadn't even noticed.

In the low hills on the north side of the property, some ugly
looking things were growing. From the truck, they looked like
white pimples on the smooth brown hill. Up close, they were
as big as melons. They were some kind of fungus, and they
pushed up through the ground like the bald heads of fat babies.
They gave off a rotten-meat stink. I would get chillbumps just
looking at them, and if I touched one, my stomach would rise.
The bulbous heads had purple streaks on them that looked like

blood vessels. I half expected to one day see human eyes clear the dirt and open. Big pale eyes that would see me and carry my image down to their deepest root. I was glad they seemed to prefer the hillside and bench and not the bottom land.

Justified or not, I blamed the growth of this fungus on the poison spray, just as I blamed it for the death of my father, the loss of our animals and the strangeness of my mother. Now the land itself was becoming strange. And I thought, what about me? How am I being rearranged by that weedkiller?

I guess I should have gotten mad, but I didn't. Maybe I *had* been changed by the spray. Where once I had been a quick-to-take-offense hothead, I was now docile and thoughtful. I could sit on a stump and think for hours, enjoying the slow and complicated intertwinings of my own thoughts. Even though I felt sure the cause of all our troubles had fallen out of the sky, I would hold arguments with myself, as if there were always two sides to every question. If I said to myself, "Big Pete Parley has poisoned my family and farm and my father is dead because of it," I would follow it up with, "But Daddy was old anyway, past 75, and he always had high blood pressure. Anything could have set off his stroke, from a wasp bite to a sonic boom."

"And what about Mama?" I would ask. "Senile with grief," came the quick answer. "Furthermore, Daddy himself used poison in his time. Cyanide traps for coyotes, DDT for mosquito larvae, arsenic for rats."

My busy mind was always doubling back on itself in this way, and it would often leave me standing motionless in a field for hours, paralyzed with indecision, sighing like a moonstruck girl of 12. I imagined myself mistaken by passersby for a scarecrow.

Sometimes I saw myself as a human weed, useless to other people in general and maybe even harmful in some weedy way. The notion wasn't entirely unpleasant. Jack Hucklebone: a weed amid the well-established money crops of life.

On my way to town with Miss Milky, I crossed over the irrigation ditch my father had fallen into with the stroke that killed him. I pulled over onto the shoulder and switched off the engine. It was a warm, insect-loud day in early June. A spray of grasshoppers clattered over the hood of the truck. June bugs ticked past the windows like little flying clocks. The 13-year locusts were back and raising a whirring hell. I was 15 the last time they came, but I didn't remember them arriving in such numbers. I expected more helicopters to come flapping over with special sprays meant just for them, even though they would be around for only a few weeks and the damage they would do is not much more than measurable. But anything that looks like it might have an appetite for a money crop brings down the spraying choppers. I climbed out of the truck and looked up into the bright air. A lone jet, too high to see or hear, left its neat chalk line across the top of the sky. Then the chalk line stopped, and there was nothing up there at all.

The sky itself was like hot, blue wax, east to west. A hammerhead sat on the south horizon as if it were an oblong gray planet gone dangerously off course.

There's where Daddy died. Up the ditch about 50 yards from here. I found him, buckled, white as paper, half under water. His one good eye, his right (he'd lost the left one 30 years ago when a tractor tire blew up in his face as he was filling it), was above water and wide open, staring at his hand as if it could focus on the thing it gripped. He was holding on to a root. He had big hands, strong, with fingers like thick hardwood dowels, but now they were soft and puffy, like the hands of a giant baby. Water bugs raced against the current toward him. His body blocked the ditch and little eddies swirled around it. The water bugs skated into the eddies and, fighting to hold themselves still in the roiling current, touched his face. They held still long enough to satisfy their curiosity, then slid back into the circular flow as if bemused by the strangeness of dead human flesh.

I started to cry, remembering it, thinking about him in the water, he had been so sure and strong, but then—true to my changed nature—I began to laugh at the memory, for his wide blue eye had had a puzzled cast to it, as if it had never before seen such a crazy thing as the ordinary root in his forceless hand. It was an expression he never wore in life.

"It was only a weed, Daddy," I said, wiping the tears from my face.

The amazed puzzlement had stayed in his eye until I brushed down the lid.

Of course he had been dead beyond all talk and puzzlement. Dead when I found him, dead for hours, bloated dead. And, this is how I've come to be; blame the spray or don't. The chores don't get done on time, the unplanted fields wait and yet I'll sit in the shade of my truck sipping on Lewis and Clark bourbon, inventing the thoughts of a stonedead man.

Time bent away from me like a tail-dancing rainbow. It was about to slip the hook. I wasn't trying to hold it. Try to hold it and it gets all the more slippery. Try to let it go and it sticks like a cocklebur to cotton. I was drifting somewhere between two kinds of not trying: not trying to hold anything, not trying to let anything go.

Then he sat down next to me. The old man.

"You got something for me?" he said.

He was easily the homeliest man I had ever seen. His bald head was bullet-shaped and his lumpy nose was warty as a crookneck squash. His little, close-set eyes sat on either side of that nose like hard black beans. He had shaggy eyebrows that climbed upward in a white and wiry tangle. There was a blue lump in the middle of his forehead the size of a pullet's egg, and his hairy ear lobes touched his grimy collar. He was mumbling something, but it could have been the noise of the ditch water as it sluiced through the culvert under the road.

He stank of whiskey and dung, and looked like he'd been sleeping behind barns for weeks. His clothes were rags, and he was caked with dirt from fingernail to jaw. His shoes were held together with strips of burlap. He untied some of these strips and took off the shoes. Then he slid his gnarled, dirt-crusted feet into the water. His eyes fluttered shut and he let out a hissing moan of pleasure. His toes were long and twisted, the arthritic knuckles painfully bright. They reminded me of the surface roots of a stunted oak that had been trying to grow in hardpan. Though he was only about five feet tall, his feet were huge. Easy size twelves, wide as paddles.

He quit mumbling, cleared his throat, spit. "You got something for me?" he said.

I handed him my pint. He took it, then held it up to the sunlight and looked through the rusty booze as if testing for its quality.

"If it won't do," I said, "I could run into town to get something a little smoother for you. Maybe you'd like some Canadian Club or some 12-year-old scotch. I could run into town and be back in less than an hour. Maybe you'd like me to bring back a couple of fried chickens and a sack of buttered rolls." This was my old self talking, the hothead. But I didn't feel mad at him, and was just being mouthy out of habit.

"No need to do that, " he said, as if my offer had been made in seriousness. He took a long pull off my pint. "This snake piss is just fine by me, son." He raised the bottle to the sunlight again, squinted through it.

I wandered down the ditch again to the place where Daddy died. There was nothing there to suggest a recent dead man had blocked the current. Everything was as it always was. The water surged, the quick water bugs skated up and down inspecting brown clumps of algae along the banks, underwater weeds waved like slim snakes whose tails had been staked to the mud. I looked for the thistle he'd grabbed on to. I guess he thought that he was going to save himself from drowning by hanging on to its root, not realizing immediately that the killing flood was *inside* his head. But there were many roots along the bank and none of them seemed more special than any other.

Something silver glinted at me. It was a coin. I picked it out of the slime and polished it against my pants. It was a silver dollar, a real one. It could have been his. He carried a few of the old cartwheels around with him for luck. The heft and gleam of the old solid silver coin choked me up.

I walked back to the old man. He had stuffed his bindle under his head for a pillow and had dozed off. I uncapped the pint and finished it. I flipped it into the weeds. It hit a rock and popped. The old man grunted and his eyes snapped open. He let out a barking snort, and his black eyes darted around him fiercely, like the eyes of a burrow animal caught in a daylight trap. Then, remembering where he was, he calmed down.

"You got something for me?" he asked. He pushed himself up to a sitting position. It was a struggle for him.

"Not any more," I said. I sat down next to him. Then, from behind us, a deep groan cut loose. It sounded like a siding being pried off an old barn with a crowbar. We both turned to look at whatever had complained so mightily.

It was Miss Milky, up in the trailer, venting her misery. I'd forgotten all about her. Horseflies were biting her. Her red eyes peered sadly out at us through the bars. The corners of her eyes were swollen, giving her a Chinese look.

Suddenly and without warning, a snapping hail fell on us. Only it wasn't hail. It was a moving cloud of 13-year locusts. They darkened the air and they covered us. The noise was like static on the radio, miles of static across the bug-peppered sky, static that could drown out forever all talk and idle music, no matter how powerful the station.

The old man's face was covered with the bugs and he was saying something to me, but I couldn't make out what it was. His mouth was opening and closing. When it opened, he'd have to brush away the locusts from his lips. They were like ordinary grasshoppers, only smaller, and they had big red eyes that seemed to glow with their own hellish light. Then, as fast as they had come, they were gone, scattered back into the fields. A few hopped here and there, but the main cloud had broken up.

I just sat there, brushing at the lingering feel of them on my skin and trying to readjust myself to uncluttered air, but my ears were still crackling with their racket.

The old man pulled at my sleeve, breaking me out of my daydream or trance. "You got something for me?" he asked.

I felt blue. Worse than blue. Sick. I felt incurable—ridden with the pointlessness of just about everything you could name. The farm struck me as a pointless wonder, and I found the idea depressing and fearsome. Pointless bugs lay waiting in the fields for the pointless crops as the pointless days and seasons ran on and on into the pointless forever.

"Shit," I said.

"I'll take that cow off your hands, then," he said. "She's done for anyway. All you have to do is look at her."

"No shit," I said.

He didn't seem so old or so wrecked to me now. He was younger and bigger, somehow, as if all his clocks had started spinning backwards. He stood up. He looked thick across the shoulders like he'd done hard work all his life and could still do it. He showed me his right hand and it was yellow with hard calluses. His beady black eyes were quick and lively in their shallow sockets. The blue lump on his forehead glinted in the sun. It seemed deliberately polished, as if it were an ornament. He took a little silver bell out of his pocket and rang it for no reason at all.

"Let me have her," he said.

"You want Miss Milky?" I asked. I felt weak and childish. Maybe I was drunk. My scalp itched and I scratched it hard. He rang his little silver bell again. I wanted to have it, but he put it back into his pocket. Then he knelt down and opened his bindle. He took out a paper sack.

"I'll give you these for her," he said, handing me the sack.

I looked inside. It was packed with seeds of some kind. I ran my fingers through them and did not feel foolish. I heard a helicopter putt-putting in the distance.

In defense of what I did, let me say this much: I knew Miss Milky was done for. Doc Nevers would have told me to kill her. I don't think she was even good for hamburger. Old cow meat can sometimes make good hamburger, but Miss Milky looked wormy and lean. And I wouldn't have trusted her bones for soup. The poison that had wasted her flesh and ruined her udder had probably settled in her marrow.

And so I unloaded my dying cow. He took out his silver bell again and tied it to a piece of string. He tied the string around Miss Milky's neck. Then he led her away. She was docile and easy, as though this was exactly the way things were supposed to turn out.

My throat was dry. I felt too tired to move. I watched their slow progress down the path that ran along the ditch. They got smaller and smaller in the field, until, against a dark hedge of box elders, they disappeared. I strained to see after them, but it was as if the earth had given them refuge, swallowing them into its deep, loamy, composting interior. The only sign that they still existed in the world was the tinkling of the silver bell he had tied around Miss Milky's neck. It was a pure sound, naked in the world.

Then a breeze opened a gap in the box elders and a long blade of sunlight pierced through them, illuminating and magnifying the old man and his cow.

The breeze let up and the box elders shut off the sun again, and I couldn't see anything but a dense quiltwork of black and green shadows out of which a raven big as an eagle flapped. It cawed in raucous good humor as it veered over my head.

I went on into town anyway, cow or no cow, and hit some bars. I met a girl from the East in the Hobble who thought I was a cowboy and I didn't try to correct her mistaken impression, for it proved to be a free pass to good times.

When I got home, Mama had company. She was dressed up in her beet-juice dress, and her face was powdered white. Her dark lips looked like a wine stain in snow. But her clear blue eyes were direct and calm. There was no distraction in them.

"Hi boy," said the visitor. It was Big Pete Parley. He was

wearing a blue suit, new boots, a gray felt Stetson. He had a toothy grin on his fat red face.

I looked at Mama. "What's he want?" I asked.

"Mr. Parley is going to help us, Jackie," she said.

"What's going on, Mama?" I asked. Something was wrong. I could feel it but I couldn't see it. It was Mama, the way she was carrying herself, the look in her eyes, her whitened skin. Maybe she had gone all the way insane. She went over to Parley and sat next to him on the davenport. She had slit her gown and it fell away from her thigh, revealing the veiny flesh.

"We're going to be married," she said. "Pete's tired of being a widower. He wants a warm bed."

As if to confirm it was no fantasy dreamed up by her senile mind, Big Pete slipped his meaty hand into the slit dress and squeezed her thigh. He clicked his teeth at me and winked.

"Pete knows how to operate a farm," said Mama. "And you do not, Jackie." She didn't intend for it to sound mean or critical. It was just a statement of the way things were. I couldn't argue with her.

I went into the kitchen. Mama followed me in. I opened a beer. "I don't mean to hurt your feelings, Jackie," she said.

"He's scheming to get our land," I said. "He owns half the county, but it isn't enough."

"No," she said. "I'm the one who's scheming. I'm scheming for my boy who does not grasp the rudiments of the world."

I had the sack of seeds with me. I realized that I'd been rattling them nervously.

"What do you have there?" she asked, narrowing her eyes.

"Seeds," I said.

"Seeds? What seeds? Where'd you get them?"

I thought it best not to mention where I'd gotten them. "Big Pete Parley doesn't want to marry *you*," I said. It was a mean thing to say, and I wanted to say it.

Mama sighed. "It doesn't matter what he wants, Jack. I'm dead anyway." She took the bag of seeds from me, picked some up, squinted at them.

"What is that supposed to mean?" I said, sarcastically.

She went to the window above the sink and stared out into the dark. Under the folds of her evening gown, I could see the ruined shape of her old body. "Dead, Jack," she said. "I've been dead for a while now. Maybe you didn't notice."

"No," I said. "I didn't."

"Well, you should have. I went to sleep shortly after your Daddy died and I had a dream. The dream got stronger and stronger as it went on until it was as vivid as real life itself. When I woke up I knew that I had died. I also knew that nothing in the world would ever be as real to me as that dream."

I almost asked her what the dream was about, but I didn't. In the living room Big Pete Parley was whistling impatiently. The davenport was squeaking under his nervous weight.

"So you see, Jackie," said Mama. "It doesn't matter if I marry Pete Parley or what his motives are in this matter. You are all that counts now. He will ensure your success in the world."

"I don't want to be a success, Mama," I said.

"Well, you have no choice. You cannot gainsay the dead."

She opened the window and dumped out the sack of seeds. Then Big Pete came into the kitchen. "Let's go for a walk," he said. "It's too blame hot in this house."

They left by the kitchen door. I watched them walk across the yard and into the unplanted field. Big Pete had his arm around Mama's thin shoulder. I wondered if he knew, or cared, that he was marrying a dead woman. Light from the half-moon painted their silhouettes for a while. Then they disappeared.

I went to bed and slept for what might have been days. In my long sleep I had a dream. I was canoeing down a whitewater river that ran sharply uphill. The farther up I got, the rougher the water became. Finally, I had to beach the canoe. I proceeded on foot until I came to a large house that had been built in a wilderness forest. The house was empty and quiet. I went in. It was clean and beautifully furnished. Nobody was home. I called out a few times before I understood that silence was a rule. I went from room to room, looking for something. The longer I searched, the more vivid the dream became.

When I woke up I was stiff and weak. Mama wasn't in the house. I made a pot of coffee and took a cup outside. Under the kitchen window there was a patch of green shoots. "Kuk-a-kuk," I said, softly.

A week later that patch of green shoots had grown and spread. They were weeds. The worst kind of weeds I had ever seen. Thick, spiny weeds, with broad green leaves tough as leather. They rolled away from the house, out across the fields, in a viny carpet. Mean, deep-rooted weeds, too mean to uproot by hand. When I tried, I came away with a palm full of cuts.

In another week they were tall as corn. They were fast growers and I could not see where they ended. They covered everything in sight. A smothering blanket of deep green sucked the life out of every other growing thing. They crossed fences, irrigation ditches, and when they reached the trees of a windbreak, they became ropy crawlers that wrapped themselves around trunks and limbs.

When they reached the Parley farm, over which my dead mother now presided, they were attacked by squadrons of helicopters which drenched them in poisons, the best poisons chemical science knew how to brew. But the poisons only seemed to make the weeds grow faster, and after a spraying, the new growths were tougher, thornier and more dertermined than ever to dominate the land.

Some of the weeds sent up long, woody stalks. On top of these stalks were heavy seedpods, fat as melons. The strong stalks pushed the pods high into the air.

The day the pods cracked, a heavy wind came up. The wind raised black clouds of seed in grainy spirals that reached the top of the sky, then scattered them far and wide, across the entire nation.

RICHARD FORD

WINTERKILL

I had not been back in town long. Maybe a month was all. The work had finally given out for me down at Silver Bow, and I had quit staying around down there when the weather turned cold, and come back to my mother's, on the Bitterroot, to lay up and set aside my benefits for when things got worse.

My mother had her boyfriend then, an old wildcatter named Harley Reeves. And Harley and I did not get along, though I don't blame him for that. He had been layed off himself down near Gillette, Wyoming, where the boom was finished. And he was just doing what I was doing and had arrived there first. Everyone was laid off then. It was not a good time in that part of Montana, nor was it going to be. The two of them were just giving it a final try, both of them in their sixties, strangers together in the little house my father had left her.

So in a week I moved up to town, into a little misery flat across from the Burlington Northern yards, and began to wait. There was nothing to do. Watch TV. Stop at a bar. Walk down to the Clark Fork River and fish where they had built a little park. Just find a way to spend the time. You think you'd like to have all the time be your own, but that is a fantasy. I was feeling my back to the wall then, and didn't know what would happen to me in a week's time, which is a feeling to stay with you and make being cheerful hard. And no one can like that.

I was at the Top Hat having a drink with Little Troy Burnham, talking about the deer season, when a woman who had been sitting at the front of the bar got up and came over to us. I had seen this woman other times in other bars in town. She would be there in the afternoons around three, and then sometimes late at night when I would be cruising back. She danced with some men from the air base, and sat drinking and talking late. I suppose she left with someone finally. She wasn't a bad-looking woman at all. Blond, with wide, dark eyes set out, wide hips, and dark eyebrows. She could've been thirty-four years old, although she could've been forty-four or twenty-four, because she was drinking steady, and steady drink can do both to you, especially to women. But I had thought the first time I saw her: Here's one on the way down. A miner's wife drifted up from Butte, or a rancher's daughter just run off suddenly, which can happen. Or worse. And I hadn't been tempted. Trouble comes cheap and leaves expensive is a way of thinking about that.

"Do you suppose you could give me a light," the woman said to us. She was standing at our table. Nola was her name. Nola Foster. I had heard that around. She wasn't drunk. It was four o'clock in the afternoon, and no one was there but Troy Burnham and me.

"If you'll tell me a love story, I'll do anything in the world for you," Troy said. It was what he always said to women. He'd do anything in the world for something. Troy sits in a wheelchair due to a smoke jumper's injury, and can't do very much. We had been friends since high school and before. He was always short, and I was tall. But Troy had been an excellent wrestler and won awards in Montana, and I had done little of that, some boxing once was all. We had been living in the same apartments on Ryman Street, though Troy lived there permanently and drove a Checker cab to earn a living, and I was hoping to pass on to something better. "I *would* like a little love story," Troy said, and called for whatever Nola Foster was drinking.

"Nola, Troy. Troy, Nola," I said, and lit her cigarette.

"Have we met?" Nola said, taking a seat and glancing at me.

"At the East Gate. Some time ago," I said.

"That's a very nice bar," she said in a cool way. "But I hear it's changed hands."

"I'm glad to make your acquaintance," Troy said, grinning and adjusting his glasses. "Now let's hear that love story." He pulled up close to the table so that his head and his big shoulders were above the tabletop. Troy's injury had caused him not to have any hips left. There is something there, but not hips. He needs bars and a special seat in his cab. He is both frail and strong at once, though in most ways he gets on like everybody else.

"I *was* in love," Nola said quietly as the bartender set her drink down and she took a sip. "And now I'm not."

"That's a short love story," I said.

"There's more to it," Troy said, grinning. "Am I right about that? Here's cheers to you," he said, and raised his glass.

Nola glanced at me again. "All right. Cheers," she said and sipped her drink.

Two men had started playing a pool game at the far end of the room. They had turned on the table light, and I could hear the balls click and someone say, "Bust 'em up, Craft." And then the smack.

"You don't want to hear that," Nola said. "You're drunk men, that's all."

"We do *too*," Troy said. Troy always has enthusiasm. He could very easily complain, but I have never heard it come up. And I believe he has a good heart.

"What about you? What's your name?" Nola said.

"Les," I said.

"Les, then," she said. "You don't want to hear this, Les."

"Yes he does," Troy said, putting his elbows on the table and raising himself. Troy was a little drunk. Maybe we all were a little.

"Why not," I said.

"See? Sure. Les wants more. He's like me."

Nola was a pretty woman, with a kind of dignity to her that wasn't at once so noticeable, and Troy was thrilled by her.

"All right," Nola said, taking another drink.

"What'd I tell you?" Troy said.

"I had really thought he was dying," Nola said.

"Who?" I said.

"My husband. Harry Lyons. I don't use that name now. Someone's told you this story before, haven't they?"

"Not me. Goddamn," Troy said. "I *want* to hear this story."

I said I hadn't heard it either, though I had heard there was a story.

She took a puff on her cigarette and gave us both a look that said she didn't believe us. But she went on. Maybe she had thought about another drink by then.

"He had this death look. Ca-shit-ic, they call it. He was pale, and his mouth turned down like he could see death. His heart had already gone out once in June, and I had the feeling I'd come in the kitchen some morning and he'd be slumped on his toast."

"How old was this Harry?" Troy said.

"Fifty-three years old. Older than me by a lot."

"That's cardiac alley there," Troy said and nodded at me. Troy has trouble with his own organs now and then. I think they all moved lower when he hit the ground.

"A man gets strange when he's going to die," Nola said in a quiet voice. "Like he's watching it come. Though Harry still was going to work out at Champions every day. He was an estimator. Plus he watched *me* all the time. Watched to see if I was getting ready, I guess. Checking the insurance, balancing the checkbook, locating the safe-deposit key. All that. Though I would, too. Who wouldn't?"

"Bet your ass," Troy said and nodded again. Troy was taking this all in, I could see that.

"And I admit it, I *was*," Nola said. "I loved Harry. But if he died, where was I going? Was I supposed to die, too? I had to make some plans for myself. I had to think Harry was expendable at some point. To *my* life, anyway."

"Probably that's why he was watching you," I said. "He might not have felt expendable in *his* life."

"I know," Nola said and looked at me seriously and smoked her cigarette. "But I had a friend whose husband killed himself. Went into the garage and left the motor running. And his wife *was not* ready. Not in her mind. She thought he was out putting on brake shoes. And there he was when she went out there. She ended up having to move to Washington, D.C. Lost her balance completely over it. Lost her house, too."

"All bad things," Troy agreed.

"And that just wasn't going to be me, I thought. And if Harry had to get wind of it, well, so be it. Some days I'd wake up and look at him in bed and I'd think, Die, Harry, and quit worrying about it."

"I thought this was a love story," I said. I looked down at where the two men were playing an eight-ball rack. One man was chalking a cue while the other man was leaning over to shoot.

"It's coming. Just be patient, Les," Troy said.

Nola drained her drink. "I'll guarantee it is," she said.

"Then let's hear it," I said. "Get on to the love part."

Nola looked at me strangely then, as if I really did know what she was going to tell, and thought maybe I might tell it first myself. She raised her chin at me. "Harry came home one evening from work, right?" she said. "Just death as usual. Only he said to me, 'Nola, I've invited some friends over, sweetheart. Why don't you go out and get a flank steak at Albertson's.' 'When are they coming?' I said. 'In an hour,' he said. And I thought, An hour! Because he never brought people home. We went to bars, you know. We didn't entertain. But I said, 'All right. I'll go get a flank steak.' And I got in the car and went out and bought a flank steak. I thought Harry ought to have what he wants. If he wants to have friends and steak he ought to be able to. Men, before they die, will want strange things."

"That's a fact, too," Troy said seriously. "I was full dead all of four minutes when I hit. And I dreamed about nothing but lobster the whole time. And I'd never even seen a lobster, though I have now. Maybe that's what they serve in heaven." Troy grinned at both of us.

"Well, this wasn't heaven," Nola said and signaled for another drink. "So when I got back, there was Harry with three Crow Indians, in my house, sitting in the living room drinking mai tais. A man and two women. His *friends*, he said. From the plant. He wanted to have his friends over, he said. And Harry was raised a strict Mormon. Not that it matters."

"I guess he had a change of heart," I said.

"That'll happen, too," Troy said gravely. "LDS's aren't like they used to be. They used to be bad, but that's all changed. Though I guess coloreds still can't get inside the temple all the way."

"These three were inside my house, though. I'll just say that. And I'm not prejudiced about it. Leopards with spots, leopards without. All the same to me. But I was nice. I went right in the kitchen and put the flank steak in the oven, put some potatoes in water, got out some frozen peas. And went back in to have a drink. And we sat around and talked for half an hour. Talked about the plant. Talked about Marlon Brando. The man and one of the women were married. He worked with Harry. And the other woman was her sister. Winona. There's a town in Mississippi with the same name. I looked it up. So after a while—all nice and friends—I went in to peel my potatoes. And this other woman, Bernie, came in with me to help, I guess. And I was standing there cooking over a little range, and this Bernie said to me, 'I don't know how you do it, Nola.' 'Do what, Bernie?' I said. 'Let Harry go with my sister like he does and you stay so happy about it. I couldn't ever stand that with Claude.' And I just turned around and looked at her. *Winona is what?* I thought. That seemed so unusual for an Indian. And I just started yelling it. 'Winona, Winona,' the top of my lungs right at the stove. I just went crazy a minute, I guess. Screaming, holding a potato in my hand, hot. The man came running into

the kitchen. Claude Smart Enemy. Claude was awfully nice.
He kept me from harming myself. But when I started yelling,
Harry, I guess, figured everything was all up. And he and his
Winona woman went right out the door. And he didn't get even
to the car when his heart went. He had a myocardial infarction
right out on the sidewalk at this Winona's feet. I guess he
thought everything was going to be just great. We'd all have
dinner together. And I'd never know what was what. Except
he didn't count on Bernie saying something."

"Maybe he was trying to make you appreciate him more," I
said. "Maybe he didn't like being expendable and was sending
you a message."

Nola looked at me seriously. "I thought of that," she said.
"I thought about that more than once. But that would've been
hurtful. And Harry Lyons wasn't a man to hurt you. He was
more of a sneak. I just think he wanted us all to be friends."

"That makes sense," Troy said, nodding and looking at me.

"What happened to Winona?" I said.

"What happened to Winona?" Nola took a drink and gave
me a hard look. "Winona moved herself to Spokane. What
happened to me is a better question."

"Why, you're here with us," Troy said enthusiastically.
"You're doing great. Les and me ought to do as well as you do.
Les is out of work. And I'm out of luck. You're doing the best
of the three of us, I'd say."

"I wouldn't," Nola said frankly and turned and stared down
at the men playing pool.

"What'd he leave you," I said. "Harry."

"Two thousand," Nola said coldly.

"That's a small amount," I said.

"And it's a sad love story too," Troy said, shaking his head.
"You loved him and it ended rotten. That's like Shakespeare."

"I loved him enough," Nola said.

"How about sports. Do you like sports?" Troy said.

Nola looked at Troy oddly then. In his chair Troy doesn't

look exactly like a whole man, and sometimes simple things he'll say will seem surprising. And what he'd said then surprised Nola. I have gotten used to it, myself, after all these years.

"Did you want to try skiing?" Nola said and glanced at me.

"Fishing," Troy said, up on his elbows again. "Let's all of us go fishing. Put an end to old gloomy." Troy seemed like he wanted to pound the table. I wondered when was the last time he had slept with a woman. Fifteen years ago, maybe. And now that was all over for him. But he was excited just to be here and get to talk to Nola Foster, and I wasn't going to be in his way. "No one'll be there now," he said. "We'll catch a fish and cheer ourselves up. Ask Les. He caught a fish."

I had been going mornings in those days, when the *Today Show* got over. Just kill an hour. The river runs the middle of town, and I could walk over in five minutes and fish downstream below the motels that are there, and could look up at the blue and white mountains down the Bitterroot, toward my mother's house, and sometimes see the geese coming back up their flyway. It was a strange winter. January was like a spring day, and the Chinook blew down over us a warm wind from the eastern slopes. Some days were cool or cold, but many days were warm, and the only ice you'd see was in the lows where the sun didn't reach. You could walk right out to the river and make a long cast to where the fish were deep down in the cold pools. And you could even think things might turn out better.

Nola looked at me, then. The thought of fishing was seeming like a joke to her, I know. Though maybe she didn't have money for a meal and thought we might buy her one. Or maybe she'd never even been fishing. Or maybe she knew that she was on her way to the bottom, where everything is the same, and here was this something different being offered, and it was worth a try if nothing else.

"Did you catch a big fish, Les?" she said.

"Yes," I said.

"See?" Troy said. "Am I a liar? Or am I not?"

"You might be," Nola said. She looked at me oddly then, but, I thought, sweetly too. "What kind of fish was it?"

"A brown trout. Caught deep, on a hare's ear," I said.

"I don't know what that is," Nola said, and smiled. I could see that she wasn't minding any of this because her face was flushed, and she looked pretty then.

"Which?" I said. "A brown trout? Or a hare's ear?"

"That's it," she said.

"A hare's ear is a kind of fly," I said.

"I see," Nola said.

"Let's get out of the bar for once," Troy said loudly, running his chair backwards and forwards. "We'll go fish, then we'll have chicken-in-the-ruff. Troy's paying."

"What'll I lose?" Nola said and shook her head. She looked at both of us, smiling as though she could think of something that might be lost.

"You got it all to win," Troy said. "Let's just go."

"Sure," Nola said. "Whatever."

And we went out of the Top Hat, with Nola pushing Troy in his chair and me coming on behind.

On Front Street the evening was as warm as May, though the sun had gone behind the peaks already, and it was nearly dark. The sky was deep beryl blue in the east behind the Sapphires, where the darkness was, but salmon pink above the sun. And we were in the middle of it. Half drunk, trying to be imaginative in how we killed our time.

Troy's Checker was parked in front, and Troy rolled over to it and spun around.

"Let me show you this great trick," he said and grinned. "Get in and drive, Les. Stay there, sweetheart, and watch me."

Nola had kept her drink in her hand, and she stood by the door of the Top Hat. Troy lifted himself off his chair onto the concrete. I got in beside Troy's bars and his raised seat and started the cab with my left hand.

"Ready," Troy shouted. "Ease forward. Ease up."

And I eased the car up.

"Oh my God," I heard Nola say and saw her put her palm to her forehead and look away.

"Yaah. Ya-hah," Troy yelled.

"Your poor foot," Nola said.

"It doesn't hurt me," Troy yelled. "It's just like a pressure." I couldn't see him from where I was.

"I know I've seen it all now," Nola said. She was smiling.

"Back up, Les. Just ease it back again," Troy yelled out.

"Don't do it again," Nola said.

"One time's enough, Troy," I said. No one else was in the street. I thought how odd it would be for anyone to see that, without knowing something in advance. A man running over another man's foot for fun. Just drunks, you'd think, I guess. And be right.

"Sure. Okay," Troy said. I still couldn't see him. But I put the cab back in park and waited. "Help me, sweetheart, now," I could hear Troy say to Nola. "It's easy getting down, but old Troy can't get up again by himself. You have to help him."

And Nola looked a me in the cab, the glass still in her hand. And it was an odd look she gave me, a look that seemed to ask something of me, but I did not know what it was and couldn't answer. And then she put her glass on the pavement and went to put Troy back in his chair.

When we got to the river it was as good as dark, and the river was only a big space you could hear, with the south-of-town lights up behind it, and the three bridges and Champion's paper, downstream a mile. And it was cold now with the sun gone, and I thought there would be fog in before morning.

Troy had insisted on driving with us in the back, as if we'd hired a cab to take us fishing. On the way down he sang a smoke jumper's song, and Nola sat close to me and let her leg be beside mine. And by the time we stopped by the river, below the Lion's Head motel, I had kissed her twice, and knew all that I could do.

"I think I'll go fishing," Troy said from his little raised-up seat in front. "I'm going night fishing. And I'm going to get my own chair out and my rod and all I need. I'll have a time."

"How do you ever change a tire?" Nola said. She was not moving. It was just a question she had. People say all kinds of things to cripples.

Troy whipped around suddenly, though, and looked back at us where we sat on the cab seat. I had put my arm around Nola, and we sat there looking at his big head and big shoulders, below which there was only half a body any good to anyone. "Trust Mr. Wheels," Troy said. "Mr. Wheels can do anything a whole man can." And he smiled at us a crazy man's smile.

"I think I'll just stay in the car," Nola said. "I'll wait for chicken-in-the-ruff. That'll be my fishing."

"It's too cold for ladies anyway now," Troy said gruffly. "Only men. Only men in wheelchairs is the new rule."

I got out of the cab with Troy then and set up his chair and put him in it. I got his fishing gear out of the trunk and strung it up. Troy was not a man to fish flies, and I put a silver dace on his spin line and told him to hurl it far out and let it flow for a time with the current until it was deep, and then to work it, and work it all the way in. I said he would catch a fish with that strategy in five minutes, or ten.

"Les," Troy said to me in the cold dark behind the cab.

"What," I said.

"Do you ever think of just doing a criminal thing sometime? Just do something terrible. Change everything."

"Yes," I said. "I think about that."

Troy had his fishing rod across his chair now, and he was gripping it and looking down the sandy bank toward the dark and sparkling water.

"Why don't you do it?" he said.

"I don't know what I'd choose to do," I said.

"Mayhem," Troy said. "Commit mayhem."

"And go to Deer Lodge forever," I said. "Or maybe they'd

hang me and let me dangle. That would be worse than this, I think."

"Okay, that's right," Troy said, still staring. "But I should do it, shouldn't I? I should do the worst thing there is."

"No, you shouldn't," I said.

And then he laughed. "Hah. Right. Never do that," he said. And he wheeled himself down toward the river into the darkness, laughing all the way, "Hah, hah, hah."

In the cold cab after that I held Nola Foster for a long time. Just held her with my arms around her, breathing and waiting. From the back window I could see the Lion's Head motel, and see the restaurant there that faces the river and that is lighted with candles where people were eating. I could see the WELCOME out front, though not who was welcomed. I could see cars on the bridge going home for the night. And it made me think of Harley Reeves, in my father's little house on the Bitterroot. I thought about him in bed with my mother. Warm. I thought about the faded old tattoo on Harley's shoulder. VICTORY, that said. And I could not connect it easily with what I knew about Harley Reeves, though I thought possibly that he had won a victory of kinds over me just by being where he was.

Nola Foster said, "A man who isn't trusted is the worst thing, you know that, don't you?" I suppose her mind was wandering. She was cold, I could tell by the way she held me. Troy was gone out in the dark now. We were alone, and her skirt had come up a good ways.

"Yes, that's bad," I said, though I could not think at that moment of what trust could mean to me. It was not an issue in my life, and I hoped it never would be. "You're right," I said to make her happy. I felt like I could do that.

"What was your name again?" she said.

"Les," I said. "Lester Snow. Call me Les."

"Les Snow," Nola said. "Do you like less snow?"

"Usually I do," I said, and I put my hand then where I wanted it most.

"How old are you, Les?" she said.

"Thirty-seven," I said.

"You're an old man."

"How old are you?"

"It's my business, isn't it?"

"I guess it is," I said.

"I'll do this, you know," Nola said, "and not even care about it later. Just do a thing. It means nothing more than how I feel at this time. You know? Do you know what I mean, Les?"

"I know it," I said.

"But *you* need to be trusted. Or you aren't anything. Do you know that too?"

We were close to each other. I couldn't see the lights of town or the motel or anything more. Nothing moved.

"I know that, I guess," I said. It was whiskey talking.

"Warm me up then, Les," Nola said. "Warm. Warm."

"You'll get warm," I said.

"I'll think about Florida," she said.

"I'll make you warm," I said.

What I thought I heard at first was a train. So many things can sound like a train when you live near trains. This was a *woo* sound, you would say. Like a train. And I lay and listened for a long time, thinking about a train and its light shining through the darkness along the side of some mountain pass north of there and about something else I don't even remember now. And then Troy came around to my thinking, and I knew then that the *woo* sound had been Troy.

Nola Foster said, "It's Mr. Wheels. He's caught a fish, maybe. Or else drowned."

"Yes," I said.

And I sat up and looked out the window but could see nothing. It had become foggy in just that little time, and tomorrow, I thought, it would be warm again, though it was cold now. Nola and I had not even taken off our clothes to do what we had done.

"Let me see," I said.

I got out and walked into the fog to where I could only see fog and hear the river running. Troy had not made a *woo*ing sound again, and I thought to myself, There is no trouble here. Nothing's wrong.

Though when I walked a ways up the sandy bank, I saw Troy's chair come visible in the fog. And he was not in it, and I couldn't see him. And my heart went then. I heard it go click in my chest. And then I thought, This is the worst. What's happened here will be the worst. And I called out, "Troy. Where are *you*? Call out, now."

And Troy called out, "Here I am, here."

I went for the sound then, ahead of me, which was not out in the river but on the bank. And when I had gone farther, I saw him, out of his chair, of course, on his belly, holding on to his fishing rod with both hands, the line out into the river as though it meant to drag him to the water.

"Help me!" he yelled. "I've got a huge fish. Do something to help me."

"I will," I said. Though I did not see what I could do. I would not dare take the rod, and it would only have been a mistake to take the line. Never give a straight pull to the fish, is an old rule. So that my only choice was to grab Troy and hold him until the fish was either in or lost, just as if Troy was a part of a rod *I* was fishing with.

I squatted in the cold sand behind him, put my heels down and took up his legs, which felt to me like matchsticks, and began to hold him there away from the water.

But Troy suddenly twisted toward me and said fiercely. "Turn me loose, Les. Don't be there. Go out. It's snagged. You've got to go out."

"That's crazy," I said. It's too deep."

"It's not deep," Troy yelled. "I've got it in close now."

"You're crazy," I said.

"Oh, Christ, Les, go get it. I don't want to lose it."

I looked a moment at Troy's scared face then, in the dark.

His glasses were gone off of him. His face was wet. And he had the look of a desperate man, a man who has nothing to hope for but, in some strange way, everything in the world to lose.

"Stupid. This is stupid," I said, because it seemed to me to be. But I got up, walked to the edge and stepped out into the cold water.

It was at least a month then before the run-off would begin in the mountains, and the water I stepped in then was cold and painful as broken glass, though the wet parts of me numbed at once, and my feet just felt like bricks bumping the bottom.

Troy had been wrong all the way about the depth. Because when I stepped out ten yards, keeping touch of his line with the back of my hand, I had already gone above my knees, and on the bottom I felt large rocks, and there was a loud rushing around me that suddenly made me afraid.

Though when I had gone five more yards, and the water was on my thighs and hurting, I hit the snag Troy's fish was hooked to, and I realized then I had no way at all to hold a fish or catch it with my numbed hands. And that all I could really hope for was to break the snag and let the fish slip down into the current and hope Troy could bring it in, or that I could go back and beach it.

"Can you see it, Les?" Troy yelled out of the dark. "Goddammit."

"It isn't easy," I said, and I had to hold the snag then to keep my balance. My legs had gone numb. And I thought: This might be the time and the place I die. What an odd place it is. And what an odd reason for it to happen.

"Hurry up," Troy yelled.

And I wanted to hurry. Except when I ran the line as far as where the snag was, I felt something there that was not a fish and not the snag but something else entirely, some thing I thought I recognized, though I am not sure why. A man, I thought. This is a man.

Though when I had reached farther into the snag branches and woods scruff, deeper into the water, what I felt was an animal. With my fingers I touched its cold, hard rib-side, its legs, its short, slick coat. I felt to its neck and head and touched its nose and teeth, and it was a deer, though not a big deer, not even a yearling. And I knew when I found where Troy's silver dace had gone up in the neck flesh, that he had hooked the deer already snagged here, and that he had pulled himself out of his chair trying to work it free.

"What is it? I know it's a big brown. Don't tell me, Les, don't even tell me."

"I've got it," I said. "I'll bring it in."

"Sure, hell, yes," Troy said out of the fog.

And it was not so hard to work the deer off the snag brush and float it up free. Though once I did, it was dangerous to get turned around in the current with numb legs, and hard to keep from going down, and I had to hold onto the deer itself to keep balance enough to heave myself toward the slow water and the bank. And I thought, as I did, that in the Clark Fork many people drown doing less dangerous things than I am doing now.

"Throw it way far up," Troy shouted, when he could see me. He had righted himself on the sand and was sitting up like a little doll. "Get it way up safe," he said to me.

"It's safe," I said. I had the deer beside me, floating, and I knew Troy couldn't see.

"What did I catch?" Troy yelled.

"Something unusual," I said, and with effort I hauled the little deer up on the sand a foot, and dropped it, and put my cold hands up under my arms. I heard a car door close back where I had come from up the riverbank.

"What is that?" Troy said and put his hand out to touch the deer's dark side. He looked up at me. "I can't see without my glasses."

"It's a deer," I said.

Troy moved his hand around on the deer, then looked at me again in a painful and bewildered way.

"What's it?" he said.

"A deer," I said. "You caught a dead deer."

Troy looked back at the little deer then for a moment and stared at it as if he did not know what to say about it. And sitting on the wet sand, in the foggy night, he all at once looked scary to me, as though it was him who had washed up there and was finished. "I don't see it," he said and sat there. And I said nothing.

"It's what you caught," I said finally. "I thought you'd want to see it."

"It's crazy, Les," he said. "Isn't it?" And he smiled at me in a wild, blind-eyed way.

"It's unusual," I said.

"I never shot a deer before."

"I don't believe you shot this one," I said.

And he smiled again, but then suddenly he gasped back a sob, something I had never seen before. "Goddammit," he said. "Just goddammit."

"It's an odd thing to catch," I said, standing above him in the cold, grimy fog.

"I can't change a fucking tire," he said and sobbed again. "But I'll catch a fucking deer with my fucking fishing rod."

"Not everyone can say that," I said.

"Why would they want to?" He looked up at me crazy again, and broke his spinning rod into two pieces with only his hands. And I knew he must've been drunk still, because I was still drunk a little, and that by itself made me want to cry. And we were there for a time just silent.

"Who killed a deer?" Nola said. She had come behind me in the cold night and was looking. I had not known, when I heard the car door, if she wasn't walking back up to town. But it was too cold for that, and I put my arm around her because she was shivering. "Did Mr. Wheels kill it?" she said.

"It drowned," Troy said.

"And why is that?" Nola said and pushed closer to me to be warm, though that was all.

"They get weak, and they fall over," I said. "It happens in the mountains. This one fell in the water and couldn't get up."

"So a gimp man can catch it on a fishing rod in a shitty town," Troy said and gasped with bitterness again. Real bitterness. The worst I have ever heard from any man, and I have heard bitterness voiced, though it was a union matter then.

"Maybe it isn't so bad," Nola said.

"Hah!" Troy said loudly from the wet ground. "Hah, hah, hah." And I wished that I had never shown him the deer, wished I had spared him that, though the river's rushing came up then and snuffed his sound right out of hearing, and drew it away from us into the foggy night beyond all accounting.

Nola and I pushed the deer back into the river while Troy watched, and then we all three drove up into town and ate chicken-in-the-ruff at the Two-Fronts, where the lights were bright and they cooked the chicken fresh for you. I bought a jug of wine and we drank that while we ate, though no one talked much. Each of us had done something that night. Something different. That was plain enough. And there was nothing to talk about to make any difference.

When we were finished, we walked outside and I asked Nola where she would like to go. It was only eight o'clock, and there was no place to go but to my little room. She said she wanted to go back to the Top Hat, that she had someone to meet there later, and there was something about the band that night that she liked. She said she wanted to dance.

I told her I was not much for dancing, and she said fine. And when Troy came out from paying, we said good-bye, and she shook my hand and said that she would see me again. Then she and Troy got in the Checker and drove away together down the foggy street, leaving me alone, where I didn't mind being at all.

For a long time I just walked then. My clothes were wet, but it wasn't so cold if you kept moving, though it stayed foggy. I walked to the river again and across on the bridge and then a long way down into the south part of town, on a wide avenue where there were houses with little porches and little yards, all the way, until it became commercial, and bright lights lit the drive-ins and car lots. I could've walked then, I thought, clear to my mother's house twenty miles away. But I turned back, and walked the same way, only on the other side of the street. Though when I got near the bridge again, I came past the senior citizen recreation where there were soft lights on inside a big room, and I could see through a window in the pinkish glow, old people dancing across the floor to a record player that played in a corner. It was a rumba or something like a rumba that was being played, and the old people were dancing the box step, smooth and graceful and courteous, moving across the linoleum like real dancers, their arms on each other's shoulders like husbands and wives. And it pleased me to see that. And I thought that it was too bad my mother and father could not be here now, too bad they couldn't come up and dance and go home happy, and me to watch them. Or even for my mother and Harley Reeves, the wildcatter, to do that. It didn't seem like too much to wish for. Just a normal life other people had.

I stood and watched them awhile, and then I walked back home across the river. Though for some reason I could not sleep that night, and simply lay in bed with the radio turned on to Denver, and smoked cigarettes until it was light. Of course I thought about Nola Foster, that I didn't know where she lived, though for some reason I thought she might live in Frenchtown, out Route 20 west, near the pulp plant. Not far. Never-never land, they called that. And I thought about my father, who had once gone to Deer Lodge prison for stealing hay from a friend, and had never recovered from it, though that meant little to me now.

And I thought about the matter of trust. That I would always lie if it would save someone an unhappiness. That was easy. And that I would rather a person mistrusted me than dislike me. Though still, I thought, you could always trust me to act a certain way, to be a place, or to say a thing if it ever were to matter. You could predict within human reason what I'd do, that I would not, for example, commit a vicious crime, trust that I would risk my own life for you if I knew it meant enough. And as I lay in the gray light, smoking, while the refrigerator clicked and the switcher in the Burlington Northern yard shunted cars and made their couplings, I thought that though my life at that moment seemed to have taken a bad turn and paused, it still meant something to me as a life, and that before long it would start again in some promising way.

I know I must've dozed a little, because I woke suddenly and there was the light. Earl Nightengale was on the radio, and I heard a door close. It was that that woke me.

I knew it would be Troy, and I thought I would step out and meet him, fix coffee for us before he went to bed and slept all day, the way he always did. But when I stood up I heard Nola Foster's voice. I could not mistake that. She was drunk. And she was laughing about something. "Mr. Wheels," she said. Mr. Wheels this, Mr. Wheels that. Troy was laughing. And I heard them come in the little entry, heard Troy's chair bump the sill. And I waited to see if they would knock on my door. And when they didn't, and I heard Troy's door shut and the chain go up, I thought that we had all had a good night finally. Nothing had happened that hadn't turned out all right. None of us had been harmed. And I put on my pants, then my shirt and shoes, turned off my radio, went to the kitchen, where I kept my fishing rod, and with it went out into the warm, foggy morning, using just this once the back door, the quiet way, so as not to see or be seen by anyone.

ELIZABETH TALLENT

WHY I LOVE COUNTRY MUSIC

Nod is a miner. He has long dark hair and owns probably a hundred different pairs of overalls; he likes to go dancing in cowboy bars. Because he weighs about two hundred pounds and is no taller than I am—about five feet four in my bare feet—the sight of Nod, dancing, has been known to arouse the kind of indignation in the hearts of cowboys that, in New Mexico, can be dangerous to the arouser. Cowboys in slanting hats—not only their Stetsons, in fact, but often their eyes are slanting, and the cigarettes stuck in one corner of their mouths, the ash lighting only with the brief, formal intake of each breath—watch Nod dancing with the slight contemptuous smiles with which they slice off a bull calf's genitals on hot afternoons in July. The genitals themselves are plums buried in soft pouches made of cat's fur; if you are not quick with the small knife the scrotum slides between your fingers, contracting against the calf's ermine-slick black belly, the whites of its eyes almost phosphorescent with fear. The cowboys—with what seems to me an unnecessary lack of tact—often feed the remains to the chickens. Sometimes, living in the desert, you understand the need for an elaborate code of ritual laws; without them, the desert makes you an accomplice in all kind of graceless crimes. They are not even crimes of passion—they are crimes of expediency, small reckonings made in the spur of the moment before the white chickens boil around the rim of the bloody, dented bucket.

"Want to go dancing?" Nod says. It is still early and he has just called. I stare at the picture on the wall by the phone: my ex-husband, standing up to his knees in a stream, holding a trout. In the picture my husband is wearing a dark T-shirt, and the water in the stream is the color of iodine. Only the trout is silver. "That job came through," Nod says. "The one in Texas, you remember? It put me in a bad mood. I want to go sweat out my anguish in a dim-lit bar. And it's Saturday night and you're a lonely woman with love on her mind. Come with me. You've got nothing else to do."

I pause. It is true, I'm not doing anything else: on the television in the other room a long-haired Muppet with a quizzical expression is banging on a black toy piano with a toy hammer. My ex-husband is in Oregon. The trout, when he had opened it, was full of beautiful parallel bones. I was amazed by the transparency of the bones, and the fact that they had been laid down so perfectly inside the fish, lining the silvery gash of its intestines. My husband was pleased that I was taking such an interest in the trout. "This is an art," he said. He showed me the minnow he had found, perfectly whole, inside the belly cavity. The minnow had tiny, astonished eyes. I wanted to put it in water. He refused. He wrapped it in a scrap of newspaper and threw it away. "It was *dead,*" he told me. When he finally called me from Oregon, I could hear a woman singing in the background. My husband pretended it was the radio.

Nod waits a moment longer. "Come on," he says. "I already told you I'm in a bad mood. I don't want to wait around on the phone all night."

"Why are you in a bad mood?" I counter. "Most people would be in a good mood if their job had just come through."

"Coal mining always put me in a bad mood," Nod says. "Now get dressed and let's go to the Line Camp. I'll be at your house in twenty minutes."

I hang up the phone and go into the other room to get dressed, pulling on my Calvin Klein jeans while the long-haired Muppet sings "The Circle Song."

The cowboys, leaning against the left-hand wall as you go in, look you over with the barest movement of the eye, the eyelid not even contracting, the pupil dark through the haze of cigarette smoke, the mouth downcurved, the silent shifting of the pelvis against the wall by which one signals a distant quickening of erotic possibility. The band is playing "Whiskey River." My white buckskin cowboy boots—I painted the roses myself, tracing the petals from a library book—earn me a measure of serious consideration, the row of Levi-shaded pelvises against the wall swiveling slightly (they can swagger standing still, for these are the highest of their art, O men) as I go by, the line of cigarettes flicking like the ears of horses left standing in the rain, movement for the sake of movement only. The cowboys stand, smoking, staring out at the dance floor. Everyone who comes in has to pass by them. My hair has been brushed until it gleams, my lips are dark with costly gels. I pay my five dollars. Nod follows me. He pays his five dollars. The man at the card table, collecting the money, has curly sideburns that nearly meet under his chin. He whistles under his breath, so softly I can't tell whether it is "Whiskey River" or something else. He keeps the money in a fishing-tackle box, quarters and dimes in the metal compartments that should have held coiled line, tiny amber flies. The cowboys shift uneasily against the wall. Nod graces them with a funereal sideways miner's glance, the front of his overalls decorated with an iron-on sticker of Mickey Mouse, giving the peace sign. There is one like it on the dashboard of his jeep. Nod is nostalgic for Mickey Mouse cartoons, which I do not remember. Fingers in their jeans, the cowboys watch us like the apostles confronted with the bloody, slender wrists: horror, the shyest crease of admiration, hope.

In Nod's arms I feel, finally, safe: a twig carried by lava, a moth clinging to the horn of a bull buffalo. Nod, you see, thinks I am beautiful—a beautiful woman—and that in itself is an uplifting experience. Nod is, for the most part, oddly successful with women; he has been married twice, both times to women you would think, if not beautiful, at least strikingly good-looking. Nod faltered through his second divorce, eking out his unemployment with food stamps, too depressed to look for work. He listened to Emmylou Harris records day and night in his bare apartment; his second wife had taken everything, even the aloe vera. In the end, Nod says, it was "Defying Gravity" that saved him. He had the sudden revelation that there were always other women, deeper mines. He got dressed for the first time in months and sent a resumé to Peabody Coal. Peabody Coal, Nod claims, knows how to appreciate a man who has a way with plastic explosives. Don't they use dynamite anymore? I asked him. Nod grinned. Dynamite, he said, is the missionary position of industrial explosives; some men won't try anything else. He described the way explosives are placed against a rock face; in the end it often comes down to a matter of intuition, he said. You just *know* where it should go. Now, in the half-dark of the Line Camp dance floor, Nod is not unattractive. I imagine him closing his eyes, counting. (Do they still count?) No matter how many times you have seen it before, Nod says, when you see rock explode it still surprises you.

He holds me tightly, we move around the floor. Night washes the Tesuque valley in cold shadow, the moon rises, the eyes of the men along the wall glint seductively behind their Camels. In the mountains the last snow of the year is falling. On the stage, the harmonica player's left hand flutters irritably, as if he were fanning smoke from his eyes; his mouth puckers and jumps along the perforated silver, anemone flow of sound rising and falling above the whine of the pedal steel. The lead singer is blond and holds the microphone close to her teeth. She is wearing a blue satin shirt, the beaded fringe above the breasts causing her nipples to rise expecantly in dark ovals the size of wedding rings.

"Aren't they fine?" Nod says. He is pleased. He sweeps me around in a tight, stylish circle, my boots barely touching the floor. Around us women dance with their eyes closed, their fingernails curving against plaid or embroidered cowboy shirts, their thoughts—who can have thoughts, in this music?—barely whispered. At the end of the set couples separate from each other slowly. There is a smattering of applause. Everyone's face looks pale and slightly shocked. A couple in a corner near the band's platform continue dancing as if nothing had happened. The woman is several inches taller than the man, who is wearing, above his black bolo tie, a huge turquoise cut in the shape of Texas. The woman gazes straight ahead into the air above the man's slick black hair. It is very quiet. Around us people are moving away, to tables, to the bar against the far wall. Nod takes me by the hand. Someone unplugs the cord of the microphone. The harmonica player is left standing alone in the light, talking to himself. He cleans the spit from his instrument with a white handkerchief so old it is nearly transparent.

In the parking lot Nod lets go of my hand. Around us headlights are coming on like the lamps of a search party—dust rising from white gravel, the sound of many car doors slamming in pairs. Nod turns me around, kissing me. Ahead of us a tall girl in a white skirt patterned with flamingos is walking on pink platform shoes, singing to herself in a voice blurred with fatigue. The skirt blows apart around her thighs; she stumbles. Nod takes her gently by the elbow. The three of us walk together to the end of the parking lot, where there is a black van with the words "Midnight Rider" painted in silver across the doors. The windows are round and seem to be made of black glass; there is a sound of drumming from within. When Nod knocks, a man gets out of the van, taking hold of the tall girl—she is still singing, her head thrown back, her eyes now tightly closed. She seems indifferent to his grasp. The man nods to us; he has a light scar across one corner of his mouth which makes him seem to be smiling ironically. He balances against the van, shifting the weight of the girl against him so that she falls inside. The floor of the interior is covered with a dark red-and-black rug. The girl lies on her side; her voice is muffled by the blond hair that has fallen across her face. The man shuts the door. He looks at us and touches the scar with one finger. "She knows the song," he says, "but not the words."

The cowboys had seen us leave together. There was this, which might have been considered an incident: a blond cowboy with a narrow mustache—it seemed to be longer on one side of his mouth than the other—kissed me on the nape of the neck as I went by him on my way to the bathroom. It was a very fast kiss and his expression never changed. The kiss left a circle of evaporation on my skin, cold as a snowflake. It was, I understood, an experiment. In the other room, far away, the guitarist rasped out a few chords, tightened his strings, rasped again, fell silent. He seemed to be taking a long while tuning his guitar. The lead singer hummed comforting sounds into the microphone: one, two, three, foah—

We stood for a moment, staring at each other. This always happens to me when I am confronted with a cowboy in a shadowed hallway; it has to do with having watched too many Lone Ranger matinees during a long and otherwise uninteresting midwestern adolescence. I thought of those Saturday afternoons, looking at him; I thought of the long white mane foaming against those black gloves, the eyes barely visible behind the mask, the steely composure in the face of evil and uncertainty. I tried for a few moments to summon my own steely composure. The cowboy leaned against the wall, cocking one shoulder jauntily. My steely composure had been abandoned somewhere between the second tequila sunrise and the third, and now it was hopelessly lost. The cowboy stared at me. I hoped that I emanated a kind of cool innocence. I understood that cool innocence ran a poor second to steely composure. His eyes were gray, his fingers in his jeans pockets, knuckles riding the ridge of the hip bone, no wedding ring (good sign). Coors belt buckle (bad sign: cliché). Boots of dark suede with tall slanting heels (good sign). Gray eyes (neutral). Slight smile (very good sign: he is not pressing the issue, neither is he willing just to let it drop). I stood there, thinking about it.

He looked at me. I looked at him. My shoulders—one shoulder only if I am to be utterly truthful—lifted of its own accord. A shrug.

He watched me as I walked away. Out of the corner of my eye I could still see him. He shook his head vaguely, stood and strolled down to the end of the hall, walking with real grace on his tall, scuffed heels. The jukebox was indigo and silver and there was a framed photograph of Loretta Lynn on the wall above it. He stood and looked at Loretta Lynn for a few moments, cocking his head like a bank clerk trying to decipher a blurred check. Loretta Lynn, it was clear, would not have refused him. He eased a quarter from his pocket, pressed several of the numbered buttons, and waited. When nothing happened, he leaned forward and nudged the jukebox suddenly with his hip. I could hear the coin drop from where I stood.

The door to the women's room says "Fillies." Inside there was a fat lady powdering her nose; she watched me from the corner of her eye. Tonight, I thought, everyone is watching everyone from the corners of their eyes. I closed the door and latched it. I could hear the fat woman sigh deeply as she clicked her compact shut.

Nod would have been a diamond miner if there had been any diamonds in New Mexico: he only missed it by a continent. He could have been in South Africa, supervising the long-fingered black men in the dank caverns, if his father hadn't been a physicist in Los Alamos. But he was, and Nod regrets it. Diamonds, he says, think of that, coming out of the earth, thinking hard, now that would be *something,* the first human being to touch a *diamond.* Of course they don't look like diamonds right away, but you can tell. In South Africa the men dig hunched over—it is "uneconomic," in the words of the mining companies, to dig away enough earth for the men to stand upright, the traditional vertical posture of *Homo sapiens,* but not, it seems, of miners. So the miners of diamonds remain for years in their position of enforced reverence, on their knees. The depths of the earth are open to them, the glinting, ancient lights buried within are retrieved and sold, only to end up on the fingers of virgins in fraternity house basements.

The night had clouded over, leaving only the moon, which followed us from behind. Nod was driving. The Toyota jeep bucked in second gear over the narrow, stony road. Below us on the left was an abyss filled with the looming, lightning-struck tips of ponderosa pines, wind stroking through the heavy branches until they roared. Occasionally a single branch glittered in the moonlight. I stared down at my boots. I had placed them carefully, toe by toe, out of the way of the gear shift. Now the toes seemed remote, indifferent as the pointed skulls of lizards. I was very tired. "No," Nod said, rubbing a clear space in the mist that covered the windshield. "That light you see over there, *that's* the moon." I looked. It was bright as a flying saucer, cold and white, full of intelligent life.

When we got to the end of the road Nod parked the jeep, pulling out the handbrake. He stood at the entrance to the mine, his hands thrust into the pockets of his overalls, looking down. "This whole mountain is honeycombed with mines," he said. I did not feel reassured. He bent and threw a small stone into the interior. It made a very small chink, like a ring tapped against a mirror. "This is one of the oldest," Nod said. "Look how they cut the wood for those braces. Look at the craftsmanship in those notches. Those fuckers are going to last a thousand years." I looked. I could see nothing except darkness.

"Smell the coal," Nod said.

He went back to the jeep for a light. Nod always carries rare and useful things in his jeep: a bottle of Algerian wine, a blanket, a light. He drove the jeep a few more feet forward so that the headlights glared down into the entrance of the mine; this was so we could find our way out. The light grew lazy only a few feet from the front of the jeep. The jeep itself seemed mystically beautiful—a lost island, an airplane after you have just jumped out.

"Minotaur," I sang out. "Come home. Ally-ally-ox-in-free." Nod laughed. I was more than a little drunk.

"We always said it different," he said. "We always used to say, 'Ally-ally-in-come-free.' " He ran the light down the curved walls. The walls were dark and seemed to have been chiseled; the light barely touched them. We did not go far. "Here," Nod said. He got down on his knees. The earth at the floor of the shaft seemed raw and gemmy, as if it had never quite healed. Nod's shadow swept along the walls. He took off his overalls and stepped away from them lightly. Barefoot, he swung the beam of the flashlight in my direction.

"Nod," I said. "Take the damn light out of my eyes."

"I love you," he said. He turned the light off. I could hear nothing. No sound from Nod. No matches in the pockets of my jeans. I cursed heatedly: the cowboy, Nod, the darkness, the mine, Algerian wine, the full moon, Calvin Klein.

"Find me," he said, out of the darkness.

I wished for a long moment that I was with the cowboy, fucking in the back of his International on an old Mexican blanket smelling of dog hair, between bales of pink-yellow hay.

"Nod," I said. "It's dark, it's cold. I'm tired. Do you want to make love or do you want to fuck around all night?"

(The idea suddenly of his agile two-hundred-pound mass moving naked down the gleam-wet corridors forever and ever.)

I lay down on the blanket. I took off my boots. "Ally-ally-in-come-free," I said. He was very drunk. Suppose he got lost, how would I ever find him? "Ally-ally-come-home-free," I called. The wine bottle tipped cool against my spine. I lifted it, held it against my cheek for the comfort of a solid object in the darkness. "You damn well better get your ass *over* here," I screamed. I waited. If he was anywhere near at all he could hear my crying.

When he came from the darkness he was different: he had small curved horns, yellow tipped with ebony, and his eyes were dark in the centers, ringed all the way around with startled white, his forehead covered with ringlets damp as a rock star's. He stared at me. I stared at him.

For a long while neither of us moved. In the light from the headlights small motes of dust danced around his horns.

"It's a lovely trick, Nod," I said. "How long have you had that thing hidden down here?"

I stood up and pulled down my jeans, tripping slightly in the process. I laid them in the corner of the blanket near my cowboy boots, feeling for the bottle again in the darkness. I held it up for him to see. He stood with his mouth half-open.

"What the hell is the matter with you?" I said. "Haven't you ever seen a naked woman before?"

He took a small step toward me. I undid my shirt, one button at a time. "I want you, O.K.?" I said. "Nod, is that what you wanted me to say? I want you. Come over here, Nod. I want you right now." He came toward me, lowering his head. He was not clumsy. Miners never are, in the dark.

Nod, like all true heroes, left in the morning for Austin. He had written down my address on the side of a carton packed full of old copies of *National Geographic*. His cat, asleep on a pile of dirty overalls in the back of the jeep, opened one eye and regarded me coldly. She was not jealous, Nod said. She just disliked being looked at while she was trying to sleep; anyone would. Nod had on a pair of immaculate white overalls over a striped T-shirt. There was a red ceramic heart pinned to the front of the overalls. He had curled the *Rand McNally Road Atlas* into a tube in his left hand, and now he swung it idly, as if it were a baseball bat. His eyes were veiled.

"I'll bring you a diamond," Nod said. "If I find any."

Of course, I thought he was lying.

I told this story to my analyst. Her hair is thick and curly and she sits in a white wicker chair in a sunny front room, listening to God knows what and nodding her head. In one corner of the room there is an old wooden carousel horse. When she first started practicing in her own house, she thought of

moving the horse into another room. The horse has faded blue
eyes, a pure, vacant stare, small curved ears. Think of the
dizzying moments that horse has known—small girls kissing its
ears, caramel vomited across its flanks, a distant smell of mountains. Every single one of her clients protested when she moved
the horse. She had to bring it back. These are crazy people? I
thought. Once, when she thought I could not hear, she made
a phone call. The conversation concerned another client. The
session she had had with this client must have disturbed her.
She whispered into the telephone.

"What is the professional term for someone who eats dirt?"
she whispered. She wrote the word down on a small yellow pad.

She must have known it, and forgotten. Here is someone,
telling her the story of how, as a child, he had eaten dirt, and
here she is, in her white wicker chair, nodding gently, knowing
she can't think of the word. When my husband calls from Oregon, the static sounds like sand blowing across glass. Against
the static I can make out a baby's crying. He asks how I am. I
ask how he is. We are both fine. I count how many months it
is that he has been gone; he pretends the baby crying is a
Pampers commercial.

A small brown paper box from Austin. The UPS man who
handed it to me looked at me queerly because my face was
painted. The neighbors' children had been here, and we all
painted our faces together. Mine is gorgeous—dark gold, indigo.
Silver false eyelashes. The little girl next door has promised to
invest her allowance in a box of Fake Nails. The UPS man does
not know what to say, handing me his slate. The pencil is
attached to the slate by a small beaded chain. His truck—the
same color as his uniform—ticks distantly in my driveway.

"Is it going to go off?" I ask.

He pretends not to get it. His name is stitched over his pocket,
approximately where his left nipple would be, and below that,
his heart. Alan. Alan leaves me the box. He shifts the gears in
his truck and drives slowly away.

I open the box.

The earth inside smells dusky, rich. There is no message. I lift it, sifting the dirt between my fingers, sniffing. I even taste a little, hoping it will taste foreign and rare, like imported chocolate. It is only faintly sour. Perhaps a square foot of dirt. It will take me all night, I think. I dig through it softly, trying to feel with the insides of my fingers as well as the tips, the way I imagine a mole feels things with the damp pink skin of its nose, its body cloistered, remote. Certain nuns are not even allowed to see the priest, they receive the sacraments through tiny jeweled windows, in darkness. Only the hand, the whisper, the little piece of bread. "Nod," I whisper. The name goes no farther than the smoke from a match. The dirt feels good, it crusts against my fingers beneath the nails. I rub a small clod against my teeth, like a child toying with an aspirin, letting it dissolve into separate bitter grains. I lift two handfuls and finger the dry clumps, breaking the soft clods apart, watching them fall.

ROBERT MAYER

THE SYSTEM

FROM *MIDGE & DECKER*

LAND OF ENCHANTMENT
LAND OF ENCHANTMENT
LAND OF ENCHANTMENT
LIVE FREE OR DIE
LAND OF ENCHANTMENT
GRAND CANYON STATE
FAMOUS POTATOES
LAND OF ENCHANTMENT
LAND OF ENCHANTMENT

There were 1,628 cars in the parking lots. (Valet parking, $1.50. Preferred parking, $1. General parking, 50 cents.) That was not an exact count but Midge's best guess. She wished you could bet on the number of cars in the parking lots. It would be more scientific than betting on the races.

Only one car was occupied besides theirs. FAMOUS POTA-TOES, the car in front of them. Inside FAMOUS POTATOES a fat, sloppy brown-and-white St. Bernard was squeezed in the back seat, its huge head in the rear window pointed straight at Midge. Its eyes were closed and its tongue was hanging out, pale pink, spotted with saliva.

Across the parking lots the warm metal voice of the track announcer drifted fuzzily. "The horses are entering the track for the running of the ninth and feature race, the Fiesta Classic."

The voice sounded as if it had its back turned. It sounded also as if it had taken a Fiesta drink.

The St. Bernard in FAMOUS POTATOES did not stir. The St. Bernard in FAMOUS POTATOES did not seem to hear the track announcer. The St. Bernard in FAMOUS POTA-TOES appeared to have died of heat stroke five minutes before.

"Decker?"

"What?"

"Can't we go in now?"

"You heard 'im."

Decker did not look at her as he spoke. He stared straight ahead through the fractured windshield with those crazy eyes of his.

Midge lifted the can of sugar-free Dr Pepper to her mouth and let the last warm drop sweeten her tongue. She set the can on the seat between them, alongside her tissues, and hunched forward against the steering wheel, raising herself slightly to unstick her purple pants from the pillow.

"Can't you sit still!" Decker said. His eyes flicked at her with annoyance.

"It's hot in here," she said.

He turned back to the windshield. The sun catching the edges of the cracks slashed at the eye like razors. Decker seemed to be staring the razors down. Then, without blinking, he drank from his can of Coors. It was his second can. He didn't seem to care that it was warm.

"Why don't you get a cooler?" she had said to him once, way back in July.

"With what money? The Frenchies drink warm beer all the time. That's what's wrong with you, you ain't got any class. Stick with me and maybe I'll teach ya some class."

She hadn't mentioned it again.

She hunched forward and adjusted the pillow. She was four feet eleven inches tall and needed the pillow to see over the dashboard, over the steering wheel. It was her car but Decker hardly ever let her drive. Driving was a man's job, he said. Except on the way to the race track. Then he insisted that she drive. On the way to the race track a man likes to have a chauffeur.

Perched high on her pillow—once solid pink, it was stained now in the shape of interesting butterflies by assorted fluids—she began to read the license plates again. Most were local, Santa Fe plates, or Albuquerque. But there were also in the row in front of them a SUNSHINE STATE, a FASTEN SEAT BELTS, and four different GRAND CANYON STATEs. Probably because of the big race tomorrow. The Arizona horse.

"Decker."

"What?"

"You see that dog up there?"

"What about it?"

"I think it's dead."

"I know."

He drank a slug of beer.

"Shouldn't we do something about it?"

"What do you want to do? It's dead."

She chewed her bottom lip. He was right. That's what she admired about Decker. His intellect.

She looked at his profile as he stared down the slits of sun: his black hair cut short, his flat nose, his strong jaw and pro-truding jaw muscles that never stopped working, bunching, committing some unseen task, as if he were chewing gum or tobacco, except that he rarely chewed gum and never tobacco. Her blouse—the lucky one, yellow with a green elephant on the pocket, the one she had been wearing the night he knocked on the door—was sticking to her back, was soaking wet under the arms, but Decker wasn't even sweating. He never sweated, he seemed incapable of it.

"How come you never sweat?" she had asked him once, in a tangle of twisted sheets, their second or third night together.

"My father was a snake," he said.

She had shivered, her sweat had turned cold, she had dried

up instantly. She had cried with pain as he forced her nonetheless. Afterward he had taken off his T-shirt and shown her
the tattoos on his upper arms. The word MOM on one arm. A
spitting snake on the other.

Midge picked up the warm can of Dr Pepper and held it to
her lips and leaned her head back as far as she could. All she
got was warm air. She crossed her eyes on the can, her Adam's
apple exposed. Decker, who thought he was a champion stud,
could never make her reach any mountaintops. Not the kind
she had read about in *Fury's Savage Sweetness*. She didn't know
why she even stayed with him.

She put the can on the seat again. She knew why she stayed
with him.

The slurred voice of the track announcer curled across the
parking lots again: "It's post time."

"Now?" Midge said.

"Now."

She pushed open the door and, holding the pillow down with
one hand, slid out of the car. The door creaked shut behind
her. She had to wait while Decker uncoiled the twisted wire
that held the passenger door closed, and got out, and lifted the
door back into place, and wired it closed again, kicking it as he
did. She crossed in front of the car, looking sadly at the huge
head of the St. Bernard in the back window of FAMOUS PO-
TATOES. The head didn't move but the two eyes blinked.

Decker hadn't waited for her. He was already ten steps toward
the concrete walkway that split the dirt and gravel field that
was general parking. Midge had to run to catch up to him.

She felt hurt. She had been crossing in front of the car to
take his hand. She put it out of her mind. Feeling hurt would
only cause trouble.

"Hey, Decker," she said, still two steps behind him, a bit
breathless.

"What?"

"You know that dog?"

He didn't answer.

"It ain't dead."

"It's dead," he said, as she caught up beside him and took his hand.

"It ain't," she said. "I saw it blink."

"So what?"

"So nothing. It ain't dead, that's all."

Decker took his hand away and rubbed his jaw muscles. An excuse, she knew. When he put his hand down again he didn't want it held.

As they walked in silence she looked at the cars broiling in every direction, like a drive-in movie with no picture playing. Endless cars from the concrete grandstand to the place where the track railing curved away, gleaming white. Behind the track across the pale desert she could see the state prison with its squat brown buildings and its tall steel water tower, set in the middle of nowhere. Just like the track was set. Far beyond the parking lots, at the end of the highway, the mountains rolled up like blue waves. Santa Fe was at the bottom of the mountains. She couldn't see it from here.

"One thousand six hundred and twenty-eight," she said.

"What?"

"Cars."

"Jesus H. Christ!"

"That's a lot, huh," she said. She was pleased by his rare enthusiasm.

Decker spat on the sidewalk.

"That's not what I meant," he said. "I meant Jesus H. Christ, can't you ever shut up."

She let him get a few steps ahead of her. From the track they could hear the crowd yelling at the ninth race.

Midget, he used to call her, when they first got together in June. Midget. Just because she was small. Eighty-seven and three-quarter pounds, to be exact. Four feet eleven inches exactly. She was happy with her size, she couldn't imagine herself being any other size. She had let him call her Midget for a week, afraid to tell him she didn't like it. Then one night, in bed, she had cried.

"Whatsa matter?" he said.

"I'm not a midget," she said. "I don't like being called a midget. My name is Beatrice."

He had stroked her hair, tender as he sometimes was back then.

"I know your name," he said. "I just say Midget 'cause I like you."

"I know," she said, sniffling through her tears. "But I'd rather be called Beatrice."

His tenderness had faded. He had swung his legs off the bed and sat on the edge in his Jockey shorts.

"I can't," he said. "I can't be seen with no Beatrice. I'd be a laughingstock. It's bad enough . . ."

He didn't finish the sentence.

A laughingstock with who, she wanted to say. We ain't never gone out with nobody but ourselves. But she didn't say it. She sniffled again, and turned over and rubbed her nose in the pillow.

For several minutes neither of them moved. Then he touched her back, her shoulder, and said: "Midge?"

With its own sweet will her whole body curved into a smile, cupped and joyous and waiting. She turned her head on the pillow to look at him.

"Is that okay?" he said.

She gazed at him with half-closed eyes, her best seductive look. And nodded.

"And nobody will know nothing else?"

She nodded again, could not stop her smile, turned in the bed to face him.

"No. Turn over," he said. "The way you was before—Midge."

The way he liked it.

It didn't matter. She understood.

As they crossed into the shadow of the grandstand she was sweating under her arms, in the small of her back, at the rec-

ollection of that night, of what had happened since, sweating
in sympathy with the extended Santa Fe summer, still 81 degrees
now at 4:57 P.M. (to be exact), Friday, September second, the
start of the long Labor Day weekend when an estimated 512
people would be killed on the nation's highways, the radio had
said in the morning.

"Four hundred ninety-eight," she said.

"What?"

"Nothing."

Sweating at the uncertain future that was growing inside her.
At what Decker wanted her to do.

He pulled open the wooden door to the grandstand. The lobby
was cool and dark. A roar went up from the crowd as the tote
board posted the results of the photo finish in the ninth race.
The track announcer's voice boomed like God over the roar:
"The winner—number three, Fair Change. Second—number
one, Go Lightly. Third—number four, Ampersand. Time of the
race—one-oh-nine and two-fifths."

"Jeez," Midge said.

"Jeez what?"

"That's two-fifths off the track record."

Decker looked at her for the first time since they had left
the car.

"How the hell do you know that?"

"Wanna bet?" she said.

"You and your numbers," he said, and turned away.

He looked toward the turnstiles. The two girls in their red
blouses were still sitting there. He couldn't imagine what was
wrong. The ninth race was over. Why didn't they leave? After
the ninth race you didn't have to pay a dollar. After the ninth
race you could get in free. See the last three races for free.
Decker was no fool. Every Friday, Saturday, and Sunday, all
summer long, they had come out after the ninth race. Without
one cent wasted on admission.

But what was wrong now? Had they changed the policy because of the holiday weekend?

The bastards!

Then he saw the man from upstairs come by, the sleeves of his white shirt rolled up, wearing his bolo tie, and nod to the girls. The girls slid off their stools and walked away. The turnstiles were empty. The man from upstairs looked across, and smiled and waved at Decker and Midge. Decker's face burned. He cursed under his breath. He hated the man to see them, to know they came in free every time. Even though there was nothing wrong with it. That's why he insisted they sit in the parking lot till the last minute. So the man would be gone. It was the damn photo finish that had delayed him.

"C'mon," Decker said, after the man had left.

Midge didn't respond. He turned to look at her, and for a moment he didn't see her. Then he spotted her bending down near the far wall, picking up a betting ticket that someone had thrown away.

"A five," she said as she approached.

They pushed through the turnstiles. A Spanish couple, the man small and tanned, the woman quite heavy in red slacks, were walking toward the exit. Decker confronted them with his needle eyes.

"You need your program?" he said.

The man shrugged, looked at his wife, and handed Decker the program.

"That, too," Decker said.

The man handed over his folded copy of the *Daily Racing Form*. Decker took it without a word and moved inside. A program cost seventy-five cents. A *Racing Form* cost a buck and a half.

"Thanks," Midge said to the couple, and she hurried after him into the grandstand. It was more crowded than usual for a Friday, because of the holiday weekend. The city would be jammed to bursting for Fiesta. Midge could hardly wait for the burning of Zozobra that night. The burning of Old Man Gloom. Her third favorite night of the year, after Christmas and Miss America. Much more exciting, certainly, than New Year's Eve.

She followed Decker to the bar, where he bought himself a paper container of beer, and followed him down an aisle between the crowded seats, to the sloping concrete area that led to the rail. People, men and women both, were standing about, talking or studying their racing forms, making marks on them with ballpoint pens or pencils. Small children were running about, unnoticed. Decker had his program and his racing form sticking conspicuously out of the back pocket of his black pants, as if he had been up all night figuring out the winners, and had made his choices then, and could now relax with his beer.

"Well, whattaya waitin' for?" he said.

Midge was standing to the right and slightly in front of him, looking across the desert-dry infield. It would be nice, she thought, if they planted some flowers there.

"Get with it," Decker said.

He shoved her in the small of the back. She stumbled forward several steps, and caught her balance. She turned and looked back at him with anger and hurt. Then she turned again, and began to scan the ground. She saw a discarded betting ticket and picked it up, and she looked some more and found another ticket and picked it up. She moved across the concrete space that way, a small woman in and among the taller people, bending down, sometimes right beside their shoes, to pick up every ticket she could find. She wished she had never told Decker about the system.

It had been back in July, when things were going good. The welfare people had gotten her a job with the state for the summer months. The Health Services Department, it was called. After a few days—after he quit his week-old dishwashing job—Decker had asked how she liked it. They were drinking soda pop and eating bologna sandwiches in the kitchen of the trailer her brother let her use when he was busted.

"It's real interesting," Midge said. "We get the plague here every summer in New Mexico. From germs carried by fleas, which live on mice and squirrels and prayer dogs and such. If the flea bites a person, they could die. So they got to keep checkin' up, to see if the plague is around. They do that by settin' up traps out in the desert, and in the bushes and things. To catch squirrels and mice and rodents. Then they test them to see if they got the plague. To see where it's around. Me and some other people, we go and set the traps and catch the animals. We wear these rubber gloves so we don't get bit."

Decker had stopped eating, and was staring at her with disgust.

"You got to tell me that during dinner?"

"You asked me," she said, looking down at the table.

"Yeah," he said. "I guess I did." Then, as if to make up, he said, "How many animals you bring in? Every day, I mean."

Midge brightened. "Fifteen, sixteen. Sometimes twenty. It depends. They got other people doing it too."

Decker pointed his thumb and forefinger toward the counter near the sink, and pulled the trigger of an imaginary gun. "Fix me another sandwich," he said. Then he quickly stood up. "Never mind, I'll fix it myself."

Midge caught on right away. "What's the matter, you afraid I got the plague?"

Decker looked at her. Almost as if he was capable of being hurt himself. "Hey, what do you think I am?" he said.

Midge smiled. She felt as if she were married.

He came back with his sandwich and set it on the Formica table. "Thing I don't understand," he said. "There's thousands of little animals out there, right? Maybe millions. They catch fifteen, twenty a day that ain't got the plague, there could be a million more out there that do, and they wouldn't know nothing about it. Sounds like another one of them government moondoggles to me."

Midge finished chewing her last bite and wiped her mouth with a green paper towel. She was flattered by his interest. Most of the men her brother told to look her up, they didn't come back a second time.

"It's the law of averages," she said.

Decker squinted at her. She couldn't tell if it was admiration or disapproval. Decker disapproved of most laws.

"Go on," he said.

"They told us all about it when we started. Seems if you catch enough animals in the right places, it's called a scientific sample. If enough animals out in the desert has got the plague fleas, enough to make it a danger, then some of them will get caught in the traps. It's the law of averages."

She could tell he wasn't convinced.

"They told us it's like with a penny," she said. "You toss up heads or tails, maybe it comes up heads. You toss up again, it should come up tails. Fifty-fifty. Only it don't have to. It could be heads two times in a row. But you keep tossing up, maybe ten times, it's got to come up tails pretty soon. It's just got to. It's the law of averages."

Decker took a small, thoughtful bite of his second sandwich. They let the subject drop. But in the middle of the night, the lights of the trailer park squaring the darkness of the shade, he shook her awake. She became aroused almost instantly.

"Listen," he said. "About that law of averages. You think it could work at a race track?"

She rubbed her eyes, trying to wake herself up. Wondering how her breath smelled. Not that Decker seemed to care.

"What do you mean?"

He was sitting up in the bed, the sheet covering his middle. It seemed as if he'd been sitting that way for a while.

"If there's eight numbers," he said. "Post positions. And the record shows they all come in about the same number of times every year. Then that should keep on happening, right? The law of averages?"

"Right," Midge said.

She couldn't see his eyes in the dark. She hiked up her nightgown and turned away from him. Ready.

They spent the next afternoon at The Downs, picking up all the discarded betting tickets they could find. Not looking for winning tickets that had been thrown away by mistake, as people must have assumed. There was no percentage in that. They got to the track after the ninth race, when admission was free, and picked up tickets that had been thrown away all day. Midge sorted them out, the ones, the twos, the threes, and so on. No matter which race they were from. When she counted them all up, they had more sixes than anything else. They had sixes from every race, which meant six hadn't won at all. Decker showed her the records in the program. It was just as he had said. Every number came up about the same number of times, the six as much as any other. So on the last race, the twelfth race, he bought a $2 win ticket on number six, Blue Lady.

The race was five and a half furlongs, which meant the starting gate was on the other side of the track. Midge had to stand on a bench to see it over the tote board. Number six was wearing yellow, the program said. A yellow shirt and a yellow cap. She could see it brightly as the horses broke from the gate, the red moving to the front, the green cutting across to second, then the white, the orange, the purple. The yellow had pulled to the rail, and was running last.

They watched as the horses moved into the turn, the red, the green, the white.

"The law of averages," she heard Decker mutter under his breath.

Then, as they came out of the turn, the yellow was moving up. It was fifth, then fourth. As they moved through the stretch it was third, and then it was alongside the leader, running neck and neck, the yellow and the red, the yellow and the red, and just as they reached the finish line the yellow seemed to leap ahead. A cute gray horse. Number six. Blue Lady.

The horse paid $14.20 to win. Decker leaned over and kissed Midge on the top of the head. He bought her dinner at McDonald's, and that night, when she turned away, he told her to turn back. He told her that he wanted to look at her.

They had returned to the track every Friday, Saturday, and Sunday afternoon since. After they lost a few bets, Decker

stopped picking up tickets. That became Midge's job alone. It
was her system, he said. Her back ached, she wanted to stop
doing it. But they won just often enough to keep him coming
back.

Bending to pick up another ticket, Midge felt that she should
hate Blue Lady. The filly who started it all. The pretty gray
horse with the blue ribbon braided into its tail. Who had won
five straight races since that day. Who would be in the big
match race the next afternoon, the Unicorn Handicap. A filly
against a colt. The best Santa Fe horse against the best Tucson
Park horse. The last big feature of the Santa Fe season, which
would be ending on Labor Day. But she knew she could never
hate Blue Lady. She loved Blue Lady. Who started everything.

If she could own a horse of her own, she would braid a ribbon
into its tail. A yellow ribbon, with a small green elephant attached. An elephant that didn't weigh too much.

She hurried over to Decker, to make sure he remembered.
He was starting on another beer. An erratic breeze had come
up and was swirling pale sand across the infield, like baby
tornados. It blew globs of foam off Decker's beer. They splattered messily on the pavement.

"What you got?" he said.

"I didn't count them yet."

"Why not?"

"You remember about tomorrow?" she said.

"What about it?"

"You promised we could pay to get in."

"The hell I did," he said, and drank from the paper cup, as
if to change the subject. Foam streaked his lips, oddly, like milk
on a child.

"You promised."

He drank again.

"Why should we do a fool thing like that?"

"So we can watch Blue Lady against that Arizona horse."

He took a long drink of the beer, finishing it, and crumpled the cup and tossed it on the ground. It seemed to hesitate for a moment, then let itself be carried off by a gust of wind.

"Blue Lady don't got a chance in hell against that Arizona horse. He'll beat her going away. You'll see."

She kissed his arm, near the elbow. She shuffled through the tickets in her hand, counting how many of each number.

"Not enough for a scientific sample," she said. "Be right back."

She moved away, scanning the ground, picking up more discarded tickets, chasing some across the area among the people's feet as they tossed and tumbled in the spinning breeze. A five, a six, a nine, a nine, a two. More and more tickets, to get a big sample. To find Decker a winner. All the while thinking about watching Blue Lady run. Paying their way in like everyone else. Wondering if she would bet. She had $2 hidden away in her elephant bank, just in case. She had never bet on anything before. Not ever. It was a waste of money, and she didn't have money to waste. She . . .

Then she got the best idea of her life.

She stopped picking up tickets. She thought and thought about it. The more she thought, the more the feeling of excitement grew inside her.

She counted the tickets and ran back to Decker, who was standing near the rail, watching the horses parade for the last race.

"Number four," she said, breathless. "On the nose."

Decker hurried off to bet. She waited by the rail, trying to calm herself. Rehearsing how to say it. Till Decker came back, carrying another beer.

"Give me a sip," she said.

He looked at her with surprise, but held the cup to her mouth. She took a sip, and wiped her lips with her sleeve. Her heart was racing like the horses, her knees were starting to shake. You bet $50 on a horse, she thought, it must feel just like this.

Her mouth was dry already, but she forced herself to speak.

"You don't think Blue Lady'll win tomorrow?"

A hint of little girl in her voice.

"No way," Decker said. "That Arizona horse will kill her. Fillies just can't keep up with colts. It's the same as with people."

She hesitated. With the plague season over, her job would end in a week. It would be back on welfare. One eleven a month. Unless Decker took a dishwashing job again.

She plunged ahead anyway.

"You pretty certain about that?"

"Damn certain," he said.

Just like a man. Not even guessing what she was driving at.

"You wouldn't want to bet on it, would you?"

He looked at her over the rim of the paper cup. That strange light that was there sometimes shining from his eyes.

"With you? What you got to bet? Your brother's trailer? That ratty old car?"

It's more than you got, she wanted to say. What you got to bet? My brother's trailer? My car? Or maybe that torn old bedroll you brought on out? But she didn't say any of those things. Together, that's how they had something. Together.

"You want to bet or don't you?" she said.

"How much?"

"What's it matter how much? You're so sure Blue Lady's gonna lose."

"I'll bet your ass," he said. "You name it."

She reached up and took the container of beer from him and drank a full gulp. The cold was good but the taste was bitter. She handed it back to him. She looked around to see if anybody was listening. Nobody was. There was a wide circle of space around them. People always seemed to allow them a wide circle of space.

"We'll bet the baby," she said.

His eyelids closed halfway, focusing the light. His jaw muscles throbbed faster.

"What are you talking about?"

She was feeling braver, now that the worst had been spoken. "If Blue Lady loses, I get it done next week, like I'm supposed. Like you want. But if Blue Lady wins, I keep the baby. And we get hitched."

Married. Why hadn't she said married, as she meant? No matter, she thought. Words don't matter at all.

Decker looked away, at the desert beyond the infield, at the penitentiary in the distance. He turned his back to her and looked up at the grandstand, at the upper deck, where the rich people sat in season boxes and ate sandwiches at tables with waitresses. The sun had sunk behind the grandstand, the breeze was starching his pants, and far down the highway the sky was gray. A storm was approaching.

"You're crazy," he said, turning to her again.

"What's the matter? You afraid you'll lose?"

He worked his jaw muscles, a pulsating nervousness building inside him. A thrilling kind of tension. The kind he used to feel driving the getaway.

"Well, yes or no?"

A bet for all time, Decker thought. To bet a life. Those rich people up in the box seats, they never made a bet like that. Even the owners of the horses. They never made a bet like that.

Besides. The Arizona horse couldn't lose.

"It's a deal," Decker said.

Midge licked the sweat on the edge of her harelip, to hide her smile. She stuck out her small hand.

"Shake," she said.

"Jesus H. Christ!"

The horses were entering the starting gate for the last race. Decker walked up toward the grandstand. A lot of people had left, to beat the traffic, to get a head start on Fiesta. He stood on a bench to have a better view of the race. To root home the four.

No need to worry about tomorrow, he told himself. The Arizona horse couldn't lose.

Besides. He could always skip town. It was getting about the time he should move along. It was getting about the time he should be alone.

Midge didn't follow him to the grandstand. She sat on the ground near the rail, her thin legs in her purple pants tucked under her. Across the dirt track the tote board loomed very large. She thought of saying a prayer, for Blue Lady. But she knew she didn't have to pray.

She had read the stories in the papers about Blue Lady. About that other big match race between a filly and a colt a few years ago. The filly was called Ruffian, and the colt was called Foolish Pleasure. Ruffian had broken a leg in the race, and had to be destroyed. Foolish Pleasure had won. That was the last such match race between a filly and a colt at a recognized track, the paper said. There had been nine such races in recorded racing history, the paper said, and the colt had beaten the filly every time. Nine times out of nine.

Midge untucked her legs and stretched out on the concrete. She extended her arms flat above her head and kicked off her sneakers and wiggled her toes. She looked up at the sky, at a bright patch of blue that was all she could see. She could tell people were watching her from a distance, giving her a wide circle of space, as always. She didn't care. She closed her eyes and let the wind and the dirt and the fading sun swirl over her, and kiss her face, her lips, again and again and again, as the pounding of the horses' hooves closed in.

ALAN PRENDERGAST
THE LAST MAN ALIVE

In the stories that are told about Claude Lafayette Dallas, Jr.,
he appears as many people. Cowboy, mountain man, fast-draw
artist, desperado, dreamer of the Western dream—the authorities, the lawyers, and the reporters have their versions of him,
all different, none complete. "What Claude did was wrong,"
one of his defenders will say, "but the way I see it . . . "—
and another version of the crime is born, like *Rashomon* in
Western garb on an endless loop. You can sweep all that aside
and grapple with the facts—hard facts, locking horns in the
mind—but facts do not always explain themselves.

Claude Dallas loved his own brand of freedom and was gen-
uinely surprised that the law tasked him as much as it did. The
first time it happened, he was buckarooing with the Nevada
wagon outfit, as remote and anonymous as any in the contiguous United States, and bothering no one. The FBI found him
anyway and took him back to Ohio on a charge of failing to
appear for military induction. The charge didn't stick, but it
seems clear that Dallas didn't care for being arrested. Whether
he didn't care for it enough to coolly gun down two Idaho game
wardens seven years later, just to avoid an arrest for misde-
meanor poaching, is another question.

That question proved to be of considerable interest to the
farmers, ranchers, and trappers of southern Idaho and northern
Nevada. In the fall of 1982, they turned out in force at Dallas's
double-homicide trial in Caldwell, Idaho—along with the reporters, the would-be biographers, and the putative represen-

tatives of Hollywood. They were in for quite a show. It is not often that a prosecutor attempts to coax a defendant into a discussion of the finer points of fast-draw technique. Not every day that a defense lawyer raises the question of a dead lawman's reputation for "turbulence, dangerousness, violence, or quarrelsomeness," as if he were describing a raft trip through Cataract Canyon. Not more than once in a lifetime, surely, that the myth of the Old West—not the West of history or even of memory but of paperbacks, movies, and mini-series—is woven and unraveled in the flesh, right before your eyes.

The New York Times called the case "a window on another era, in which mountain men trapped a desolate frontier and fought those who threatened to bring law and order to their lives." But the Dallas case is a window on this era and no other. It is a story about guns and dreams of freedom and the choices we make, the lies we tell ourselves, to survive with our dreams intact. It begins and ends with the country, which is not a frontier but the desperate illusion of a frontier. And it invites more questions than answers, which is as Western as you can get.

The Owyhee country begins in southwestern Idaho, where the green swath of the Snake River changes direction and sweeps north, shunning the badlands to the south. Across the river is Owyhee County: rolling desert twisting into arid mesas and shapeless buttes, with only the occasional roadside proclamation (DANGER! WATCH OUT FOR WHITE HORSES IN SNOWSTORMS) to suggest a human presence somewhere up the road. The county is roughly the size of New Jersey, but New Jersey has seven million people and a few good roads. It can take a full day to drive through the heart of the county to the Nevada border— a convenient demarcation but a false one, since the desert is the same on either side. It is all Owyhee, named for some Hawaiian fur trappers who left the green comfort of the Snake and never came back.

On the Nevada side, along the back roads between Jackpot

and Winnemucca, are trailer camps, cattle ranches, potato farms, former mining and livestock centers, a bare scatter of settlements, some of them scarcely distinguishable from the ghost towns plundered by tourists. Humboldt and Elko counties claim an average of one person per square mile. The rest is mostly sagebrush, prairie grass, wind-swept hills and alkali flats.

The desert is for hermits. With the right kind of promotion, it attracts others, too. Men who want to take the measure of themselves. Women who love good air and horses. Losers who have bought the Western romance of starting over. Prospectors. Religious cranks. And, of course, cowboys. Claude Dallas was one of them.

He was a true Westerner, which is to say that he came from somewhere else, with a hunger for empty places. He was born in Virginia and raised in northern Michigan and central Ohio. His father was a dairy farmer, and it is said that Claude started hunting and trapping with several of his brothers at an early age. In high school he made no secret of his desire to go West.

After graduation Dallas fed cattle on a ranch in California. It was not real buckarooing, with the rawhide reata and the green woollies, the chuckwagon and the sweat-stained bedroll. For that he had to move on to the wagon outfits of Oregon and Nevada, where men and women still work horseback on spreads as large as half a million acres. In the summer of 1970, at the age of twenty, Dallas rode into Paradise Hill, Nevada, a misnamed trailer-town north of Winnemucca. He stayed there off and on for the next ten years and worked for several of the outfits in the area.

Among the braggarts, boozers, and brawlers of the buckaroo camps, Dallas was a different breed altogether—quiet, dependable, a man of particular skills. He filed his own spurs, collected books about the West, and even made a pilgrimage of sorts to the Charles M. Russell Museum in Great Falls, Montana. When the National Geographic Society published its popular coffee-table tome *The American Cowboy in Life and Legend* in 1972, there was Claude in full regalia: bandanna and leather chaps, wire spectacles, and the beginnings of a beard. He had arrived.

The following year the FBI arrested him on the draft evasion charge, but the case was soon dismissed; Dallas hadn't received the required second induction notice. He returned to Nevada and discovered that the joy had gone out of buckarooing. Some ranchers say that only a man in need of a tax shelter can afford to run a ranch the old-fashioned way; sooner or later, the curse of modernity gains a foothold, and in march the corporate, absentee owners, the trucks, the branding tables, the whole mechanized fall from grace. It happened to a number of the Nevada operations in the seventies. Claude Dallas moved on to other things.

He took odd jobs on farms and watered cattle for smaller outfits, in return for the privilege of wintering on the land. He grew his hair long, trapped bobcats and coyotes, and made the rounds of the fur sales. It would appear that the life suited him better than cowboying, which requires a certain gregariousness, a family spirit of cooperation. A trapper, if he is earnest about making a living mixes his own scents, stakes out his own territory, and competes in a lonely game of nerves.

As a rule, game wardens don't care much for trappers. Trappers are on the land too much and tend to get proprietary about it. Their livelihood is at stake, and that makes them more argumentative than Joe Sportsman. In the past decade their ranks have multiplied, along with the complaints of vandalism, theft, and encroachment from old-timers, all directly attributable to the number of amateurs rushing to cash in on a fleeting boom in the price of most long-fur pelts. Add to that the fact that many of the amateurs outfit themselves with absurdly impractical pig-stickers and large-gore sidearms—the greater the amateur, the larger the arsenal—and you can see why the Nevada Department of Wildlife was particularly leery of Dallas. To them he was a "type": a bearded, pony-tailed bozo with a surplus of fire power and insufficient manners, a real way-out-Westerner. They fined him once for using illegal bait and tried unsuccessfully to catch him straying from the book in other ways. When he reportedly told one conservation officer to leave his badge outside or stay clear of his camp, the story spread throughout the department.

The man must have misunderstood. Dallas knew a thing or two about guns, hell, yes, but—as he tried to explain at his trial—that was because he found them to be a "useful tool" in his line of work. You get thrown by a horse, and a pistol might come in handy. You could signal for help—or make a meal of the sonofabitch, if it came to that.

He wasn't flirting with yesterday. He was more interested in making it through tomorrow. He had been in places "where I had no one to fall back on but myself." So he carried a .22 trap pistol in a shoulder holster and a .357 magnum revolver on his right hip. He sighted in guns for his friends and talked about being prepared for war. Not prepared to enlist, perhaps, but prepared to take to the hills and defend himself. That would explain the items found among his other guns and gear in an old trailer and schoolbus in Paradise Hill—a gas mask, a bulletproof vest, police manuals, and books on combat shooting, with titles like *Kill or Get Killed* and *No Second Place Winner*. All practical and necessary equipment for the way he expected to live, the way of a survivor.

Even a solitary man has friends. Dallas had three, whose loyalty to him would one day pose great conundrums for them: George Nielsen, who ran a bar in Paradise Hill; Jim Stevens, a potato farmer from Winnemucca; and Craig Carver, a self-employed fence-builder. All three joined the expedition when, in December of 1980, Dallas took his mules and traps across the Idaho line, into Owyhee County. He pitched his tent along the South Fork of the Owyhee River, on a stretch of public land called Bull Camp. His friends wished him luck and left him to his traps, knowing this would be his last winter in the game. The country was getting too cramped for Claude. He'd been talking about Canada and Alaska—places where the caribou roam, where the idea of a frontier gleams like the aurora borealis, receding into the mystery of the north.

On New Year's Eve, a trapper named Ed Carlin rode into Dallas's camp. The two had crossed paths before: in 1979, Carlin and his father had abandoned a camp in Star Valley, 14 miles away, at the landowner's request to make room for Dallas. The Carlins had since become caretakers for the neighboring 45 Ranch, and Ed Carlin wanted to discuss a matter of territorial rights. He eyed a bobcat pelt and some deer meat hanging in Dallas's camp—both evidently taken out of season—and mentioned that he had been turning in poachers in the area. He quickly added that he wouldn't tell on Claude, but he implied that Fish and Game already knew about him. Dallas said he would be ready for them.

Five days later—January 5, 1981—Jim Stevens returned to Bull Camp. Seven years older than Dallas, Stevens had been an admirer of the trapper ever since the two worked together on a farm in 1976. Dallas "intrigued" him—that was the word he used—and taught him some back-country lore. Dallas had invited him to visit in this last winter in the desert, and Stevens made the five-hour drive through fog and chill with pleasure.

The sun appeared and burned off the fog, and the day had all the promise of a boys' adventure in Owyhee. Stevens arrived around noon, bearing fruit, baked goods, and pistachio pudding. "We're going to have a real good time," Dallas told him.

The farmer went off in search of arrowheads. The trapper hiked up to the plateau above his camp to unload more supplies from Stevens' truck. Waiting on the rim were officers William H. Pogue and Wilson Conley Elms, enforcement division, Idaho Department of Fish and Game. That morning they had already cited two other trappers in the area; Dallas they had saved for last. Over breakfast at the 45 Ranch, Ed Carlin had warned Pogue that Dallas was not to be trusted and always carried a revolver on his hip.

Pogue, a former Winnemucca police chief and 16-year vet-
eran of Fish and Game, carried a .357 on his hip, too. Elms, a
younger, bigger man with a well-known sweet disposition, preferred the shoulder holster. They marched Dallas back to camp.
On the way they relieved him of the pistol in his shoulder
holster. Somehow they neglected the hip-gun that Carlin had
talked about, which might have been partially hidden by Dallas's
windbreaker.

Pogue brought along a pair of handcuffs and did most of the
talking. If Dallas's account is correct, the conversation ran
something like the dialogue in an Audie Murphy oater:

POGUE: We're Fish and Game, Pogue and Elms. We heard you
have some meat hung up in your camp.
DALLAS: I'm 150 miles from town. I've got to hang up meat. If
you've come 150 miles to give me a citation for hanging up
meat, well, I can't see it.
POGUE: Dallas, you can go easy or you can go hard. It doesn't
make any difference to me.

Jim Stevens was summoned back to camp and asked to sur-
render his piece, another .357 revolver, favored tool of sportsmen and peace officers throughout the West. Pogue removed
the bullets and poured them into Stevens's shirtpocket. Over
Dallas's objections, Elms searched his tent and emerged with
two bobcat pelts. Stevens, uncertain about whether his friend
was being cited or arrested, drifted away from the discussion
between Pogue and Dallas in front of the tent.

He had wandered off only a few feet when Dallas crouched
and fired his revolver. Two bullets for Pogue. One for Elms.
Two more for Pogue. One more for Elms. Then a lightning
rush into the tent for his .22 rifle, and a finishing shot in the
head for each of the downed men.

"My God, I'm an eyewitness," Jim Stevens told himself.

Stevens ran. Dallas caught up with him and apologized for

"getting you into this." He said something about justifiable homicide. "They had no business in my camp," he said.

Dallas loaded Pogue's body into Stevens's truck. Elm's body was too heavy to carry up to the rim, even on a mule. Dallas dragged it to the river. It occurred to Stevens to reload his pistol—just in case. It occurred to Dallas to take the gun away from him—just in case. James M. Cain would have understood.

After dark they drove to Paradise Hill and awakened George Nielsen and his wife. Dallas transferred Pogue's body to Nielsen's truck and drove away. He returned with an empty truck, borrowed one hundred dollars from Nielsen, and headed off on foot into the Silver State Valley. Stevens changed clothes, went home, and told his wife a tale. She didn't believe him. The next morning, almost twenty-four hours after the shootings, Stevens and the Nielsens walked into the county sheriff's office in Winnemucca.

A manhunt was launched, drawing on the available pool of talent in Owyhee County and northern Nevada. They didn't find Claude Dallas or the body of Bill Pogue. They did find Conley Elms, floating face-down in the Owyhee River. At the campsite they found bloodstains and the mules and gear Dallas left behind. In one of his traps was a golden eagle, helpless but still alive.

The chase lasted fifteen months—plenty of time for the newspapers, television stations, and hunting magazines to get in on it. A tale took shape, a tall tale about a mountain man born a century too late, a man who lived by his own rules, alone, in the wilderness. The reward fund swelled to over $20,000, and suddenly his phantom was everywhere. Rumor had it he was in Mexico. No, Alaska. Handwritten confessions or challenges to the law, supposedly authored by Dallas, surfaced in Wyoming, Texas, and Maine. They were all shams.

A year passed. The press lost interest. Then someone in need of $20,000 made a phone call. On a Sunday afternoon in April

1982, a small army of county, state, and federal agents surrounded Craig Carver's trailer on Poverty Flat, four miles outside of Paradise Hill. This time it was Dallas's lever-action .22
rifle, a .38 with speed-loaders, and yet another .357 magnum
revolver against M-16s, shotguns, SWAT teams, a rocket
launcher, a helicopter, and a surveillance plane. After attempt-
ing to escape in an old truck and being wounded in the left heel,
Dallas gave up. A deputy said it was "just like in the movies."
Maybe he was thinking of Kirk Douglas in *Lonely Are the
Brave*.

Dallas's attorneys, Michael Donnelly and Bill Mauk of Boise,
had a history of representing unpopular clients and causes. But
they had never tangled with myth before. They surveyed one
hundred Owyhee County residents and discovered that sixty of
them believed Dallas deserved the death penalty. The trial was
moved to Caldwell, the seat of neighboring Canyon County.
Donnelly received anonymous phone calls at his home. Death
threats reached Dallas in the solitude of his cell.

The case went before a jury in the fall. Matrons clutching
needlework lined up outside the courtroom each morning, to
be teased and inspected by bailiffs clutching metal detectors.
Despite the banter security was tight, and death threats were
not the only reason. It was whispered that Claude was sizing
up his captors, waiting for an opening, one last dash for daylight.
The armed men who escorted him in and out of the courtroom
had the wary, why-me look of apprentice snake handlers.

By contrast, Dallas seemed relaxed. Dressed in blue jeans
and a Western shirt, his hair and beard neatly trimmed, he
followed the proceedings closely, took notes, and traded odd
pleasantries with his lawyers. He did not acknowledge the ma-
tronly stares, whether they came from the crowd or the jury,
which was made up of ten women and two men. If he was
looking for an opening, it might have been a crack in the pon-
derous case assembled by Owyhee County prosecutor Clayton
Andersen and Idaho Deputy Attorney General Michael Ken-

nedy. He found one in an unlikely place—the testimony of the state's star witness, Jim Stevens.

Stevens did his best for Dallas. He praised his friend's work habits: "he does more than his share." But his testimony was laced with damning statements he said Dallas had made in the frantic hours after the shootings: "They had handcuffs. I swore I'd never be arrested again." "I would have taken them on the rim, but they would have killed me up there." "This is murder one for me."

Yet when asked about the moment of horror, Stevens recalled seeing Bill Pogue's hand dropping to his side—and the officer's gun lying on the ground, free of its holster, in the still aftermath. It wasn't much, Pogue's split-second motion toward his gun, but it was doubt.

Dallas took the stand and explained, in the cool, idiomatic drawl of the buckaroo, that Bill Pogue had come on strong. Pogue was "on the fight," he claimed. He kept patting his holster, he was "itching to use that gun." And Pogue's tone was hostile, Dallas said—his words the tough words of a man who has seen too many movies and no longer knows where his true interests lie.

DALLAS: That tent's my home. I don't want you in there without a search warrant.
POGUE: We don't need a warrant. . . . We're taking you in. You can go easy or you can go hard.
DALLAS: I can't go. I have my mules and my equipment, and I can't leave them.
POGUE: Then you can go hard.
DALLAS: You're out of line. You're crazy. You can't shoot a man over a game violation.
POGUE: I'll carry you out.

Pogue drew his gun and fired one shot, Dallas claimed. He fired back, and by that time Conley Elms was going for his gun, so he shot Elms, too, and, still in fear of his life—"out of my head"—he fetched the rifle and shot them again. "I reacted the only way I could," he said.

He said he had buried Pogue near Daveytown, in the shadow of the Bloody Run Mountains. Nevada authorities located the skeleton that afternoon. They did not find the officer's gun.

After Dallas testified, the facts were more elusive than ever— and those that did turn up seemed treacherous or beside the point. A handwriting expert helped to establish that the mountain man had worked on an assembly line in Sioux Falls, South Dakota, less than a month after the killings, and then had disappeared again. There was one pathologist who believed that Elms was shot in the back, and one who insisted he was not.

What remained was reputation. Nevada conservation officers took the stand to expound on Dallas's alleged lawlessness. Friends and former bosses of the trapper painted an entirely different picture. Colleagues eulogized Pogue as a seasoned, conscientious officer. Others, including hunters and fishermen who claimed to have had run-ins with Pogue over suspected violations, described a swaggering, badge-happy bully with a chip on his shoulder.

The focus had shifted from the act itself to the personalities involved. It wasn't really a murder trial any more, it was an investigation into the psychology of gunfighting. And everyone knows something about that: the irreconcilable clash of wills and principles—especially principles—the tempo building as the showdown approaches, the tall dance of death, the arm whipping down, the lightning response, the slower hand twitching in the dust. It had happened thousands of times on the great screen of public imagination; why couldn't it happen in real life, at the end of a boys' adventure in Owyhee?

If you accepted the state's theory of the crime, then you had to believe that Dallas decided upon murder the moment he encountered Pogue and Elms on the rim, took them by surprise with a concealed weapon, and ruthlessly finished the job with the rifle from his tent—all to save himself a few dollars and a few hours of inconvenience. If you sided with the defense, then you had to believe in gunfights. You had to believe that Bill Pogue came to Bull Camp looking for a shootout, defied procedure and common sense by leaving his adversary with a loaded gun, fired from six feet away and missed, then paid for his foolishness with his life and the life of Conley Elms.

On the final day of argument, Michael Donnelly stood in the center of the overheated courtroom, mopped his brow, and made one last appeal to principle. "What this case is about is fate. What this case is about is freedom of action, the right to privacy, freedom from unwarranted assault and threat," he said. "Could you say that when the gun was pulled, that shot fired, and Conley Elms was going for his gun, you could have done anything differently?"

The jury deliberated for a week. On the seventh day Judge Edward Lodge dismissed one woman from the panel, explaining that she had brought "extraneous" information into the jury room; reportedly, the information concerned Dallas's previous arrest. An alternate juror replaced her, and within hours the deadlock was broken.

Claude Dallas was guilty, they decided, of two counts of voluntary manslaughter, concealing evidence, and the use of firearms in the commission of crimes against the power, peace, and dignity of the state of Idaho. It wasn't murder one, but it wasn't justifiable homicide, either. That business of Claude being out of his head, running into his tent for a rifle to shoot men already wounded and dying—that had bothered them. It didn't square with the accepted rituals of gunfighting. And it was difficult to imagine Claude Dallas being that afraid. They could credit him with passion, the outrage of a private man provoked in his own camp—"that tent's my home," he had said—but not fear. Cowboys don't spook.

The director of the Idaho Department of Fish and Game called a press conference: "We feel that the jury has told us some people can live off the land without social responsibility . . . that when a peace officer is killed, it is the officer who is on trial and not the accused killer . . . or at least, that the last man alive is the one telling the truth."

Members of the jury began to receive threatening phone calls.

On January 4, 1983, the eve of the second anniversary of the deaths of William Pogue and Conley Elms, Claude Dallas made a brief statement to the court before receiving his sentence. "I do regret what happened at Bull Camp," he said, "but I feel I reacted the only way I could under the circumstances."

"I do not believe the issue of self-defense arose at Bull Camp," Judge Lodge said. After listening to Dallas and assorted character witnesses, he handed down a sentence of thirty years in prison, believing that Dallas had acted and talked the way Jim Stevens had said he did, but still at a loss to explain why. "It's difficult for me to understand how you can do these atrocious things, and yet be described the way you are—as a compassionate, thoughtful, well-liked, honest, loyal person. It's not in your character to do what you did."

That was one way of settling it; when a man of good reputation does atrocious things, he must be acting out of character, if not out of his head. But we expect more from the West, even the modern West. We expect a gunfight to be a revelation of character, and the mystery to be a mystery of character. We have only Dallas's word that his survival was at stake, that he reacted the only way he could—yet isn't that a statement of character?

Perhaps Claude Dallas did believe that Pogue had come to Bull Camp to kill him. It takes a certain kind of man to have no doubt about where all that tough talk was heading, to decide that "going hard" means going dead. That decision is not made on the basis of reason or fear but something deeper, something along the lines of instinct. And the man who reacts fastest to— what? a shot? a sudden drop of the arm?—is probably a man who believes in his own survival and little else, a man who has banished doubt, a man who is prepared to meet death at every turn and consequently finds it.

That man might live in a trailer, read *Soldier of Fortune*, and store guns in caves in the mountains. He might also live in the suburbs, read *Fortune*, and hoard food and ammunition in the basement. But his natural habitat is the back country of the American West, where people keep to themselves and the myth of frontier adventure lives on. Under the spell of the country, it is easy to indulge in a few hackneyed notions that you have left all obligations behind, that what lies ahead is freedom and the sweet promise of danger—an acid test of character in a place where you can rely on no one but yourself.

Claude Dallas lives in a cell at the Idaho State Penitentiary. He could become eligible for parole within ten years. His lawyers are contemplating an appeal. Jim Stevens has resettled in Idaho. The remains of Bill Pogue were cremated, the ashes scattered from an airplane over the Sawtooth National Forest.

In the buckaroo camps of today there is a chronic shortage of skilled, reliable, all-purpose cowboys, but there is no lack of raw material. "We still get kids from all over the place," one rancher told me, "looking to have a real good time."

DAVID LONG

HOME FIRES

Longer than anyone knows, fir and tamarack had clung to the sharp slopes of the canyon, ravaged by lightning fires and bark beetles and gravity, their tenacity witnessed only by the moody northwestern clouds, by birds of prey whose serrated wings bore them on the tricky thermals, by families of deer carefully following trails beside the fast gray water. In this century Jeep roads intruded until the entire eighty miles could be traversed by a strong rig, though it was never thought of as a way to get from one place to another. Then in the 1960s dynamite and giant earth-movers left a two-lane blacktop highway that matched the river's twists, ascending in places hundreds of feet above it through unguarded switchbacks.

It was an early morning in the dregs of a September that had frosted early. Scattered stands of aspen and weeping birch fluttered in the shadows. Down in the heart of the river, kokanee salmon were making their first run, a few now to be followed by great numbers, swimming upstream toward the waters of their spawning—surely it was a kind of miracle that they should ever find their way back, no longer feeding, their bodies already soft and pulpy in preparation for death.

Traffic on the highway was sparse, relieved of the sluggish flow of motor homes and top-heavy camper outfits from other states. A few feet past mile marker 44, where the road climbs into a smooth northeasterly bank, a fresh pair of double tire tracks continued straight that morning, through the chunks of

227

reddish clay, into the dry brush and the feathery upper branches of firs.

The truck lay upside down, back end crushed like a soda can, cab folded into so dense a bolus of steel it would take Search & Rescue better than two hours working with welding torches and hydraulic jaws to discover it contained no body. Up slope, scattered among the outcrops of shale and limestone, in the trees and resting here and there on the flaps of freshly gashed topsoil, white packages of frozen fish were strewn, still rock-hard, though the exposed sides would feel mushy to the fingers of the first county deputy to huff down the slope, midafternoon. The truck had nearly made it to the river, stopped only by a slug of granite twice its size, where now the man named Pack squatted, head between his knees, glancing up every few seconds at the wreckage.

He could not understand why it did not include him. He should not have survived such a mistake, should not first have made it. He tried to picture the night just elapsed, the route that had led him to the lip of the road. He had no precise memory of it. Surely he had fallen asleep. Drivers fear the graveyard hours, though that fear is so close to the heart of what they do that it remains unsaid. They ride behind the wheel, pumping Dentyne or cigarettes or Maalox, half-thrilled by the power of the diesel and the reach of the headlamps, half-terrified by their limitations. They flick cassettes into the tape player and set the volume so high the treble jars them out of that dreamy hypnotic mood that comes just before the moment their heads drop. They sing, they banter with one another on the CB, they juggle weights and distances and velocity in their heads. Anything to keep them sharp until it is light again. In the end, though, the fear itself provides the energy.

But Pack was never like that. Driving those hours he found a kind of peace, a solitude that was its own reward. The darkness outside seemed to illuminate his loneliness, seemed to tell him it was only the natural way of the world. He aimed the passenger mirror inward at his own face so he could watch his eyes in the halo of dash lights. He never used the radio except sometimes to tune in an all-night talk show from the coast and listen to the paranoia and longing that gave the voices their peculiar timbre. He kept to himself at the truckstops, letting his cup be filled and refilled as he watched other drivers kill their nights off under the acid lights. He would be privately pleased when the phone would ring and the waitress would wipe her hands and grab for it. It would never be for him.

He could not remember choosing to be a driver. He had fallen into the pattern of it a job at a time, found it suited his disposition. He had been to college but picked up nothing lasting there except the taste for reading, another solitary pastime. Sometimes on long nights he thought about his wife, but it was in the same drowsy distant way he thought about what he had read. He did not doubt that he loved her, but he could not remember choosing her. She had been with him as long as he could recall—the adolescence she'd marked the end of only a blur now, dotted by occasional points of shame and excitement. When he came home to her, his desire quickened and he'd hold her and listen to her deep sure voice and be happy, but driving again, at night, he knew that the two were not one, after all, but two.

Pack sat on the crown of the boulder, surrounded by the quiet and bird songs, trying to make sense of what had happened. He saw himself popping out the driver's door as the nose of the truck first hit, his body flipping backward through the branch tips, pitching like a dead weight into the snarl of laurel where he'd come to.

He ran his fingers up and down his legs, over his ribs and back, finally touching around his skull, searching for the fatal exception to his good luck. Though he was dizzy and his forearms were devilled with long scratches, he could find nothing dreadful.

He climbed off his perch and bent over a sheltered pool. His face was thin and droopy-eyed, fringed with a beard the color of clay dirt. His eyes were the blue of an undeclared predawn sky. He smiled into the calm water, and it was then he saw that his front teeth were gone, ripped out by the roots. He touched the gums delicately, felt the clots forming over the holes, withdrew his hand and saw the fingertips evenly stained, as if his body were nothing but a bucket of blood.

At that moment the sun first crossed the ridgeline and Pack squinted up the steep slope, bathed now in keen September sunlight. The dizziness gave way to a rush of clarity, as if he'd only now begun to wake up, not just from the accident and from the night, but from ten years of living in the dark. He looked at the crumpled truck, the torn earth. Clearly he was supposed to be a dead man.

He *knows his loneliness better than he knows me*, Elisabeth Pack, called Willie, wrote her sister who had moved east. *Maybe I am a jealous woman after all.*

She put her pen down, stared impatiently out the side window where the two pear trees dropped their yield into long sweeps of grass. The leaves were brittle and gold. The road dead-ended here. If there had been children, it would have been a safe place for them to play, away from the hazards of through traffic. But there were none. In the distance, the parched foothills hung in a blue morning haze, curving out of sight toward the mouth of the valley where the river flowed wide and tame, accompanied by the tracks of the Burlington Northern and the placid interstate.

But I doubt it, Willie wrote.

She was a handsome woman, six feet even—slightly taller than Pack—with clear hazel eyes and soft lines around the mouth. At thirty she wasted no time mourning the woman she was or might have been. In uniform her presence was striking. Intensive-care patients were guarded by her skills, comforted by her manner, perhaps mistaking her reserve for serenity or

for a larger, more merciful view of things, one in which the sick
always healed and the grieving were granted peace. It was good
consuming work; with Pack gone so often she was happy
for it.

His homecomings have become unbearable, she wrote, frowned
at the words and stopped. It was not exactly what she meant
to say. She preferred her letters to remain simple and full of
news; even in the ones to her sister she was seldom confidential.
She was embarrassed by the heaviness of her words. The fact
was, though, his returns *had* become more difficult to cope with.
She had long-ago accepted that Pack—for all her love of him,
for all her willingness not to judge him—was a man who came
and went. In the ten years of their marriage he had gone off on
the fire lines their first summers, after that had shuttled rental
cars back to the Midwest, traveled with a bar band called *Loose
Caboose*, and in recent years driven truck on the long interstate
routes.

He was always edgy just before he left, and she would have
to turn away from him to avoid a fight. He always returned
with a high-spirited exhaustion, coming to her bed for a spell
of love-making, hard and wonderful for Willie, though lasting
too long now, leaving her body sore and her spirit cut by re-
sentment. She saw his passion soon spoiled by restlessness, as
if she were not an object of love but of release. It had not always
been like that, but she had to admit, privately, it was now. Still
she forgave him that. What worried her more was that even
between jobs he seemed to come and go, as though tracing an
elliptical orbit around her and the part of his life that remained
fixed. Sometimes she believed he might swing too far, snap
loose, and keep sailing out into space.

"How do you put *up* with it?" her friends sometimes asked
over coffee.

"I don't see that it's really a problem," Willie said, willing
to defend Pack from loose talk. She could handle the Pack whose
nature it was to come and go, who hadn't settled into a life's

work the way she'd imagined he might, who seemed an odd
character put up against their husbands. But she knew they
also meant: *How can you trust him to be faithful?* Faith was private,
Willie thought. It irritated her the casual way her friends rated
their husbands' performance, almost eager to see them fail and
at the same time scared to death of losing them, especially to
someone else. She was not afraid of losing Pack to another
woman.

Once she told him: *I don't mind sleeping alone.* "No?" Pack
said, smiling at the darkness, rubbing her wide damp stomach.
She had meant that it kept her from taking him for granted,
that the emptiness of her bed, at night and again in the morning,
stayed with her as a reminder even when he held her and
warmed her. And she meant it as a kind of triumph, too, because
it had not been easy for her at first; she had needed to learn
to be alone.

Unbearable, she had written.

She craned her neck and squinted through the white sunlight
at the clock on the kitchen wall, saw that it was already afternoon. She finished the letter quickly, dismissing her remarks
as a morning's bad humor, sealed it, and laid it by her purse.

Though it was still early, she grabbed her uniform from the
hook back of the bathroom door and slipped into it. She sat on
the edge of the bed and double-knotted her white-polished Clin-
ics, rising then for a quiet inspection in the big mirror. She
liked to see herself in the white uniform, her wheat-colored hair
drawn smoothly over the ears and gathered in a silver clip at
the neck. She liked not worrying about the quirks of fashion,
but more than that, the whiteness itself pleased her.

She closed up the house and walked out to the Volvo and
idled it lightly in the driveway, a kind of nervousness overtaking
her, the feeling that she'd left something undone. The afternoon
light seemed suddenly frail, as if this were the exact moment
the season turned. Her thoughts about Pack troubled her. She
wished he were here, she wished he could walk down the hos-

pital corridors beside her, feeling what she felt: the terrible precariousness of the lives and their links to one another. She wished he understood that.

Veins of worry began to dart through the halo of bright amazement surrounding Pack as he studied the ruined truck. The tires pointed absurdly in the air, splayed and flattened; the painted lettering emerged without meaning from the jammed aluminum. Unignited gasoline mixed with freon from the fractured cooling unit and gave the air a gray stink. It was past time for precaution, but Pack was overwhelmed with being too close. All the sounds he had missed in his flight now swarmed into his ears. His stomach balled up like a fist.

He backed along the silt-caked stones, hands tucked into the tops of his jeans, staring at the wreckage as it diminished and began to blend with the other debris along the river. He walked upstream until the current bent sharply around a deposit of harder rock and he could no longer see the truck, kept walking a long time, the click of the small hard stones ringing in the narrow canyon. The roadway was high above him, out of sight; he wanted no part of it.

When he stopped, the sun was nearly overhead, its light broken into rich shadows by the low-hanging limbs of the cedars. As he knelt he felt the shakes coming on strong. He got up again quickly and caught the glint of orange rip-stop nylon, across the river and a short ways up a feeder creek. Above it rose a thin braid of smoke, the first sign of life Pack had seen. He waded into the shallows, the water rising over his boottops, then out where it was deeper, bending his knees against the current. Approaching, Pack saw two women crouched by the fire, for the moment unaware of him. The one facing him was slight —*wasted*, his wife would have said—even in a down vest. She pulled her blue stocking cap down over strands of pale hair as she leaned to flip a pair of fish skewered above the coals. The campsite looked small and orderly. The other woman, who

had been sitting back smoking, head down, suddenly caught
sight of Pack and grabbed up a shotgun he'd not seen resting
beside her.

"*Hey!*" Pack said, freezing.

The woman aimed the gun at Pack's midsection and appeared
willing to squeeze off a shot.

"There's been an accident," Pack said, hands lifted in a victim's posture.

"There could easily be another," the woman said. "You alone?"

"No trouble," Pack said. "OK?"

The woman in the vest got to her feet and squinted at Pack's
face, turned, and shook her head at the gun. Her companion
slowly lowered it until it pointed at the pine needles around
Pack's feet.

"Tell us what happened," she said.

Pack moved in gingerly, squatted, and told them what he
could remember. "I was headed home," he began. It sounded
like somebody else's story, though the throbbing in his mouth
reminded him it was neither made-up nor borrowed.

The women seemed to listen with special attention. Finally
the one with the gun cracked a smile, but it was thin-lipped
and made Pack more nervous. "It should be that easy," she
said.

Pack looked at her, not understanding, not knowing what to
do next.

"Here," the other said. "You want some food?"

Pack shook his head. He was beginning to feel truly bad.
"You think it would be all right if I maybe laid down?" he said.

The women checked with each other. The one in the stocking
cap nodded toward the tent. As Pack stood she caught his arm
and said, "Let me . . . ," dipping a corner of her towel in a
pan of hot water, then dabbing at the blood dried around his
mouth.

"Don't you get weird on us," the woman with the gun said.
"You understand?"

Pack nodded. He crawled heavily into the tent, slid across

the warm nylon and collapsed, watching the leaf shadows twitch above him.

While Pack slept the truck was spotted by a young man who had stopped above the ravine to photograph the eagles circling above the salmon run. He trained the long lens of his Nikon down the embankment, scanned the river bank for signs of life, and wondered what the little squares of white were. After a while he walked back to his van, dialed the CB to channel 9, and began calling for help. He was joined eventually by two county deputies, the highway patrol, Search & Rescue, and the coroner. The photographer followed the police down to the wreck and stayed until the light failed, snapping pictures of the truck and the broken slope and the faces of the workers, listening to their speculations, pleased to be so close to it all. The plates of the truck were checked through the Department of Motor Vehicles and identified. In Pack's darkened house the phone rang every hour, beginning at dinner time, continuing late into the evening.

Pack woke abruptly and saw that it was fully dark. It seemed as if a great flood of time had swept him away. He thought for a moment that he had dreamed but realized what he had seen and heard was the power of the fall itself, magnified and re-iterated in the stillness of his mind. He ached everywhere; his lips and gums swollen hard around the missing teeth. Peering from the tent flap, he saw the woman who had cleaned him sitting alone by the fire. Pack joined her. She smiled in an easy, sisterly way. It was as if they had gone in and studied him as he slept, reading into the man he was and deciding he was not a danger to them.

"Rita believes these are desperate times," she said. "She believes it's important to be armed and ready. Are you any better?"

"I don't know."

"That was a miracle," she said.

"I don't know," Pack said again.

She laughed, her cheeks glowing round in the firelight. "Any fool could see that."

"*Kyle* . . . ," Rita said, breaking the circle of light, armed now with a load of firewood, her voice reedy and careful. She knelt and dumped the wood, looked back at the two of them.

"Kyle," she said, "what have you told him?"

Kyle stared into the flames. "I just told him that it was a miracle."

"Yes, that's true," Rita said. "But what will he do with it?"

"I don't think he knows yet," Kyle said gently.

Rita dusted the wood flakes from the front of her sweatshirt, then stooped and poured coffee into a tin cup and handed it to Pack, its steam puffing into the cold air. Pack nodded and took it, and it felt good between his hands.

"They'll be looking for you, of course," Rita said in a minute. "They'll figure your body fell into the river and was carried downstream. You could have gone several miles by now. It's not uncommon. For a while you'll be called missing, then presumed dead."

She stopped a moment to let that sink in. Kyle moved closer to Pack.

"I was missing once," Kyle said, quiet excitement in her voice. "My husband looked all over for me. No telling what he would have done if he'd found me. He'd done plenty already."

"Beaten her," Rita said.

"At first I was hiding upstairs at the hotel with a wig and a new name. I didn't know what I was going to do exactly. I couldn't sleep. Sometimes I could see his truck going down the main street and one night I saw it parked outside the Stockman's Bar, and he came out with someone else. I wasn't surprised. The next morning I took the bus to Pocatello."

"Yes," Rita said. "He was a bad man. A real prick."

Pack heard the tinkling of a brass windchime hung in the tree, drank his coffee in small careful sips.

"Still," Rita went on, "Kyle was smarter in the heart than I was. I waited until I was barely alive, barely able to help myself. But all that's changed now, as you can see."

"Can you eat yet?" Kyle asked Pack. "I saved a fish for you." She tugged a bundle of tinfoil from the edge of the coals.

"You'll need strength," Rita said. "Whatever you decide."

Pack took the fish into his lap and cracked it open and lifted out the long limp spine and tossed it into the fire. The meat crumbled in his mouth.

"But you're not a bad man, are you?" Rita said.

"What do you think?" Pack asked her.

"I think you're a lucky man," Kyle said. "But luck's only the start of it."

"Let me be blunt about this," Rita said. "They will be looking for you, but they don't have to find you."

As she spoke she stood behind Kyle, her fingers lightly stroking the shoulders of the down vest. The smoke twisted up before them, through the fringe of trees to a wedge of sky overcome with autumn constellations.

"Brother," Rita laughed, "have a new life."

Right then Pack stopped chewing and looked hard at the two women. *"New life . . . ,"* he said.

"Clean slate," Rita said. "Maybe you have the nerve, maybe not."

"I don't know," Pack said. "I can't tell you exactly how I feel."

"That's right," Kyle said. "That's how it is at first. You feel sick."

"You get this unmoored feeling," Rita said. "But then you start to see destinations and you go ahead." Her soft white face shone with patience. "Don't tell me you wouldn't like another chance."

Pack was silent.

Rita stood over him a moment, then said, "Now, we're going to bed. You can stay with the fire as long as you need, but it's going to be very cold here soon. Believe me."

Passing by, Kyle whispered to Pack, "Don't think it was an accident," and disappeared toward the tent.

"Thanks," Pack said.

He stayed watching the fire until the last cedar log burned through, showering the air with fine embers, stayed remembering the fires of his life, the blue-gray smoke of branding fires and the stink of burnt hide, the scattered fires of his childhood. He stayed listening to the steady clamoring of the creek, imagining the water's descent, how it wept from remote snowfields, came together, and followed high country drainages to the wide rivers that passed under the city's bridges disappearing west toward the sea. He thought of all the lighted places where he had stopped, the extravagance of his curiosities, and the careless ways he had broken faith with his wife. When he bent later to crawl into the tent, he heard the powerful contentment of the women sleeping. They had left one bag empty for him and were together in the other, holding each other like twins. Pack backed out and stood alone in the cold, measuring the foolish turns his life had taken.

The phone back in its cradle, Willie Pack let her uniform drop to the linoleum of the downstairs bathroom, wrapped herself in a terry-cloth bathrobe, took the Valium bottle from her purse and carried it to the kitchen, lit the gas under the tea kettle, stared at the clear blue flame until the water steamed, turned it off, and sat finally at the breakfast table, surrounded by the bright enamel, the saffron scalloped curtains, lacing her long fingers together in front of her, sure that this moment of control was a fast-fringing lifeline.

Save your tears, she could hear her mother saying. As a child she'd imagined great fetid reservoirs of unshed tears. *Save them why?* How lame and remote her mother's efforts were. Yet Willie knew, perched in the solitude of her own kitchen, that she had grown so much like that woman, believing life was best treated with caution and reserve, believing that loved ones could suddenly trade places with darkness.

Missing, the sheriff had stressed, his voice like fresh gauze.

All her life she'd wanted the exact names of things. Beneath his words she heard this: We haven't found a body yet—in country this wild we may never.

"What does *missing* mean?" Willie said.

"Anything's possible," the sheriff said. "I'm sorry."

"Thank you," Willie Pack said.

So in that time before the confusion and the shouting and crying took possession of her, she held her own hand and rested in an aura of clarity not unlike the one that had settled around Pack hours earlier, as he contemplated the boundaries of his good fortune. This is what tears were saved for.

She had long-ago accustomed herself to his absence, but though it looked the same as always it was not. She felt a flush of shame, to think she had ever enjoyed having him gone. Solitude meant nothing if it was infinite. She thought about death, the way it was taught to her in school, the predictable steps the minds of the living and the dying took in confronting it. Month by month she practiced its sacraments, sometimes finding in her discipline an antidote, mostly not. The farm wife died whispering: *Tell them.* . . . The twenty-year-old logger witnessed the bright splashing of his blood with a pure and wakeful knowledge. She heard the halting voices of old husbands turn suddenly eloquent in the white hallways, reciting an Old Testament catalogue of suffering and accommodation.

She thought then of Pack's missing body. She remembered the feel of her fingers sliding down over the arch of his ribs, she pictured his beautiful hip-swinging gait through the downstairs rooms, the angle of his fingers resting across this table from hers. The image of that body torn and broken rose in her like a searing wind, bringing a wave of sadness—for Pack's body having to die so far away and alone.

She drew a long, controlled breath. For the first time since the telephone call she forced herself to see Pack's face, straight on. It was then, in a burst, she understood what she'd hidden from herself: that she had not seen Pack as he actually was in

a long time. What she saw now was not the face she had guarded
in her imagination, the one she had married as a teenaged girl,
the one she had always reckoned her own happiness by. What
she saw now was a face with eyes crimped and glazed, a mouth
constantly biting at something, a thumbnail or an emery board
or the inside of his lip. It told her Pack had been missing long
before this night.

She lurched to the sink and threw up and kept heaving though
there was little in her stomach except the dark residue of caf-
eteria coffee. She ran the water and watched it swirl over the
grate, gradually washing away her nausea. In a few minutes she
straightened and snugged her bathrobe.

She spilled the blue pills on the table, spacing them evenly
with her finger, imagining the sleep they would bring, each one
clarifying it like sudden drops in the thermometer, until the
muscles no longer flexed and the heart beat indifferently. The
rooms were still dark around her: the front room where Pack's
book was spread flat on the carpet beside his coffee mug, a book
on snow leopards and survival; their bedroom where his work-
shirt had been carelessly thrown; the bathroom where Pack
taped messages to the mirror—no longer the boyish love notes
he'd once left, more like the one there now:—*and this our life,
when was it truly ours, and when are we truly whatever we are?* from
something he had read.

Another chance, she thought, sitting again. She studied the
pills lying before her, the tears beginning to burn her eyes. She
scraped her hand across the tabletop, scattering the pills across
the kitchen, spilling back the chair as she stood and ran out
into the darkness of the house, turning on lights, screaming
Goddamn it at the tears, screaming *No* at the treads of the stairs.
Goddamn it. Goddamn it, throwing open doors, flipping switches,
every one she could lay a hand on, until the whole house was
burning and raging with life.

It was dawn again. Dawn of the husbands, Pack thought. He
had been quiet all the way back, not letting on to the trucker

who'd stopped for him who he was: the man presumed dead. It was still a private affair. The driver played a Willie Nelson tape, mostly ballads, and hummed along in fair harmony, blinking constantly at the road beyond his windshield. Pack hugged his arms inside the sweatshirt the driver had lent him. This was always a nervous and transitional hour, one kind of thought giving way to the next. Pack remembered how much of his life had disappeared working like the driver beside him, only with less sense of destination than this man surely had. He remembered the few times he had left a woman at that hour, the sadness of strange doorways and words that disappear like balloons into an endless sky, the whine of his engine as it carried him away. He thought of Kyle and Rita waking together in their tent, joined by affection and the belief that the only good road leads away from home.

Pack thanked the man and got down from the truck at the edge of town. He walked slapping his arms. The full white moon floated above the unawakened houses, above the familiar rise and fall of the mountains. In the next block somebody's husband had gone out and started a pickup in the semidark. Steam flared from the exhaust. Soon the heater would throw two rings of warm air at the frosted windshield. Pack broke into a run, loping through the empty intersections, cold air slamming into his lungs.

He stopped in the mouth of the short street that deadended at his house. Men on the road talk about coming home religiously, though they are not religious men or even, Pack thought, men who are at peace being there. What they want is to be welcomed each time, their return treated like the consummation of something noble, which is too much to ask. Unnecessary risks, Pack thought, too great and foolish to be rewarded with love. He had somehow thought he was immune.

Panting hard through the gap in his teeth but warm for the first time in many hours, Pack looked up to see the lights blazing from his house, even from the twin attic dormers and the areaway at the basement window. He could never know the fullness of his wife's grief, how it came with as many shades of diminishing light as a summer twilight, just as she would never know why his lonely disposition took him always away from her, or precisely what had happened to change him. Sometimes it is a comfort to believe that one day is like another, that things happen over and over and are the same. But accidents happen, and sometimes a man or a woman is lucky enough to see that all of it, from the first light kiss onward, could have gone another way. Pack ran to the front door of his house, alive, thinking *dawn of homecoming, dawn of immaculate good fortune.*

WILLIAM KITTREDGE

WE ARE NOT
IN THIS TOGETHER

This time it was a girl Halverson knew, halfway eaten and her hair chewed off. She had been awake in the night; she'd been afraid and whimpering as the great bear nudged at the side of the nylon tent like a rooting hog. She held to the other girl's hand, and began to scream only when the long claws ripped her out of her sleeping bag, continuing to scream as she was being dragged away, the feathery down from the sleeping bag floating above the glowing coals of a pine-knot fire. This time it was someone he knew; and he lay still in the darkness and the warmth of his own bed and tried to understand the feeling of knowing you were killed before you were dead.

Thinking was beyond the point. The last time Halverson lay awake like this, the first weekend the hard wind-drifted snow was plowed off the Going-to-the-Sun Highway over Logan Pass, it had been a fetus—not a fetus really, a child, stillborn, a baby girl dropped in a roadside trash container at the east end of Two Medicine Lake and found by workmen. A dead baby wrapped in a pink motel towel and thrown into a garbage can. It could not have been anything like indifference which brought someone to such a burial. More like the need to get rid of what can happen. Walk into the wind and your eyes will water.

But in the beginning there was Darby, and the way Halverson saw her avoiding mirrors. There was no explaining it to Darby, but early in May, when the aspen leaves along the middle fork of the Flathead were lime-green and just emerging, Halverson began to think he saw what Darby was seeing when she quickly looked away from the long mirror she'd hung in his bedroom. Halverson would glance up on the evenings when she was home and see Darby with her stockinged feet up on the hearth before the fire, intent on one of her magazines—the old issues of the *National Geographic* she brought with her when she came to live with him—and he would see her as she would look when she was old. Her eyeglasses would be thicker and distorting her eyes until they were strange as the eyes of owls; eventually, he knew, she would be fumbling and blind. Her hands would touch at things she could not see, tentative and exploring. If he stayed with her long enough there would be the time when she fell, the cracking of bone, a sound he imagined as he watched her turn the magazine pages; and some indeterminate time after that, he would be alone and old, his hands touching and exploring each thing in this familiar room as he talked to some memory of his father about sharpening a knife or the color of hatchery trout.

Halverson told Darby that he would never have children if he had anything to say about it. He told her that he could not go on living with her, and that he would not ever try living with another woman. He told her they were better off alone.

"I'm sorry," he told her, expecting her to argue. But she only looked back to her magazine.

"No," she said. "It's not that."

The next night, when he came home from hauling cedar logs, his cabin was filled with chairs and tables made of twisted and shellacked bamboo. Bright patterns of lavender and orange tropical flowers were splashed across the cushions. His old furniture was piled out in the pole barn where he sheltered the truck in winter. "Don't you think about worrying," Darby said. "This is all in my name. I'm making the payments. Fifty-seven dollars a month." There was a new canvas drop cloth over the chair on his side of the fireplace, so the fabric would stay clean.

"While I pay for every bite there is to eat," Halverson said. There had been nothing kind he could say.

"I always wanted this," Darby said. "It's like the South Pacific, don't you think?"

"Pretty close," Halverson said. He didn't mention the notion of her leaving again.

That which is not useful is vicious: in needlepoint, those words had been framed on his grandfather's wall, attributed to Cotton Mather. Halverson's father burned the plaque along with the bedding heaped on the bed where his grandfather had shivered away his last months. The blankets smelled of camphor as they burned. Halverson's grandfather had died angry, refusing to eat and starving himself. His father had never helped his mother try to make the old man eat, but had sat in the kitchen glaring at the snowfall outside the window over the sink while the persuading went on. Halverson had been six or seven, but he could still hear his mother's voice murmuring from the old man's room at the back of the house.

"There is only so much sin for each of us," his mother had repeated over and over. Halverson had never thought of it much until now, but he knew the old man had not been sinning.

In the bedroom, the digital clock atop Halverson's Sony TV showed the time to be 12:52. The pint of Jack Daniel's was empty and Halverson was nowhere near sleep. He always tried to be sleeping when Darby came home late from her bartending shift. He didn't want to hear who had gone off with the wrong partner at closing time, or which children slept in the car while their parents drank and quarreled after the drive-in movie.

But tonight there was the girl; she was young, and now she was dead, the round slope of her tight belly eaten away by the grizzly. Her hair, which hung down her back in a tangled red-tinted rope, had been gnawed off her skull. Park rangers were searching with rifles. Halverson got up and went into the bathroom and turned the shower to steaming hot, then down to cold while he stood under the spray, trying not to gasp or flinch. He shaved for the second time that day, and then pulled a flannel shirt from his closet, turned the cuffs up, and dragged on his work pants and laced his boots. His face was smooth and slick as he rubbed at his eyes, thinking: just this one time, just tonight, another drink.

The girl who died had worked in the bar where Darby worked. Halverson stopped there each evening for his pint of Jack Daniel's and a glass or two of beer. He'd joked with the girl only a few nights ago about how she was going to be stuck in this country if she stayed much longer. "Five years . . . you can't help going native." It had been something to say while she rang up the pint. She was a dark and not exceptionally pretty girl who had come West from a rich suburb of Columbus, Ohio. She had quit the Wildlife Biology School down in Missoula and come to Columbia Falls with a boy who sold cocaine to the skiers in Whitefish and spent his summers climbing mountains. Halverson wondered what happened to you with cocaine. When the boy was caught and sentenced to five years in the state prison at Deer Lodge, maybe three years with probation, she took the barmaid job and said she was going to wait. According to Darby, she had been; there hadn't been any fooling around.

Halverson drove down the canyon from his cabin toward the neon thickness of light over Columbia Falls. Outside the tavern he parked and listened to the soft racketing of the tappets in his Land-Rover.

Halverson sat watching the beer signs flicker on and off, and then he drove home. Below the cabin, he parked the Land-Rover beside the shadowy bulk of his 350 Kenworth diesel log-hauling truck. Halverson spent his working days drifting the truck down the narrow asphalt alongside the Flathead River, hauling cedar logs to the shake mill below Hungry Horse. The amber-hearted cedar smelled like medicine ought to smell. The work was a privilege, mostly asphalt under the tires and those logs. And now he was quitting.

Halverson climbed up and sat in the Kenworth, snapped on the headlights so they shone into the scrub brush at the edge of the timber. He was not going out the next morning. The truck was ready, log bunks chained down for the trip into the mountains before sunrise, but he was not going to work come morning.

He was imagining the bear. The dished face of the great animal would rear up simple and inquisitive from vines where service-berries hung thick as wine grapes. The dark nose would be a target under the cross hairs. The sound of the shot would reverberate between the mineral-striped walls of the cirque, where the glaciers had spent their centuries eating away rock. Far away a stone would be dislodged and come rattling down over the slide. The square-headed peaks would dampen the sound to silence.

Halverson could hear the stone clattering on other stones after the echo of the shot diminished to nothing. But he could not imagine the animal falling. He couldn't imagine anything beyond that first shot. Halverson shut off the headlights on the Kenworth and went into the cabin and punched off the alarm, and was satisfied to sleep.

The girl had died two nights ago in the back country of Glacier Park. With another girl, she'd camped at the distant eastern end of Quartz Lake in the Livingston Range. Here there were no trails cut through the deadfall lodgepole along the shore, the section of the park kept closest to true wilderness, miles from other campers. It was territory Halverson knew, from those late summer encampments his father had called vacations. All his working life Halverson's father had drawn wages from the park: trail crew supervisor in the summer and snow clearance in the winter; feeding baled hay to the elk and deer during the really bad winters. Each September after the Labor Day tourists had gone home, his father took time to camp in the backcountry, to hide out, as he said, and let his whiskers grow and learn to smell himself again. You go and forget who you are, his father said, when you never get wind of yourself. The time that don't count, his father liked to say, meaning a thing John Muir said about wandering the mountains: *the time that will not be subtracted from the sum of your life.* But something had been subtracted. His father died of a heart seizure, defibrillation the doctors called it, when he was thirty-nine years old. There was a winter morning when Halverson's mother stood in the lighted bedroom doorway, saying to Halverson, "Don't you come in here!" Then there was the door closing, and her shrieking. *You don't come in here!* After a while she was quiet. And then she came out of the bedroom and closed the door and washed her face. Then she turned to Halverson and said, *he is dead.*

Halverson was forty-two now, three years older than his father had been when he died. He had not been in the park except to shortcut through, since the funeral. What year could that have been?

The girl who survived told of awakening to hear the bear grunting outside the tent, and the other girl whimpering. What I thought, the girl said, is *thank God it is out there.* That was all I could think, like I knew there was a bear outside, but it was *outside,* you see. The girl who survived told how she and the other girl held hands, and tried to stay quiet. Then the nylon tent ripping away, and the vast dark animal dragging the other girl from her sleeping bag; and the beginning of the screaming, really just long breathless shrieking as the bear killed her. That was the way she told it, the girl who survived; *he just dragged her away and killed her.* After a while, the girl said, I climbed a tree. The insides of her thighs were torn by the bark. But it didn't make any difference, the girl said, he didn't come for me, he didn't want me.

The girl spent most of the next day making her way out along the six-mile rocky shoreline of Quartz Lake, back toward the trails and other hikers. Before nightfall the hunt began. Rangers with rifles dropped at the shore of the lake from helicopters and discovered the half-eaten body. Halverson burned the newspaper in his fireplace, and looked around at Darby's flowered furniture, remembering her notion of making a getaway to some Pacific island. "Marlon Brando did it," Darby said.

— — —

"Three or four days," Halverson told Darby. "You do some bowling or something." He didn't tell her he was heading out of Montana, over to Spokane where nobody would know him, to buy a rifle.

"Which one is it?"

"Nobody," he said. "I wouldn't be chasing a woman."

Halverson spent two days talking to gun men in the surplus houses and sporting goods stores, and ended up spending $440 for a falling block Ruger #1, fitted out with a Redfield 3 × 9 variable wide-angle scope, and firing a .458 Winchester magnum bullet. One reasonably placed shot would kill anything native to North America, really anything anywhere, the salesman said, except for maybe a whale. Except for maybe a blue whale, and there were not many of them left. The salesman laughed, but then shook his head like there was nothing funny about dead whales.

The walnut stock swung hard and secure against Halverson's shoulder, and the mechanism worked with heavy, poised delicacy. The series of simple firing motions could be performed in two or three seconds, which was important, because the grizzly is as fast as a thoroughbred horse: three hundred yards in twenty seconds on level ground. But the rifle was extravagantly accurate at distance. Breathe, hold, and fire with the soft draw of the fingertip; and the animal would be dead. There should be no need for speed.

Late the second afternoon, Halverson drove to a gun club north of Spokane, beyond the industrial park around the Kaiser aluminum plant. At the gun club he fired nine rounds at range targets, three more for pleasure. The pattern of the last three rounds, at two hundred yards, was smaller than the spread of his fingers: all into the back of the throat, inside past the carnivorous fangs and into the soft and vulnerable flesh above the dark palate. Halverson could see the leafy boughs with their clusters of red and purple berries whipping after the animal fell, and then quiet in the noontime heat. When he finished firing, his shoulder ached like it had been struck a dozen times with a heavy mallet. The next day he outfitted himself with a light, down-filled sleeping bag and a one-man sleeve tent, a light-weight butane GAZ stove that nested with cooking pots, a spoon and fork and an elaborate Swiss Army knife, a Buck skinning knife, packets of freeze-dried food in heavy aluminum foil, and detailed hiker's maps of Glacier Park. He knew the park well enough, but the maps, with their shaded precision, were like verification of his accuracy. The bill for the heavy-duty back-pack and the traveling gear was almost as much as he'd paid for the rifle, but that was fine with him. Halverson had worked twenty-three years to earn a paid-off Kenworth, and now his time had come and he could just write checks. The gear would start with him, new and clean, and would wear and stain and become his in the wilderness.

Darby was awake. Just out of the shower and blow-drying her hair at the kitchen table while she sipped instant coffee. Halverson had driven back from Spokane in the early morning hours. Now he stood in the doorway with the rifle in his hands. Darby nodded her head, as if acknowledging some premonition. "Who on earth," she said, "can you think you are making plans for?" She was staring at the rifle, the hair-dryer aimed at the ceiling. "Why in the world?" As if this could be his way of making up for her flowered furniture.

So Halverson told her. Just killing one bear, for a head, to mount on the wall, to get things even. Anyway, he said, I never killed one. I am owed one. And no, he told her, she could not come along.

"The rangers killed one," she said. "An old one, a cripple."
Halverson told her it wasn't enough.
"I'm going," Darby said. "I'm going and you can't stop me. I'll just follow."

"Why in the hell?" Halverson said. "This is not any of your concern." No, he told her, she was not going.

"So half the head will be mine," she said.

Halverson mimicked her voice. "What about me?" he said. "How about mine?" He told her she would never make it.

"I got boots," Darby said. "I walk more on a night shift than you walk in three weeks. You better worry about yourself. Back and forth on them duckboards behind that bar is more than you ever think about walking. What you should do is get in some running. Before the moon comes back, you should get in better shape than you are. I can carry extra food, think of that, and you could quit shaving." The hair-dryer looked like a thick-barreled weapon as she shook it while she talked; and the silence after she shut off its whirring let Halverson see how loud their voices had been. There had been the years of climbing through the brush, setting three-quarter-inch cable choker behind the D-8 skid Cats when he was breaking in; and then more years bucking a chain saw up those mountains and falling timber, all those years until he had the money for the down payment on the Kenworth, and he was hard as he would ever need to be. Halverson thought of telling her about how many years he had worked to be in shape for this, but after she shut off the hair-dryer, he didn't say a thing. He kept quiet.

"You come out here." Halverson crossed the kitchen and stood at the open back door, fishing in his coat pocket for a cartridge, and then slipping the round into the firing chamber. "You shoot this thing and see. You just see." Darby followed him barefoot out into the weedy lot where he showed her how to hold the rifle, her hands small and white against the stained walnut stock. She almost couldn't reach the trigger.

"Where?"

"Anywhere."

Halverson was surprised by how quick she fired, the roar as she cast a shot toward the timbered hillside. She stepped backward from the recoil. But only for a moment, crouched and regaining her balance, did she look bewildered.

"You should know something," she said. "You are not the

first one to try that trick. I been mixed with before by you wise-assed boys." She grinned like a child in the morning sunlight.

"Have it the way you like."

For three weeks, while they waited on the full moon, Halverson kept on driving his truck while Darby went on pulling her bartending shift. He gave up on the Jack Daniel's and slept anyway. He lost weight and quit smoking, and felt he was becoming less than himself.

They crossed at Polebridge over the North Fork of the Flathead River almost at midnight, under a full moon as they'd planned, carrying enough food for several weeks; the freeze-dried stuff in aluminum packets, a half pound of salt, a brick of cheese; potatoes and onions to fry with the fish he'd catch; and even a heavy uncut side of bacon, Darby's idea. Halverson wanted to travel light. But there was no arguing. "We can camp and you can travel out. We are not going to be moving around. We will make a place." She was carrying her share, and she bought her own gear, every few days bringing home something new to show him: a frameless pack, a Dacron insulated sleeping bag she claimed would dry better than his goose feathers, an expensive breakdown fly rod. She would smile and fondle each thing, as if this was part of her plan to move away across the Pacific Ocean. As a last gesture, she trimmed his beard. Halverson wanted to shave it off after the first week, because of the itching, and because the gray in it surprised him. "You leave it grow," she said. "It makes you look like a movie star." After the second week the itching stopped and Halverson got used to it and stopped leaning out to see himself in the huge rectangular mirrors hung on either side of the truck cab. What Darby said was true; he looked like some visitor who might be in town for only a night or so.

The walking was easy in the moonlight, along the twisting roadway past the ranger station at the lower end of Bowman Lake and then on the wide park service trail over Cerulean

Ridge toward Quartz Lake, stepping in and out of the shadows of moonlight. Presently, the early midsummer sun rose in a great blossom over the cirque wall beyond Quartz Lake, near the blunt peak Halverson figured from the map had to be Redhorn, light coming down at them and the shadows receding like tide. Halverson felt as if he could be walking into his childhood where he might find the strange thin-armed boy in his mother's box camera photographs, himself at thirteen, solemnly holding aloft a small trout; the person he had been, real and turning over stones in a creek, searching for caddis fly larvae, or in a hot meadow catching grasshoppers with his hat. The boy would pay him no attention, intent on catching bait, wearing no shirt under raggedy bib overalls. A boy who existed only in tones of photographic gray.

They got themselves off the trail before there was a chance of meeting other hikers, and made a cold camp. As they wove out through the open brush, Halverson deliberately stepped on the clustering mushrooms, like he was balancing rock to rock across a stream; and as he slept in the afternoon stillness, he dreamed of the mushrooms crackling under his boots. They looked poisonous, wide caps sprinkled with virulent red. Over twenty years since he had been inside this park, and now, bad dreams.

The next night they worked past the camps at the lower end of Quartz Lake, tents and the sparking remains of a fire, the end of any sort of trail. They made maybe five or six hundred yards up the north side of the lake, even with moonlight coming bright over the water, stepping along in the shallows, in and out of shadows cast by the timber, afraid their splashing would be heard by the campers down the shore where the fire still glowed. In the grassy opening between deadfalls they laid their packs against a log, and Darby unbuttoned her shirt and dropped it and stood naked to the waist. "You better get some dry socks," Halverson said.

"I never did this before," Darby said. "I never stood like this in the moon before."

Halverson looked away. "Now is not the time for these things.

You just worry about changing your socks." While he lay listening to her breathe in her sleep and watched the stars make
their slow way around the moon, Halverson reflected on how
long it had been since he and Darby had been after one another.
The first night when he went into the tavern and she was there,
tending the bar, Halverson drank late, rolling dice in a long
game of Ship, Captain, and Crew; and toward closing time she
looked at him and said, fine, all right she would, after she
counted out the till, when he asked her if she had ever gone
riding in a logging truck. Even though she invited herself into
his bed after she found out he owned the truck and cabin, what
they got from each other was not founded on any financial
considerations; she kept her job and nobody was bought or sold.
But now they were stopped, these months since spring; and
maybe the way they slept without touching was causing the
changes in her, thin white hands lifting her breasts in the moonlight, if she was changing and hadn't always been ready for
anything secretly. Darby was from a town named Wasco, in the
great central valley of California; and her breasts were lined
faintly by stretch marks. There had been other men and probably
children. He wondered how much she told him, and why they
could live together and not tell each other what was true.

After sunrise, picking their way along where that lone surviving
girl had fought her way back toward the world, Halverson followed Darby and wished there could be some sign of that girl,
a rip of cloth he could lift off a snag and tuck into his breast
pocket as a sign of his intentions. But there was no hurry, and
they went slowly, heading up to the swampy creek-water flat
between Quartz and Cerulean lakes, willow ground, and thick
with ferns and berry brush where the bear would come to feed.
Up there he would be deep below the rough high circle of
hanging wall peaks, looking up to those spoon-shaped cirques
carved by the ancient glaciers to the remnants of ice which
would show faint white under the moon on these clear nights,
and into the country where his business waited. There was no

hurry and this walk was more and more a trip back into someone he had been. In the afternoon Halverson surprised himself as they stood resting on a rocky point overlooking the lake—he put his arm around Darby and held her to his side. She smelled of a deep sour odor, but it was not entirely unpleasant; it was as if all the stench from the barroom was seeping out of her. Most importantly, he was trying to figure just when he had stood in this very place before. The complex green and yellow etching of lichen on the rocks was familiar. What if you could recall even the look of the clouds from every moment of your life? There was too much of himself he was bringing along, so much he felt dizzy holding onto Darby; and he shut his mind against it.

The third night they camped a quarter mile up from Quartz Lake, toward Cerulean, north of the swampy willow ground in an open grove of stunted black cottonwood on a little knoll. The fire, their first fire, was in the ashes of another fire—where those girls might have built their fire. The beaver trappers had come into this country close to 150 years ago, when there was no one else in this high country, to this place which had no history except for the Blackfeet. But the beaver trapping must have been poor, because beaver never lived above timberline where the little creeks froze to the bottom in winter, except for the deep holes where the trout survived. There had never been enough beaver to draw the trappers. Maybe the only past here was the one he brought, him and Darby, what they remembered.

Their first open fire, they were alone finally, up toward the head of the fifteen or so mile trough the ancient glacier had eroded and left for the lakes, more than 2,000 feet below the ring of peaks which had shown east of them like a crown when touched by the last sunlight. Darby was frying four small cutthroats caught from the ripple where the creek slipped into Quartz Lake when a loon called, its mournful laugh echoing over and back into the settling coolness under the mountains before moonrise, a sound Halverson had not heard since one of the far places of his childhood, but perfectly known and expected, not surprising as it came back off the shadowed walls above them. As the moon turned through the sky those shadows moved as if the mountains were going to fall out over the fire and the creek water below.

"What were they doing here?" Darby asked.

"Who?"

"Those children." Halverson was astonished when she turned from the fire; there were tears in her eyes, lighted by the flames. "If what I'm thinking about is any of your business," she said, and she rubbed at her face and went to turn her sleeping bag open.

In the morning, Halverson set up a business of camp-tending meant to last. Where they could listen to the water of the creek falling through a raft of deadwood as they perched themselves each morning after coffee, he picked a fallen barkless lodgepole to serve as toilet seat, and spooled a roll of yellow paper on a dead branch like a flag. In the afternoon he shot and butchered a yearling mule deer and ran the meat high in a tree, out of the reach of any bear, the carcass wrapped in cheesecloth to keep away the flies. In the gray light after sunset the dead animal in that white wrap of cloth turned slowly on the rope. "They ain't going to get to it," Halverson said. "But they will be coming to see."

"The bears and squirrels," Darby said. "And the park rangers. You are going to draw a crowd."

"Everybody who is interested," Halverson said. The intestines from the slaughtered yearling had been warm and slippery, and the odor of the kill had been acrid in the late afternoon warmth. Halverson smiled for the first time, smelling his hands, where the faint odor of deer remained.

How long had he refused returning into these mountains? Why had that girl come here from that rich place on the outskirts of Columbus, Ohio? Why come hunting a place where there is no one else?

The girl had used the excuse of school for getting away from whatever crowded life she had been born to, then quit her wildlife biology studies down in Missoula and gone off to Columbia Falls with that boy who delivered cocaine and climbed in the summer, and now she was dead in these mountains.

"What do you guess she was up to?" Halverson said.

"You wait and you wait," Darby said, "and everything takes all the time it can. Then it all comes in a hurry." She shook salt over the venison steaks in the frying pan. "You . . . " she said and waited. "Why don't you ever fuck me?"

"Why are you talking like shit?" Halverson said. "You tell me what fucking has to do with this?"

"Nothing. I'm just wondering. She never talked anything serious to me, like I never knew anything, or come from anywhere, and all the time I could have told her."

"You could have told her what?"

"About how we go looking for some one thing to be, and there's nothing to find."

The biggest trouble, he understood, was that he was not afraid. Halverson tried to center himself into that frail girl, the girl who died, and then he shook his head. He wished he had brought a pint of whiskey so that this single night, when everything was ready, he could rest here with his common sense turning circles and be inside that girl and feeling the warmth from this fire and the cool night on her back, drifting in someone else—a rich girl estranged from the rich part of Ohio—and no rifle.

Maybe that would have worked—no rifle. At least he might have been a little bit afraid and not sitting here with thoughts of his dead father, and his mother living her life out in San Diego. His mother in a wicker chair on the front lawn and sunset over the warships in San Diego harbor; Halverson saw her, and some dim memory of his father kneeling in the snow to fasten the straps on her snowshoes, a logging road and larch in the background.

"Why don't you ever?" Darby said.

"What?"

"You know."

"Because you talk like you do."

Picking along the edge where the lodgepole timber leveled into
the swamp, scouting the new territory, Halverson was walking
alone when the old she-bear reared herself out of thick brush
only a hundred or so yards before him. Listening but no doubt
unable to make him out with her weak eyes, she was maybe
ready to come at him and find out what he was, but more likely
to drop and lope away. Halverson heard her snuffling; and as
he had planned, but before he was able to understand this was
not what he wanted, not this easiness, he centered the cross
hairs just beneath her dark uplifted nose and fired. As he slipped
his finger across the trigger, he was astonished by the noise,
which hadn't mattered when he killed the doe, the hard jolt of
the rifle stock against his shoulder and the crack that went
echoing, the massive head jerking away, gone from the scope.
Halverson thought he had missed, levered in another shell,
thinking *nowhere*, then lifted his eye from the scope to see the
bear floundering backward and sideways into the leafy brush,
and falling as he had imagined. With such thoughtless luck he
was done with it now, and had killed his grizzly, too quickly
for recall, except for the diminishing echo of the rifle shot; and
he was already sorry, knowing this one was wasted. There had
to be another, stalked and properly confronted and then killed.
There had to be time for thinking, and time for the bear, for
hoping the animal might dimly sense the thing happening.

Halverson waited, listening, expecting Darby, who did not
come, hearing nothing but the buzz of insects. Soon the birds
began moving and calling in the trees once more, and then he
went to the bear. The odor was rancid, and Halverson was
surprised by the smallness of the dead animal, the raggedness
of her coat, because already he could see it was a she-bear, an
old one who looked to be shedding in midsummer, the gray-
tipped pelt ragged and almost slick to the hide around the rear
haunches. An old one. The wrong one. The .458 magnum slug

had entered her mouth and blown away the back of her skull. Halverson cupped his fingers into the wound and there was nothing to be felt but pulpy flesh and sharp bone fragments and warm blood, like thick soup.

He tasted the salty blood.

Kneeling beside the carcass, Halverson tried again to think of the dead girl in these mountains. The stench of the animal beside him was like a part of the air. Off in the willows a frog was croaking; and then he heard the first sounds of the helicopter, rotor blades cutting at the stillness as the aircraft came up along the length of Quartz Lake, the thunking louder until the helicopter hung between walls of the stippled rock face above him.

Downstream that roll of yellow toilet paper was spooled onto the dead branch like a flag. The helicopter turned and lifted, moved a half mile away. Halverson brought the rifle to his shoulder and through the eye of the scope watched the two men up there searching for him with binoculars. Don't find me, Halverson thought. This is none of your business, and it is not finished. We are not in this together.

It had to have been the echoing of the shot that drew the men in the helicopter. The afternoon of the day before he'd killed the yearling mule deer; and now, another shot, echoing down the length of the lake, they were after him. Only when the helicopter lifted and turned in three wide fluttering circles, and then bore off down the lake, going away, did Halverson pay attention to what came next. He would have to build a silencer.

Darby would not leave. "You got me here," she said, "so you are going to have trouble getting me out, even if they come looking." She was talking about the park service rangers. "There won't be the rifle, so there is nothing against the law with me being here." The carcass of the gutted doe was hanging a quarter mile away, wrapped in cheesecloth. Halverson thought of that, but didn't say anything. Let her learn, if this is what she wants. Halverson went out of the park the next morning, carrying only the rifle, and drove back to his cabin in the canyon above Columbia Falls. Even without the pack it was a hard, daylong march. Darby would be all right, or else she wouldn't. She had insisted on coming along, and she was into it.

The silencer turned out to be a reasonably simple piece of business. Halverson slipped an eight-inch section of heavy plastic hot water tubing over thick rubber washers on the end of the rifle barrel; and when it was securely in place, he cut pipe threads on the outside of the tubing. This was a mount for the silencer. The thing itself consisted of two cylinders, a small perforated core of metal tubing inside a larger section of steel pipe, the space between them packed with sound-absorbing steel wool. Halverson brazed it together in the pole-walled shed back of his cabin, where he kept the Kenworth in winter, then screwed the silencer onto the threaded plastic pipe fixed to the end of the rifle barrel. It was like a small metal can hanging out there. He fired the rifle into the hillside back of the cabin, and the contraption worked. There was the crack of the magnum slug passing the sound barrier, he lost none of his muzzle velocity, but the explosive roar was absorbed in the steel wool. He was ready again. This time he would hunt quietly, secretly, and choose and get this properly done with. He called and had the telephone shut off, and the power, and the newspaper. Through it all he felt as if he were acting on precise instructions for going away that he did not need to understand. That night he thought of Darby up there alone in her sleeping bag, the frogs croaking in the darkness. He wondered if she was frightened, or if she was walking around naked amid the trees. If she touched herself in the night, who would she be thinking about? Before driving back to the park in the morning, he went into Columbia Falls and bought a newspaper to read with breakfast; and again acting on what seemed to be directives for survival somewhere else, a guidebook to edible species of mushrooms.

Darby had moved the camp. She found another fire ring a couple of miles upstream from their first camp, and said the ashes were fresh and no doubt it was the place where the girls had camped. "It was the right place, being here where they were," she said. Halverson had found her late in the afternoon, and now it was dark.

"Which one will you be?" Darby said. "One night you can be one, and I'll be the other, and then we can switch around. We can see which one gets eaten worst." She smiled as though this lewdness was very funny, and turned back to her work, frying three trout. "Maybe this is the place. When I was here alone, I tried to think what that girl was thinking, and it felt like the place."

"What did she think?"

But Darby didn't answer, and Halverson took the whiskey from his day-pack. Along with the book on mushrooms, he had brought a quart of Jack Daniel's. The firelight shone through the liquid like a dim lantern. "There was a man here, really a boy, the second night you were gone," Darby said. "One of those park service boys, just last year out of college in Vermont. He was looking for you. At least he was looking for someone with a rifle. He was frightened. That's what he said. Probably some lunatic son of a bitch, is what he said. I didn't say anything. I don't think he wanted to find anybody, least of all a man." She salted the frying fish. "He talked about how this park is open ground for crazies. What he said is lunatics. He said there was no control, and lunatics clustered in places where there was no control."

"Maybe he got it right. We might stay here forever. All the goddamned helicopters do no good. We might stay right here," Halverson said. "You know what I did? You guess . . . I got back and there was a week's newspapers all over the porch." He was going to lie, there had been the newspapers, but the rest of this was going to be a lie. "I didn't call them and have the newspaper shut off, or the power company shut off the lights, or the telephone. Those things are going on back there, without us, to remind them. I could have shut it off, but I didn't." Halverson waited for her to look away from the fire and back toward him.

"Who are they reminding?" Darby said. "About what?"

When Halverson didn't answer, she went on. "What I did is, I slept with that boy. In his sleeping bag and mine zipped together. He was frightened and I felt like his mother, holding to him all night." Darby finally turned and looked at Halverson. "It was the right thing to do," she said.

"Did you fuck him?"

She nodded. She did not seem disturbed. "It was the right thing to do. I wanted to be with somebody, and it made him feel better."

Halverson was not frightened, and he was not angry. Maybe she did do the right thing, for her. It was not anything he could get himself to think about. "I guess we could have a drink together," Halverson said. Maybe each thing they were doing was the right thing to do. He poured them each a shot in the steel Sierra Club cups, and didn't say anything about how he was going to sit drunk in the night and see if he could see what it could maybe feel like to be that girl as the bear began nudging at the tent walls. He would get drunk and think he was alone and begin whimpering; and when he woke up and the hangover was gone, he would begin hunting.

Late in the night, sipping at his whiskey and sharpening his skinning knife by firelight, Halverson surprised himself. Darby was curled in her sleeping bag, maybe sleeping and maybe not, when Halverson for the first time in all this surprised himself absolutely by drawing the knife along the tender flesh inside his left forearm, careful to avoid the veins as they stood out, just softly tracing and watching the painless slide of the blade and the immediate welling streak of blood, holding himself so he did not force the blade deeper, pulling away just as he reached the wrist. After a moment of watching the blood gather and begin to drip, he held the knife low over the coals until the cutting edge began to glow red, and then breathing through his teeth, he seared the wound. The next morning, when Darby asked, he told her it had only been a test.

"Just practicing, I thought about cutting off a finger," he

said, which was a lie, "but then I thought, there is nothing to grieve over, so I didn't cut off no finger."

"That's fine," Darby said.

"The first blood," Halverson said, "was always mine."

"Never in this world," Darby said. "That story I told, about fucking with that boy, was a lie. I've had plenty of that. It didn't happen."

What Halverson did not tell her was that the whiskey worked: he finally dreamed of the girl who died. At least it was a dream he had never witnessed before, and it must have come from someone nearby. It must have been waiting. Below in some street there was the snow melting as it fell on wet black asphalt that flared under the headlights of a red Olds convertible which was backing out of a long driveway. In the street, the convertible did not move. The motor stopped and the headlights dimmed, and Halverson, in his sleep, thought: which window is this I am watching from?

Then he was awake and the fire was burned down to embers; and he listened to the snapping of pitch and Darby's breathing, and heard the rasping of brush against brush and stillness; and knew it was the girl's dream he was in because for the first time he was afraid. The rifle was there, he could touch it by reaching out, but he was trembling.

Another sound, and he lay there, not calling out to Darby because this was not her business, feeling his forearms tremble as a pine limb flared, and waiting for the rooting hoglike sound which never came. There was a whisper of air high in the yellow pine. The moon was gone. Off east the high wall of the cirque hung in delicate outline against the fainter blue of what had to be the sky turning toward morning. Nothing had happened, and as the dream began to fade there was nothing to do but rebuild the fire.

After breakfast, as she watched him scrubbing their plates with sand in the cold water at the edge of the stream, Darby got started talking about what was fair. She wanted seriously to try the rifle, not just firing off at nothing on a hillside, but killing. "You slice at your arm like that, you might cut your throat. Where would I be, when there was trouble?"

"What would you kill?"

Darby didn't answer, but turned her back to Halverson, un-buttoned her wrinkled blue work shirt and dropped it off her shoulders and sat facing the morning sun on a grassy ledge above the creek, slumping, as from the weight of her breasts. "No wonder you draw crowds," Halverson said, "sitting around bare-assed like that."

"Maybe I already did. Maybe I had a boatload of cowboys, and there is more coming in tonight, and maybe I am just warning you." The stretch marks on her breasts and over her hips were a silvery network of light. So I was never pretty, she said, after their first night together, talking about the marks, tracing them with a fingertip after she turned on a light, showing them to him like some wound, but never explaining. I never been pretty because of these, she said, and he never asked where they came from.

"You are going to sunburn your tits," Halverson said, and he went off to the half-rotten cored-out deadfall where he kept the rifle hidden. Quietly he slipped a cartridge into the firing chamber and raised the rifle and fired without aiming, as she had that morning behind the cabin, only he was firing toward the grayish snowpack in the ravines of Redhorn Peak.

"I heard you," she said when he came back to where she sat in the sun. Halverson was carrying the rifle and her shirt was on and buttoned. "You missed," she said, and she looked around and bit at the tip of her index finger as she watched him eject the empty casing. Halverson put in another shell.

"Not now," she said. "I changed my mind."

There were no clouds anywhere in the long sky reaching off south and west from the peaks; and far off in the trough to the west, Quartz Lake shone under the late afternoon sun. Early that morning, standing over the darkness of Cerulean Lake,

Halverson had looked down from the logjam at the creek outlet to trees floating upright far below the surface, his face mirrored among them, then spent the morning climbing along the southern rise of the drainage. He was resting in the noontime warmth on a rotting log, listening to the silence which whispered of insects, when he heard the dry cracking of a limb breaking out onto this open burn-slope.

But this was Darby, not a bear. She had followed him all this way. Halverson watched as she came from the timber into the sunlight maybe 150 yards down slope, stopped and looked around and didn't see him. Halverson watched as she undid the buttons on her blue work shirt again, took it off and knotted the sleeves around her waist. This time she was wearing the orange top to her swimming suit over her breasts. Watching her through the scope on the rifle, the magnification bringing her up to only fifteen or so yards. Halverson was surprised how tanned she was from this last couple of weeks lying naked in the afternoons while he was off hunting. There it was, this other person she had become. What was she following, all this way into his idea of what he had to do?

It was Darby, after he whistled softly to her and waved, who first saw the bear. She sat beside him on the rotting log, not saying anything, as if there was no reason to explain why she spent this long day trailing him, and then she said, "Do you see him?"

"Who?"

"Down over there."

There it was, down the length of her pointing arm, the bear thrashing in the berry brush, head down and only the dark hump flashing at them occasionally. Halverson watched through the scope, and saw the animal roll a great rotting log for the grubs on the underside, the casual movement of enormous strength like that of a man moving driftwood on a beach. This sunny quiet day. Halverson wondered what he should do now, which move to make. Rest the rifle solidly on the log, shout, and when the animal stands, breathe one last deep steady time, and fire. That is how close you must be. It was all too easy.

"What you can do is go down there with your knife," Darby said. "You can slide up closer and closer, and I will do the shooting."

"Yeah, sure," Halverson said.

"Otherwise there's no point. We can shoot him right now and go home, if that's all you want, to kill a bear." She wet her index finger and marked a cross on the air. "That does it. One bear." He understood she wanted something here more than he did. What did she want?

Halverson understood what he was going to do. Darby was right, this was not any kind of getting even, and making things even was not what he was about. *He didn't want me.* Those were the words of the girl who survived. As if the bear possessed some gift, and had withheld it from her.

"See if you can do it," Halverson said, and he slid a cartridge into the firing chamber, and handed the rifle to Darby. She took it like she had been waiting. Halverson gave her three cartridges. "See if you can do it," he said again.

Only when he was fifty or so yards downhill, with his skinning knife in his right hand, did Halverson wonder at all about what he was doing. He could feel the eye of the scope on his back, and as he moved carefully through the brush, Halverson thought, *now who is the hunter?*

Not even yet was he afraid. He had been afraid in the night, after dreaming, when he lay in his sleeping bag and trembled and nothing happened but the eventual sunrise. But that was gone, and nothing was left of the terrible anger he felt the first night in his cabin, if it was anger, when he heard the girl was dead. Halverson felt small and weak, but not afraid. Brilliant deep pinkish-lavender stalks of fireweed grew waist-high from long-rotted roots of an overturned alpine fir. Puffball mushrooms, overripe by now, clustered under them. Halverson bent and punctured the gray-white skin of a mushroom with a forefinger. It had looked like a little balloon on the ground. The skin broke; the spore rose like gunpowder smoke. The odor of the spore was that of clean earth, slightly acid, as was the taste when he licked his forefinger. Halverson felt himself touching one thing at a time with great slowness. The rasp of a wasp in the air before him was abrasive against his eyelids as he hesitated. One thing and then another. He moved carefully over the spongy lichen-covered and mossy ground between clumps of deep saw-edged grass, crouching and pushing through slowly, reaching for one of the red-purple berries that hung in clusters around him, tasting it, pulling a handful that were sticky in his palm as he crouched there eating them one at a time. The aftertaste was like a sour ache in his mouth. So, he thought, this is the way you are feeding.

Halverson stood quiet amid the buzzing of insects, listening. He heard the bear stirring just ahead in the brush. The smell of it was like an odor of clean rot in the sunlight, tangible as something to taste, the air filled with bright floating specks like infinitesimal crystalline butterflies which would settle and flutter on the tongue after drifting on currents of light. He could hear the bear's chuffing—a grunting sound which was more like slow, heavy breathing rather than anything eating. Only when he moved closer, crouching again and stepping forward slowly, did Halverson at last see the animal. Low to the ground, looking upward through leafy green brush, he saw the dark belly, and realized he was being watched. The grunting had stopped and Halverson looked up and saw the bear reared and gazing down on him, black lips curled over the fangs as though the animal was smiling, and nothing but curious.

The bear shook its head against the flies crawling on its lips in the thick juice of the berries. Halverson stepped back and stood upright, seeing that shake of the animal's head as an acknowledgment, almost a greeting. Halverson was not sure what to do except wait; he was this close, he should always have been this close. The bear lifted its muzzle, weaving its head from side to side, looking upward as if there might be some tiny thing to be seen far off in the sky, then lowered its head and dropped slowly forward, the decision made, and after a great slow bunching of itself, moved at him, hidden a moment in the brush, and then at him, before him. The leaves shook as if there had been a wind to accompany the rush. The animal stopped and reared again. Halverson lifted the knife.

With forelegs raised, the bear looked down at him. The dark eyes were soft, and the terrible odor was a stench. With the knife still upraised, Halverson waited: *this close.*

What do you do with the knife? Do you step closer, toward the embrace, and where do you plunge the blade? There was no knowing; Halverson began to move forward, stroking the blade of the knife through the air with small tentative motions while he waited to know what he should do as the bear lifted its forelegs higher, and then Halverson was no longer wondering as in the slowness of what was happening he tasted the sweet fecal breath of the animal, Halverson touching his tongue to his teeth. One thing and then another. The clean long pelt over the breast of the animal was ruffled by what had to have been a breeze in the afternoon stillness. Softly it ruffled, like a woman's hair as Halverson tried to imagine it later, except that it was really like nothing but that yellowish silver flutter before him, not like a woman's hair at all. And then there was a shot, the crack as the lead slug from the rifle broke over his head, the flat splattering sound; and Halverson saw what he had been unable to imagine, the head jerking back, the terrible involuntary slackness as the jaws gaped open, the spasm in the eyes, the flowering of blood, and the bear going down in the brush, dead with a great final rush of breath.

Halverson lowered his knife. There was nothing to defend against; there hadn't been, not unless he courted it, and the anger he felt, the trembling in his forearms, was not so much at anything as it was at loss; and he did not know what was lost. He stood over the bear, now a mere dead animal, however large, and looked at his knife. There is the least you can manage, he thought, and he dropped to his knees, enveloped in the hot stench, and began hacking, dismembering, cutting off the head. It was a long job, and he broke the knife blade prying between the vertebrae, but finally the head rolled free, a couple of turns down the slope, coming to rest beneath the clusters of red-purple berries.

When Halverson stood, his back ached and his arms and chest were sloppy from his wallowing at his job, in the blood. All the time feeling the scope on his back, Halverson rested and smoked a cigarette, and then with his arms wrapped awkwardly around it, smelling it, Halverson began transporting the head back up the slope to Darby. He wondered fleetingly if she would let him reach her. At last she lowered the rifle.

"I waited long enough, didn't I?" she asked. He stood before her, legs braced against the fleshy weight of the head. She stood on the grayish rotting log where she had rested the rifle, which she had let fall into the matted grass. Halverson set the head at her feet, so it grinned up at them—great carnivorous teeth closed and the black lips slack. He dropped the broken knife, watching it fall through the tangled grass to the mossy ground. "That will do," he said. The head of the bear could rest there on that log, the insects could have it until it was a skull, looking west.

Halverson brushed away a fly that was crawling on the fingers of his hand. Seven cartridges were heavy in the loops of his belt. One by one he took them out and fired them away toward the peaks; the crack, the rush of the slug, then nothing. All this was one act of trust after another. The far white sky to the west was reflected from the lake below in its trough. They were inside a place where each thing irrevocably followed another, and the only hesitations were those that could be reckoned with.

Back at their camp Halverson fired the rest of his cartridges, then gave Darby the rifle and asked her to take it out and hide it in some place where it couldn't be found.

"You know that old one, that cripple the rangers killed," she said. "Well, they killed the right one. The belly was full of hair."

Halverson told her that didn't make any difference. He built a fire and sat with his back to it, watching the line of shadow rise on the peaks as the sun descended. Then he heard her coming back. "Darby," he said.

"I'm here," she said.

THOMAS McGUANE
THE EL WESTERN

Lucien's father died down in Arizona the same year Lucien lost custody of his son. The old man had insisted that a member of the family call every day. He did not want to die and have someone discover his remains at the end of a long holiday. Yet that is exactly what happened. Lucien arranged a small funeral, left some money with the priest and came home. Snow whirled in the windows, and eating was just kind of hit and miss right up until Lucien was fairly unrecognizable. He couldn't keep from thinking.

When the funeral was over and before he left to go back to Montana, Lucien stopped to see his brother and his wife. His brother had been pretty much of a goner since Parris Island. That was twenty years ago and Arizona hadn't helped. His wife moved like a scared fly, and Lucien's brother just kept smoking real slow and saying quietly, "I guess they're all together now." His fingers rested on the clouded glass top of a wrought-iron table. There were toys tipped over against the sliding door. No one seemed to know just how mad to be. The brother looked up at Lucien in his fogged-out way and said, "It's like some deer hunter got him."

When Lucien was very young, he read all of the sporting magazines; and one of these, he now remembered, had a feature called "This Happened to Me" in which awful things happened to sportsmen because of ice and cliffs and wild animals, things which were terrible but which the sportsmen survived by thinking of something fast and at just the right moment. Or they were saved by the inexplicable. For instance, the polar bear sees his mate float past on an iceberg and therefore releases your skull. These things were very much like divine intervention and were meant to leave you thinking that the sportsman is most directly exposed to feeling the big flywheel, the eternal gear. What gave "This Happened to Me" its special brimstone quality, apart from the illustrations of sportsmen dangling, sliding or being pursued, was that each segment was signed by the survivor. "Art Clancy, Acme, Michigan," or somebody. And for a long time, Lucien identified himself with these nearly anonymous sportsmen, that is to say with *all* of them, and began seeking out ways of living which would produce civilian versions of "This Happened to Me," combining the episodic, the anecdotal yield and, best of all, the deep and abiding smell of brimstone. When he tried to get away from that, he sensed nothing was going on; when he gave in to it, he found he required a steady, deepening effort in the episodes to produce a real "This Happened to Me" effect of sportsmen against the flywheel with a geniunely sulphuric atmosphere. Then everything happened to Lucien. He got rich and lost his family. He grew savage in his loss. He sought crimes against nature the way a normal man will roll a cart through the supermarket. But at the same time it held his attention, and after each purple connivance, Lucien would think, This Happened to Me.

Now, however, it had happened to him. Familiar remedies were not at hand. So he spent all his time out at the cow camp, as he called it, a cattle ranch with a small white house, whose high pastures were shattered by ancient earthquake faults and brush canyons that turned upon themselves like seashells. Inside these canyons the sun or moon rose and fell inside an hour's time; a shadow would race at you like a guillotine. Insects were magnified in the angular light, and the rock walls seemed to have been cleaned with vinegar. Coyotes stole through the sequestered Byzantium, not knowing Lucien was there eating cold fried trout in these one-hour days which let him emerge into a larger day, feeling he had stolen time.

Lucien saw the sun move up toward him on the surface of the river. The river edged up in the bend as a cresting glare. His sedan was a luminous tear of terrific paint parked on the bank. If he rowed long enough he would be tired, and usually he was shaking. But he felt that there was only so much that his mind could do to him because he had arranged a weariness for himself that was as plain as he could make it.

He folded the oars within the gunwales and stepped out onto the bank with the bowline in hand. The drift boat ran off a bit on the eye of the current, then came to shore. He dragged the bow up on the cold pebbles and lit a cigar.

Lucien had taken the position that he was growing to meet himself, that he was ascending to a kind of rendezvous. He had placed himself on trial but would make the odd exception, because he had seen what little things break our parole from eternity. Last night's paper revealed that a man had been badly beaten, then shot to death guarding a Royal Doulton Toby jug collection. A quiet type met his end in a welter of ceramics and lead. Everything that meant anything was being sold to guitarists and pants designers. He was going to fish quietly and sweat it out.

The road was hot. Birds had dusted in its course and disappeared once again into the brush along the creek. Aquatic insects drifted from the creek and speckled the windshield of the sedan moving between alternating panels of light, vegetation and sky. The sedan's luster was magnificent with nature's passing show. Lucien and a new friend were finishing a long night together; they didn't quite know how.

"I'm going to shut it down here," Lucien said. The woman

sat across the front seat staring at him with a slightly swollen
look about her lips. It was sunup.

Lucien lit a cigar and sighted around himself before directing
its smoke toward the leafy staggered shadow from which the
movement of cold water could be heard. He could feel himself
speeding up. He felt he was being run to earth.

"Maybe I can catch a fish," he told her and got out. He
strung the line through the guides of the rod and stared at the
brushy enclosure through which the moving water announced
itself.

"There's bugs," she said from inside, her head displayed on
the wiper arcs. "Now they're on the dash. Can I play the radio
while you do that?"

"Go ahead. Try and pick up the news."

Blue duns drifted over the tops of the willows. By the time
he waded to the spring he could no longer hear the radio. He
caught four small cutthroats before turning his attention to the
end of this small escape. He thought, I have only myself to
blame. He closed the lid to the compartmented English fly box
with its hundred treasures, and the escape was over.

"Did you get a fish?"

"I got three fish. Can you turn that thing down?"

"Three fish. That's nice. You got three fish. There it's down.
Happy?"

"Yes, very."

"That was a top ten crossover."

"You see, it gives me no special feeling. It's like being rolled
around in a barrel."

"Uh huh. Y'know, I just imagine my old man's alarm went
off about an hour ago." To Lucien daybreak had made her look
like one of the monuments at Easter Island. "But here's the
deal," she said, opening her compact, then throwing it back
into her purse hopelessly. "Let's find a way to get this over
with. My aunt will let me in through the garage. Nobody'll be
the wiser."

Lucien started the car and moved down the road toward town.

He tried to put some diplomacy and gratitude in his voice. "This sounds best for both of us," he said.

"You sickening fuck," she said. "I feel like a sewer."

The ranch house had a springy floor. Lucien's grandmother's house in town also had a spring to it. When Lucien was a child he could run through the first floor and cause the china to tinkle in the cabinets for a minute and a half. A train on the bridge would do the same; and the second-story sitting porch trembled at traffic or even, it seemed, the shouts of the neighbors from down the street. But this was a different motion, less the consequence of human pounding than some catarrhal moan from the ground, borne through the timbers of the house.

Part of the problem was that Lucien had got rid of the furniture. There was plenty of it too. And behind the two mortifying unsprung beds, there were hair-oil spots on the wall. Lucien didn't know who made the spots, but he thought, We've got plenty of haunts without this.

It was the last spring storm, a perfect day to burn furniture without fear of starting a grass fire. It was wet, and croaking ravens hung on the telephone wires, black and unassembled, like rags. He wasn't supposed to drink; but he did anyway. Then he hauled the brutal beds, the all-knowing sofas, the crazed mechanical La-Z-Boy prototype which some solitary *Popular Mechanics* reader had put together and whose experiment Lucien made a shambles of. These, surmounted by chrysanthemum print linoleum in quarter-acre lots, doused with number-two diesel fuel, took only a match. The fire lit up the fine, dense snow and produced the effect of sunny fog; anything at a middle distance—horses, trees, fences—shone through with an intense gray like spirits banished from the furniture. It did not seem then to Lucien as he paced around the draconic snow-licking flames with his bottle that there could be a way to call him unlucky; or, upon consideration, to subject him to opinions of any kind.

A half year later, the house was still empty of everything
except what would furnish a dormitory room; and the vacancy
seemed more rueful and eloquent than the furniture had. And
there were bullet holes in the mystery circles of hair oil. But
nobody is improved by having his child taken away.

The sound of snow slumping from the barn, the chinook winds
at night, coyotes below the house competing with noisy ball
games on the television, wood smoke and the moan of tractor
engines, serious flotation of the river in his drift boat, generally
good behavior if you omit one five-hundred-mile blackout on
the interstate. Which nobody got wind of.

Dear Herbert:
   I have been made aware of your and your client's version
as to why I would like to see my boy before winter and
why I would like to see his report cards, school projects,
drawings, and so on. I am made to understand that you
and your client imagine that I am building some sort of
case to reverse a decision which I have with some considerable difficulty learned to accept. I am further led to
believe that you have encouraged your client in this kind
of thinking.
   Herbert, I must assume that this is a false idea; and that
whoever generated such a diseased piece of reasoning has
either the ability to correct his thinking or the common
sense to recognize that people who are wronged seek whatever remedies that there are available to them.
   I know you will understand what I am saying.
                                        Sincerely yours,
                                        Lucien Taylor

Wick Tompkins had his small law offices across from the
monument to the fallen cavalryman, a grimacing bronze fighter
already dead, falling on an already dead horse, seizing the shaft

of the arrow which pierced his tunic, suggesting that the last man still left alive in the world was the bowman. Wick liked to point out that the chap would have had to be standing somewhere right close to his secretary's desk when he got the trooper.

The secretary winked up from her new data processor, then rolled fresh boiler plate onto the screen. This machine had made Wick a man of leisure: Wick now weighted 240 pounds. He smiled all the time, and his smile said, This better be funny.

"Lucien, come in here and close the door. I don't want anyone to see you. Your hat, give me your hat."

Lucien reached his Stetson to Wick, who hung it on a trophy for the champion mare at the Golden Spike show in Utah.

"Herbert Lawlor informs me that you have threatened him with a letter."

"I did not. I wrote him a letter."

"I've seen the letter."

"So you know that Herbert Lawlor is hysterical."

"The letter has threatening overtones. It is a pissing fight with a skunk. It is the very thing you are not to do. You're having fun out on your crummy cow camp, aren't you?"

"I'm making repairs."

"And you are floating on the river?"

"Almost every day."

"I think that's grand. Especially if you let me do the communicating with Mister Lawlor. It's demeaning for you to take these things into your own hands. I am paid to demean myself, though I dream of glory as well as weight loss and sex miracles with strangers."

"I'll do better at everything if I can see my boy."

"You will see him at Christmas and you're going to have to get used to that."

"Christmas."

"That's the next time, not the *last* time."

"How do you know when the last time is?"

Wick Tompkins drew on his cigarette, made a tentative gesture to stub it out, decided that too much of it remained, and said, "I think that is a disastrous remark."

"It's not a remark. It's what I think."

"It's a disaster."

When young girls learn the new dances, thought Lucien, it is the last time the new dances are interesting. I am in town, thought Lucien, why not make the most of it?

He sat down at the counter at Pop's Place, a hangout for people dramatically younger than himself, and drank coffee, the fastest beverage in the house. He drank as much of it as fast as he could and watched a two-by-four opening at the end of the room where the young girls danced together to a jukebox. Their movements were strange and formal, glassy and distant; and everything wonderful about their bodies was under twenty-four months old. They moved toward the bellowing music, then moved away, gazes crisscrossing. They arced toward the surrounding columnar tables and quick-swigged pop without losing the beat. Though much of this struck a deep chill in Lucien, part of him desired to be a shallow boy with a sports car. Anything he'd ever done seemed like old tickertape.

Lucien knew that he had to practice an upright existence. He was being watched, not by everyone as he imagined, but fairly closely watched.

When he emerged from Pop's, he immediately spotted people he knew; and he felt as though his trousers were undone, or that his face and neck were a mass of hickeys. He saw two people he knew. One was the messianic Century 21 realtor, H. A. "Bob" Roberts. Bob cried out a greeting. He coasted past Lucien with a marathoner's stride, but kept his face on a locked rotational axis in Lucien's direction.

The other was Mrs. Hunt, Lucien's mathematics teacher of years back. She had been retired for a long time and now stalked Main Street reproaching former students, some of whom were grandparents and had had quite enough of this from her over the years.

"Aren't you a little old for that place?" she asked Lucien.

"I guess I am," Lucien said, staring at a smile that revealed three-quarters of a century of cold fury. "I'm kind of chipper when I'm in a spot like that. What d'you think?"

"We're talking about self-control, aren't we, Lucien."

It was the perfect setting. Lucien sat with her at the first table this side of the closed-circuit television screen, an immense thing which stood huge and pale in the dark room. Along the wall were dark, empty, intimate booths, and they seemed as infested with ghosts as Mexican catacombs. The bartender put so much shaved ice in the blender drinks that Lucien never knew why his head was numb and his wrists ached. All he had to go by was mood swing.

"What in God's name am I doing here with you?" she said.

"I couldn't guess." He stared in fear at his drink.

"Did I tell you how glad I was you were able to catch a few fish the other day?"

"No you didn't, but thank you."

"So this is love."

"Well, it's very nice, isn't it."

"So this is your capital F love."

"No, frankly, it's not. But it has a nice side. Barkeep may I have a black olive?"

"For your *margarita*?"

"Precisely."

The bartender arrived and dropped the olive from about two feet right into the Sno-Kone.

"Thank you," said Lucien, staring straight at him.

She was actually pretty, except that, to Lucien, her neck seemed a little strong, a little sculptural. A blue vein crossed it like something hydraulic. Perhaps if her head had been a trifle bigger . . . Then everything else would have been out of whack.

Lucien had been through this before: change shoe sizes, hollow the ankles a bit along the tendon line, rotate the ass a few degrees north. After that you might as well load it out in a wheelbarrow. The thing's lost its magic. Then where are you?

"I ran into my old math teacher. She was cruel and made me feel old."

"I've got a good buzz now."

"I hadn't been doing anything wrong and she kind of nailed me." Lucien watched her with a wary gaze.

"Le Buzz Magnifique!" she cried.

"So as to what you're doing here, I don't know and I don't care. This old broad made me feel like a bum waiting for his heart to blow up in some bus station."

She stared at Lucien for a long moment.

"Say my name."

"Oh, darling." Lucien felt panicky.

" 'Cause you don't know the goddamned thing, do you. What do you take me for, a Kleenex?"

Lucien made a smile. It looked right and understanding. It looked okay.

"Stay right there," she ordered him. "Don't move."

She went to the bar and had a word with the bartender. He leaned on the hand that held a towel. From Lucien's distance, the bartender looked like Father Time. He blinked while she talked to him, nodded, wiped at the bar suddenly, and she curved on back to the table.

"Don't worry about a thing. I've got a late date with the bartender. He dearly loves to party."

"So everything's fine . . . ?"

"Yeah," she said, feeling in her purse for a Virginia Slim. "Said it'd be about half an hour."

A Kleenex. It was astonishing that she could make a remark like that, whatever her bitterness. Lucien, with not a little delusion, attempted to picture her husband, the background of the bitterness. Her husband belonged, by all Lucien could tell, to that class of people, usually vainglorious cuckolds, who chain-saw through trailer houses, use dump trucks for revenge upon their wives and girlfriends, and who are eventually captured, lambs with anomalous records, by baffled authorities, accorded treatment for stress, and released into a new world.

Lucien stopped at his office in the old railroad station to pick up his messages. Five sighs, fifteen hangups, some overdue bills, horrid beeps and strains upon the telephone system and the following unidentified voice. "Keep it up, fella. Just keep 'er on up." He thought about that for a moment, then punched up another message. It was his estranged wife. Her beautiful, slightly teasing voice made him ache. "Lucien, it's me. God, I hate these things. How much time have I got? After talking to Herbert Lawlor, I think you had better speak directly to me. Surely we can find something that will make you less unhappy."

Lucien drove up the valley. The purling creeks glittered in the hillsides. It is still heartening, he thought, that the water goes on going downhill.

So he launched his drift boat again. He floated and smoked between the chalk cliffs. For a couple of hours, he let the river take him away, toward the bubble of the ocean, toward teeming populations with women who looked like they came from Egypt, who did not seem to have been raised on pancake mix. For a while, he felt the nation and its people coming to him, and then he dragged the boat out on a gravel bar, spooking eight fledgling ducks whose takeoffs failed. They pinwheeled into the reeds and disappeared.

I am a family man, thought Lucien, despite what you have stolen.

Please send one tall bottled spirits of oleander. The north wind is tearing this joint up. Please send one sentimental war memorial heated by the sun and suitable for emplacement on coastal Bermuda grass. Am anxious to review above-captioned properties with canal and floating coconuts as pistol targets. Guard dog an unnecessary extravagance, also dismantle hydroponic tomato system as I am in all respects devoid of a green thumb especially as it applies to my own life.

Lucien thought, Possibly I should not have thrown out all the furniture. The wind has a bit of a run at things as is, don't you think? Of course it has. It's like being left in the barn.

He sat bolt upright in the cane rocker, an amber shooter in his hand. The cruelest thing I did on my father's death was to request "no keening" of my relatives. We could start from there. Sixty-six years of his wreaking havoc did not seem an appropriate background for some loud Celtic attempt to grease the boy to heaven. I'll take my lumps; he'll have to take his. If he's going to heaven, it will have to be as an exemplary criminal, a figure of pathos, there to give the chiaroscuro effect to happy souls who have everything.

As to my child, maybe I am doing no better. Perhaps I *should* deal with principals only, phone it in without too much English on it, looking at myself with the instrument to my ear in the wind-shuddering front window and ascending foothills enameled on the darkness. Punch in this yankee doodle area code, digits falling through the computer. If I get a boyfriend, I'll sing how's my ex treating you with castrati enthusiasm. Calm down.

"Suzanne?"

"Yes?"

"It's me."

"What time is it?"

"About eleven here. I can't see my watch."

"Huh. One here. What's up?"

"Are you having company?"

"What's up, Lucien?"

"I'm afraid I've been rude to your lawyer."

"Oh, so I'd heard, You're going to have to stop that."

"I have already. On advice."

"Where are you?"

"I'm out at my camp."

"Did you ever get water in there?"

"Months ago."

"Seemed like you were kind of torturing yourself going without running water. What time did you say it was?"

"Almost nine."

"Huh. Must've dozed off."

"Where am I?"

"What?"

"Where am I?"

"Luien, I'm sure if *you* don't know—"

"Remember years ago New Blue Cheer?"

"Yes—"

"They still make that stuff."

"All right, pal. That's enough."

"I was playing our old tune, Suzanne."

"What was our old tune?"

" 'My Girl.' "

"This is news to me."

"Anyway, I listened to it and it was good. It was clear and it was good."

"Okay."

"I demand to see James."

"You will have to demonstrate to a neutral party that you are worthy."

"I ought to brain you."

"See what I mean? Besides you're in a completely other time zone. So that is a sick fantasy. It would be ill enough if you said it to my face, but this is ill-on-ill. And every time you light into my attorney you look slightly less good to neutral parties."

"Am I to understand that I have to get a gold star from every potlicker who cares to evaluate me or I don't see him?"

"That's probably the best way for you to view it. James is not something which you picked out of a litter. He is a little person entitled to the usual assortment of human rights. It's my job on earth to see that he gets them. It's also my job to be at work in about seven hours. It's not nine o'clock. Not here, not there. Not anywhere. I'm going before you get your tail into a worse crack than it's already in. Goodbye."

She hung up. There was no smack of black plastic, just the buttons going off, a regular hangup. Lucien could tell he had not particularly gotten under her skin. Then suddenly he was clear. What he had done had made it a little harder for him to see his child. It had been a long day and now it was over.

He called back.

"Sorry."

"Okay, I accept, goodbye."

Lucien put on his coat, went outside and felt for the porch rocker.

He sat in the dark with his hands in his sleeves and looked at the grayish silhouettes of cattle along the creek. He startled some bird when he first moved in the rocker, and the papery awkward rush of wings near his head made him nervous. All of him seemed out of the moonlight except his shoes, which shone disconnected before the rocker. He moved his eyes from the knuckles of his left hand to the knuckles of his right hand. There was a little light on them. I'm still here, he thought.

Before his father had died and he had asked everyone to refrain from keening, in fact many years ago, Lucien had gone on a fishing trip to the Bear Trap on the Madison River with his father, a man named Ben Rush and a man named Andrew McCourtney. Each night his father and Ben Rush would go to the bar and tell fish stories, then come home and pass out till halfway through the next morning. They'd wake up and tell fish stories right through their hangovers, which they would cure with bourbon chilled in the icebox. Andrew McCourtney was a fragile Irishman who had been shell-shocked, and his face had sudden unwilled movements. McCourtney seldom drank because it threw him into the Second World War and he'd screech about booby-trapped German cameras, snipers in bombed châteaus, and law school: he'd flunked his bar examination and become a salesman, working for Lucien's father and Ben Rush, a former prizefighter from Chicago.

So McCourtney got up early while the other two slept, and awoke young Lucien to take him out for the morning mayfly hatch; and Lucien would be completely and unquestionably happy.

Lucien's father and Ben Rush liked to play tricks on Mc-Courtney and one night they took Lucien aside. Here's a good one, they breathed on him: when McCourtney comes round in the morning, tell him you're not in the mood to fish; tell him to find somebody else. Lucien lay up long after the two came crashing in, worrying about the joke. He assumed at least that his father knew what he was doing. So, when McCourtney came to the door, he piped, "I'm not in the mood to fish. Find someone else." And McCourtney was gone.

He waited around the camp until his father and Ben Rush woke up and told them he had delivered the joke to McCourtney. Neither of the men could remember how it began. When McCourtney came back to camp with his rod and a full creel, Lucien hurried to explain the joke. "That's all right, Lucien. We leave tonight." But McCourtney was no longer there, not in his bright twitching expectant face of the early morning, or in any other way. His remoteness lasted Lucien indefinitely.

Tonight on the windy porch, features of the darkness began to emerge to his adjusting eyes. He thought, I wonder if this is it. He considered his child's decent circumstances. I couldn't do as good a job, he thought, and went inside for a drink. Find somebody else.

When he awoke, he could hear car engines starting just past the curtains. He didn't know where he was, but this had happened before. He went to the window and looked out upon a parking lot and beyond to the jerky movement of early traffic. He sat on the edge of the bed, picked up the phone and dialed the desk.

"What's the name of this place?" he asked.

"It's the El Western," said the voice. "This is the El Western. May I help you?"

RUSSELL MARTIN

CLIFF DWELLERS

There beyond the comforting country, past still and grassy stock ponds, past the folds of irrigated fields, beyond the hot black ribbon of highway, Paul Ruthers's place is anchored to the thin soil at the sandstone lip of the canyon. His gray Butler silos stand empty at the flank of the farm yard; the big red Ferguson combine, his Ford Flex-O-Hitch harrow, the seed drills, rod weeders, and rusted moldboard plows stand in a straight line against the curved corrugated roof of the Quonset; a derelict Deere tractor is parked beside a blue Ford 4100 diesel whose color has just begun to go. A beige Chrysler is shaded by the crabapple that is rooted by the back door of the house, and an Australian shepherd named Sampson is shaded by the bulk of a battered International pickup that stands exposed to the sun.

Paul Ruthers at the kitchen sink, pouring the contents of two soup cans into a saucepan, preparing a lunch that he will take into the bedroom to his wife, stands in his stocking feet and looks out the open window across the bare yard and into the west. His broad bean fields give way to a stand of piñon and juniper trees, gnarled and stunted, as stubborn as the advance of age. Then the timber thins and gives way to bald and baking rock that sweeps still farther west before it drops suddenly into the canyon. Paul Ruthers watches a red-tailed hawk lift up from the branch of a juniper snag, sees it find the thermal at the cliff's edge, then circle higher into the sky before its wings peel back and it plunges into the canyon's open cut. He waits at the sink, watches to see if the hawk will circle up again, its prey in its fierce talons, thinks he will tell Margaret about the hawk when he takes in her lunch, imagines her eyes briefly bright with the image of the bird, wonders if Tom and the girl have watched it hunt from the ruin below the rim.

Beneath the sheer overhang of smooth rock, buff-colored sandstone streaked black by oxidation, tear-stained by weather and the worry of time, Tom Ruthers sits on a low stone wall shaped out of the cliff's rubble at least eight hundred years ago, mortared with mud by the Old Strangers, people who lived above the dry cliffs and beneath them, who built walls and houses and whole towns out of the rock before they walked away. Tom Ruthers imagines for a moment how the Old Ones, called Anasazi now, lived out their days inside this cave as he watches Helen Beech climb up from the talus below the ruin. He watches her move tentatively toward him—anxious about the loose rock, checking the placement of each foot, checking the scrapes on her palms, repeatedly tucking a loose strand of light brown hair behind an ear.

"This lunch won't wait forever," Tom calls when she stops and stretches her pale legs out to rest, her back bent against a pie-shaped slab of rock.

"It'll have to," she sighs, her head turned to the still air suspended in the narrow canyon. But soon she is climbing again and soon is in the shadow of the overhang, leaning comfortably against Tom Ruthers, hugging his head against her damp shirt, cradling it between her breasts.

"When can we go, Thomas?" Helen asks as Tom pulls his head away. When he doesn't answer she adds, "I just don't feel right about it."

"We'll go as soon as we can," Tom says. "I know what you mean. I'd go crazy in time."

"How long do you think she has?"

"Dad thinks she'll hang on a long time, says as long as she

can stay at home she'll tough it out. Once she's back in the hospital, it'll just be a matter of days, I'm sure."

"I just wish I could help. I wish I didn't feel so guilty about being so bored."

"You're a big help," Tom says as he rolls a slice of salami around a bite of yellow cheese. "They like having you. And you're my only real proof that I've ever amounted to anything."

"Some achievement. A divorcee with her tubes tied who speaks in some strange accent, who can't even cook nor stomach their beloved dried beans."

"You're right," Tom laughs. "You are a fairly sorry specimen." He turns to plant a sudden and comic kiss and glimpses a hawk drop over the cap rock and trail away toward the canyon floor. "I do appreciate your staying, though, when you ought to be off checking out this brash young nation of ours, taking it all in."

"It's not as young as all that, is it? How old is this cliff house?"

"Nearly a thousand years. But they weren't Americans. They weren't even what you'd call Indians. 'Anasazi' is just Navajo for 'Those Who Were Here Before Us,' somebody's ancestors."

"Why did they leave?" Helen asks.

"Maybe their mothers died," says Tom.

In the truck on the way to town, Paul Ruthers pushes against the steering wheel with the butt of his hand while he lifts the top off a tin of Skoal and tucks a bit of moist tobacco inside his lower lip.

The lip bulges and he presses it back against his teeth when he speaks.

"Your mom appreciates Helen staying with her like this," he says. "I think women kind of relax a little when there's just other women around."

"She's glad to," Tom says. "She likes to feel she can help out." A hot wind whips into the cab from the vent window and

Tom looks out at the rows of beans that stretch away from the gravelled road, running straight as rifle shots across the rolling brown earth as if they reach all the way to the haze-blue, timbered base of the mountain, its high and hump-backed summit rising abruptly up from the flat plateau. He sees the canal close at hand, sluggish and brimming with brown water, crossing beneath the road at a sharp angle, feels the truck bounce across the county bridge, notices the sudden change the water makes —the irrigated fields below the canal lush with late-summer growth, the alfalfa in bloom and ready to cut again, oats going golden, fat cattle feeding in thick pastures, lazy, heat-struck horses with their heads at each other's swishing tails in shared efforts to keep the flies away.

"Plenty of water this summer," Tom says, his words a passive kind of question.

"Plenty for these guys. Just turn their rain out of the headgates." Paul Ruthers combs his eyebrows flat with his thumb and forefinger, then pulls once at his narrow jaw. "But they still piss about not having enough. They ought to try it the dry way sometime."

"You're still supposed to get water when they get the new canal built, aren't you?"

"Yeah, but I'm not sure I'll buy it. Be an awful big cost to me to get equipped for it." He spits into a plastic cup that hangs from the door in a plastic holder, then reaches to turn the radio off. "Fact, I may give it up, Tommy. After your mother's gone. It's already too much for me, with her. By myself out here, I don't know. Delbert McCabe says I could truck hay for him. Hauls it to Arizona all winter long." Paul begins to grin. "I could get a little place in town and high-tail it to Arizona in the middle of the snowstorms."

"I can't really imagine you in town," Tom says, "with a square of grass and a garden the size of a sandbox."

"Person can get used to anything, Tommy. People can live damn near any way you can imagine."

Tom Ruthers tries to imagine his old man hauling the huge loads of one-ton bales down to the Salt River Valley, flirting with Flagstaff truck stop waitresses, pounding his huge tires with a ball bat at Tuba City, jabbering on the CB with commuting Navajo coal miners as he crosses the red sand plains on the reservation. But the image won't hold for long. And it disappears completely when they pass a big rig pulling Safeway produce on the highway into the tin and cinderblock town that is tacked into place at the base of the ragged northern wall of Mesa Verde.

They pass the International Harvester dealer and Paul Ruthers makes a one-fingered wave at a farmer who waits to turn his truck onto the asphalt; pass the junk yard whose skeletal, paint-peeled cars fill forty acres; pass the feed mill and sale barn, the John Deere and Massey Ferguson lots, the Ford farm dealer and the drive-in theater before they reach the Sears catalog store. Paul Ruthers turns off the engine, then says, "But who knows? I'll probably farm that ground for another twenty years," before he opens the door of the cab.

They load the cardboard-crated hospital bed into the back of the truck.

"Sure think Mother'll be more comfortable with this," Paul says.

"Couldn't you have rented one of these?" Tom asks as he shuts the tail-gate.

"Oh, probably. But . . . I guess I might use it sometime. Or Pops. None of us is going to stay on our feet forever."

Vernon Ruthers in bib overalls, the grizzled grandfather called Pops, his bald head freckled with brown spots, his eyes glazed behind the lenses of the big black glasses, leans back in a naugahyde lounger that is liberally patched with duct tape, surveys his visitors across the worn toes of cordovan leather slippers.

Tom and Helen sit beside each other in the sofa, her hands folded and placed in her lap, his bare arm stretched out along the back of the couch, her hair brushing a narrow scar that circles his forearm and ends in the crease of his elbow.

"You bring Sampson?" Pops asks.

"He's outside chasing prairie dogs," says Tom. "Dad says he only has to say 'Pops' to him and he goes into a dither, dog-dreaming about finally catching one of those little farts."

"He's had his practice," Pops says. "God knows, I got plenty for him to have a crack at." Pops directs his words at Helen, his eyes awakening with his story, his dry lips unable to suppress the hint of grin. "Prairie dogs is my only cash crop, you know. I tan their little hides and sell them to this big outfit in California. People think this leatherette is just plastic, but really it's prairie dog cured with engine oil." He picks up the top book from a stack of six new volumes, identically bound in brown leatherette, that lie on the dusty table beside his chair, turns the book over in his swollen hands, then lays it on his pant leg and rubs it with his palm as if to iron it flat. "Books, chairs, cars, pretty near everything has got leatherette. And guys like me make out like bandits."

Helen furtively glances at the expression on Tom's face, then smiles at the old man as she cups her hand around Tom's knee. Tom shakes his head, careful not to laugh, hiding his pleasure with a practiced smirk.

"Where did you get all those?" he asks his grandfather.

"Paul and Maggie give them to me for my birthday," Pops says. "They're Zane Grey. I hadn't ever read none of his. Hardly read any of them cowboy books. But I'll tell you what. For a guy from somewheres back East, that son of a buck sure knew this country. Right here I mean. I know exactly where he's writing about lots of times. He writes down the canyons and washes and the timber just so. And here. Listen to this. He even has Moqui ruins in this one."

Pops finds *Riders of the Purple Sage* in the stack, thumbs the gilt-edged pages, goes too far and flips back to the dog-eared page he had hoped to find. "Here. This is it," he says and begins to read, haltingly at first, his voice unsure of the words when they are spoken aloud, then stronger and more steadily as he becomes accustomed to the cadence of his sounds.

It was a stupendous tomb. It had been a city. It was just as it had been left by its builders. The little houses were there, the smoke-blackened stains of fires, the pieces of pottery scattered about cold hearths, the stone hatchets; and stone pestles and mealing-stones lay beside round holes polished by years of grinding maize—lay there as if they had been carelessly dropped yesterday. But the cliff-dwellers were gone!

Vernon Ruthers lifts his eyes from the page and looks expectantly at his grandson and at the woman he has brought home with him from Britain. He waits only a moment before he says, "Isn't that just like it? Hell, so many times when I've been tinkering around I've come across something like a metate with little dry kernels of corn still lying in it. And you think, by God, these people must have just gone away in the middle of the afternoon. Doubt it was really like that, but it sure seems like it sometimes."

"You ought to take Helen over to your ruin," Tom says.

"Yes, I'd like that sometime," she tells him.

"Well, sure. Be glad to, if you'd like to. Went down there with your mom, Tom's mom, one time after she got back from Denver. She was still able to get around pretty good and her and me spent a whole afternoon down there. Got caught in a thunderstorm and had to crouch way up under the rock to keep dry. While we was sitting there, she asked me how the Moquis took care of their dead."

Tom sees his grandfather's eyes cloud up, sees him pull two long breaths into his nostrils, then hears him say, "Funny kind of a world that makes a woman like Maggie go through this kind of thing." Tom nods, tries to find something to say in response, makes a soft and steady hissing sound with his teeth pressed against his upper lip, gives up his search for a statement, and bends his forearm back to place his hand on Helen's head.

"Did they bury them?" Helen asks.

"They find lots of skeletons buried in their trash dumps," Pops says. "Kind of like once they was dead a body didn't mean nothing to them and they just threw it away."

"Maybe it was easier to dig in the dumps than in the hard ground," Tom says. "It would have been awfully tough to dig a grave in the winter dirt with just a digging stick."

Pops nods, then bends his head to both sides before it stops. "Jesus. Would have been hard anytime," he says, then rubs the book he holds flat against his leg.

Still brown sage sparrows rest in long rows on the powerline that stands at the edge of the dirt road. The air is cool in the twilight; the last of the orange hues of sunset hang on the western horizon and cap the canyon with a thick and gloaming light. Sampson trots ahead of Tom and Helen who walk slowly along the half-mile of hardpan that links Vernon Ruthers's house to Paul's distant farmstead—only a huddled blur of buildings in the nascent night. The dog pokes its head into a culvert that passes beneath the road, pees on a band of tire tread that lies in the borrow ditch, then dashes away toward home. Tom walks with his hands in the pockets of his jeans; Helen locks her arm in his, holds his wrist and forearm with her fragile hands.

"Your mother told me this afternoon that your father hopes you'll stay and farm," she says; but Tom is silent. "Has he talked to you about it?"

"No. He won't. I don't think he'd bring it up. It's just a dream of his anyway. He knows this place couldn't support both of us. The price of beans has gone to hell, and this soil's almost shot."

"She said in a couple of years you could irrigate it and grow alfalfa and build the soil back."

"He said he thinks he'll become a truck driver."

"You mean sell it? Where would Pops go?"

"I doubt he'd go anywhere. Dad says he could live in town, but Pops couldn't. Wouldn't. He's tied right here with pretty heavy rope."

"And what about you? Where are we going to go?"

"Back to the U.K., aren't we? Back to soggy socks and window mold."

"Do you dread it?"

"No. 'Course not. It sounds good and bad in parts."

"I'd love to see San Francisco and Santa Fe before we go."

"I'd like to see what happens to Dad," Tom says.

"And he'll want to know what happens to you, I'm sure."

The crucifix carved out of walnut is lit by the morning light that angles in through the window and sprays across a painted wall. Photographs of Tom and Darlene as children, seated on bundled carpet in a portrait studio in town, hang on the blue wallpapered wall; on the dresser are photographs of a camera-shy couple on their wedding day and a stern-faced woman, her hair pulled severely back, who must be more than seventy. Above the single bed that stands in the space where the double bed has been, its head tilted upward, its steel rails hanging at its sides, is a print of an Alfred Bierstadt painting that makes the Rocky Mountains look strangely elusive, somehow exotic.

The closet door is open, but Paul Ruthers closes it when Tom enters the room. Tom sets a cup of tea on the stand beside the bed, kisses his mother's forehead, and asks how she feels as he moves toward the window.

"Pretty good," says Margaret, her voice a veiled whisper, her dark eyes sunk into a face that has been worn by fear but is now only drawn by weakness. She wears a floral-printed polyester robe, her legs tucked beneath a cotton blanket, a scarf tied to her head to hide the wisps of hair. "Looks like a pretty day. Are there clouds?"

"Yes," Tom says, "above the mountain. But they won't amount to anything."

"Such a shame we never get rain when we need it," she says, but Tom doesn't respond this time. He watches Helen, who sits in a tire swing suspended from a branch of the sprawling cottonwood, a swing that Paul has hung to humor Darlene's children, a swing they seldom sit in, the one in which Helen slowly twists and arcs across the yard.

"We'll make it," says Paul, who picks up the tea and holds it for his wife. "No reason to pine about things we don't get."

"I'm wishing, not pining," she says after she takes a sip. "More like a dream than a complaint. Isn't it Tommy? I'm dreaming about lots of rain." She is spent by the few words and slumps her head against the pillow.

"You rest," Paul says. He helps her with another sip, then sets the saucer down again and gets up to go away. "You see she gets some rest, Tom. I'll be back about noon."

Tom turns and watches his father go out the door and down the hall, watches his mother lie motionless in the new bed, sees the slick fabric of the robe rise as she breathes, sees her open her eyes, watches as they try to focus.

"Wish I didn't have to be so doped up," she says. "If I was stronger, I wouldn't have to take it all. It makes me so sleepy."

"You're plenty strong," he says as he sits on the edge of the bed. "I'm amazed."

"But not strong enough to lick it, am I?" Then silence before she says, "Did I tell you I really like that girl? I think she's good for you."

"Yes. I'm glad. You did tell me."

"We never thought you'd live in England, though."

"Never thought I would either."

"I bet it's beautiful. All lush and rolling. The tidy little towns."

"It's not all beautiful. Some of it's hideous. Gray factory towns that you'd think would make people just give up. But you'd love the Sussex farm country. It feels . . . reassuring. I wish we could take you. You and Dad."

"Wouldn't it be nice if after people were gone they could see places they've never been? Maybe that's one of the consolations."

"If you could see things, everything, and understand everything, it would be more like a prize than a consolation."

"It would be a prize," she says. She winces suddenly and holds her breath, then gives up the breath with a slow and quiet sigh. "Have you told Dad yet that you're going back?" she asks after the wave of pain has passed.

"It hasn't come up yet."

"Bring it up. So he'll know. His mind's full of his wondering what's going to happen—to everybody. Better he doesn't hope you'll stay."

"I'd stay if there was any logic in it. I could live here. I could farm and read—turn into an Anasazi buff like Pops. I could do it. But the place has had it, Mom. His yields have gone to hell. Equipment's worn out. You couldn't recoup the cost of getting the irrigation."

"He's like any father," Margaret says. "If you took over it would seem to mean he's done something that lasted. But he knows you can't, that it wouldn't be right for you. He just needs to hear you say so."

"I'll tell him," Tom says when he goes to the window again. "But Jesus, he's talking about getting out of it himself. How can he expect me to want to take it on?"

"He doesn't expect, Tommy," Margaret says, straining against the pain to make her point. "He's just dreaming. Like me and the rain and the consolation."

"I know," he says, and goes to the table, pushes the button that lowers the head of the bed. "I should go, and you should sleep."

She nods, closes her eyes, keeps them closed when she asks, "If you stayed, which you won't, would Helen stay too?"

"No," Tom says.

"I didn't think so," says his mother.

— — —

Darlene Bauer in cut-off jeans and a chambray shirt, the front tails of the shirt tied in a knot at her navel, turns hamburgers on the black barbecue grill; sweet and greasy smoke curls up from the charcoal, stings her eyes; the torrid air of the early evening draws beads of sweat that slide from the nape of her neck.

"Hamburgers must seem kind of strange to you," she says to Helen, who sits at the picnic table in the shade of the house and slices two fat white summer onions.

Helen laughs. "Oh, I've had a few hamburgers. I think they're fun."

"We don't think of them as fun; more like essential to the survival of the species," Tom says, mounted on Jason's small bicycle, his feet flat on the concrete walk that reaches to the garbage cans by the back gate and divides the narrow lawn in equal halves. "I'm not going to break this thing, am I?"

"You do and you'll have a vicious little six-year-old on your hands."

"Be careful," Helen says.

"Oh, he won't hurt it. Bobby rides it, and he weighs more than Tom." She flips the seven hamburgers, tops them with slices of cheese, glances toward the back door, checks herself in the reflection of the kitchen window as she turns. "I'll have to get him out here in a minute. He's watching some game on cable. We've just had cable about a month and he's still glued to it."

"You ought to go see what a baseball game looks like," Tom tells Helen.

"Football. It's exhibition season already," Darlene says.

"Even better. You'll think it's definitely crazy."

"You don't like football anymore?" Darlene asks.

"Don't get a chance to see much."

"Let me have a look," Helen says, the slicing finished. "I'll bring him back out with me."

"Tell him five minutes," Darlene says as Helen opens the

screen door. "I'll get the kids at the Simmons's." She listens
to Helen crossing the kitchen before she says, "It's so cute the
way she talks, Tommy. I love it. You know, you've picked up
a little."

"I hope not," he says. "The Americans I know with British
accents aren't my favorite people."

"How's Mom today?"

"Not good. She's getting pretty weak. The doctor was due
about the time we left. Dad's afraid he's going to want her back
in the hospital."

"Well, if she has to, at least I can get over to see her a lot
more if she's here in town."

"She won't last long at the hospital."

"Tommy."

"I don't think she will."

"Maybe the sooner the better for you so you can take off
again."

"Shut up, Darlene."

"I don't like you talking about her like that."

"I know it's—"

"Why'd you even bother to come back? Dad and me and Pops
have taken care of her just fine."

"I know you have," Tom says. He twists himself off the
bicycle, goes to the table, idly lifts the stack of paper plates, lets
each plate drop into the one below it, lifts the plates and lets
them drop again. "You've all been great. 'Course you have. But
she's dying. She's not going to get better."

"And if we act like we're waiting for her to die, she will."

Tom looks up at his sister. "She's the one who really understands what's happening. There's not very much we can do."

"You could get married." Darlene lays her sentence bluntly
in front of Tom as she lays the meat on a metal tray. "You
know it would mean a lot."

"I'm not sure it's that important."

"It hurts her that you guys aren't. She wouldn't say anything
to you, but she's told me."

"There are a lot of things you aren't aware of."

"I was just saying it was something you could do. It's no big deal to me, Thomas. She calls you Thomas, doesn't she? Just a second. I've got to go get those kids."

Tom watches his sister go out the back gate and down the alley, wishes she didn't live here, wishes she didn't make him feel so sad, wishes he had told her how much his mother means to him as she disappears behind the neighbors' inboard boat.

The legs of Pops's overalls are stuffed into the tops of his boots. His straw stockman's hat is pulled down onto his ears as he climbs through the big boulders that block the head of the canyon, that stand at the end of the two-track road where his Chevy pickup is parked. Helen follows close behind him, a blue bandanna tied into a scarf, her T-shirt tucked into khaki trousers. She watches the placement of Pops's feet, waits for a piñon branch to snap back across the trail before she pushes it out of the way again and continues.

"They showed up about the time of Jesus," Pops says as they descend into the shade of the sandstone wall. "It was dry country, like it is now, 'course, but the ground was good so they stayed and tried to farm it. Corn and beans. Built these little houses—half in and half out of the ground—right by their fields. Pretty damn primitive. But they was good stubborn farmers evidently, and stayed on and did all right. Must have. And they sure learned how to build." His motion and his words are enough to bring hard breaths, and the old man stops, lifts the hat brim and wipes his brow with his sleeve in a single unconscious motion, then continues his story while he stands.

"Used rock and this mud adobe mortar. They built big towns with kind of apartments. All stacked together, three and four stories. But that was still up on top, like where the truck is, the towns out in the open. The reason they come down under the cliffs is hard to guess at."

"Thomas said they might have wanted protection from attack," Helen says.

"That and winters would have been warmer under the rock, I suppose. But good God, it must have been a struggle to haul that rock and timber, and to climb up those fields every day. Here was people that had already lived here about ten times longer than white people have been here. Some places they had roads and reservoirs and irrigation, good places to live. They must have been awful worried or spooked or something to come down to the cliffs. Let me show you this place," Pops says.

They walk down the dry wash on the canyon bottom, then skirt left onto a talus slope when the cut deepens, move slowly across the litter of rock above the shaggy timber, and stop when the ruin becomes visible beneath a suspended arch of sandstone. Mortared walls rise up from the bedrock base of the cave in square and rectangular patterns. Roofs supported by juniper beams have given way; roof rubble and collapsed stone from the walls are scattered across the smooth rock floor. The walls at the back of the cave, protected from centuries of callous weather, still rise high, showing the doors of three successive stories. At the far right, a thin cylindrical tower stands erect and undamaged, its cap stones still touching the haughty overhang of rock.

"Amazing," Helen says, her face flush with surprise. "It's beautiful."

"Isn't it? I call it Five Finger House. See that broad wall just to the left of the tower? About a third of the way up, next to the doorway, see that red hand painted there? It's just a tiny bit smaller than my hand. Funny that somebody painted it there."

"And this is your ruin, is it?"

"Oh, it's on our property. So it's legal for me to poke around in it, but it's the Moquis' ruin."

"Why do you call them Moquis?"

"That's what everybody called them back before the place got thick with archaeologists. They say 'Anasazi,' but that's Navajo, and the Moquis wasn't Navajo."

"Wouldn't it have been easier to fight than to move into the cliffs?" Helen asks as she ties a new knot in the scarf.

"That's what you'd think. It had to be more than that. Maybe they thought things got out of whack with their gods and thought they could put things right down here. Maybe few enough people was doing the farming and heavy carrying that the majority was just happier down in the warm rock, out of all the weather."

"Did building the villages down here have anything to do with why they finally left?"

"I don't know," Pops says. He takes a plastic bottle out of the big back pocket of his overalls, opens the cap, hands the bottle to Helen. "They say there was a long hard drought over all this country about the time they took off—out here, Mesa Verde, over in Utah. The farming would have got awful tough. Springs would have dried. But by then they'd been here for twelve hundred years or so. They must have had hard, bad times before. I think maybe they just decided, or their religion told them, that nothing here was good anymore. Because they wasn't nomads. This was where they'd always, always been."

He leads the way through sage and rabbit brush and the scattered rock to a narrow shelf of sandstone that forms a passageway into the wide mouth of the cave. Inside it the midday summer sun is blocked by the rock canopy, and the air is cool, almost damp. Pops sits down on a decrepit wall, reduced by time to only seven courses of stone, takes his glasses off, wipes his face with a white handkerchief, softly begins to whistle. Helen walks into the dim light at the rear of the ruined village, through the maze of mortared walls and dry debris. She looks out through a thin rectangular window cut out of the curving wall of the tower, sees Pops leaning back on his palms, taking silent stock of the place, sees the dark stains streaking the opposite wall of the canyon, notices how the canyon courses away to the west, sharply bending back on itself before it vanishes.

Tom Ruthers sits on the shaded back step of the house in canvas shorts, his feet bare and his wavy hair brushed back, when Pops pulls his truck to a stop beside the Quonset shop. Tom gets up, walks gingerly across the gravelled driveway, and waits for Helen and his grandfather to get out of the cab and come toward him.

"Mom died about two o'clock," he says, his voice calm and quiet, his words carefully measured, as if he has long known what he has to say. He purses his lips for a second, looks at the two of them, sees Helen's blank and unbelieving look, sees Pops turn and walk back toward the truck.

Tom and Helen embrace, hugging each other for a long time—a brace against the shock, the surge of sadness, and a sudden draining relief. Then they turn toward the truck where Pops sits on the running board beside the bald spare tire, his elbows on his denim knees, his forehead in his hands.

"I'm sure sorry you weren't here," Tom says to his grandfather, whose face is now wet and suddenly sallow.

"How'd it happen?" Pops asks.

"She had a little lunch and then Dad gave her a bath. She took a nap. When he came in to get some iced tea we checked on her and she was gone."

"I'm glad," Helen says, "that it was in her sleep."

"It was pretty easy, I think," Tom says. "Then Dad called the mortuary. He called the priest, but he didn't come out."

"Where's Paul?" Pops asks.

"He drove to town. Followed the hearse in. I think he felt like he wanted to get her settled there. He said he'd pick out a coffin."

"What will happen now?" Helen asks; she holds her arm around Tom's bare, sweat-dampened waist.

"Dad and the priest arranged a requiem for tomorrow night, and the funeral mass the following morning. While we were waiting for the guy from the mortuary, he told me she'd planned everything out."

"How is he doing?" Helen asks.

"He was quiet. He didn't cry. He was real warm toward me, toward her. He got her dressed before they came. Guess he didn't want her going in her nightgown."

"It was like this when Frances died," Pops says when he looks up at Tom and Helen. Helen extends her hand to him;

he takes it, squeezes it, presses it against his whiskered cheek. "I was out drilling seed, and the doctor said she must have just slumped over at the kitchen sink. Said she probably didn't feel anything though." Pops sighs, his breath long and slow, carrying regret. "Maybe Maggie'll have some relief now."

"She was hoping she'd see new things when she died," Tom says. He struggles with the words.

"That's like her," Pops says. "Most people just want peace and quiet. Maggie's heaven'd have excitement."

High clouds cannot shelter the tawny ground, and the air is anvil-hot after the funeral. Shining black limousines and the sleek hearse with smoked-glass windows lead a slow procession of cars away from Our Lady of Victory church, across the dry arroyo and out of town. The highway cuts across the plateau's upland fields, through alfalfa and oats and the yellow stubble that still stands from the winter wheat. The long line of cars crosses the rock dam of the reservoir, crosses the last canal, crosses the green grids of the beanfields before it stops at the small cemetery laid out in a glade of juniper trees at the edge of the open canyon.

Faded plastic flowers grow out of the brown ground beside the headstones; the hot breeze rustles the berry-tipped branches of the trees. A coyote barks below the rim, barks again, and finally whines like a wistful child. Then the cars begin to disperse and the waxed black vehicles move a mile north on the dust-caked county road to Paul Ruthers's place.

At the house, Darlene in sunglasses greets the farm women in satin dresses who come to the door singly and in pairs carrying casseroles in paper sacks. She hugs each of them, hugs those she barely knows. The women embrace Paul Ruthers in a black suit and Vernon in a blue suit, tell them how good they look, tell them just to give a call, before they hurry out the door and drive away.

Helen puts the food on the dining room table, finds forks and serving spoons. Bob Bauer stands alone by the big coffee pot and drinks from a styrofoam cup, his white shirt stretched across his chest, his tie in the breast pocket of his coat. He sees the kids climb on the tractor through the picture window, goes out to the porch and shouts at them to come inside.

In the kitchen Tom has taken off his jacket and rolled up the sleeves of his oxford shirt. He takes the iced tea out of the refrigerator, notices the beer and grabs two cans, goes to the living room to find Pops and his father, tells them the food is ready.

They sit on the sofa and in overstuffed chairs to eat, paper plates in their laps, cups and glasses cradled between their feet. Darlene says how nice she thought it was; Pops is surprised at all the people. Paul puts down his plate and wonders if there is anything else they ought to do today. Helen sits on the upholstered arm of a chair beside Tom. She picks slowly at her food; he abandons a heaping plate.

Later, Pops falls asleep against the upright back of the rocking chair. Darlene and Helen cover the casseroles and wash silverware and empty pans. Bob pushes the children in the tire swing; they take impatient turns and squeal as the tire reaches out to the height of its arc. Paul changes his clothes, goes to the shop to change the oil in the combine.

Tom takes Sampson in the truck and drives around the head of the canyon, then follows the rutted track along the opposite rim to a jutting, treeless point of rock. He opens the door, lets the dog jump over his legs and out, sees through the bug-splattered windshield across the canyon, finds the green roof of the house and the gray outbuildings against the timbered skyline. He sees the strong afternoon sun reach into the small ruin below the house, looks up the canyon to see if he can spot Pops's ruin, Five Finger House, in the glaring light. But the big ruin is hidden by the curving canyon wall. He cannot find it. And he slaps the center of the steering wheel with his palm, holds it down with the weight of his arm, with the weary weight of the afternoon. The blaring sound of the horn echoes off the rock, bounces between the walls, then carries across the tilted farmland.

— — —

"I still wish you'd come with me," Helen says, her eyes fixed on the asphalt road, her hands wrapped around the Chrysler's steering wheel, the car cresting a barren hill.

"I wish I could," Tom says from the passenger seat. "But this way you won't have to cool your heels here while I help Dad. See? You're doing fine. I told you it wasn't any big deal to switch sides."

"I'm still afraid I'll pull out onto the left after a stop."

"You won't. Just keep it in mind. Follow the other cars. In Santa Fe you can park it and walk."

"Sounds lovely. This feels like such a huge machine to me."

"Yeah, but it's a treat on the open road. There's a lot of highway between here and there."

"Five hours at home would get us all the way to Yorkshire."

"Maybe clear to Edinburgh," Tom says. "Lots of territory out here, Limey. Okay, you're all checked out. Drop me off and you're on your way."

"I could wait a couple of days for you," Helen says as she turns through an empty intersection and pulls down the visor to block the slanting morning sun. "I'd really be glad to wait."

"Quiet," Tom says. "We're just going to sort through her things, figure what to do with them, get the house straightened out. It's a perfect time for you to enjoy yourself for a change."

"You make me sound so spoiled. I'd be glad to help, you know."

"You wanted to go to Santa Fe."

"With you."

"I'm not going to make you go. You've got a car, you're all set. If you want to go, go. This is stupid."

Helen is silent as she turns onto the dirt road and heads toward the house. Tom is silent, staring out at the bundled clouds that spill over the crest of Mesa Verde and spread across the sear and sweeping ground. He watches two magpies play chase in the air above his father's stalwart silos as Helen pulls the Chrysler to a stop.

"It's only two nights," he says. "Nobody thinks you're abandoning us."

"It will be good for you to be alone with your father, I'm sure." She starts to shape a grin and turns in the seat to face him. "And good for me to get away from you for a bit."

"Just me and Dad and Pops and Darlene's clan. That sounds a little spooky, doesn't it? It'll be odd without you," Tom says.

"I hope so," Helen says before she drives out of the yard and down the road, trailing dust like a billowing brown goodbye.

Three men walk westward between boot-high rows of bean; the low light of the evening casts no shadows. The air is still; birds have found their roosts.

Tom Ruthers in a cowboy hat walks between his tall, square-shouldered father and his grandfather—shorter, rounder, stooped by his longer string of years. Paul Ruthers's red-billed cap reads RANCHWAY FEEDS; Vernon's cap says CO-OP. Paul bends down and tears off a light green pod, splits it with his fingernail, quickly studies the beans inside, puts one in his mouth.

"I'd say you're going to be all right," Pops says. "You get a decent storm or two and they'll finish off pretty good."

"Got to weed them one more time," Paul says. "Then wait. Pray like hell the market improves."

"I guess Mexico still isn't buying beans, huh?" Tom asks.

"If they are, I haven't heard about it," his father tells him. "Shows you how bad it is when we're dependent on the poor broke Mexicans."

"Noticed Delbert McCabe at the funeral," Pops says. "You still thinking about trucking for him?"

"I've got a harvest to worry about first," Paul says. "I'll give it some thought this winter."

"Ain't sure I'd agree to put the place on the market," Pops says solemnly.

"Am I asking you to?"

"Well, that's what you might expect if you quit farming it. I'm sure as hell not up to it."

"Jesus, Dad," Paul says, "nobody's making any big decisions. You can't farm it, Tommy's smart enough to stay out of it, so it's kind of up to me, isn't it? If I ever start trucking hay, it's because that's what I decide I've got to do."

"No chance you'd stay, huh Tommy?" his grandfather asks.

"It's not that. There's just not enough here to support both of us. And Helen needs to be at home. I guess we can both keep teaching little kids in short pants and neckties till something better comes along. Sometimes I feel like I kind of ought to be here, but I do fine over there."

"We're none of us no different from the damn Moquis," Pops says; his hands clutch the front straps of his overalls, his head is bent toward the beans.

"Yeah, we are," Paul says. "They quit this country because they were afraid. I'm not afraid; Tommy's not. Mom's dead; now Margaret's gone."

"Maybe they was afraid of starving to death," Pops says. "Afraid of the drought and all the bad omens. That ain't so different."

"That's what it comes down to, I guess," Tom says. "Everything sooner or later goes to hell."

"These beans look like they're going to hell to you?" Paul asks, his voice suddenly loud and challenging. "I may not make a dime off them, but I'm still getting something done here. Your mother may have died, but that doesn't mean her life wasn't worth nothing, for Christ's sake."

Tom stops walking. He waits, then chooses his words carefully, speaks them slowly. "All I mean is what you told me the day we went to get the hospital bed . . . that people can handle anything. That they have to. Everything changes."

"Well, I'm too old to change," Pops says. "Count me out on that. You two go gallivant off wherever you want to."

Paul pays no attention, walks ahead to the edge of the field, to the shallow draw in the furrowed ground that leads to the lip of the canyon. He stands with his hands in his pockets, his head turned toward the sudden depression in the earth, toward the distant hump of mountain, toward the stand of haggard trees that hides the headstones. When Tom and Pops approach him he says, "I've probably been in this very spot on two-thirds of all the days I've been alive. Lots of people'd think that's pretty pathetic."

"I don't, Dad," Tom says. He tries to think of something else to say to the two of them, watches the canyon angle away like the slow, sad flight of the Anasazi, sees his father turn toward the house.

JAMES WELCH

FROM

WINTER IN THE BLOOD

"Hello," he said. "You are welcome."

"There are clouds in the east," I said. I could not look at him.

"I feel it, rain tonight maybe, tomorrow for sure, cats and dogs."

The breeze had picked up so that the willows on the irrigation ditch were gesturing in our direction.

"I see you wear shoes now. What's the meaning of this?" I pointed to a pair of rubber boots. His pants were tucked inside them.

"Rattlesnakes. For protection. This time of year they don't always warn you."

"They don't hear you," I said. "You're so quiet you take them by surprise."

"I found a skin beside my door this morning. I'm not taking any chances."

"I thought animals were your friends."

"Rattlesnakes are best left alone."

"Like you," I said.

"Could be."

I pumped some water into the enamel basin for Bird, then I loosened his cinch.

"I brought some wine." I held out the bottle.

"You are kind—you didn't have to."

"It's French," I said. "Made out of roses."

"My thirst is not so great as it once was. There was a time . . ."
A gust of wind ruffled his fine white hair. "Let's have it."

I pressed the bottle into his hand. He held his head high,
resting one hand on his chest, and drank greedily, his Adam's
apple sliding up and down his throat as though it were attached
to a piece of rubber. "And now, you," he said.

Yellow Calf squatted on the white skin of earth. I sat down
on the platform on which the pump stood. Behind me, Bird
sucked in the cool water.

"My grandmother died," I said. "We're going to bury her
tomorrow."

He ran his paper fingers over the smooth rubber boots. He
glanced in my direction, perhaps because he heard Bird's guts
rumble. A small white cloud passed through the sun but he said
nothing.

"She just stopped working. It was easy."

His knees cracked as he shifted his weight.

"We're going to bury her tomorrow. Maybe the priest from
Harlem. He's a friend . . ."

He wasn't listening. Instead, his eyes were wandering beyond
the irrigation ditch to the hills and the muscled clouds above
them.

Something about those eyes had prevented me from looking
at him. It had seemed a violation of something personal and
deep, as one feels when he comes upon a cow licking her new-
born calf. But now, something else, his distance, made it all
right to study his face, to see for the first time the black dots
on his temples and the bridge of his nose, the ear lobes which
sagged on either side of his head, and the bristles which grew
on the edges of his jaw. Beneath his humped nose and above
his chin, creases as well defined as cutbanks between prairie
hills emptied into his mouth. Between his half-parted lips hung
one snag, yellow and brown and worn-down, like that of an old
horse. But it was his eyes, narrow beneath the loose skin of his
lids, deep behind his cheekbones, that made one realize the old

man's distance was permanent. It was behind those misty white eyes that gave off no light that he lived, a world as clean as the rustling willows, the bark of a fox or the odor of musk during mating season.

I wondered why First Raise, my father, had come so often to see him. Had he found a way to narrow that distance? I tried to remember that one snowy day he had brought me with him. I remembered my mother, Teresa, and the old lady commenting on my father's judgment for taking me out on such a day; then riding behind him on the horse, laughing at the wet, falling snow. But I couldn't remember Yellow Calf or what the two men talked about.

"Did you know her at all?" I said.

Without turning his head, he said, "She was a young woman; I was just a youth."

"Then you did know her then."

"She was the youngest wife of Standing Bear."

I was reaching for the wine bottle. My hand stopped.

"He was a chief, a wise man—not like these conniving devils who run the agency today."

"How could you know Standing Bear? He was Blackfeet."

"We came from the mountains," he said.

"You're Blackfeet?"

"My people starved that winter; we all starved but they died. It was the cruelest winter. My folks died, one by one." He seemed to recollect this without emotion.

"But I thought you were Gros Ventre. I thought you were from around here."

"Many people starved that winter. We had to travel light— we were running from the soldiers—so we had few provisions. I remember, the day we entered this valley it began to snow and blizzard. We tried to hunt but the game refused to move. All winter long we looked for deer sign. I think we killed one deer. It was rare that we even jumped a porcupine. We snared a few rabbits but not enough . . ."

"You survived," I said.

"Yes, I was strong in those days." His voice was calm and monotonous.

"How about my grandmother? How did she survive?"

He pressed down on the toe of his rubber boot. It sprang back into shape.

"She said Standing Bear got killed that winter," I said.

"He led a party against the Gros Ventres. They had meat. I was too young. I remember the men when they returned to camp—it was dark but you could see the white air from their horses' nostrils. We all stood waiting, for we were sure they would bring meat. But they brought Standing Bear's body instead. It was a bad time."

I tapped Yellow Calf's knee with the bottle. He drank, then wiped his lips on his shirt sleeve.

"It was then that we knew our medicine had gone bad. We had wintered some hard times before, winters were always hard, but seeing Standing Bear's body made us realize that we were being punished for having left our home. The people resolved that as soon as spring came we would go home, soldiers or not."

"But you stayed," I said. "Why?"

He drew an arc with his hand, palm down, taking in the bend of the river behind his house. It was filled with tall cottonwoods, most of them dead, with tangles of brush and wild rose around their trunks. The land sloped down from where we were sitting so that the bend was not much higher than the river itself.

"This was where we camped. It was not grown over then, only the cottonwoods were standing. But the willows were thick then, all around to provide a shelter. We camped very close together to take advantage of this situation. Sometimes in winter, when the wind has packed the snow and blown the clouds away, I can still hear the muttering of the people in their tepees. It was a very bad time."

"And your family starved . . ."

"My father died of something else, a sickness, pneumonia

maybe. I had four sisters. They were among the first to go. My mother hung on for a little while but soon she went. Many starved."

"But if the people went back in the spring, why did you stay?"

"My people were here."

"And the old—my grandmother stayed too," I said.

"Yes. Being a widow is not easy work, especially when your husband had other wives. She was the youngest. She was considered quite beautiful in those days."

"But why did she stay?"

He did not answer right away. He busied himself scraping a star in the tough skin of earth. He drew a circle around it and made marks around it as a child draws the sun. Then he scraped it away with the end of his stick and raised his face into the thickening wind. "You must understand how people think in desperate times. When their bellies are full, they can afford to be happy and generous with each other—the meat is shared, the women work and gossip, men gamble—it's a good time and you do not see things clearly. There is no need. But when the pot is empty and your guts are tight in your belly, you begin to look around. The hunger sharpens your eye."

"But why her?"

"She had not been with us more than a month or two, maybe three. You must understand the thinking. In that time the soldiers came, the people had to leave their home up near the mountains, then the starvation and the death of their leader. She had brought them bad medicine."

"But you—you don't think that."

"It was apparent," he said.

"It was bad luck; the people grew angry because their luck was bad," I said.

"It was medicine."

I looked at his eyes. "She said it was because of her beauty."

"I believe it was that too. When Standing Bear was alive,

they had to accept her. In fact, they were proud to have such beauty—you know how it is, even if it isn't yours." His lips trembled into what could have been a smile.

"But when he died, her beauty worked against her," I said.

"That's true, but it was more than that. When you are starving, you look for signs. Each event becomes big in your mind. His death was the final proof that they were cursed. The medicine man, Fish, interpreted the signs. They looked at your grandmother and realized that she had brought despair and death. And her beauty—it was as if her beauty made a mockery of their situation."

"They can't have believed this . . ."

"It wasn't a question of belief, it was the way things were," he said. "The day Standing Bear was laid to rest, the women walked away. Even his other wives gave her the silent treatment. It took the men longer—men are not sensitive. They considered her the widow of a chief and treated her with respect. But soon, as it must be, they began to notice the hatred in their women's eyes, the coolness with which they were treated if they brought your grandmother a rabbit leg or a piece of fire in the morning. And they became ashamed of themselves for associating with the young widow and left her to herself."

I was staring at the bottle on the ground before me. I tried to understand the medicine, the power that directed the people to single out a young woman, to leave her to fend for herself in the middle of a cruel winter. I tried to understand the thinking, the hatred of the women, the shame of the men. Starvation. I didn't know it. I couldn't understand the medicine, her beauty.

"What happened to her?"

"She lived the rest of the winter by herself."

"How could she survive alone?"

He shifted his weight and dug his stick into the earth. He seemed uncomfortable. Perhaps he was recalling things he didn't want to or he felt that he had gone too far. He seemed to have lost his distance, but he went on: "She didn't really leave. It was the dead of winter. To leave the camp would have meant a sure death, but there were tepees on the edge, empty—many were empty then."

"What did she do for food?"

"What did any of us do? We waited for spring. Spring came, we hunted—the deer were weak and easy to kill."

"But she couldn't hunt, could she?" It seemed important for me to know what she did for food. No woman, no man could live a winter like that alone without something.

As I watched Yellow Calf dig at the earth I remembered how the old lady had ended her story of the journey of Standing Bear's band.

There had been great confusion that spring. Should the people stay in this land of the Gros Ventres, should they go directly south to the nearest buffalo herd, or should they go back to the country west of here, their home up near the mountains? The few old people left were in favor of this last direction because they wanted to die in familiar surroundings, but the younger ones were divided as to whether they should stay put until they got stronger or head for the buffalo ranges to the south. They rejected the idea of going home because the soldiers were there. Many of them had encountered the Long Knives before, and they knew that in their condition they wouldn't have a chance. There was much confusion, many decisions and indecisions, hostility.

Finally it was the soldiers from Fort Assiniboine who took the choice away from the people. They rode down one late-spring day, gathered up the survivors and drove them west to the newly created Blackfeet Reservation. Because they didn't care to take her with them, the people apparently didn't mention her to the soldiers, and because she had left the band when the weather warmed and lived a distance away, the soldiers didn't question her. They assumed she was a Gros Ventre.

A gust of wind rattled the willows. The clouds towered white against the sky, but I could see their black underbellies as they floated toward us.

The old lady had ended her story with the image of the people

being driven "like cows" to their reservation. It was a strange
triumph and I understood it. But why hadn't she spoken of
Yellow Calf? Why hadn't she mentioned that he was a member
of that band of Blackfeet and had, like herself, stayed behind?

A swirl of dust skittered across the earth's skin.

"You say you were just a youth that winter—how old?" I
said.

He stopped digging. "That first winter, my folks all died
then."

But I was not to be put off. "How old?"

"It slips my mind," he said. "When one is blind and old he
loses track of the years."

"You must have some idea."

"When one is blind . . ."

"Ten? Twelve? Fifteen?"

". . . and old, he no longer follows the cycles of the years.
He knows each season in its place because he can feel it, but
time becomes a procession. Time feeds upon itself and grows
fat." A mosquito took shelter in the hollow of his cheek, but
he didn't notice. He had attained that distance. "To an old dog
like myself, the only cycle begins with birth and ends in death.
This is the only cycle I know."

I thought of the calendar I had seen in his shack on my
previous visit. It was dated 1936. He must have been able to
see then. He had been blind for over thirty years, but if he was
as old as I thought, he had lived out a lifetime before. He had
lived a life without being blind. He had followed the calendar,
the years, time—

I thought for a moment.

Bird farted.

And it came to me, as though it were riding one moment of
the gusting wind, as though Bird had had it in him all the time
and had passed it to me in that one instant of corruption.

"Listen, old man," I said. "It was you—you were old enough
to hunt!"

But his white eyes were kneading the clouds.

I began to laugh, at first quietly, with neither bitterness nor humor. It was the laughter of one who understands a moment in his life, of one who has been let in on the secret through luck and circumstance. "You . . . you're the one." I laughed, as the secret unfolded itself. "The only one . . . you, her hunter . . ." And the wave behind my eyes broke.

Yellow Calf still looked off toward the east as though the wind could wash the wrinkles from his face. But the corners of his eyes wrinkled even more as his mouth fell open. Through my tears I could see his Adam's apple jerk.

"The only one," I whispered, and the old man's head dropped between his knees. His back shook, the bony shoulders squared and hunched like the folded wings of a hawk.

"And the half-breed, Doagie!" But the laughter again racked my throat. *He wasn't my mother's father; it was you, Yellow Calf, the hunter!*

He turned to the sound of my laughter. His face was distorted so that the single snag seemed the only recognizable feature of the man I had come to visit. His eyes hid themselves behind the high cheekbones. His mouth had become the rubbery sneer of a jack-o'-lantern.

And so we shared this secret in the presence of ghosts, in wind that called forth the muttering tepees, the blowing snow, the white air of the horses' nostrils. The cottonwoods behind us, their dead white branches angling to the threatening clouds, sheltered these ghosts as they had sheltered the camp that winter. But there were others, so many others.

Yellow Calf stood, his hands in his pockets, suddenly withdrawn and polite. I pressed what remained of the bottle of wine into his hand. "Thank you," he said.

"You must come visit me sometime," I said.

"You are kind."

I tightened the cinch around Bird's belly. "I'll think about you," I said.

"You'd better hurry," he said. "It's coming."

I picked up the reins and led Bird to the rotting plank bridge across the irrigation ditch.

He lifted his hand.

Bird held his head high as he trotted down the fence line. He was anxious to get home. He was in a hurry to have a good pee and a good roll in the manure. Since growing old, he had lost his grace. With each step, I felt the leather of the saddle rub against my thighs.

It was a good time for odor. Alfalfa, sweet and dusty, came with the wind, above it the smell of rain. The old man would be lifting his nose to this odor, thinking of other things, of those days he stood by the widow when everyone else had failed her. So much distance between them, and yet they lived only three miles apart. But what created this distance? And what made me think that he was Teresa's father? After all, twenty-five years had passed between the time he had become my grandmother's hunter and Teresa's birth. They could have parted at any time. But he was the one. I knew that. The answer had come to me a if by instinct, sitting on the pump platform, watching his silent laughter, as though it was his blood in my veins that had told me.

I tried to imagine what it must have been like, the two of them, hunter and widow. If I was right about Yellow Calf's age, there couldn't have been more than four or five years separating them. If she was not yet twenty, he must have been fifteen or sixteen. Old enough to hunt, but what about the other? Could he have been more than hunter then, or did that come later? It seemed likely that they had never lived together (except perhaps that first winter out of need). There had never been any talk, none that I heard. The woman who had told me about Doagie had implied that he hadn't been Teresa's father. She hadn't mentioned Yellow Calf.

So for years the three miles must have been as close as an early morning walk down this path I was now riding. The fence hadn't been here in the beginning, nor the odor of alfalfa. But the other things, the cottonwoods and willows, the open spaces of the valley, the hills to the south, the Little Rockies, had all been here then; none had changed. Bird lifted his head and whinnied. He had settled into a gait that would have been a dance in his younger days. It was only the thudding of his hooves and the saddle rubbing against my thighs that gave him away. So for years the old man had made this trip; but could it have been twenty-five? Twenty-five years without living together, twenty-five years of an affair so solemn and secretive it had not even been rumored?

Again I thought of the time First Raise had taken me to see the old man. Again I felt the cold canvas of his coat as I clung to him, the steady clopping of the horse's hooves on the frozen path growing quieter as the wet snow began to pile up. I remembered the flour sack filled with frozen deer meat hanging from the saddle horn, and First Raise getting down to open the gate, then peeing what he said was my name in the snow. But I couldn't remember being at the shack. I couldn't remember Yellow Calf.

Yet I had felt it then, that feeling of event. Perhaps it was the distance, those three new miles, that I felt, or perhaps I had felt something of that other distance; but the event of distance was as vivid to me as the cold canvas of First Raise's coat against my cheek. He must have known then what I had just discovered. Although he told me nothing of it up to the day he died, he had taken me that snowy day to see my grandfather.

A glint of sunlight caught my eye. A car was pulling off the highway onto our road. It was too far away to recognize. It looked like a dark beetle lumbering slowly over the bumps and ruts of the dusty tracks. I had reached the gate but I didn't get down. Bird pawed the ground and looked off toward the ranch. From this angle only the slough and corral were visible. Bird studied them. The buildings were hidden behind a rise in the road.

The clouds were now directly overhead, but the sun to the west was still glaring hot. The wind had died down to a steady breeze. The rain was very close.

It was Ferdinand Horn and his wife. As the dark green Hudson hit the stretch of raised road between the alfalfa fields, he honked the horn as if I had planned to disappear. He leaned out his window and waved. "Hello there, partner," he called. He turned off the motor and the car coasted to a stop. He looked up at me. "We just stopped to offer our condolences."

"What?"

Ferdinand Horn's wife leaned forward on the seat and looked up through the windshield. She had a pained look.

"Oh, the old lady!" It was strange, but I had forgotten that she was dead.

"She was a fine woman," Ferdinand Horn said. He gazed at the alfalfa field out his window.

"Teresa and Lame Bull went to Harlem to get her. They probably won't get back before dark."

"We saw them. We just came from there," he said. He seemed to be measuring the field. "A lovely woman."

Ferdinand Horn's wife stared at me through her turquoise-frame glasses. She had cocked her head to get a better look. It must have been uncomfortable.

"We're going to bury her tomorrow," I said.

"The hell you say."

"We're not doing anything fancy. You could probably come if you want to." I didn't know exactly how Teresa would act at the funeral.

"That's an idea." He turned to his wife. She nodded, still looking up through the windshield. "Oh hell, where's my manners." He fumbled in a paper sack between them. He punched two holes in the bottom of a can of beer. It had a pop-top on top. He handed it to me.

I took a sip, then a swallow, and another. The wine had left my mouth dry, and the beer was good and colder than I expected. "Jesus," I gasped. "That really hits the spot."

"I don't know what's wrong with me. What the hell are you doing on that damn plug?"

"I was just riding around. I visited Yellow Calf for a minute."

"No kidding? I thought he was dead." He looked at the field again. "How is he anyway?"

"He seems to be okay, living to the best of his ability," I said.

"You know, my cousin Louie used to bring him commodities when he worked for Reclamation. He used to regulate that head gate back by Yellow Calf's, and he'd bring him groceries. But hell, that was ten years ago—hell, twenty!"

I hadn't thought of that aspect. How did he eat now? "Maybe the new man brings him food," I said.

"He's kind of goofy, you know."

"The new man?"

"Yellow Calf."

Ferdinand Horn's wife pushed her glasses up, then wrinkled her nose to keep them there. She was holding a can of grape pop in her lap. She had wrapped a light blue hankie around it to keep her hand from getting cold or sticky.

"You have a low spot in that corner over there."

I followed his finger to an area of the field filled with slough grass and foxtail.

"Did you find her?" The muffled voice brought me back to the car.

"We're going to bury her tomorrow," I said.

"No, no," she shrieked, and hit Ferdinand Horn on the chest. "Your wife!" She hadn't taken her eyes off me. "Your wife!"

It was a stab in the heart. "I saw her . . . in Havre," I said.

"Well?"

"In Gable's . . ."

She leaned forward and toward Ferdinand Horn. Her upper lip lifted over her small brown teeth. "Was that white man with her?"

"No, she was all alone this time."

"I'll bet—"

"How many bales you get off this piece?"

"I'll bet she was all alone. As if a girl like that could ever be alone." She looked up like a muskrat through the thin ice of the windshield.

"We just came by to offer our condolences."

"Don't try to change the subject," she said, slapping Ferdinand Horn on the arm. "Did you bring her back?"

"Yes," I said. "She's in at the house now. Do you want to see her?"

"You mean you brought her back?" She sounded disappointed.

"You want to see her?"

"Did you get your gun back?" Ferdinand Horn was now looking at me.

"Yes. Do you want to see her?"

"Okay, sure, for a minute," he said.

His wife fell back against the seat. She was wearing the same wrinkled print dress she had worn the time before. Her thighs were spread beneath the bright butterflies. I couldn't see her face.

"We're late enough," she said.

"Well, just for a minute," Ferdinand Horn said.

"We just came by to offer our condolences."

Ferdinand Horn seemed puzzled. He turned toward her. Her thighs tightened. He looked up at me. Then he started the car. "How many bales you get off this piece?" he said.

As Bird and I rounded the bend of the slough, I could hear the calf bawling. It was almost feeding time. We passed the graveyard with its fresh dirt now turning tan beneath the rolling clouds. Bird loped straight for the corral, his ears forward and his legs stiffened. I could feel the tension in his body. I thought it was because of the storm which threatened to break at any time, but as we neared the corral, Bird pulled up short and glanced in the direction of the slough. It was the calf's mother.

She was lying on her side, up to her chest in the mud. Her good eye was rimmed white and her tongue lolled from the side of her mouth. When she saw us, she made an effort to free herself, as though we had come to encourage her. Her back humped forward as her shoulders strained against the sucking mud. She switched her tail and a thin stream of crap ran down her backside.

Bird whinnied, then dropped his head, waiting for me to get down and open the gate. He had lost interest.

I wanted to ignore her. I wanted to go away, to let her drown in her own stupidity, attended only by clouds and the coming rain. If I turned away now, I thought, if I turned away—my hands trembled but did nothing. She had earned this fate by being stupid, and now no one could help her. Who would want to? As she stared at me, I saw beyond the immediate panic that hatred, that crazy hatred that made me aware of a quick hatred in my own heart. Her horns seemed tipped with blood, the dark blood of catastrophe. The muck slid down around her ears as she lowered her head, the air from her nostrils blowing puddles in the mud. I had seen her before, the image of catastrophe, the same hateful eye, the long curving horns, the wild-eyed spinster leading the cows down the hill into the valley. Stupid, stupid cow, hateful in her stupidity. She let out a long, bubbling call. I continued to glance at her, but now, as though energy, or even life, had gone out of her, she rolled her head to one side, half submerged in the mud, her one eye staring wildly at the clouds.

Stupid, stupid—

I slid down, threw open the corral gate and ran to the horse shed. The soft flaky manure cushioned the jolt of my bad leg. A rope hung from a nail driven into a two-by-four. I snatched it down and ran back to the gate. Bird was just sauntering through. I half led, half dragged him down to the edge of the slough. He seemed offended that I should ask this task of him. He tried to look around toward the pasture behind the corral.

The red horse was watching us over the top pole, but there was no time to exchange horses. Already the cow lay motionless on her side.

I tied one end of the rope to the saddle horn to keep Bird from walking away, then threw open the loop to fit over the cow's head. But she would not lift it. I yelled and threw mud toward her, but she made no effort. My scalp began to sweat. A chilly breeze blew through my hair as I twirled the loop above my head. I tried for her horn but it was pointing forward toward me and the loop slid off. Again and again I threw for the horn, but the loop had nothing to tighten against. Each time I expected her to raise her head in response to the loop landing roughly against her neck and head, but she lay still. She must be dead, I thought, but the tiny bubbles around her nostrils continued to fizz. Then I was in the mud, up to my knees, wading out to the cow. With each step, the mud closed around my leg, then the heavy suck as I pulled the other free. My eyes fixed themselves on the bubbles and I prayed for them to stop so I could turn back, but the frothy mass continued to expand and move as though it were life itself. I was in up to my crotch, no longer able to lift my legs, able only to slide them through the greasy mire. The two or three inches of stagnant water sent the smell of dead things through my body. It was too late, it was taking too long—by leaning forward I could almost reach the cow's horn. One more step, the bubbles weren't moving, and I did clutch the horn, pulling myself toward her. She tried to lift her head, but the mud sucked it back down. Her open mouth, filling with slime, looked as pink as a baby mouse against the green and black. The wild eye, now trying to focus on me, was streaked with the red threads of panic.

By lifting on her horn, I managed to raise her head enough to slide the loop underneath, the mud now working to my advantage. I tightened up and yelled to Bird, at the same time pulling the rope against the saddle horn. The old horse shook his shoulders and backed up. He reared a few inches off the

ground, as though the pressure of the rope had reminded him
of those years spent as a cow horse. But the weight of the cow
and mud began to pull the saddle forward, the back end lifting
away from his body. It wouldn't hold. I gripped the taut rope
and pulled myself up and out of the mud. I began to move hand
over hand back toward the bank. Something had gone wrong
with my knee; it wouldn't bend. I tried to arch my toes to keep
my shoe from being pulled off, but there was no response. My
whole leg was dead. The muscles in my arms knotted, but I
continued to pull myself along the rope until I reached the edge
of the bank. I lay there a moment, exhausted, then tried to get
up but my arms wouldn't move. It was a dream. I couldn't move
my arms. They lay at my sides, palms up, limp, as though they
belonged to another body. I bent my good knee up under me,
using my shoulders and chin as leverage.

Once again I yelled at Bird, but he would not come, would
not slack up on the rope. I swore at him, coaxed him, reasoned
with him, but I must have looked foolish to him, my ass in the
air and the sweat running from my scalp.

Goddamn you, Bird, goddamn you. Goddamn Ferdinand Horn,
why didn't you come in, together we could have gotten this
damn cow out, why hadn't I ignored her? Goddamn your wife
with her stupid turquoise glasses, stupid grape pop, your stupid
car. Lame Bull! My stepfather. It was his cow, he had married
this cow, why wasn't he here? Off riding around, playing the
role, goddamn big-time operator, can't trust him, can't trust
any of these damn idiots, damn Indians. Slack up, you asshole!
Slack up! You want to strangle her? That's okay with me; she
means nothing to me. What did I do to deserve this? Goddamn
that Ferdinand Horn! Ah, Teresa, you made a terrible mistake.
Your husband, your friends, your son, all worthless, none of
them worth a shit. Slack up, you sonofabitch! Your mother
dead, your father—you don't even know, what do you think of
that? A joke, can't you see? Lame Bull! The biggest joke—can't
you see that he's a joke, a joker playing a joke on you? Were

you taken for a ride! Just like the rest of us, this country, all
of us taken for a ride. Slack up, slack up! This greedy stupid
country—

My arms began to tingle as they tried to wake up. I moved
my fingers. They moved. My neck ached but the strength was
returning. I crouched and spent the next few minutes planning
my new life. Finally I was able to push myself from the ground
and stand on my good leg. I put my weight on the other. The
bones seemed to be wedged together, but it didn't hurt. I hobbled
over to Bird. He raised his head and nodded wildly. As I touched
his shoulder, he shied back even further.

"Here, you old sonofabitch," I said. "Do you want to defeat
our purpose?"

He nodded his agreement. I hit the rope with the edge of my
hand. I hit it again. He let off, dancing forward, the muscles in
his shoulders working beneath the soft white hair. I looked back
at the cow. She was standing up in the mud, her head, half of
it black, straight up like a swimming water snake. I snapped the
rope out toward her, but she didn't move. Her eyes were wild,
a glaze beginning to form in them. The noose was still tight
around her neck.

As I climbed aboard the horse, I noticed for the first time
that it was raining. What I thought was sweat running through
my scalp had been rain all along. I snapped the rope again,
arcing a curve away from me toward the cow. This time the
noose did loosen up. She seemed surprised. A loud gasp, as
harsh as a dog's bark, came from her throat. As though that
were her signal for a final death struggle, she went into action,
humping her back, bawling, straining against the sucking mud.
Bird tightened up on the rope and began to back away. The
saddle came forward; I turned him so that he was headed away
from the slough.

The rain was coming hard now, the big drops stinging the
back of my neck and splattering into the dusty earth. A magpie,
light and silent, flew overhead, then lit on a fence post beside

the loading chute. He ruffled his sleek feathers, then squatted to watch.

The rope began to hum in the gathering wind, but the cow was coming, flailing her front legs out of the mud. Bird slipped once and almost went down, doing a strange dance, rolling quickly from side to side, but he regained his balance and continued to pull and the cow continued to come. I took another dally around the saddle horn and clung to the end of the rope. I slapped him on the shoulder. Somewhere in my mind I could hear the deep rumble of thunder, or maybe it was the rumble of energy, the rumble of guts—it didn't matter. There was only me, a white horse and a cow. The pressure of the rope against my thigh felt right. I sat to one side in the saddle, standing in the right stirrup, studying the rough strands of hemp against the pant leg. The cow had quit struggling and was now sliding slowly through the greasy mud. Her head pointed up into the rain, but her eyes had lost that wild glare. She seemed to understand this necessary inconvenience.

It was all so smooth and natural I didn't notice that Bird had begun to slip in the rain-slick dirt. He turned sideways in an attempt to get more traction. He lowered his rump and raised his head. He lowered his head again so that he was stretched low to the ground. I leaned forward until I could smell the sweet warmth of his wet mane. Then I felt the furious digging of hooves, and I realized that he was about to go down. Before I could react, he whirled around, his front legs striking out at the air. His hind legs went out from under him. It was only the weight of the cow on the end of the rope that kept him from falling over backwards on top of me. His large white butt thumped the ground in front of me, he tottered for an instant, then he fell forward and it was quiet.

A flash of lightning to the south of me. I couldn't or wouldn't turn my head. I felt my back begin to stiffen. I didn't know if it was because of the fall or the damp, but I wasn't uncom-

fortable. The stiffness provided a reason for not moving. I saw
the flash in the corner of my eye, as though it were mirrored
countless times in the countless raindrops that fell on my face.

I wondered if my brother and father were comfortable. They
were the only ones I really loved, I thought, the only ones who
were good to be with. At least the rain wouldn't bother them.
But they would probably like it; they were that way, good to
be with, even on a rainy day.

I heard Bird grunt twice as he tried to heave himself upright,
but I couldn't find the energy to look at him. The magpie must
have flown closer, for his metallic *awk! awk!* was almost con-
versational. The cow down in the slough had stopped gurgling.
Her calf called once, a soft drone which ended on a quizzical
high note. Then it was silent again.

Some people, I thought, will never know how pleasant it is
to be distant in a clean rain, the driving rain of a summer storm.
It's not like you'd expect, nothing like you'd expect.

We buried the old lady the next day. The priest from Harlem,
of course, couldn't make it. So there were the four of us—
Teresa, Lame Bull, me and my grandmother. I hadn't told them
about Ferdinand Horn and his wife, but they wouldn't show
up anyway. I had to admit that Lame Bull looked pretty good.
The buttons on his shiny green suit looked like they were made
of wood. Although his crotch hung a little low, the pants were
the latest style. Teresa had shortened the legs that morning, a
makeshift job, having only had time to tack the original cuffs
up inside the pant legs. His fancy boots with the walking heels
peeked out from beneath the new cuffs. His shirt, tie, handkerchief and belt were various shades of green and red to match
the suit. He smelled of Wildroot and after-shave lotion. I felt
seedy standing beside him. I was wearing a suit that had belonged to my father. I hadn't known it existed until an hour
before the funeral. It was made out of a cream-colored wool
with brown threads running through it. The collar and cuffs

itched in the noonday heat, but the pant legs were wide enough
so that if I stood just right I didn't touch them, except for my
knee which was swollen up. It still didn't hurt. The necktie,
which I had loosened, had also belonged to my father. It was
silk with a picture of two mallards flying over a stand of cattails.

Teresa wore a black coat, black high heels, and a black cup-
cake hat. A black net extended down from it to cover her eyes
and nose. It stopped just above her upper lip. She had painted
her stern lips a bright red. Once again she was big and handsome—except for her legs. They appeared to be a little skinny,
but it must have been the dress. I wasn't used to seeing her
legs.

The old lady wore a shiny orange coffin with flecks of black
ingrained beneath the surface. It had been sealed up in Harlem,
so we never did find out what kind of makeup job the undertaker
had done on her.

The hole was too short, but we didn't discover this until we
had the coffin halfway down. One end went down easily enough,
but the other stuck against the wall. Teresa wanted us to take
it out because she was sure that it was the head that was lower
than the feet. Lame Bull lowered himself into the grave and
jumped up and down on the high end. It went down a bit more,
enough to look respectable. Teresa didn't say anything, so he
leaped out of the hole, a little too quickly. He wiped his forehead
with the pale green handkerchief.

"Well," he said. It was a question. He looked at me and I
looked off toward the slough, fingering the tobacco pouch.

Teresa began to moan. She wavered back and forth as though
the heat were getting to her.

"What do you think, pal?"

The air was heavy with yesterday's rain. It would probably
be good for fishing.

"I suppose me being the head of the family, it's up to me to
say a few words about our beloved relative and friend."

Teresa moaned.

Lame Bull clasped his hands in front of him. "Well," he said. "Here lies a simple woman . . . who devoted herself to . . . rocking . . . and not a bad word about anybody . . ."

I shifted my weight to my bad leg. It was like standing on tree stump.

"Not the best mother in the world . . ."

Teresa moaned louder.

". . . but a good mother, notwithstanding . . ."

I would have to go to the agency and see the doctor. I knew that he would try to send me down to Great Falls to have it operated on. But I couldn't do it. I'd tell him that. I would end up in bed for a year. By that time the girl who had stolen my gun and electric razor would have forgotten me.

Teresa fell to her knees.

". . . who could take it and dish it out . . ."

Next time I'd do it right. Buy her a couple of crèmes de menthe, maybe offer to marry her on the spot.

". . . who never gave anybody any crap . . ."

The red horse down in the corral whinnied. He probably missed old Bird.

I threw the pouch into the grave.

NOTES ON THE CONTRIBUTORS

RICHARD HUGO

Richard Hugo, who was born in 1923 and died in 1982, was a poet, essayist, novelist, and teacher. His volumes of poetry included *The Lady in Kicking Horse Reservoir, What Thou Lovest Well Remains American,* and *The Right Madness on Skye.* He also wrote *The Triggering Town,* a book of essays on poetry and writing, and *Death and the Good Life,* a novel. His work was nominated for a National Book Award and the Pulitzer Prize, and he was director of the creative writing program at the University of Montana.

N. SCOTT MOMADAY

N. Scott Momaday, a Kiowa Indian, spent his childhood on various reservations in the Southwest. He is the author of a book of poetry, *The Gourd Dancer;* an autobiography, *The Names* (1976); and a novel, *House Made of Dawn,* which won the Pulitzer Prize for Literature in 1969. Married and the father of three daughters, he teaches English at the University of Arizona and continues, through poetry and lyric prose, to delve into the personal significance of his ancestry. The selection here is the introduction to his much-acclaimed collection of tribal and familial legends and history, *The Way to Rainy Mountain* (1969).

LESLIE MARMON SILKO

Although "white ethnologists have reported that the oral tradition among Native American groups has died out," says Leslie Marmon Silko, herself a Laguna Pueblo Indian, "I hear the ancient stories very clearly in the stories we are telling right now." Born in 1948, Silko attended law school before deciding to write full-time. She is currently on leave from the University of Arizona in Tucson, after receiving a five-year MacArthur Foundation prize fellowship. Her books include *Laguna Woman* (1974), *Ceremony* (1977), and *Storyteller* (1981), in which "Yellow Woman" appeared.

IVAN DOIG

Ivan Doig was born in White Sulphur Springs, Montana, in 1939. His father was a sheeptender; his mother died shortly before daybreak on his sixth birthday. Descended from a family of homesteading Scots who settled into the gray Montana foothills, he grew up—as a *New Yorker* reviewer described it—"on a stark succession of hardscrabble, sheep-and-cattle ranches, and in little, lost one-street towns." Trained as a journalist, Doig has written three books of nonfiction—*Utopian America* (1975), *This House of Sky* (1978), and *Winter Brothers* (1980)— as well as one novel, *The Sea Runners* (1982). "Flip" is excerpted from *This House of Sky,* which was nominated for a National Book Award.

NORMAN MACLEAN

Norman Maclean was born in Montana in 1902. A former William Rainey Harper professor of English at the University of Chicago, he retired to write his first collection of stories, *A River Runs Through It* (1976), which received critical and popular acclaim around the country. The book, which was singled out by *The New York Times* for its "acerbic, laconic, deadpan" voice that "rings out of a rich American tradition," has won him legions of fans, who are captivated by his deft winding of stories around life's odd, incidental details. He is currently at work on his second book.

JOHN NICHOLS

"For some reason, the East had overwhelmed me," says John Nichols, referring to his move west after the early success of his first novel, *The Sterile Cuckoo* (1969). This first book was followed by *The Wizard of Loneliness* (1966), *The Ghost in the Music* (1979), *The Last Beautiful Days of Autumn* (1982), *If Mountains Die* (1979), and the screenplay for the Costa-Gavras film *Missing.* Nichols is best known, however, for a trilogy of richly peopled novels, sketching the evolution of the small backwater Hispanic town of "Chamisaville"—a thinly veiled version of Taos, New Mexico, where Nichols now lives. The selection here is excerpted from *The Milagro Beanfield War* (1974), the first book of the trilogy, which includes *The Magic Journey* (1978) and *The Nirvana Blues* (1981).

RUDOLFO ANAYA

Born in the high plains of eastern New Mexico in 1937, Rudolfo Anaya credits growing up amid the Hispanic oral storytelling tradition for his fascination with "the magic of words." An associate professor of English at the University of New Mexico, Anaya is the author of two short-story collections, a Corporation for Public Broadcasting teleplay, *Rosa Linda*, and three novels—*Heart of Aztlan* (1976), *Tortuga* (1979), and *Bless Me, Ultima* (1972), from which this selection is taken. Evoking the world of seven-year-old Antonio Marez—a world full of sensual dreams, unexplained phenomena, and the dark might of Latin American Catholic theology—Anaya explores a young boy's maturation with the eye of a mystic and the keen ear of a fabulist.

DAVID QUAMMEN

David Quammen was educated at Yale and Oxford; then, as he puts it, "mildly horrified," he moved to Montana and "disappeared." His recent novel, *The Zolta Configuration* (1983), is a "semi-historical thriller" about the development of the American H-bomb, which *The New York Times* called "ironic and riveting." Quammen, who alternates his time between the Sonoran desert and Ennis, Montana, writes science-related nonfiction for *Audubon* and *Outside* magazines. "Walking Out" first appeared in *TriQuarterly*.

GRETEL EHRLICH

California-born Gretel Ehrlich landed in Wyoming at age thirty as the result of a film assignment, and a planned stay of a few months turned into eight years. She has produced two books of poetry—*Geode/Rock Body* (1970) and *To Touch the Water* (1981)—and four documentary films. The recipient of a 1982 National Endowment for the Arts creative writing fellowship, she has written for *The Atlantic, Vanity Fair, The New York Times,* and *New Age Journal.* At present, she lives with her husband on a cattle ranch in north-central Wyoming, where, she writes, "the truth and consequences of ranch life" have taught her "the importance of humor." The essay here first appeared in *The Atlantic.*

EDWARD ABBEY

Born in 1927 in Home, Pennsylvania, Edward Abbey twice flunked journalism in high school, hitchhiked across the country at seventeen, fought in Italy, studied philosophy in Edinburgh, Scotland, worked in New York City as a welfare caseworker, and spent sixteen summers alternating as a park ranger and a fire lookout through the span of the Rockies. The author of eight books of nonfiction and six novels—the most notorious one, *The Monkey Wrench Gang* (1975), has become a sort of "eco-guerrillas' " handbook—Abbey lives in the open desert outside of Tucson, Arizona. Edward Hoagland has called Abbey "a war horse, a wild horse, and one of a kind." "Cape Solitude" is excerpted from *Abbey's Road,* a 1979 collection of essays.

RICK DeMARINIS

Rick DeMarinis is the author of three novels—*A Lovely Monster* (1975), *Scimitar* (1977), and *Cinder* (1978)—as well as *Jack and Jill* (1979), a collection of short stories. Born in 1934 in New York City, he came to Montana in 1955 and studied with poet Richard Hugo at the University of Montana. Of living in the West, he writes, "The climate is hard, but it satisfies something in me; the sparsity of population is wonderful for the nervous system." DeMarinis has written for *Esquire, The Atlantic,* and *Rocky Mountain Magazine,* where "Weeds" first appeared.

RICHARD FORD

"I have nothing fancy or even interestingly close-mouthed to say about my stories or my novels or essays," reports Richard Ford, "nothing to add to my curriculum vitae beyond that I'm married, have no children, and was born in 1944 in Jackson, Mississippi." He was educated at Michigan State University and the University of California; he is the author of two novels, *A Piece of My Heart* (1976) and *The Ultimate Good Luck* (1981); his short stories have appeared in *Harper's, Esquire, The Paris Review,* and *TriQuarterly,* as well as in the anthologies *Matters of Life and Death* and *Dirty Realism: New Writing from America.* He currently lives in Missoula, Montana, and is working on a new novel titled *The Sportswriter.*

ELIZABETH TALLENT

Elizabeth Tallent moved to Santa Fe, New Mexico, after graduating from the University of Illinois. She began writing fiction, she says, "as a detour from anthropology." She is the author of *In Constant Flight* (1983), a collection of short stories, and is the recipient of a National Endowment for the Arts creative writing fellowship. She has recently moved back to Santa Fe, but says of a recent sojourn in the small town of Eaton, Colorado, "I like knowing the limits, and I enjoy the dead quiet."

ROBERT MAYER

Robert Mayer was born in 1939 in New York City, where he eventually worked as a journalist and *Newsday* columnist, winning a National Headliner Award and two Mike Berger Awards. Since moving to Santa Fe, New Mexico, more than a decade ago, he has written three novels: *Superfolks* (1977), *The Execution* (1979), and *Midge & Decker* (1982), which the *Washington Post* called "pure, undiluted magic." "The System," which first appeared in *Rocky Mountain Magazine*, is an excerpt from *Midge & Decker*, and introduces one of the most unusual romances in recent fiction.

ALAN PRENDERGAST

Alan Prendergast is a native of Denver, Colorado. After graduating *summa cum laude* from The Colorado College in 1978, he worked at a variety of jobs in the West and in New York City—proofreading, cabdriving, and yeoman duties at *The New Yorker*. He now lives in Denver, from which locale he has reported for *Rolling Stone*, the *Denver Post*, *Rocky Mountain Magazine*, *New Age Journal*, and the *Columbia Journalism Review*. In early 1981 Prendergast became interested in the case of Claude L. Dallas, Jr., then a fugitive being sought in connection with the slaying of two game wardens in southern Idaho. Following Dallas's capture in April 1982, Prendergast went to Idaho to report on his trial for *Rolling Stone*. His essay "The Last Man Alive" is based on the trial proceedings and many subsequent interviews.

DAVID LONG

Born in Boston in 1948, David Long received an M.F.A. from the University of Montana in 1974. He now makes his home in Kalispell, Montana, with his wife and two sons, Montana and Jackson. He has published one book of poetry, *Early Returns*, in addition to *Home Fires* (1983), a collection of short stories. Long writes: "One morning a few summers ago, a truck ran off a mountain highway not far from here. The authorities, unable to find a body, labeled the driver *missing*. I was in the Stockman's Bar the next day and overheard two guys speculating that the man had staged his own disappearance; they sounded like they wouldn't mind disappearing themselves. This story came up after some mulling over accidents and second chances."

WILLIAM KITTREDGE

William Kittredge is one of the deans of modern Western fiction. A professor of creative writing at the University of Montana, he has, as one reviewer wrote, "genuine cowpoke credentials, albeit dusty ones" from his youth spent in the Owyhee River country of southeastern Oregon. He has published fiction and nonfiction in such magazines as *The Atlantic, Harper's, New Age Journal, TriQuarterly, Rocky Mountain Magazine, Outside,* and *Rolling Stone.* His first book of short stories, *The Van Gogh Field,* won the Fiction International Prize for 1979. A second book of stories, *We Are Not in This Together,* was recently published. With Steven M. Krauzer, he is coauthor of the *Cord* series of Western novels, and is now completing a novel titled *Sixty Million Buffalo.*

THOMAS McGUANE

Thomas McGuane is a former Wallace Stegner Fellow at Stanford University, a prize-winning cutting-horse trainer, and one of the original "new settlers" of Montana's Paradise Valley. "The West is a wreck," he avers. "I'd like to document that without getting totally depressing." A former Yale Drama School student, McGuane has proceeded with almost ferocious élan: His 1971 novel, *The Bushwhacked Piano,* won the Richard and Hilda Rosenthal Foundation Award from the American Academy and Institute of Arts and Letters; its successor, *Ninety-two in the Shade,* was a 1973 nominee for the National Book Award. In addition to his three other novels, *The Sporting Club* (1969), *Panama* (1978), and *Nobody's Angel* (1982), he has written three screenplays—*Rancho Deluxe, Tom Horn,* and *The Missouri Breaks.* "The El Western" first appeared in *Vanity Fair.*

JAMES WELCH

James Welch was born in Browning, Montana, in 1940, of mixed Blackfeet and Gros Ventre Indian parentage. He received his early education in reservation schools, later going on to study business at

Northern Montana College. Welch, who was appointed to the Literature Panel of the National Endowment for the Arts in 1970, is the author of three books—*Riding the Earthboy 40*, poems, and two novels, *The Death of Jim Loney* (1979), and *Winter in the Blood* (1974), from which this selection is excerpted. *Winter in the Blood*, wrote Jim Harrison, "is deeply and strangely 'American' in a way that very few of our novels are."

ACKNOWLEDGMENTS

Grateful acknowledgment is made to the following for permission to use copyrighted material:

A & W Publishers, Inc.: "The System" from *Midge & Decker* by Robert Mayer. "The System" appeared originally in *Rocky Mountain Magazine.*

Rudolfo Anaya: A selection from *Bless Me, Ultima* by Rudolfo Anaya. Copyright © 1972 by Rudolfo A. Anaya, Tonatiuh-Quinto Sol International Publishers, P.O. Box 9275, Berkeley, CA 94709.

The Atlantic Monthly Company: "The Solace of Open Spaces" by Gretel Ehrlich. Copyright © 1981 by The Atlantic Monthly Company. "The Solace of Open Spaces" appeared originally in *The Atlantic Monthly.*

Don Congdon Associates, Inc.: "Cape Solitude" from *Abbey's Road* by Edward Abbey. Copyright © 1979 by Edward Abbey.

Rick DeMarinis: Weeds" by Rick DeMarinis. Copyright © 1979 by Rick DeMarinis. "Weeds" appeared originally in *Rocky Mountain Magazine.*

Richard Ford: "Winterkill" by Richard Ford. Copyright © 1983 by Richard Ford. "Winterkill" appeared originally in *Esquire.*

Harcourt Brace Jovanovich, Inc.: "Flip," abridged from *This House of Sky* by Ivan Doig. Copyright © 1978 by Ivan Doig.

Holt, Rinehart and Winston, Publishers: A selection from *The Milagro Beanfield War* by John Nichols. Copyright © 1974 by John Nichols.

William Kittredge: "We Are Not in This Together" by William Kit-